THE STREET WAS MINE

THE STREET WAS MINE

WHITE MASCULINITY IN
HARDBOILED FICTION AND FILM NOIR

MEGAN E. ABBOTT

palgrave
macmillan

First published 2002 by
PALGRAVE MACMILLAN
175 Fifth Avenue, New York, N.Y. 10010 and
Houndmills, Basingstoke, Hampshire, England RG21 6XS.
Companies and representatives throughout the world.

PALGRAVE MACMILLAN is the global academic imprint of the Palgrave Macmillan division of St. Martin's Press, LLC and of Palgrave Macmillan Ltd. Macmillan® is a registered trademark in the United States, United Kingdom and other countries. Palgrave is a registered trademark in the European Union and other countries.

ISBN 0–312–29481–6

Library of Congress Cataloging-in-Publication Data
Abbott, Megan E., 1971-
The street was mine : white masculinity and urban space in hardboiled fiction and film noir / by Megan E. Abbott.
    p.   cm.
Includes bibliographical references and index.
ISBN 0–312–29481–6
    1. Detective and mystery stories, American—History and criticism.
2. Detective and mystery films—United States—History and criticism.
3. Film noir—United States—History and criticism.   4. City and town life in motion pictures.   5. Private investigators in literature.   6. City and town life in literature.   7. Masculinity in literature.   8. White men in literature.   9. Men in motion pictures.   10. Race in literature.   11. Men in literature.   I. Title.

PS374.D4 A23   2002
813'.087209321732—dc21
                                                                    2002068408

A catalogue record for this book is available from the British Library.

Design by Letra Libre, Inc.

First edition: November 2002
10 9 8 7 6 5 4 3 2 1

Printed in the United States of America

To my parents

For 1578 Anita Avenue

And for Josh

"It's a wonderful thing, dinner for two."
—*Jack Lemmon,* The Apartment *(1960)*

CONTENTS

ACKNOWLEDGEMENTS

I CANNOT IMAGINE EMBARKING ON THIS PROCESS WITHOUT THE SUPPORT and motivation of Carolyn Dever, whose utterly indispensable criticism has challenged and inspired me, and whose kindness and patience has been a beacon throughout this project. Likewise, I would like to thank Phillip Brian Harper, who was so influential and inspiring throughout my research and who offered me the crucial encouragement to pursue the non-canonical texts that so fascinated me. And I want to thank Lisa Duggan, whose key insights and crucial historian's perspective has tightened and focused this project, and whose encouraging advice guided me.

In addition, I would like to thank Corrine Abate, Sarah Stevenson, Joe Nazare, Ezra Cappell, Kyung-Sook Boo, all of whom were endlessly helpful in workshopping my chapters at New York University.

My parents Philip and Patricia Abbott provided unconditional support, insightful critiques, and, perhaps most important of all, an excitement about my work. Their generosity overwhelms me. Thanks also need to be extended to my brother Josh Abbott and sister-in-law Julie Nichols for their affection and kindness, and to my grandparents, Ralph and Janet Nase, for infusing my years on the East Coast with warmth and tenderness. And, finally, to my dearest friend Christine Biretta, whose long-distance support and generous ear-bending never wavers.

But most of all, I can't fathom completing this project without my husband, Josh. At work on his own book, he kept one maddening chapter ahead of me for twenty-four months. He watched (and continues to watch) all things noir with me, and even more importantly, he understood the pains and pangs of the process, nurturing me along with love and with an expansive generosity of spirit.

CHAPTER ONE

INTRODUCTION

"The street was mine, all mine. They gave it to me gladly and wondered why I wanted it so nice and all alone."

—Mickey Spillane, *One Lonely Night* (1951)

IN 1953, SENATOR JOSEPH MCCARTHY CALLED DASHIELL HAMMETT BEFORE a congressional subcommittee convened to investigate charges that so-called pro-communist books, including Hammett's, had been found in the State Department's overseas libraries. McCarthy asked Hammett,

> [I]f you were spending, as we are, over a hundred million dollars a year on an information program allegedly for the purpose of fighting communism, and if you were in charge of that program to fight communism, would you purchase the works of some 75 communist authors and distribute their works throughout the world, placing our official stamp of approval upon these works?[1]

Hammett rather audaciously replied, "[I]f I were fighting communism, I don't think I would do it by giving people any books at all."[2] Not long after his testimony, Hammett's books were removed from State Department libraries (though only temporarily; Eisenhower would reinstate them). As Woody Haut suggests, Hammett, having already served a six-month prison term for refusing to answer questions about indicted communist leaders threatened with deportation, certainly realized that "books are, in themselves, investigations and, if one seeks mass distribution and a mass readership, one acknowledges the dominant cultural narrative or suffers the consequences."[3]

McCarthy's raid came only a year after an extensive inquiry into the pocket book market by the House Select Committee on Current Pornographic Materials. The committee's primary targets were comic books and the newly dominant mass market paperback industry, the latter a phenomenon driven in large part by the popularity of "hardboiled" literature. Cold War assaults on mass market or popular literature obviously reflect a governmental fear that such books could communicate potentially subversive viewpoints. But what perhaps differentiates these efforts from the expurgations of more blatantly politically charged literary productions is the question of readership. The new paperback industry had made books suddenly affordable to a wide spectrum of American readers, and these erupting congressional investigations sounded the rising alarm that such paperbacks might not be merely escapist entertainment but an unruly simulacrum of the anxieties and desires of its readers.

This book, then, derives in part from one of the central premises on which these investigations operated: popular literature can be dangerous. The confluence of the pulp paperback industry and its hardboiled bestsellers with Cold War fears of political and moral contamination came at the apex of a twenty-year-long rise of a new, remarkably influential sensibility: that of the "hardboiled" novel. In their depiction of the crises of the modern white American male trapped in a battered and enclosing American city, hardboiled novels embodied, assuaged, and galvanized an array of contemporary anxieties: Depression-era fears about a capitalism-defeated masculinity, anti-immigrant paranoia, Cold War xenophobia, and the grip of post–World War II consumerism.

Specifically, this book locates and analyzes the significance of a distinctive literary and cinematic figure in 1930s–1950s American culture—namely, that of the solitary white man, hard-bitten, street-savvy, but very much alone amid the chaotic din of the modern city. Generally lower-middle or working-class, heterosexual, and without family or close ties, he navigates his way through urban spaces figured as threatening, corrupt, even "unmanning." The idea of the solitary white man trekking down urban streets has forerunners in like-minded navigators of Western space or wilderness, but a relocation to the industrialized American city, combined with the influence of modernist themes of fragmentation and alienation, created a unique new figure—a figure we can locate in Hemingway's Jake Barnes (*The Sun Also Rises*) and Harry Morgan (*To Have and Have Not*), Nathanael West's Miss Lonelyhearts, the marginal men of Nelson Algren and others, not to mention later incarnations in Henry Miller and Norman Mailer.

This iconic figure thrives, however, in its hardboiled incarnation, in the form of the archetypal "tough guy." Hardboiled magazines and novels afforded this figure a mass audience, their popular circulation dwarfing that of its more "literary" manifestations.[4] In the works of popular, or pulp, fiction, the tough guy saturated the literary market—in particular, the flourishing new paperback industry—resulting in a paradigmatic American type with a palpable gritty appeal and an encompassing influence on the American lexicon with a fresh and inescapably "modern"-sounding hardboiled slang.

Characterized in terms of the murky space he occupies between conventional society and a criminal underclass, the tough guy, as Liam Kennedy asserts, is "at once a liminal, rootless figure—modernist thematics of alienation, homelessness and melancholia recur in the writings—and a democratic anti-hero, a classless and self-reliant man able to traverse areas of American society."[5] While his purported classlessness—not to mention his self-reliance—is, I will argue, more a dreamed-for ideal than a defining characteristic, the tough guy's discomfort with traditional roles or bourgeois values of home, family, and friends is fundamental to his self-concept. But the question begs, why does this lonely figure so haunt mid-century America? This book will attempt to answer that question through a consideration of the cultural crises that both produced and perpetuated the hardboiled white man, as well as the very real national and political hysteria that eventually pointed the finger at hardboiled fiction as a source of mass corruption and contamination.

The Street Was Mine then aims to trace the transformation the tough guy underwent from the 1930s, when he became prominent in the hardboiled novels of mystery and crime writers, through the 1940s, when Hollywood absorbed the figure in a series of movies that would come to be known as film noir, to the 1950s when, in the face of public pressure and Cold War hysteria, he transmutes either into figures like Mickey Spillane's Commie-baiting detective Mike Hammer, or into icons of nostalgia from an era already recreated and reconstituted

Through its analysis of this iconic model of white masculinity, *The Street Was Mine* hopes to contribute to two recent critical interventions in the study of American literature. First, this book enters into the discussion of American whiteness—in particular, the growing theoretical insistence that the construction of American whiteness is crucial to our understanding of American literature and culture. Second, this book joins the increasing critical focus on the ways American whiteness is linked to the production and reproduction of American masculinities and femininities.

Sylvia Wynter, Toni Morrison, Eric Sundquist, bell hooks, Harryette Mullen, David Roediger, and Eric Lott, among others, have demonstrated the importance of investigating the relationship between whiteness and blackness in American culture—specifically, the consolidation of an American whiteness through a conceptual dependence on the creation of an "othered" blackness. This consolidation is repeatedly elided in the persistent recapitulation of the idea that white is transparent, a totality, the norm—an elision Judith Butler terms the "hegemonic presumption."[6]

This book seeks to intercede in the theoretical discussion of whiteness, but to do so by considering the ways whiteness functions in concert with the construction and deployment of normative gender binaries. Informed by the work of Butler, who famously argues that there is "no gender identity behind the expressions of gender; that identity is performatively constituted by the very 'expressions' that are said to be its results,"[7] this project pursues the tangled discursive production of both gender and race. Indeed, in the study of American literature these two critical discourses of race and gender beg to be investigated in tandem. As we find in the important recent work by, for example, Robyn Wiegman, Hortense Spillers, Lauren Berlant, and Ann Pellegrini, the American construction of masculinity and femininity is linked fundamentally to racial ideology: race and gender operate by and through each other, each using the other to seal up fissures, suture gaps, and naturalize their own performance of whiteness, blackness, masculinity, and femininity.

My particular point of entry into this theoretical intervention models the work of theorists such as Eric Lott, who importantly argues for an ambiguous and complex relationship between blackface minstrelsy and its predominantly white, male, working-class audiences. What makes Lott's project so trenchant is in large part his insistence that we attend to the role of the "popular," the texts of mass culture, as a "crucial place of contestation, with moments of resistance to the dominant culture as well as moments of supersession."[8] Sharing this belief in the need to investigate and interrogate what is too often dismissed as "low culture artifacts," I locate my intervention within texts repeatedly dismissed as "pulp."

To allow for a deeper focus and to allow for considerations of both detective novels and crime novels, this book focuses primarily on the famed Philip Marlowe novels of Raymond Chandler (*The Big Sleep, Farewell, My Lovely*) and the Los Angeles sex-and-sin sagas of James M. Cain (*The Postman Always Rings Twice, Double Indemnity*). These novels, all set in tensely xenophobic 1930s–50s Los Angeles, occupy central roles in our popular conception of the tough guy figure and were fundamental to the construction of a string of dark and fatalistic Hollywood productions that would come to be called film noir. Further, Cain and Chandler provide more troubled and fragmented white male heroes than the less introspective and decidedly more self-contained heroes of Dashiell Hammett. As Geoffrey O'Brien notes, the Hammett hero is "completely externalized—interior monologue has no place in his world."[9] By contrast, both Chandler and Cain rely heavily on first-person narratives, allowing the authors to anatomize this urban white male sensibility from within. Further, I will also look to the ensuing revisionary attack on the tough guy tradition through a focus on African American novelist Chester Himes, whose series of crime novels (called *romans policiers* when they were first published in France) evince a crucial critique of this white hardboiled sensibility, while also recapitulating much of its problematics.

It is my contention that the crime novels of Raymond Chandler, James M. Cain, and Chester Himes offer up a figure—the white man wandering the urban streets, threatened and alone—whose compulsive representation can help us examine the troubled and troubling consolidation of white masculinity in pre- and post–World War II American culture. In turn, by attending to the celebrated and canonical film adaptations of Cain and Chandler, we can scrutinize the ways these films attempt to consolidate a secure white masculinity through visual means—and thereby shore up identity formulations that remain unsure and unwieldy in the more ambiguous source texts. Examining the translation especially of novels written prior to U.S. entry into World War II (*Double Indemnity, The Postman Always Rings Twice, The Big Sleep, Farewell, My Lovely*) to World War II and post–World War II screens helps us to read the two decades' race and gender politics in productive ways. Much as Kaja Silverman reads post–World War II texts as reflecting the trauma of male lack,[10] I aim to show how contemporary anxieties about masculinity and whiteness—deriving from off-screen realities such as women entering the workforce and wartime xenophobia—are rehearsed and ultimately effaced within these hardboiled adaptations.

My argument then proceeds from the way the growing market for these books and the even more popular films in the 1930s–50s can help us read much of the era's race and gender politics: the hysterical efforts we find in Cain and Chandler to shore up a threatened white masculinity in the face of a racist and misogynist urban dread; Himes's absurdist and apocalyptic vision from within that feared urban space, through which Himes revises and deconstructs Cain and Chandler's race and gender paranoia, while offering new, anxious efforts at a consolidation of a black masculinity in the face of violent 1960s social change.

The Street Was Mine ultimately hopes to introduce a new range of texts into American literary studies and, in particular, into the analysis of the powerful representation of American white masculinity within American literary studies. To neglect pop culture texts like those of Cain, Chandler, and Himes, is to miss the crucial insight into mid-twentieth-century American attitudes toward whiteness, blackness, masculinity, and femininity, and especially the constantly shifting relationships between these constructions. Through analyses of the figure at the heart of these highly influential texts, we can forward our investigation into America's fraught vortex of race and gender politics. The urban white male loner can in fact tell us things.

The World You Live In

The constitutive attributes of the tough guy figure—his maleness, his whiteness, and his urban isolation—and the means by which these attributes are constructed, maintained, threatened, and restored serve as the main structuring element of this book. As such, I would like to begin by offering a brief roadmap of these gender, racial, and geographic identifications. From these identifications emerge the tensions and fears that lead to perhaps the tough guy's most important characteristic of all: his fundamental isolation. His refusal to attach himself to a woman, a family, a social network, a community, a business, a country and its ideals—all these things cast this seemingly privileged (he is white; he is male) figure as a potential transgressor, a social renegade.

Robert Sklar, in his work on the careers of film tough guys James Cagney, Humphrey Bogart, and John Garfield, argues that the cowboy of nineteenth-century American mythology is replaced, beginning in the late 1920s, with the "city boy." While Sklar's "city boy" is a broader term—it includes such filmic types as the gangster, the boxer, or the city beat reporter, and is characterized largely as any urban type fully embodied by Cagney, Bogart, and Garfield—his reflections on the relationship between such hard-boiled types and the cowboy tradition is apt. Both the cowboy and the city boy or the tough guy wrestle with the tension between individualism and community responsibility, but there is also a significant difference. The cowboy is characterized through his relationship to the past, and his persistent ahistoricity, which dooms him as a "man whom time and change must ultimately defeat."[11] In sharp contrast, the city boy is a "contemporary," a recognizable type, who changes with the city he inhabits.[12] Likewise, the tough guy ultimately is a figure of modernity, from his up-to-the-minute speech to his fast, unsentimental lifestyle. However, Raymond Chandler's honorable detective Philip Marlowe shares with the cowboy a deep connection to a possibly imagined past in that he conceives of himself as a knight trapped in a world where knightly values no longer seem to belong; as the novels progress into the 1950s, Marlowe remains the same and seems increasingly anachronistic, an artifact from another era.[13] Yet, in contrast to the fading cowboy receding on the horizon, Marlowe remains working and living in the compulsively changing city, which perhaps changes him more than he wants to acknowledge.

Further, unlike the nineteenth-century models of the American individualist hero who liberates himself from suffocating society in the wilderness, the tough guy finds no freedom, perhaps is not even looking for it, as it is no longer an option in the modern city, for the modern man.[14] The (urban) wilderness is never the tough guy's utopian dream realized or temporarily realized. It is instead the landscape of both street crime and high-level corruption, crooked hoods and the degenerate wealthy. He finds entrapment not only in the potentially domesticating and potentially lethal women, as we see in the nineteenth-century model, but also within his own troubled mind and body. Everything is a trap, not the least of which his own disturbing drives, his own pleasure in transgression.[15]

Jopi Nyman has recently argued that hardboiled fiction strives for "an affirmation of a disrupted masculine social order . . . from the privileging of a masculine language to a vision of social order based on masculine authority."[16] Nyman reads tough guy novels as reflections of a "masculine will to power," arguing that their characters "seek power and domination" amid disruptive social change.[17] This analysis rests on a link between masculinity and an individualist ideology, but such a claim concretizes the very masculine ideals that the texts themselves often throw into question, unsettle, and even (temporarily) deconstruct. That is, I hope to demonstrate the extent to which this figure's masculinity is shown to require constant maintenance and reconstitution. These men repeatedly find themselves dissembling, fainting, unconscious, overpowered, and out of control while their ideals of masculinity continue to require of them self-discipline, toughness, and the quintessential hardness that gives the genre its name.

Those few critics who have confronted issues of gender in hardboiled fiction in any substantial way have tended to do so largely in the context of the femme fatale, and primarily as a way to show these texts to be emblematic of a genre- or historically specific misogyny. It is rarer still to see any extended discussion of how masculinity in particular is configured in these texts; instead, femininity is explored through the text's masculine lens—its insistently male protagonist—as if that lens were so typical, so universal as to be not worth pursuing in its own right.

If masculinity is broached, it is typically limited to the "toughness" of the tough guy, the hardboiled loner, wisecracks always at hand, fists ready for any violent encounter that may come his way.[18] (This impression may say more about the film adaptations of hardboiled novels than the novels themselves, a point about which I will have more to say in chapter five.) When a critic does reckon with a more problematic or complex view of these protagonists' masculinities, however, the argument generally limits itself to how masculinity operates in relation to the sexual wiles of the femme fatale.

Without question, a central characteristic of hardboiled fiction is the configuration of gender through binary structures—in particular, binaries produced in the service of constituting a fearless and potent maleness. Two binaries in particular predominate, that of the private eye/femme fatale and that of the sap-driven-to-crime/femme fatale—the former binary operating in Chandler, the latter in Cain, and both within Himes.

The relationship between the tough guy and the femme fatale will be a concern in this book, as hardboiled masculinity constructs itself in large part through this relationship. My hope, however, is to extend consideration beyond this relationship, and to foist the view of masculinity out of the hardboiled tradition's tightly rendered perception that masculinity is the norm and femininity, a lethal perversion. I aim to show that, far from generic and stable, masculinity in these novels is a fraught and tentative thing, and not merely as a result of the femme fatale's betrayal. Indeed, I will argue that the protagonists' reaction to the femme fatale derives from an already existing threatened and threatening configuration of masculinity. Further, what we find in the works of Chandler and Cain is not the tough guy of yore, confident in his ability to shoot or punch his way out of danger; instead, he is a dissembling figure constantly on the verge of nervous collapse or even hysteria, a figure that often finds himself the victim of claustration and sequestration not because of his (actual or mistaken) criminal guilt, but because of his questionable behavior, his deviance from gender norms or expectations.

This threat to normative masculinity is enhanced by the location in which hardboiled protagonists find themselves: the American city, where criminal dangers, aggressive modern women, crooked juridical systems, and urban decadence lurk around every corner. Even when he travels to the outer regions of the city for the roadside setting of James M. Cain's crime classic *The Postman Always Rings Twice,* he remains only twenty miles from Los Angeles, and that city's presence looms heavily over the text as the place the femme fatale's Hollywood dreams first failed, sending her, fatefully, to work in a "hash joint."

Indeed, it is not just any city that serves repeatedly as the setting for the white male loner. It is the "last city," the frontier's end, the supposed promised land: Los Angeles. The majority of hardboiled writers—Horace McCoy (*They Shoot Horses, Don't They?*), Paul Cain (*Fast One*), Raymond Chandler, James M. Cain, and later Ross McDonald—use Los Angeles's multiple significations and evocations in their construction of this white male figure. As Ralph Willett notes, "the disparity between the promise and abundance of the region and the reality of its neon/plastic decadence (symbolized by Los Angeles) is continually present like a dark trace."[19]

Moreover, the symbolic weight of Hollywood is crucial in these novels. Cain and especially Chandler use Los Angeles proper as a sign for Hollywood artificiality and the endless tales of failed starlets and would-be luminaries as recurrent symbols of modern inauthenticity and shattered dreams. Mike Davis refers to hardboiled fiction and film as the "great anti-myth," naming James M. Cain's *The Postman Always Rings Twice* as the first in a "succession of through-the-glass-darkly novels—all produced by writers under contract to the studio system—that repainted the image of Los Angeles as a deracinated urban hell."[20] Indeed, both Cain and Chandler worked as Hollywood screenwriters during their careers (Chandler even co-adapting Cain's *Double Indemnity* for the screen), and their novels bristle with hostility for that myth-making industry and its commodification of illusory dreams, its siren song promise of stardom. The murderess-heroine of Cain's *The Postman Always Rings Twice* originally came to Hollywood after winning a screen-test in a Des Moines beauty pageant. Likewise, Chandler's *The Little Sister* (1949) concerns a Kansas-bred rising starlet concealing her past and a lethal faux-Mexican screen temptress concealing her own Midwestern roots. As Liahna Babener writes,

> Chandler's Los Angeles is a metropolis of lies. Artifice is everywhere. . . . The architecture of Los Angeles—often derivative, insubstantial, and tasteless— attests to the city's preoccupation with façade. . . . Throughout the novels, the documents of daily life are seen to be false constructs. . . . Most important, personal identity is portrayed as unstable and uncertain. In a society of second chances and new beginnings people are not what they seem or what they used to be.[21]

The perception of artifice and deceit obviously provides the ripe atmosphere for the chicanery and lurid crime that drive these novels, but the fear of a dangerous insubstantiality looms larger than the imposture and corruption that offer the putative plots of hardboiled fiction. The tough guy inhabits a world without authenticity and potentially without meaning or personal identity, with nothing onto which he can hold.

In addition to this unnerving hollowness, Los Angeles is overdetermined as both the newest of all cities but also the dropping-off of the American frontier. Its Depression-era status as the destination of many poverty-stricken Americans immediately gives way to dead-end realities for those who flocked there. Manifest Destiny has reached its endpoint and remains stagnant in a never-ending network of modern freeways wrapping around each other in hopeless repetition.[22] David Fine suggests that Cain importantly uses Los Angeles County's extensive freeway system, its growing reputation as a "city on wheels," to reflect his characters' disastrous desires for speed and escape.[23] Certainly Cain's *The Postman Always Rings Twice* uses the rest-stop culture of the Los Angeles area to pinpoint a kind of rotting purgatory for its characters: a failed Hollywood starlet and her hobo lover, both trapped in a place through which others merely pass.

But perhaps most crucially, the Los Angeles setting affords a particularly volatile xenophobic atmosphere in which this hardboiled hero's whiteness is very much up for grabs. Nineteen-thirties and forties Los Angeles was experiencing both an increasing ethnic diversity and an increasing segregation, the two combining to create an ambience of pointed racial tensions, often flaring up in violence (such as the Zoot Suit riots of 1943). These tensions play out vividly in the novels of Cain and Chandler, in which the white male hero asserts his whiteness through distancing himself from perceived encroachment by, most especially, Mexican Americans, African Americans, and Asian Americans. In turn, these novels use signifiers of the Other to heighten the exoticism of the narrative and setting, and to carve out the hero's liminal space teetering delicately between center and margin. The Los Angeles setting allows for and encourages a lethal mix of illusion and artifice, racial and ethnic upheaval, political segregatory efforts, and echoes of frontier and Western ideology.

In the late 1940s and before he began his famous "*roman policier*" series, Chester Himes set two novels in Los Angeles, where he lived miserably in its unbearable post-war racial climate before relocating to Paris.[24] Shifting the location of his *romans policiers* to Harlem has a distinct effect: the frontier myth and the aura of movie-made artifice are eliminated. Himes, however, still focuses on the notion of a racial enclave—yet the portrait comes from within the enclave, not from the intruding white tough guy. Harlem's status as a "world apart" from the wealth and exploitation of the rest of Manhattan mirrors depictions of the African American Central Avenue neighborhood in Los Angeles, which provides the setting for many hardboiled novels, from the neighborhood's racist-exoticist representation in Chandler's *Farewell, My Lovely* to the milieu of Walter Mosley's contemporary Easy Rawlins series. But more important, Himes' choice to set his radically revisionary novels in Harlem allows him to contrast the area's rich artistic and cultural legacy with its crippling civil rights–era poverty and violence. In so doing, Himes excavates the stealth and oppressive whiteness of both detective fiction and hardboiled crime fiction as a whole

Hardboiled: The Genre Question

This book shares with Himes the pursuit of the ubiquitous white male figure who repeatedly looms at the center of a series of detective novels, crime fiction, and Hollywood films, all emerging in the America of the 1930s through the 1950s, all eventually categorized as "hardboiled."

Considerations of the hardboiled protagonist often mistakenly conflate hardboiled fiction with one of its variants: the private eye novel. Such a conflation neglects the crime novels that constitute a large part of the hardboiled tradition—crime novels that focus not on detectives but petty hoods, rough-and-ready hobos, saps, and everyday men-turned-murderers.[25] Tony Hilfer offers a compelling analysis of the differences between the hardboiled detective novel and crime novels like those of James M. Cain, writing that the "alienated posture of the tough detective becomes a reassurance about how to live, with style, in a job-centered, emotion-denying society. In contrast, the American crime novel protagonist will give all to love *or destroy himself by not so doing*, shatter into schizophrenia, and confront a world either stubbornly enigmatic or too corrupt to be borne."[26] While it seems Hilfer imposes an overly slick gloss on the ambiguities of detectives like Raymond Chandler's Philip Marlowe, he does highlight the important distance that, for instance, Marlowe forces between himself and the contaminating forces of corruption; this distance contrasts with the doomed murderer-heroes of James M. Cain's *Double Indemnity* (1936) and *The Postman Always Rings Twice*, who are fated to plunge into that contamination headfirst. The point here is that there are significant thematic and ideological differences between the crime novels of men doomed by their own lusts and greed, and the detective novels of Chandler, in which the private eye seeks to save the innocent while remaining true to personal ideals. And yet in both types of hardboiled fiction, the central figure, who is more often than not the first-person narrator as well, is a white male loner traversing a modern urban city, crippled by perceived threats to his whiteness, his gender, his sexuality, and, simultaneously, tantalized by those threats.

Scores of critics have traced the evolution of American hardboiled fiction, creating a thick web of disputed and agreed-upon influences (see appendix).[27] As such, my aim is not a genre study or a thorough historical overview of hardboiled roots. I do, however, want to offer a brief consideration of the ways in which the origins of hardboiled fiction suggest a significant history for this white male loner traversing the urban streets, eschewing ties, responsible only to himself, a man whose survival appears to depend on his ability to remain alone, untainted and unquestionably white, unquestionably masculine. Further, this need to affirm his whiteness, his conventional masculinity, is not mere means of identification but, as we will see, crucial to the mechanisms by which he distances himself from "Others," from social change, from modernity, from growing ethnic diversity, from the empowerment of women, from the threat of femininity or feminization.

First, I want to consider the earlier incarnations of the detective figure who dominates much of hardboiled fiction. While much genre study overstates the connection between the Dupin/Sherlock Holmes detective and private eyes like Philip Marlowe and Sam Spade (as we will see, the differences far outweigh the debt), a brief consideration of genre development offers important insights, particularly as these early ascetic, upper-class detective models were often precisely what writers like Raymond Chandler and Dashiell Hammett were critiquing through their violent, inescapably modern tales.

Strains of nineteenth-century literary tradition chart the development of what would come to be known as the "classic" detective model. In addition to the influences of gothic romances and sensation novels (perhaps most famously, Wilkie Collins's *The Moonstone*), the detective tales of Edgar Allen Poe and Arthur Conan Doyle helped establish the paradigmatic ratiocinative detective and the so-called drawing room murder mysteries that Hammett, Chandler, Chester Himes, and others would parody and subvert in the next century.

The popularity of "classic" detective fiction grew even more in the early twentieth century, reaching ever-growing audiences in the 1920s when writers such as S. S. Van Dine (the Philo Vance series) and Agatha Christie dominated the market, soon joined by the Ellery Queen series in the 1930s. While these models clearly have some bearing on hardboiled detective novels, they are secondary to the influence of pulp sensibility. The classic detective is generally characterized by a bourgeois or even upper-class background, intellectualism and bookishness, and a strictly remote relationship to the criminal milieu. Additionally, classic detective novels tend to be set in well-off homes or country estates, and the murders typically derive from personal conflicts. All of this is in stark contrast to what we find in the hardboiled detective novel, wherein the loner white male hero is lower-middle-class or working-class, tough-talking, intuition-driven, and very easily contaminated by the crimes that surround him. The crimes, in turn, are driven by economics, greed, rage, social-climbing, thuggery, and the settings are almost entirely within the American city, its wealthy surroundings, and its most debased and downtrodden centers and margins. In his introduction to "The Simple Art of Murder," Chandler refers to this new model as the moment when detective fiction "went native."[28] Attempting to define the appeal of the iconoclastic hardboiled style, Chandler notes that while the writing itself was limited by editorial staff tampering and the plots were often "rather ordinary," the stories stirred readers. He speculated,

> Possibly it was the smell of fear which these stories managed to generate. Their characters lived in a world gone wrong, a world in which, long before the atom bomb, civilization had created the machinery for its own destruction, and was learning to use it with all the moronic delight of a gangster trying out his first machine gun. The law was something to be manipulated for profit and power. The streets were dark with something more than night. (1016)

Then, the atmosphere of the hardboiled detective novel, likewise the crime novels that emerged with it, is distinctly urban, distinctly menacing, distinctly redolent with cynicism about American industrial modernity.

It is no accident that Chandler's language is infused with a vague late-imperialist sentiment ("went native," "dark with something more than night"). Such heart-of-darkness rhetoric discloses the tough guy's connection to

America's own racial history. Hardboiled fiction, particularly its private eye variant, has been repeatedly traced to both American frontier and Western literature. The primary connection seems to be the focus on a white figure of European descent who operates among "primitive Others," with the lines of demarcation between the white man and the "natives" often shown to be not so clearly drawn. Dennis Porter writes,

> [T]o the extent that [American private eyes] stand between two cultures, that of respectable society, on the one hand, and the criminal underworld, on the other, their situation is equally as ambivalent as that of the Indian fighter and hunter of colonial times. . . . [J]ust as the process of "Indianiza-tion" led to a marginal existence for the Indian fighter and hunter in fron-tier narratives, so too the private eye is represented as no longer at home among settled, property-owning citizens.[29]

Likewise, in his article linking early American frontier ideology with the "urban frontier" of white hardboiled fiction, Robert Crooks points to both traditions' emphasis on the individual hero, alone and unfettered by bonds or the demands of a group. He writes, "Produced by a familiar trope of in-dividualizing the European-American self against collectivized others, the 'lone white man' would be a recurring image suggesting that the struggle of European-Americans against the wilderness was not even a 'fair fight,' but rather a heroic battle against the odds."[30]

Many of these critical efforts rely heavily on the influential work of his-torian Richard Slotkin. Slotkin was among the earliest to link the hardboiled detective in particular to figures like James Fenimore Cooper's Hawkeye. Further, Slotkin charts the shift from the frontier to the city, suggesting that the "race war" of the frontier novel thus becomes a "class war" in the hard-boiled novel.[31]

But Slotkin's notion of a shift away from race to class is a bit too broadly rendered. Class war is certainly a recurrent theme in the dime detective nov-els he references, from the anti-union Pinkerton novels, in which the "sav-age proletariat" replaces the "savage Indians," to the more oblique class antagonism expressed in Chandler and Hammett, which tends to take the form of mockery of the bourgeois but most often a disgust for the rich.[32] The claim that "race war" dissolves in the shift from frontier hero to tough guy, however, is difficult to maintain in the face of the racial and ethnic rup-tures that emerge in hardboiled fiction. Among the key characteristics of this white male figure is his fear of encroaching Others, the use of racial and eth-nic stereotypes to create hardboiled exoticism, and, perhaps most important of all, the figure's obsessive attention to the consolidation of his own "white-ness." Throughout hardboiled fiction, whiteness is compulsively constructed and reconstructed in opposition to binarized and conflated Others: Mexicans, Chicanos, African Americans, Asian Americans, Greek Americans, Chilean Americans, Italian Americans—all grouped together, all racialized in opposition to the "raceless" universality of the white protagonist.

Although the connection to racialized frontier ideology is most frequently posited in reference to detective fiction, it also applies to hardboiled crime novels such as those of James M. Cain.[33] Cain's murderer-protagonists do not, however, serve as lone fighters against the dangers of the urban wilderness; instead, they live *entirely within that wilderness,* which also lies within them. The otherness projected onto Native Americans is explicitly presented as lurking within these white male loners: constructions of a racial or ethnic otherness function as metaphors for their isolation and illicit desires, their own "transgressions." But this perception may be equally true of the private eye hero. While the Philip Marlowe narratives, for instance, may be structured in large part around images of a lone knight ferreting out corruption, they also bristle reflexively with expressions of fearsome pleasure over that encroaching, internalized, and projected wilderness of otherness and desire. Race becomes a trope for a difference that is both threatening and appealing, a compelling metaphor for the hero's own marginal status, his own uninterpellated position. As Liam Kennedy writes about "blackness" in particular, the white hardboiled hero "appropriates signs of blackness to signify his liminal isolations and difference."[34] Or, more potently, Manthia Diawara has recently suggested that film noir is driven by the image of blackness as "a fall from whiteness";[35] specifically, its main characters have "lost the privilege of whiteness by pursuing lifestyles that are misogynistic, cowardly, duplicitous, that exhibit themselves in an eroticization of violence" (262). The tough guy's flirtation with non-whiteness offers him the kicks of liminality but without the more pedestrian tyranny that comes from actually being a minority in racially oppressive Los Angeles.

For Cain's eminently guilty male heroes, for Chandler's wayward characters, and even for Philip Marlowe himself in his covert enjoyment of the pleasures to be found in the dark city, whiteness and blackness reveal themselves to have little connection to ethnicity or even skin color. Instead, whiteness and blackness operate as yet another binary that both shields the hero through an invented distance, and increases the illicit gratification available through his own marginal position.

In part because of these "othering" gestures, the common view is that the hardboiled novel is, at heart, conservative or reactionary. Dennis Porter writes that the hardboiled novel offers "a radicalism of nostalgia for a mythical past. If any political program is implied at all, it is one that looks forward to the restoration of a traditional order of things, associated retrospectively with the innocent young Republic and its frontier, a traditional order that was destroyed with the advent of large-scale industrialization."[36] I hope to show that this view actually limits the very real ambiguities in these texts—ambiguities that suggest a more conflicted relationship between the hardboiled hero and urban otherness. Indeed, when one considers the other significant set of influences on hardboiled fiction—dime novels and pulp magazines—the relationship between the tough guy and otherness becomes even more complicated.

The race-beset Western and frontier forerunners to hardboiled fiction appeared regularly in perhaps hardboiled fiction's most important precursor, the dime novel. Immensely popular among Civil War soldiers, dime novels emerged in the 1860s, joining the already-popular "story papers"— eight-page weekly newspapers containing "serialized stories, as well as correspondence, brief sermons, humor, fashion advice, and bits of arcane knowledge."[37] Growing increasingly widespread with the rise of newspaper circulation in the 1870s, dime novels were actually pamphlets of about 100 pages containing narratives that had often already been serialized in the story papers.[38] The most popular dime novel series, the fabulously successful Nick Carter installments, began its long run in 1891.[39] Carter was a detective with both an upper-class pedigree and physical strength and prowess. As Larry Landrum points out, he "combined attributes of the urban gentleman detective with those of the Western adventure hero" (7). The emergence of Carter marks an important shift in the dime novel. In his important study of dime novels, Michael Denning has pointed out a "contradictory political meaning" in the late-nineteenth-century popularity of detective fiction, noting the move from a wide array of formulas (seduction stories, Westerns, working girl romances, tales of nobles-in-disguise, Molly Maguires, tramps, and outlaws) to the increasing dominance of detective stories—a shift he attributes to a larger "fragmentation of working-class culture at the turn of the century."[40] Denning suggests that the rise of Nick Carter and sleuths like him can be attributed to their ability to assume any disguise—one Carter cover shows him as "a Chinese boy, a dandy, a woman, a farmer, an Irish political boss and a black boy"—while still retaining an unimpeachable "young muscular white Anglo-Saxon" core.[41]

But while heroes like Nick Carter, well-bred and utterly unambiguous, dominated the market for several years, the rise of hardboiled novels and stories overturned this model as unmistakably as they did the Sherlock Holmes ratiocinative model. The hardboiled heroes of Chandler and Cain, not to mention Hammett, Horace McCoy, or even Hemingway or

Nathanael West, generally derive from working- or lower-middle- to middle-class origins. Further, hardboiled detectives rely not on dilettantish and clever disguises or even analytical skills but intuition, "gut," uninterpreted emotion, or even brute force. While hardboiled novels do not, in any programmatic or overt way, recuperate the potential class warfare Michael Denning locates in the dime novels, they do present the modern city as corrupted by the poisonous wealth of the exploitative businessmen who own it.

It is this emphasis that leads many critics to link hardboiled novels with the earlier urban fiction of Jack London, Upton Sinclair, and Theodore Dreiser and the "proletariat" novels of authors working during hardboiled fiction's rise in the 1930s, such as John Dos Passos, John Steinbeck, James T. Farrell, Waldo Frank, and Nelson Algren. David Madden has written extensively of the link between proletariat and hardboiled novels in the 1930s, and Woody Haut has connected Cold War–era hardboiled novels to early proletariat fiction, writing, "pulp culture writing retained the basic themes of proletariat writing: the corrosive power of money, class antagonism, capitalism's ability to erode the community, turning its citizens into a disparate band of self-centered and alienated individuals. . . ."[42]

Between the dime novels of the nineteenth and early twentieth century and pocket paperbacks of the 1940s and 50s, however, lies the most recognizable incarnation of the urban white male loner who comes to dominate hardboiled novels. Pulp magazines, as their name indicates, were made through a new wood-pulping procedure that enabled slick covers to be made cheaply. Designed for newsstands and thus for an urban population, these magazines came to replace dime novels and story papers in the early twentieth century. As the years passed, pulp magazines became increasingly specialized to meet the interests of an explicitly urban population; the crime stories dominated by "puzzles, refined heroes, and isolated settings" (*cf.* Nick Carter) shifted to tougher characters and a gritty urban milieu (Landrum, 10). One specific pulp, however, proved most crucial to the development of the hardboiled protagonist: *Black Mask*.

Originally a project of H. L. Mencken and George Jean Nathan to generate money for their literary magazine, *Smart Set, Black Mask* (1920–1951) published a range of stories, from Westerns and science fiction, to crime and detective fiction until 1933, when it moved exclusively to detective stories.[43] Mencken and Nathan sold the magazine a few months into its publication, and it eventually came under the influential leadership of editor Joseph "Cap" Shaw. Shaw created the magazine's signature style, which exhibited the influence of Hemingway's prose style in its sparse, dialogue-driven, clean narrative lines (Hemingway would in fact write a novel often considered as "hardboiled" as any *Black Mask* story, his *To Have and Have Not*). Shaw also nurtured its pet writers, the immensely popular Carroll John Daly, whose detective Race Williams was instrumental to the hardboiled model, and especially Dashiell Hammett, who published dozens of stories and his novel *Red Harvest* in the magazine. Beginning in 1933, Raymond Chandler's stories began appearing in *Black Mask,* and in other magazines modeled close to it, particularly *Dime Detective.*

Black Mask's promulgation of the whiteness of its protagonists is suggested by the fact that one of the magazine's first issues was devoted to Ku Klux Klan–themed stories that the editors recruited, professing not to care whether the Klan was portrayed as villainous or heroic. The magazine's perception of the gender model its readers were seeking is reflected in the fact that, by the mid-1920s, it began listing "The He-Man's Magazine" as its subtitle. Although under the editorship of a woman in its earlier years, publishers were careful to list her name with initials rather than reveal her gender (Nolan, 20). Of particular note, too, is Chandler's characterization of the new style inaugurated by these pulps. He speaks in explicitly gendered terms when he proposes that the hardboiled style has such "authentic power" that, "even at its most mannered and artificial, made most of the fiction of the time taste like a cup of luke-warm consommé at a spinsterish tearoom" ("Introduction to 'The Simple Art of Murder,'" 1016).

Shaw, in a 1933 editorial, envisioned the *Black Mask* protagonist thusly: "He is vigorous-minded . . . hating unfairness, trickery, injustice . . . responsive to the thrill of danger, the stirring exhilaration of clean, swift, hard action . . . [he is] a man who . . . knows the song of a bullet, the soft, slithering hiss of a swift-thrown knife, the feel of hard fists, the call of courage" (quoted in Nolan, 28). One can hear similar chords in Chandler's famous rendering of the hardboiled detective, but there are noteworthy differences:

> [D]own these mean streets a man must go who is not himself mean, who is neither tarnished nor afraid. . . . He is the hero, he is everything. He must be a complete man and a common man and yet an unusual man. He must be, to use a rather weathered phrase, a man of honor, by instinct, by inevitability, without thought of it, and certainly without saying it. He must be the best man in his world and a good enough man for any world.[44]

Shaw's figure, in his pleasure in violence and unmitigated delectation in danger, is actually a closer precursor to Mickey Spillane's violent Mike Hammer than to Chandler's Philip Marlowe, who rarely commits acts of violence and whose relationship to pleasure of any kind is deeply measured and troubled, as we will see in chapter two. If we can see the appeal of pulp as vicarious adventures in high-carnage violence and (although Shaw does not mention it here) salacious descriptions of women, readers approaching writers like

Chandler and Cain were also forced to confront more ambiguous expressions of white male urban existence—visions of bodies out of control, conflicting and even transgressive desires, complicated racial dread, and a persistent yoking of pleasure and revulsion in the face of otherness. Chandler's evocations of "strained and blocked emotions"[45] and Cain's evocations of the grotesque bodily toll of released emotions suggest a far more complicated relationship with its readers, whose escapist desires were to be both met and unmasked in these novels.

The readership of these magazines was high, but the genre was to be eclipsed in the 1940s with the rise of the paperback industry. The inauguration of Pocket Books in 1939 dramatically changed the publishing industry and access to and dissemination of hardboiled (and other popular) literature. Pocket Books heralded their first ten releases with a full-page ad in the *New York Times* that read, "OUT TODAY—THE NEW POCKET BOOKS THAT MAY REVOLUTIONIZE AMERICA'S READING HABITS."[46] Those ten releases were a mix of what we might call "high" (Shakespeare), "middlebrow" (Agatha Christie), and "low" (Dorothea Brande's *Wake Up and Live!*). In the 1940s, Avon Books, Popular Library, Dell, Bantam, and others followed Pocket Book's lead, with Avon, for instance, publishing Raymond Chandler and James M. Cain's 1930s hardcovers, along with works by William Faulkner and Noel Coward.

Sales soared during World War II, and dropped off in the years following, as television came to dominate, but also as government attention turned disastrously to the paperback industry. Geoffrey O'Brien catalogues the hysteria, noting the efforts of "vigilante groups" like the National Organization of Decent Literature and the seizure of paperbacks by vice squads. The climax of these efforts came with the aforementioned 1952 House Select Committee on Current Pornographic Materials, which focused on the paperback industry, "girlie" magazines, and comic books.[47] The fear of the mass audiences for paperbacks along with the messages potentially disbursed within them created an atmosphere of hysterical repression. Representations of sexual license and explicit and sexualized violence both within the texts and in their often lurid cover art were the putative concern of much of these repressive campaigns. A characteristic quote from the 1952 Congressional Committee expresses outrage over the use of the paperback for the "dissemination of artful appeals to sensuality, immorality, filth, perversion, and degeneracy. The exaltation of passion above principle and the identification of lust with love are so prevalent that the casual reader of such 'literature' might easily conclude that all married persons are habitually adulterous."[48] The Committee openly decried what they saw as representations of "homosexuality, lesbianism, and other sexual aberrations" as well as narcotic use.[49] However, as Dashiell Hammett's abuse at the hands of a congressional committee attests, much of this anxiety is more broadly over the potential of these novels to subvert or merely fail to bolster Cold War visions of Americanness.

This book then argues that the tough guy proved increasingly menacing amid the rise of World War II and Cold War models of what it meant to be American, or, specifically, to be a white American male. The urban white male figure who dominates Chandler and Cain's novels and is radically revised by Chester Himes actually posed a significant threat to cultural hegemony not for his reactionary misogyny, homophobia, or racism, nor even for his potential violence or his class critiques, but instead for his refusal to take up his newly aligned position within a patriarchal, heteronormative, and industrialized capitalistic system. His whiteness and maleness offer and even require in consumerist, nuclear family–focused Cold War America a more socially acceptable position than that of an unmarried, childless loner with no social ties, no community responsibilities, no patriotic or nationalist commitments.

This is not to suggest that the loner white male is a dramatically radical figure, eschewing larger societal oppressiveness against minorities and gay men and lesbians. Chester Himes, after all, clearly exposes at least the racist foundation of the tough guy, demonstrating his reliance upon the containment of black men, who are presented as docile, empty service employees or faceless symbols of degeneration and decay. In exposing and overturning the whiteness of the hardboiled tough guy, Himes confronts the abuse of black men in the genre and the larger social containment of black men that hardboiled novels reflect. He seizes the generic attributes and pushes them to absurdist heights while asserting a dazzlingly potent black hetero-masculinity. This assertion is often at the expense of black women and black gay men— just as white hardboiled fiction asserts white hetero-masculinity often at the expense of white women and white gay men.

But despite the tough guy's reactionary elements, what I want the ensuing pages to show is the extent to which this hardboiled figure is no less ambiguous and threatening than the femmes fatales he confronts. And in fact he serves as a catalyst for just as firm a containment rhetoric as that which he imposes on the spider women he encounters. While, as I will demonstrate, Chester Himes foregrounds precisely what was occluded by hardboiled fiction and contained by 1950s xenophobia and racism—agentic black male heroes—Cain and Chandler radically isolate precisely the figure meant to be interpellated: white men. If white men do not assume their appropriate position of power, who will?

CHAPTER TWO

"I CAN FEEL HER"

The White Male as Hysteric
in James M. Cain and Raymond Chandler

IN APRIL 1932, DEMOCRATIC PRESIDENTIAL NOMINEE FRANKLIN DELANO
Roosevelt gave a ten-minute radio address foregrounding a figure he called
the "Forgotten Man." The term was borrowed from an 1883 speech by free-
market social scientist William Graham Sumner, but, in the hands of Raymond Moley, a key member of FDR's brain trust and the speech's primary
architect, the term's meaning underwent significant revision.

For Sumner, the Forgotten Man was the industrious model citizen who
went unnoticed: "He works hard, he votes, generally he prays—but he always
pays—yes, above all, he pays."[1] Society depends on him, as he is the "one who
keeps production going" (491). Unlike those of whom the putative do-
gooders make "pets"—specifically, the "poor," "the weak," "the laborers"—
the Forgotten Man asks for nothing, causes no trouble, imposes no burden.
Because he is not a "problem (unlike tramps and outcasts); or notorious (unlike criminals); or an object of sentiment (unlike the poor and the weak); or
a burden (unlike paupers and loafers)," he is unjustly forgotten (491–92).

Moley and FDR's revision, perhaps with a defiant wink, replaces this
model self-supporting citizen (in many ways, a precursor to Nixon's "Silent
Majority") with the American at the "bottom of the economic pyramid."[2]
Such an overt reckoning with socioeconomic class in America led to strong
reactions against the speech, perhaps most famously by Al Smith, who accused Roosevelt of declaring class warfare.

The address itself begins with Roosevelt invoking the Great War, recalling his own role and asking listeners to remember the larger national mobilization. He cites the "united efforts of 110,000,000 human beings,"

asserting that such a dazzling mobilization was a "great plan because it was built from bottom to top and not from top to bottom" (66). He then goes on, "In my calm judgment, the Nation faces today a more grave emergency than in 1917" (66). In particular, like Napoleon, who lost Waterloo "because he forgot his infantry," the current administration "has either forgotten or it does not want to remember the infantry of our economic army" (66). Roosevelt thus calls for a new model for governing the nation, one that "rest[s] upon the forgotten, the unorganized but the indispensable units of economic power, for plans like those of 1917 that build from the bottom up and not from the top down, that put their faith once more in the forgotten man at the bottom of the economic pyramid" (66). FDR focuses on restoring the farmer's purchasing power, providing relief to homeowners and small banks (to the "little fellow" who is the local lender), and revising tariff policy (67–68). Repeatedly, he emphasizes the need to rethink the nation in terms of the "bottom up," attending to the forgotten man who won the Great War and can defeat the Great Depression.

In addition to its wildly divergent political agenda, FDR's Forgotten Man differs from Sumner's in another telling way. Sumner asserts, "the Forgotten Man is not seldom a woman" (491), going on to speak of the plight of the hardworking seamstresses who are taxed for the spools of thread they use. FDR does not openly gender the underclasses on which he focuses, but the tale he relays is of an implicitly masculine path from combat veterans to the "economic army" to the "little fellow" to the language of battle and the infantry.

Soon after the "Forgotten Man" address, the term's masculine signification was concretized as it slipped quickly into popular usage, appearing, for instance, in letters written by Americans to the Roosevelts, Harry Hopkins, and the Federal Emergency Relief Administration and other government administrators.[3] Further, Hollywood would almost immediately appropriate the term, perhaps most memorably in the immensely popular musical *Gold Diggers of 1933*. Now legendary for its glittering "We're in the Money" opening number, the film centers on a group of Broadway producers, writers, and performers struggling for parts and for financing amid the Depression. Inspired by the dire conditions around him—and by the penniless Broadway performers whose shows keep closing due to the economic crisis—a young songwriter (Dick Powell) stages a new musical called "The Forgotten Man."

The film climaxes with the Busby Berkeley–choreographed musical extravaganza, "Remember My Forgotten Man," in which actress Joan Blondell, in provocative streetwalker garb, sings the sharply rendered Harry Warren lyrics about the man she loves, lost in the economic downturn. She reminds the audience, directly invoking World War I sacrifice, "You put a rifle in his hand/You sent him far away/You shouted, 'Hip-hooray!'/And look at him today." As with the seminal early 30s song "Brother, Can You Spare a Dime?," the ghost of World War I looms large: these are the men who sacrificed all for their country and now their country and their fellow citizens have forgotten them.

This direct echoing of FDR's rendering is continued when Blondell next accuses the audience of forcing her Forgotten Man to "cultivate the land" until "sweat fell from his brow." All this sacrifice and yet, "look at him right now," she warns us. The pointed criticism then turns to a lament: her man used to take care of her and now he is gone, possibly leading her to walk the streets.

The lyrics ring with the fear of a loss of masculine potency, and with a female desire for returned virility and sufficiency. While the dependence of the woman on the man is clear, it is the woman singer who frames the demands, who presents the case and calls for action. The charges are leveled, presumably, at the impersonal and not-explicitly-gendered government who has sent the Forgotten Man off to war, who has demanded his sweat and labor—and the larger culture that allows for or endorses this treatment: the "you" Blondell addresses. The perceived threat to masculinity resounds heavily and points to larger cultural fears—the fears that drove FDR's rhetoric and that transformed his term into a resonant metaphor for Depression-era gender anxiety.

The term did not lose resonance quickly. In 1936, the Forgotten Man figures interestingly in the popular screwball comedy *My Man Godfrey*. The story begins with Park Avenue socialites embarking on a scavenger hunt in which one of the goals is to bring back a "Forgotten Man." Irene (Carole Lombard) comes upon Godfrey (William Powell) in a Hooverville by the docks and gleefully announces that she has found her Forgotten Man. Explaining to Godfrey what a scavenger hunt is, she likens it to a treasure hunt, except "with a treasure hunt you try to find something you want and in a scavenger hunt you try to find something that nobody wants."

Smitten and desirous of a mentoring role, Irene hires Godfrey as a butler for her eccentric and fabulously wealthy family. The film's screwball humor rests on the notion that Godfrey is far more intelligent, upstanding, and deserving of wealth than anyone in Irene's decadent and frivolous family—a family overrun by women (two daughters and a mother with a preening male protégée) whom the hapless family patriarch cannot control. Midway through the film the audience discovers (though Irene does not) that Godfrey is actually an upper-class child of wealth who gave all his money to the woman he loved after their affair ended. Intending to end his life in the East River, he came upon the shacks of the Forgotten Men on the city dumps and struck up friendships with them, remaining with them as a fellow vagrant.

After a time as the family butler, Powell's Godfrey manages to embark on a successful business venture, opening a posh nightclub on the very ash dump he had called home. At the film's end, Godfrey is no longer in hobo gear nor in the butler's tails; he dons the slick tuxedo of a successful entrepreneur. His self-respect regained, he can safely make the closing love match with Carole Lombard's socialite. Further, his employees are his former fellow Forgotten Men, who now have service jobs working for Godfrey, an appropriate class order restored.

As befits screwball comedies of the era, it is the flighty heroine who engineers the final coupling, but such a match "works" for the film because Godfrey has elevated himself from his butler servitude (and in fact never belonged in such a role to begin with), but even more importantly from his tramp's clothes and whiskers. In an early scene, Irene puts money in his pocket to buy clothes for his new butler job and Godfrey, embarrassed, watches as the money slips through the holes in his coat pocket onto the floor. Further, Irene designates Godfrey her protégée despite his age (he is significantly older than she) and obvious sophistication. Irene's patronage is essentially the film's running joke, given her capricious ways, but the inevitable coming together of the couple does not occur until gender and class structures fall into alignment: Godfrey re-establishes himself as a man of breeding and more important of prospects and he is no longer the helpless figure who requires a woman to put money in his pockets.

The Forgotten Man, then, operates significantly as a figure not so much of emasculation but as a warning sign of the pressing need to re-masculinize the American man rendered impotent during the economic crisis. Despite his wayward condition he is shown as not deserving of such a helpless state, having proven his masculine credentials in past war and work efforts. Significantly, however, it is up to the woman—Joan Blondell, Carole Lombard—to highlight this disjuncture and to assert the Forgotten Man's highly valuable manhood. Such a choice suggests a further impotency (not only is the man powerless, he needs a woman to help him), but also the reverse: these women *need* re-masculinized men. Even as women, driven by financial duress, enter the workforce, they can never take the place of men and would not want to. A desire for a more secure gender binary of male power and sufficiency and female dependency ripples through these Forgotten Man representations.

Robert McElvaine, in his influential history of the Depression era, argues that the economic crisis "feminized" American society, claiming that the "self-centered, aggressive, competitive 'male' ethic of the 1920s was discredited. Men who lost their jobs became dependent in many ways that women had been thought to be," finding themselves "much more often in the traditional position of women—on the bottom, in a state of dependence."[4]

McElvaine then seems to be slipping from an argument about dependence to one about feminization. He goes on to suggest that, when, with the New Deal, men moved "beyond passivity and became active in their quest to improve their situation, [they] tended to do so through 'female' values. They sought to escape dependence not through 'male,' self-centered, 'rugged' individualism, but through cooperation and compassion" (340–41).

McElvaine describes this shift toward feminine values in ways that suggest that, for McElvaine, gender distinctions are constituted primarily through the lens of a capitalist versus communitarian ethos. For instance, his model of masculinity is characterized by aggression and competition and his model of femininity by passivity and cooperation—models that surely carried cultural coinage but are deeply limited even within the 1920s–30s context in which he situates them. After all, constructions of femininity in the 1920s underwent significant overhauls, not the least through the flapper figure and rising women's rights efforts.

Philip Abbott's recent work takes issue with McElvaine, arguing that one could more easily characterize the era not by a feminization but by a "patriarchal reassertion that suffused all discourse in the Thirties."[5] Certainly the oft-quoted array of firsthand accounts of men on relief during the Depression attest to persistent fears of emasculation.[6] As Abbott offers, "Deprived of the authority that emanated from control of the household, men retrieved a sense of autonomy by creating a new masculine public space." Abbott locates the creation of a new masculinity—"public, collective, informal"—in the "guiding spirit" of Works Progress Administration and other New Deal efforts (12). In FDR's rhetoric, Abbott argues, we see a redefining of masculinity that suggests, "To be a man no longer rested upon material acquisition but public stewardship, no longer on speculation but public adventure. Strength too was invoked but it was strength derived from discipline rather than self assertion" (3–4). Susan Faludi likewise argues that the New Deal's "masculine ideal" was the "selfless public servant" devoted to the needs of the community over the self. In other words, while McElvaine recapitulates associations between dependence and femininity and competitiveness and masculinity, one might more easily see definitions of masculinity and femininity being rewritten to match the exigencies of the day; if financial success is no longer accessible to define maleness, then public works and discipline may take its place. Such a model, according to Faludi, transmuted into Henry Wallace's model of the "Common Man"—a figure characterized by a sense of personal integrity and a deep responsibility to the community and the world at large. This progressive model, outlined by Wallace in his famous "Century of the Common Man" speech in 1942, offered a masculinity focused on "contributing to the needs of the world rather than simply aspiring to dominate it."[7]

But while the New Deal conception of masculinity carried significant cultural weight (impacting other highly influential purveyors of masculine models including, as Faludi points out, journalist Ernie Pyle and also Hollywood directors such as Frank Capra), it stands in contrast to another model rising at the same time: the tough guy. Deriving more from the beset Forgotten Man's isolation and marginalization than the New Deal's disciplined and selfless public servant, the tough guy retains the individualist spirit of nineteenth-century models of American white masculinity, but with an added sense of a particularly urban and distinctly modern mood of alienation.

The tough guy, whose roots lie in the 1920s (and earlier) and whose popularity accelerates during the 1930s, is deeply significant in relation to the Forgotten Man figure and the climate from which it rises. Much has been made of the popularity of opulent Hollywood musicals in the early 1930s as an escape from the miseries of the Depression, but one might extend that notion to consider connections between the cultural anxieties over manhood—as emblematized by the Forgotten Man figure—and the rise of the tough guy. Consider, for instance, the fact that, while scores of historians, perhaps most famously Warren Susman, see the 1930s as an era of a belief in the collective and community, the tough guy is, in contrast, constituted in large part through his isolation, his refusal to be a part of community, society, family, or nation. Further, consider that the striving and often deviant protagonists of James M. Cain's novels hungrily *consume* (overwhelmed, as they are, by their own greed and desires) at a time of thwarted consumption. And consider that Raymond Chandler's detective hero struggles to remain hermetically sealed from his surroundings at a time when public servitude was a seeming masculine ideal; further, he struggles with transgressive desires at a time when the needs for a restorative and strong masculinity seemed to allow little space for such play. We can then see a split in masculinity models between the public rhetoric and national ideals—ideals also given substantial cultural coinage through Hollywood and popular literature and magazines—and the embattled and embittered tough guy gaining in audience as the decade wore on.[8]

Thus, we have a curious conjunction in which the tough guy emerges at a time of needed re-masculinization but also at a time when gender instability provided curious freedom of expression for less fixed gender constructs. If masculinity can no longer be defined solely through patriarchal function or breadwinner roles, given the economics of the day, then it is no surprise that there emerges a twisty fusion of both a reassertion of a hard-edged, uncompromising masculinity and a persistent strain of fleeting pleasure in gender collapses—collapses that, however, do eventually demand restoration.[9]

It is through these lenses that I want to approach the so-called tough guy novels, in particular those by hardboiled detective novelist Raymond Chandler and crime novelist James M. Cain. These books offer a vision of masculinity that revises its era's range of ideals of maleness in compelling ways, offering a conception of gender that, while deeply invested in a traditional masculine-feminine binary, also locates pleasure and desire in a destabilization of that binary. Further, an ensuing re-stabilization of the traditional gender roles is presented as forced, awkward, but utterly necessary. Although it would be difficult to argue that the masculinities posited in these works pose a radical challenge to conventional gender constructions, at the same time, they are far from traditional. Their subversiveness reinforces sexual difference, but in doing so, redefines what that difference means, and from what shadowy places it may derive.

Upon taking a closer look at Raymond Chandler's detective hero Philip Marlowe and James M. Cain's classic "sap," insurance salesman Walter Huff (*Double Indemnity*), a textual pattern emerges in which notions of male agency are thrown into doubt, and male subjectivity constantly threatens to unravel. Masculinity is situated as weak, changeable, even hysterical, with the feminine characterized as potentially lethal in strength and amoral will.[10] But this unsettling binary is thrown into question, as it is through weakness that these protagonists often find pleasure and eventually solidify power. Such episodic male pleasure in infirmity or temporary loss of agency, however, unsettles certain basic hegemonic structures—most notably the patriarchal family, a structure that rests on potent masculine control offsetting any exogamous threat.

As we will see, Marlowe, Walter Huff, even Frank Chambers (the murdering protagonist of *The Postman Always Rings Twice*) defy conventional patriarchal positions. All are single men with shadowy class backgrounds. However, these characters—who never marry, never become fathers, never attach themselves to any authoritarian system[11]—do not fulfill the role of glamorous and successful bachelor (later exemplified by Chandler friend Ian Fleming's James Bond), instead existing as loners with few ties and little money. Failing to adopt the role of father and husband, these men operate in what Kaja Silverman might call "deviant" ways: they "eschew Oedipal normalization, while nevertheless remaining fully within signification, symbolic castration, and desire."[12] Entrance into the family seems forbidden to these men, or, more clearly, they never seek access to such a structure, yet at the same time it is their anxious realization of this marginal position, with its attendant risks of feminization or impotence, that so unsettles and destabilizes these characters.

It is Cain's insurance salesman Walter Huff who comes closest to a traditional valuation of the Oedipal family. The conceit of *Double Indemnity* is that the narrative consists wholly of Huff's first-person confession. Huff confides to the reader how he met Phyllis Nirdlinger, the alluring wife of a client, on a routine sales call and conspired with her to murder her husband for the insurance money. In so doing, Huff enters into a family romance, both through his murder of the family patriarch, Mr. Nirdlinger, and through his relationships with the patriarch's wife and daughter. The murder offers Huff a pseudo-consummation of the Oedipal phantasy of killing the father and marrying the mother. The Oedipal drama, however, is marvelously deconstructed. The seemingly powerful patriarch is on crutches due to an injury, suggesting a literal impotence to match the cuckolding. Therefore, when Huff needs to impersonate the patriarch in order to carry off the murder plot, he is forced to take on the crutches, thereby inheriting the patriarch's weak (castrated) position. As the plot deepens, Nirdlinger's literal handicap is shown to be a symbol of his larger impotence: he is the in-name-only head of a family dominated by two strong women—one a murderous Clytemnestra (Phyllis), the other a vengeful Electra (Lola). For all Walter Huff's greedy and lust-driven criminality, the depth of his desire cannot match theirs. Both terrify him when he is afforded revelatory glimpses into the extent of their will and aspirations. And, perhaps most important, Huff ultimately recognizes that his consuming desires (for the lethal Phyllis, for the murder-for-profit scheme, for the pure daughter of the man he has killed), which he considers perverse, afford him no place in that conventional structure.[13]

Then, hardboiled novels such as those by Chandler and Cain, even when they veer closely toward an engagement with the family, end up either evading or deflating Oedipal structures and the promise of a potent male subjectivity through a standard patriarchal position (or through an unencumbered but uncomplicatedly virile male of the American individualist tradition, as we will see later). If, as Silverman suggests, a positive Oedipal complex is the apparatus by which male interpellation is achieved, "thereby . . . produc[ing] and sustain[ing] a normative masculinity" (16), then we find neither a successful interpellation nor a successful embodiment of normative masculinity in these texts. Instead, we are offered first-person accounts of deviant masculinities that not only fail but often outright reject the Oedipal model. As we will see with a closer engagement with these novels, the system into which one might be interpellated either forbids the protagonist access, or appears to the protagonist to be not a system at all, but a corrupt chaos.

One might ask, however, whether the rejection of an Oedipal mode constitutes a genuine subversion of normative masculinity. As a means of approaching this question, I want to delve more fully into *Double Indemnity* by suggesting that we find in Cain's novel a struggle between two systems:

the Company, a system of knowledge, and the Body, a system of desire but also of uncontrollable reflex.

Walter Huff's employer, General Fidelity, looms large in the novel and operates as a dominating system that encompasses or even comprises Walter's whole world. In fact, General Fidelity's very name serves as a portentous signifier of systemic expectations. The Company system, as emblematized by General Fidelity, operates in the novel as a kind of Lacanian Symbolic, consisting of language, reason, logic—all defined by bourgeois values, set in motion by a corporate economy, and ruled by the family romance model of power dynamics. As with the traditional family structure, the Company is overseen by a patriarch, and like the Nirdlinger family of *Double Indemnity*, the Company is experiencing a threat to its endogamous structure.

In binary opposition to this structure lies Walter's other primary force: the system of the Body, which can scarcely be considered a system by Company standards. It consists of unspeakable desire, consumption, the mouth, intuition, what cannot be said. The body speaks what words cannot express (much like the classic psychoanalytic formula for the hysteric, as we will discuss). Within this system, the family romance and the Company carry no regulatory or juridical power. The Body does what it wants.

As we will see later in the chapter, Raymond Chandler's detective hero Philip Marlowe is situated in uneasy opposition to either kind of system, uncomfortable in his own skin and yet an explicit outsider to any system but his own set of harassed ethics. But first let us consider Cain's Walter Huff, who tries to beat both systems, coming to realize he cannot. The differences between the two systems have disappeared; the binary has collapsed. Moreover, he realizes he has tried to defeat the very forces that constitute him, that give him his gender, class, and race, and thereby his whole identity.

General Fidelity: Taking on the Man

Walter Huff, made even more famous by Fred MacMurray's portrayal in the 1944 Billy Wilder film, is often set forth as the prime example of the fall guy seduced and betrayed by the murderous femme fatale. I would like to problematize this notion by teasing out the unsteadiness of the traditional hardboiled gender binary of masculine/sap and feminine/femme fatale. Conventional gender constructs of male strength and female weakness are not simply reversed in *Double Indemnity*, as they are in so many hardboiled texts where the male is duped by the castrating vamp.[14] Instead, we find a far pricklier process at work, where masculinity reveals itself as a hysterical structure, displacing its own anxieties onto an undefined, empty femininity.

From the start of the novel, Walter Huff presents himself as a man who operates in a universe of men—an office of salesmen, male insurance investigators, male executives, male security guards. The only woman in his daily existence is his nondescript secretary, Nettie. The rules and regulations govern this masculine space and, within that space, Walter knows all the angles to every routine, every process, every bureaucratic procedure. Clips on folders signify dubious clients. Logbooks record every call. Rate books catalog various charges. There are explicitly delineated rituals to filing claims. Everything operates according to a well-worn system. Even when Walter fabricates a rule (inventing a system called multiple-card bookkeeping to avert suspicion about his shady paperwork), it sounds so plausible that we believe it; but Walter is so obsessive about the rules of the system that he cannot let it go without assuring the reader that "[i]t was all hooey" (32), going on to explain how the actual process works.[15]

Walter's narration of the insurance business in the larger sense is characterized by a compulsive explication of its nuances, its philosophy—the novel serving a secondary function as a primer on the industry. Walter's crime, then, constitutes more of a transgression because the system is so tight, so controlled, so regulatory. As his excessive description of the insurance business conveys, Walter's decision to collude with the femme fatale Phyllis to murder her husband and file a false insurance claim sets him up to conquer a system he knows inside and out. It has trained him so well he believes he has the discipline to control it, to predict every twist and turn in the path of the false claim he originates. Frank Krutnik writes of the film adaptation, Walter "transgresses against a closed regime of masculine economic power—an insurance company, headed . . . by a powerful figure of male authority . . . [the] deceased 'Symbolic Father' Old Man Norton."[16] It is important to note, however, that the novel's Huff never sees Company founder Old Man Norton as a father; Norton's legacy means nothing to pragmatic Walter. It is not the head of the system, but the system itself that matters, that it would mean something to defeat. The system of the Company never becomes individualized for him, thereby allowing him to see it as a game to beat, not a Father to overthrow. The Oedipal drama, it appears, does not apply in the new corporate economy. Unlike the freighted family romance, the field of power is seemingly level in the American capitalist regime where all (white men) are encouraged and expected to rise, to overcome all competitors. Moreover, the Company system Huff has absorbed is not regulated by taboo, but via its panoptical structure in which discipline derives from knowing that all transgressions can be found out. Indeed, the Company serves as the primary juridical system in *Double Indemnity*, far more so than the law, which does not have the stake the Company does in solving the putative crime. The Company drives the law to act, and in the end serves as the primary punisher of Walter, in place of the slow and potentially messy path of the justice system.

William Marling argues that, in confessing to his crime, Huff reveals that, although he has "serial desires," he has also come to realize that "some degree of self-discipline is necessary in order to consume" (178); he must pay for his transgression by entering the disciplinary structure of another system, that of the Law. While I would argue that the Company supercedes the Law here, it is also difficult to argue that Huff is ever without self-discipline per se. He seems instead to apply his self-discipline to the task at hand: in the murder plot, he employs the same ingenuity, intuition, and wiles that aid him in selling insurance. These skills ultimately fail him, however, as self-discipline means little in the system of the Body he enters, where he faces perpetual threats to the self, his contained whole, his masculine stability. His hardboiled, world-weary guy routine disintegrates in the face of Phyllis and what lies (in one of the book's favorite idiomatic constructions) "back of" her, or so it first appears.

If Walter brings his savvy confidence with him when he exits the Company structure to commit the crime, he loses it fairly quickly in the face of his guilt and Phyllis herself. Instead of clips on files and logbooks, Walter must allow intuition, bodily warnings, and superstition to guide him.[17] William Marling figures the shift a bit differently, distinguishing between a narrative of desire unfettered and the ensuing juridical process that overtakes that narrative. He writes that in both *Double Indemnity* and in Cain's *The Postman Always Rings Twice,* the narrative's first half functions as the "'realistic' narrative of the reasons. Then, in place of the initial sign system of desire . . . Cain substitutes a system representing the forces of techno-economic production, highly mechanical and logical: the legal system, the insurance industry, or business economics" (183–84). While I want to bear Marling out to an extent here, I also want to begin to problematize the ease with which he distinguishes between the two parts of the narrative. As we will see, the systems Walter volleys between are not the binary he imagines. His sin lies not in a crossing-over, but in his arrogant belief that he can defeat either.

But first let us consider the differences between the two realms that the Company and the femme fatale Phyllis represent. Walter in many ways is the object of dual gazes: the Company's disciplinary gaze (which resembles Foucault's Panopticon in the extent of its surveillance, more metaphoric than literal) and Phyllis's potentially castrating gaze. Walter has developed multiple strategies for eluding the former but seems to have no way to avoid the latter. While Nino Sachetti, the son of one of Phyllis's victims, investigates Phyllis, wants to penetrate her, locate her secret, Walter does not want to know; his body tells him and he does not want to hear it. To listen to his body would mean he would have to acknowledge the darkness of his desire for that which so clearly threatens his very manhood, not to mention his life.

In her reading of several films dealing with returning World War II veterans, Kaja Silverman locates a persistent female role: that of the "good girl" who nurtures men traumatized by war experiences, men who feel so "scarred by lack" (53) that they cannot return to a dominant masculine position. To facilitate the re-entry into what Silverman terms the "dominant fiction," both the male veteran and the woman who supports and heals him must "deny all knowledge of male castration by believing in the commensurability of a penis and phallus, actual and symbolic father" (42). In *Double Indemnity* we see several of the same dynamics at work. While Phyllis may, as we will see, signify for Walter his own potential lack, effectively hystericizing him, her stepdaughter and the text's "good girl," Lola Nirdlinger, serves to buoy Walter's manhood, acknowledging his potential as a protector, thereby serving as a comforting beacon to Huff. However, Huff ultimately must confess in order to save her. In the end, Lola represents a system (the family) to which he has no access.[18] The Company remains the only system to which he belongs, and it is one where he remains a wheel in the larger machinery, no match for the Company as Father.

In turn, Phyllis clearly embodies the antithesis of the Company's closed regime for Walter. She is unpredictable, to be sure. Something lies "back of it," of all she does and says, something that makes Walter shake, stutter, jerk to his feet. And while the Company's interiors can be navigated through cunning, knowing the rules, logic, and rational thinking, Walter's dynamics with Phyllis are about feeling, sensing, bodily responses, intuition, flight or fight. These seemingly separate spheres collide after the couple's murder of Phyllis's husband. The murder, fueled by the "unnatural" excitement, the uncanny kick, the deathly risk, must then go through the cogs of the "system," the juridical process of the insurance company, which Walter knows will consistently play the odds according to the most winnable course of events. The act committed with Phyllis courses through the system Walter knows so well it is as if it were part of him, his own introjection—and the effect is violently dissembling. That is, the crime tracking through the Company's system parallels Phyllis's contamination of Walter, and then the parallels are conflated. Indeed, fixing the Company and Phyllis as distinct but commensurate powers becomes increasingly difficult as we consider whether Phyllis's gaze is as potent as the Company's, or merely an echo of it, a construction of Walter's own internalized Company-paranoia.

Specifically, the question I want to pursue here is whether Walter's involvement with Phyllis is truly distinct from his relation to the Company, or whether both are invested in the same kind of Oedipal logic. Is the Company just another family, and is Walter's desire just another family romance? Phyllis's libidinal circuit and the Company's bureaucratic regime seem oppositional, two irreconcilable systems tugging at the fundamentally split Walter. Ultimately, however, they function *as the same system,* a system Walter has introjected and, in turn, projected onto Phyllis. That is, while Phyllis may embody a lethal system of disciplined transgression, Walter's reaction to that system may actually be essential to constituting it. His physical responses reveal what he cannot: the extent of his own absorption in the system he seeks to swindle.

Of course, Walter is not, on the surface, a "Company Man." For instance, he does not view his attempt to swindle the Company as a betrayal. It is no fall from Company loyalty because he has never felt any loyalty. His only twinge of what could be work-related remorse comes when he hears pseudo-mentor and claims investigator Barton Keyes (portrayed so memorably in the film by Edward G. Robinson) defend him in a memo to the Company president: "I lifted the needle and ran [the memo recording] over again. It did things to me. I don't only mean it was a relief. It made my heart feel funny" (77). This brief moment of Huffian introspection is so compelling because, instead of examining or reflecting upon his response to Keyes's defense of him, Walter instead *feels* something and chooses not to analyze or even identify it. It is a sheer visceral, bodily response, just as his response to Phyllis is preeminently a physical reaction. It is a crucial moment of unreflective bodily reaction. Walter chooses not to interpret it because it lies deeper than the game of chance, beneath the murder-for-money scheme. But precisely what Walter has subsumed he cannot name to himself or to the reader, the interlocutor of his narrative confession.

As his reflexive bodily reaction suggests, Walter, in exiting the Company through his crime, enters the realm of outlaw desire where the body dominates; there are no rules, no probability statistics. It is a realm he cannot represent in the way he can obsessively recount and analyze the details of the insurance industry. He cannot tell us what Keyes's defense does to him, how it makes him feel, because that defense has approached the realm of the unrepresentable, the bodily. We see this new realm through Walter's bodily reactions, through *what he does not say,* rather than through traditional narrative representation. This combination of bodily revolt, uninterpretibility, and gender confusion Walter undergoes points us irresistibly to that controversial figure, the hysteric. Much as William Marling's historicist reading figures Huff as the ultimate consumer, the figure of the hysteric, as revised or re-envisioned by feminist discourse, has been portrayed as "want[ing] everything."[19] The question becomes, is Walter's move from the Company structure and into a realm of unregulated desire a gendered move? Is it a move from the masculine to the feminine and, if so, is Walter's hysteria synonymous with his feminization?

Walter Huff's Body

I put my crutches under one arm, threw my leg over the rail, and let myself down. One of the crutches hit the ties and spun me so I

almost fell. I hung on. When we came square abreast of the sign I
dropped off.

—James M. Cain, *Double Indemnity* (1936)

As a way of investigating *Double Indemnity*'s unusual construction of masculinity, I want to consider the extent to which we can view Walter Huff as a
"hysterical" figure. It is with caution that I use the theoretically freighted term
"hysteric," with its thorny history in psychoanalysis and gender studies. But
it is precisely this difficult history that I think offers us a unique perspective
from which to consider Walter Huff's gender and bodily confusion and his
narrative convolutions. As with the "hysterical text" of lore, Huff's body and
his bodily reactions strain at the seams of the narrative, a narrative that will
only document—but never analyze—the symptoms—even though (or perhaps because) the narrative is Walter's own, is in fact his criminal confession.

Conceptions of hysteria have a long history of being seen through the
lens of gender confusion or as a challenge to normative gender constructions, particularly since the Charcot-Breuer-Freud period. Without recounting Sigmund Freud's controversial history with hysteria, it is crucial to note
that, throughout his career, Freud articulated in various ways a relationship
between gender development and hysteria. His most famous hysterical patient, Dora, affords a particularly provocative example—perhaps more for
theorists since than for Freud himself (who famously struggled with the
case). Theorists arguing for sexual difference as a cultural construction look
to Dora as the embodiment of a refusal to accept normative gender and sexual identifications and desires. As Peter Brooks writes, hysteria "manifests a
basic confusion about the identity of one's sexual body. Dora's homosexual
desire, constructed on the original bisexuality of all human eros, puts into
question the very gender distinction on which social life and expected com-
portment are based. The hysteric body in this manner threatens a violation
of basic antitheses and laws, including the law of castration and the conditions of meaning."[20] The hysteric then can unsettle meaning, essentialist
gender structures, and heteronormativity through his/her body and speech.
While for Freud, as for many others, this wrestling with sexual difference is
primarily a woman's battle, men too have been "afflicted" with hysteria, including Freud himself. Yet despite the substantial number of male cases, hysteria has been largely considered a female "malady" or, more recently, a
female protest. Scores of feminist readings of hysteria have focused on the
hysteric as a woman fighting social constructions of acceptable femininity.[21]
This reading has been recently expanded to considerations of male hysteria
by film theorists such as Paul Smith and literary critics D. A. Miller and,
most extensively, Elaine Showalter, who recently asked if hysteria might "also

be the son's disease, or perhaps the disease of the powerless and silenced" of either gender.[22]

There is a distinct political difficulty with detaching hysteria from women, as women have been the victims of hysteria's pathologization, and therefore the heroes of its re-inscription as a subversive protest. If we accept hysteria as the bodily revolt of the socially powerless, then dare we consider Walter Huff, murderous salesman, as suffering from powerlessness and an occluded voice? Although Walter is, in many ways, an impotent cog in his company, he suffers from far less oppression than the silenced Victorian woman-as-pawn role from which we see Dora bursting. After all, he is a bourgeois white man in a white-collar job, suffering no race, gender, or obvious class victimization. In turn, Walter, through his confession, is not "silenced" in any fundamental way. I offer, however, that if we consider Huff's relation to the hysterical figure, we can start to unravel his mysterious transformation from canny salesman out to beat the system, to frightened rabbit in the jaws of an "Irrawaddy cobra"—a transformation that may itself be gendered.

To examine Huff's potential hysteria, we need to look at his body and his text; both offer symptoms and each problematize what the other tells us. As Walter loses control over the narrative, he simultaneously loses control over his own body. His text, with its gaps and fragments, is in fact far more manifestly "hysterical" than those that Paul Smith, for example, locates in his article on Clint Eastwood films, where Smith must strain to tease out any variation from genre expectations and traditional masculine representation. Smith contends that within "hysterical" texts the "male protagonist's control of the narrative situation is never matched by control of his own body."[23] This framing is useful in relation to *Double Indemnity*. Walter Huff begins with a compulsive, even excessive narratorial control, as emphasized by his obsessive plotting and backtracking on both the diegetic level and as the "author" out to control the transmission of plot to the reader. But although Walter plays an agentic role until after the murder, and even afterward manages to direct many events, he cannot "read" Phyllis's narrative. Ever the duplicitous femme fatale, she is plotting a narrative all her own, one that is methodical and adaptable. As her narrative adjusts to meet new circumstances and Walter's own neurotically shifting plottings, Walter's discipline dissipates into a hysteria that is both narrative—the story turns gothic as Walter does—and bodily.

Paul Smith defines the "hysterical" as that which "exceeds the phallic stakes," that which somehow "jumps off," and therefore becomes unrepresentable: "The hysterical is marked by its lack of containment, by its bespeaking either the travails or the pratfalls of a body, and by its task of carrying what is strictly the unsayable of male experience. That is, what escapes the terrible simplicity of male heterosexual experience and the crude simplicity of homocentric narratives is always something that cannot or should not be represented or spoken."[24] We can see this notion of the unsayable in Walter's narrative. His body speaks to the reader in ways he cannot. Events transpire that defy his narrative capabilities, that "jump off" and, as such, he cannot represent them: specifically, he cannot represent the murder, the meaning of his bodily condition, or what Phyllis explicitly "does" to him. He can only relay uninterpreted effects. Consider this section's epigraph, taken from a moment just after the murder, when Walter has effectively taken his victim's wounded state, impersonating him and revising his death by jumping off the train. Walter tells us, "I put *my crutches* under one arm, threw my leg over the rail, and let myself down. One of the crutches hit the ties and spun me so I almost fell. I hung on. When we came square abreast of the sign I dropped off" (emphasis added, 49). Of course, these crutches are not Walter's—they are Nirdlinger's, Walter's victim. As stated earlier, Nirdlinger is a figure of threatened power or even impotence due both to his broken leg, which requires crutches, and to his seeming inability to control his wife (who cheats on him and plots his death) or his daughter (who sees the forbidden boyfriend behind his back). Walter, in killing Nirdlinger, has had literally to "become" him by posing as him, and therefore, as pointed out earlier, assumes his powerless position. As his inability to narrate the murder ("I won't tell you what I did then" [44]) underlines, Walter has left the realm of representation. He has exited the Company, a place where acts can be represented, where structures regulate. And he has entered a place where narrative and bodily control no longer exist. Just as Smith defines the "hysterical" as that which "jumps off," Walter has "dropped off."[25]

This "dropping off" is terminal for Walter. He never regains his statistically assured control. This is not to say that, prior to the murder, Walter exhibits no hysterical symptoms, narrative or bodily. From his first meetings with Phyllis, Walter experiences inexplicable physical reactions to her, up his spine, on his neck. Although he also experiences a comparatively uncomplicated sexual desire for her, Walter's primary bodily reaction to Phyllis is one of ghastly horror.

Walter's hysterical symptoms cluster in two places, the spine and the throat. After the murder, Walter describes feeling "something like a drawstring pull in my throat, and a sob popped out of me" (53). His voice has become independent from his consciousness; his sob has the agency here, not Walter, suggesting a cognitive dissonance of sorts. His voice's subjectivity signals Walter's lack of mastery over his own body; he notes, "It was getting to me. I knew I had to get myself under some kind of control" (53). To regain control over his voice he decides to sing, hoping it will "make me snap out of it" (53). The effect is chilling as he attempts to croon "The Isle of

Capri," and after two notes "it swallowed into a kind of wail" (53). He ends up mumbling the Lord's Prayer as a seemingly more solid, stabilizing choice, but gets through it shakily twice before he suddenly forgets "how it went" (53). Walter proceeds to dig his fingernails into his hands, "trying to hold onto [him]self" (54) and ends up vomiting and experiencing a violent shaking fit. His body is a rash of vibrating, convulsing entities, all operating independently. There is no center.

This experience is a virtual smorgasbord of hysterical symptoms. Walter repeatedly attempts to forestall the fragmentation, the sense that his body is splitting from his consciousness. He survives the night, resolving never to see Phyllis again, but the symptoms persist through the rest of the text, whether as chills, an inability to eat, or uncontrollable or inappropriate fits of laughter. The common interpretation of Walter's physical maladies after the murder is that they are merely a representation of racking guilt.[26] This interpretation, however, overlooks the extent to which Walter's hysteria remains curiously distant from the murderous deed itself, which remains unsayable, the confession lacking an actual divulgence of the deed itself: "I won't tell you what I did then" (44). Instead, as we will see, the hysteria inheres in what Phyllis inspires or stimulates in Huff—a sexual dread that is both appealing and repellent.

A Shape to Set a Man Nuts

Mary Ann Doane argues that the femme fatale is "not the subject of power but its carrier . . . if the femme fatale overrepresents the body it is because she is attributed with a body which is itself given agency independently of consciousness. In a sense, she has power despite herself. . . ."[27] In other words, Phyllis herself does not even matter; her force is constituted through others. Walter refers to his attraction to Phyllis at one point as "some kind of unhealthy excitement that came over me just at the sight of her" (86). He contrasts this response with the feelings the innocent Lola inspires in him: "[A] sweet peace . . . came over me as soon as I was with her" (86). Phyllis is all agitation for Walter, while Lola is safe, *heimlich,* the expected family romance. Their different brands of femininity appear to be defined primarily by Walter's bodily reaction in their presence. His body constitutes their gender; his hysterical response casts Phyllis as a lethal femme fatale.

Interestingly, however, Phyllis fails to fulfill physical/aesthetic expectations of the glamorous femme fatale.[28] She is not "beautiful," but merely "pretty." She dresses simply—but also androgynously. No seamed stockings, tight dresses, or veiled hats. She wears lounging pajamas on first meeting Walter, later a sailor suit, then a sweater and slacks. She is characterized as appearing "sweet" rather than seductive. Walter first describes her as having a "washed out look" (5) and later as having teeth that are "big and white and maybe a little buck" (11). In a text fixated on the lure of an economic pay-off, the linking of Phyllis's mouth with slang for money ("buck") is surely telling: Phyllis is a literal consumer of dollars in Walter's eyes, as well as his key to a financial windfall. Her mouth signifies money hunger, not a *vagina dentata* or a siren's lure. Moreover, though small, Phyllis displays a decidedly "unfeminine" bodily might: She manages to shock Walter with near-super-human strength, carrying her 200-pound dead husband on her back like a lioness. Walter finds the scene horrific, "like something in a horror picture" (51). Phyllis's lure then does not lie in staggering beauty or the appearance of a hyperfemininity (as masquerade or otherwise), both of which we have come to expect in the femme fatale.

But while Phyllis falls strangely short of the aesthetic criteria, she seems to represent in excess the femme fatale's deathly aura. In what reads as a near-parody of the femme fatale, Phyllis offers a gothic monologue in which she self-identifies as Death.[29] She tells Walter, right after they have agreed to murder her husband,

" . . . [T]here's something in me, I don't know what. Maybe I'm crazy. But there's something in me that loves Death. I think of myself as Death, some-times. In a scarlet shroud, floating through the night. I'm so beautiful, then. And sad. And hungry to make the whole world happy, by taking them out where I am, into the night, away from all trouble, all unhappiness. . . . Wal-ter, this is the awful part. I know this is terrible. I tell myself it's terrible. But to me, it doesn't seem terrible. It seems as though I'm doing something—that's really best for [my husband], if he only knew it. Do you understand me, Walter?" (18–19)

We might note the image of consumption in Phyllis's speech here: she is "hungry," insatiably so, wanting to devour the whole world. Just as Phyl-lis's teeth are "big and white and maybe a little buck," she presents herself here as "consuming everything," a walking oral cavity. Further, in addition to its financial connotation, consider that the word "buck" also appears in the context of Walter stating he wants to "buck" the system, the Com-pany's regime. Phyllis's consuming mouth is then freighted with a sense of subverting and embodying the Company; she wants everything, and promises both "bucking" and "bucks" for Walter, but in the end offers nei-ther. Phyllis's mouth belies a link to the Company Walter thought he had left behind.

Walter responds to the question ("Do you understand me, Walter?") that ends Phyllis's bizarre speech with an unadorned "No," never reflecting for us on his reaction to it, the narration providing no space for this kind of horror. But the speech stunningly articulates the subtext of the femme fatale—the deathly lure at the center of its seductive shell—while also working to "spin" the murderous drive as potentially benevolent, a kind of noir euthanasia. One might even notice an interesting parallel between Phyllis's efforts to justify and glorify her murderous urges and Walter's description of the insurance industry. The horribly mistaken popular conception of the insurance industry, Walter says, is that it is "friend of the widow, the orphan, and the needy in time of trouble" (23).[30] This conception is a blinding gloss on a crude reality, just as Phyllis glosses over her dark desires. Then, the insurance industry—the Company—and Phyllis are paired again, with Walter caught between two systems that will prove to be one, a point to which I will return.

But what do we then make of Walter's intense bodily connection to Phyllis, who is conflated with castration and death? Indeed, the "feeling" Walter experiences in the presence of Phyllis, both literally or as a subject of conversation, persists throughout, even in the post-confessional last chapter. Walter, in exchange for his confession, has been given a chance to escape via a ticket to "points south." On the cruise ship, Walter sits on the deck, hears a "little gasp beside me" and, before he "even looked I knew who it was. I turned to the next chair. It was Phyllis" (112). This "feeling" of Phyllis behind, or back of, Walter serves as the novel's primal scene: the prickle up the spine or neck, sparked by Phyllis's look or words, or merely words about Phyllis articulated by another.[31] The last scene carries this sensation to its logical conclusion. As Walter is finishing his "text," he feels Phyllis behind him in the aforementioned red death garb, ready to drown with him: "I didn't hear the stateroom door open, but she's beside me now while I'm writing. I can feel her. The moon" (115). Let there be no doubt as to the text's (or Walter's) conflation of death with femininity. The text's last line seals it: "The moon." The image stands in for Phyllis, as the moon signals a universal femininity, and that all-too-familiar equation of femininity with death.[32]

We see Phyllis therefore as both failing to meet the aesthetic criteria of the femme fatale yet over-representing the femme fatale in parodic lethality. Hollowed out and even ironized, the femme fatale consequently is made to appear less and less an independent figure than a constitutive projection performing a crucial function for Walter. Readers are not given salivating descriptions of Phyllis's body or face, and consequently do not participate in Walter's desire so directly, thereby enabling readers to see Walter's projection more clearly. In fact, it is Walter's (hysterical) body that receives far more exhaustive attention than Phyllis's curves. His body is the over-represented one. As Slavoj Žižek suggests in reference to Hitchcock's femmes fatales, Phyllis exists primarily as a "symptom" of the man.[33] The sharp focus on Phyllis and her femme fatale status, then, conceals the forces constructing that representation. We must look at what the representation of Phyllis tells us about Walter. If Phyllis is the symptom of Walter, what is Walter?

After the night of the murder, Walter, out of newly born hatred, rarely sees Phyllis. As far as his narrative offers us, she is just a disembodied voice on the other end of the phone. By this point in the text, however, he no longer requires Phyllis's physical presence to trigger bodily reactions in him. He has subsumed the effect. Her illness is within him—maybe it always was. Walter tells us early on: "[I] was peeping over the edge, and all the time I was trying to pull away from it, there was *something in me* that kept edging a little closer, trying to get a better look" (emphasis added, 14). Instead of bowing out when Walter hears Phyllis say she regrets their kiss and loves her husband, Walter pushes forward, confiding to the reader, "*the thing was in me,* pushing me still closer to the edge. And then I could feel it again, that she wasn't saying what she meant" (emphasis added, 15). Again, Walter locates the drive within himself, as something he "feels." In what we may see as a stereotypically feminine construction, he is attuned to his emotions, every intuition announcing itself.

It is important to note that while Walter's fraught relation to his body appears to originate in meeting Phyllis, Walter has always "listened" to his instinct, gut—what Keyes in the film version will term "the little man"—as part of his job, his salesman identity. Walter relies heavily on instinct for his sales work, claiming, " . . . you sell as many people as I do, you don't go by what they say. You feel it, how the deal is going" (6). The wording is interesting here for several reasons. First, instead of "selling to" his customers, Walter speaks of *selling* his customers, as if they were the commodities, not the consumers—an equation that gives him the agency, the power in the transaction. Second, Walter is effectively telling us that what one says means nothing; how then do we read his confession? As a hysterical narrative that shows the most where it bursts through representation's seams? Third, Walter uses the phrase "You feel it," emphasizing the visceral, sensate experience that his "selling" involves.

The reliance on intuition is tested when Walter meets Phyllis for the first time. They have only spoken for a few minutes when Walter begins to suspect that Phyllis may, in hardboiled parlance, have an angle (though he mistakes what the angle is). It is at this moment when, he confides, "all of a sudden she looked at me, and I felt a chill creep straight up my back and into the roots of my hair. 'Do you handle accident insurance?'" (6). Note that Walter feels the creeping chill before the damning question about accident insurance comes. All Phyllis has done is look at him. It seems quite a powerful look and quite a powerful instinct on Walter's part. It fixes Walter, even when Phyllis changes the subject. While he refers to her look's potency, it is actually his look that seems compulsive and insistent as he "trie[s] to keep [his] eyes off her, and couldn't" (7).

Later, in his car, Walter composes himself, "bawling [him]self out for being a fool just because a woman had given me one sidelong look" (7). It is a curious moment. He acknowledges that the look, not the question, unnerved him. But we have no description of that look, whereas we do have the content of the question. The look is not presented as seductive or suggestive at the time: "she looked at me." Only here, in retrospect, is it even dubbed, relatively tamely, "sidelong." As D. A. Miller reminds us, with hysteria, "what the body suffers, the mind needn't think."[34] Walter's relaying of his bodily contortions, his very excess of physical response, is generally the extent of his reflection on them. Rarely does he proceed to analyze the response.

So then for what is Walter "bawling" himself out here? Was he a fool by being abrupt with her, or for becoming unnerved? It seems the latter, but if so, the connection seems to be between sexual attraction and Walter's visceral unraveling. However, what kind of sexual attraction is it? We know that Walter had, before the look, noticed with pleasure Phyllis's body, her figure. But it appears that this look has offered something far more—something so intense that it sends chills up Walter's back and through his hair. We might recall Freud's discussion of the uncanny, and his limning of the ways the uncanny can reveal our secret belief in the "omnipotence of thoughts."[35] Walter seems to believe that Phyllis's look carries all he feels or believes about Phyllis and himself. The look creates it, the body feels it, and nowhere is language, structure, or reason involved. The difference, however, is less about the knowledge gained than the means by which Walter gains it. The system of the Body ends up offering Walter a more potent brand of knowledge, but his agency is not heightened in the process.

Working from Freud's "Medusa's Head" essay, in which Freud likens the paralyzing sight of Medusa to the male's paralyzing first sight of female genitalia, Jacques Lacan writes, "The gaze is presented to us only in the form of a strange contingency, symbolic of what we find on the horizon, as the thrust of our experience, namely, the lack that constitutes castration anxiety."[36] Has Phyllis's look lifted the veil from the phallus? Surely, the episode suggests that Phyllis has effectively unmanned Walter with her look precisely at the moment before she allows her deadly plans to skate, just barely, above the surface. But as we have set up a pattern where Walter projects onto Phyllis his own anxieties, we must consider how much Walter is having her "look" signify what his narrative cannot express: his own unstable masculinity.

The next seemingly hysterical response we see in Walter comes when he makes the follow-up sales trip. Phyllis asks him if it would be possible to take out an accident policy on her husband without his knowledge. Walter knows what this means, and prepares to "get out of there, and drop those renewals and everything else about her like a red-hot poker" (13). But he does not get up and leave: "She looked at me, a little surprised, and her face was about six inches away" (13). The look, and what it carries "back of it," drives Walter to kiss Phyllis "on the mouth, hard" (13). But far from feeling manly or powerful or even pleasingly aroused, Walter instead is "trembling like a leaf" (13). The response feels stereotypically—even generically—feminine, as if he is swept away and the force of it frightens him. In response to his fearful shaking, Phyllis returns the kiss with "a cold stare, and then she closed her eyes, pulled me to her, and kissed back" (13). Phyllis's cool regard signals her ceaseless composure. She can both inspire hysterical fear and also remain coolly involved, even directive. Beside her controlled poise, Walter seems a neurasthenic mess.

Mary Ann Doane writes that the femme fatale is an "articulation of fears surrounding the loss of stability and centrality of the self, the 'I,' the ego. These anxieties appear quite explicitly in the process of her representation as castration anxiety" (2). Phyllis's presence surely "unmans" Walter here—but the "unmanning" is multi-leveled. The two take part in a dance in which Walter attempts to control the situation, while Phyllis plots behind the scenes; just when he thinks he has the power, it is revealed to be a sham, not just because Phyllis is more clever or more malevolent, but because her very presence can literally destabilize Walter.

Phyllis's plotting is only the most manifest way she unnerves Walter. There is another mode of destabilization that is explicitly gendered, and it is negotiated through Phyllis's appearance. As noted earlier, Phyllis, while delicate, displays an alarming and unfeminine physical strength. Along these same lines, Walter seems to view Phyllis's clothes as though part of a perpetual striptease, but a drag striptease—masculine exterior, feminine interior. Her pajamas cling to her body as she moves in such a way that he can suddenly discern the appealing curvy shape beneath: " . . . I saw something I hadn't noticed before. Under those blue pajamas was a shape to set a man nuts" (6).[37] Her sailor suit pulls over her hips, hinting at her figure. Her raincoat and swimming cap promise even more hidden pleasures—but, after Walter "[gets] her peeled off," he finds she's wearing "just a dumb Hollywood outfit" of slacks and a sweater, though even there "it looked different on her" (14). Phyllis's femininity is not the lure—it is her androgyny. Lola's "sweet" and feminine appearance reassures Walter, while Phyllis's unstable gender position destabilizes him.

Phyllis's appearance then involves a hypnotic dance, a topsy-turvy striptease where the final reward comes in the outfit she wears at the novel's end, the "awful-looking" death robe: "one big square of red silk that she wraps around her, but it's got no armholes, and her hands look like stumps underneath it . . ." (114). In other words, she ends up wearing a virtual sartorial representation of a castration wound: male turned female. The androgyny, the boyish clothes hiding the feminine figure, the constant play between attire and body, have exploded into an excess of castration signification, leading one to guess that such signification was there all along for Walter. Walter has entered the Freudian family romance in spite of himself, suddenly positioning himself as the young boy stripped of a belief in a maternal phallus and made to realize sexual difference, gender itself. As such, all Walter can respond with is an essentializing characterization of femininity: "The moon." The femme fatale then is unveiled to be less hyperfemininity concealing a masculine will, than a destabilizing and therefore threatening dance between genders. The gender dance threatens a collapse of gender, figured as castration. With the phallus unveiled and no secure position available for masculine interpellation, Walter has no place, and as such joins Phyllis in death.

What we see, therefore, is less Phyllis destabilizing Walter than Walter revealing his own essential destabilization by triangulating it through Phyllis. Walter's own anxiety about his masculinity emerges most blatantly with the signification accorded crutches in the text, as referenced earlier.[38] William Luhr notes about the film version of *Double Indemnity* (scripted by Billy Wilder and Raymond Chandler), "The image of the crippled man on crutches applies to three men [Huff, Sachetti, Nirdlinger]. . . . The broken leg, the crutches . . . symbolically point to a phallic injury, an emasculation suffered by men who became involved with this black widow. . . . [T]he film links this image of debilitation, deformity, death to sexual association with Phyllis."[39] Locating the origin of anxiety in the femme fatale is a persistent critical stopping point—and it is a cursory conclusion. As we have seen, Walter is not merely threatened by the femme fatale, but his masculinity is configured such that he identifies with, desires, and doubles the femme fatale. This complication leads us to ask if, in fact, the femme fatale is nothing more than Walter himself.

Paul Smith locates a "residual, barely avowed male hysteria" lurking beneath the confident, formulaic action pictures of Clint Eastwood, noting that it is "often expressed narratively as the sensation of the dangers inherent in *identification with* women or homosexuals (of either gender)" (emphasis added, 103). The question begs, does Walter identify with Phyllis? Clearly, they share a common goal as they plot Mr. Nirdlinger's death. They share a mercenary desire for a financial payoff. But where Walter is racked with guilt, Phyllis seems to have barely registered the murder.[40] Further, while Phyllis turns out to be a multiple murderer motivated by a seemingly pathological greed, Walter seems to forget about the money entirely, and becomes caught up in swooning love for Lola. Where we do, however, recognize a fear of identification is through the contagious, infectious feeling Phyllis, and the idea of Phyllis, seems to be able to produce in Walter. It affects him on nearly every bodily level: his spine, his stomach (he vomits), his voice (he can't speak), his composure (he finds himself hysterically laughing), his sleep patterns (he becomes an insomniac). And it is a bodily reaction he was primed to exhibit before Phyllis even revealed herself.

This bodily response finds an echo in the straining at the seams of Walter's narrative, wherein he cannot or will not analyze what is happening to him. He is markedly vague about his nervous reactions. He tells the reader his symptoms, but remains general about the cause: " . . . all through the spring, believe me I didn't get much sleep. You start on something like this, and if you don't wake up plenty of times in the middle of the night, dreaming they got you for something you forgot, you've got better nerves than I've got" (34). The "something like this" refers to the murder plot wherein the couple needs to beat the Company and get the insurance payoff, but is that the extent of the "this"? It might also, however, refer to the far larger "plot"—Walter's exit from one system (the statistically ruled, mercenary insurance business) and his entry into another (the body, or even the feminine). The narrative refuses to surrender this information to the reader. While, as the text is a confession, the reader appears to be in the powerful position of interlocutor, the reader is more accurately doctor to hysterical patient, trying to fill in the gaps.

"I Won't Tell You What I Did Then": The (Partial) Confession of Walter Huff

Confessions are ostensibly written because authority demands it. In *Double Indemnity*, Barton Keyes requires Huff to write one in exchange for letting him flee. According to Michel Foucault, a confession is a "ritual that unfolds within a power relationship, for one does not confess without the presence (or virtual presence) of a partner who is not simply the interlocutor but the authority who requires the confession, prescribes and appreciates it, and intervenes in order to judge, punish, forgive, console, and reconcile. . . ."[41] But while Keyes bids Huff confess to the murder and fraud, Keyes does not control the confession's substance and, as Huff admits, his confession is "more than [Keyes] bargained for, but I wanted to put it all down" (112). The power seems to be at least partially Walter's here; he controls both the confession itself (he will only write it if his demands are met) and its content. In turn, the interlocutor is not easily defined either. Although the interlocutor would seem to be Keyes or the Company's "top brass," Walter admits that he hopes Lola "will see it some time" (112), thus she is evidently part of the imagined audience as well.

But whatever the extent of Walter's personal narrative flourish, the confession and its juridical qualities reinscribe Walter into the Company—or remind Walter that he has never actually left his inscribed role in that structure. In Cain's *The Postman Always Rings Twice,* Frank Chambers writes the confession predominantly for religious reasons, to fulfill his concern for redemption, as well as for posterity in that he wants it known that he did not kill Cora, wants whomever reads it to know that he loved her. But in *Double Indemnity,* the confession exists because Claims Investigator Keyes demands Walter write it. Moreover, Keyes terms it a "statement," emphasizing its secularity and its juridical quality: "You're to give me a statement. You're to give me a statement setting forth every detail of what you did, and have a notary attest it. You're to mail it to me, registered. You're to do that Thursday of next week, so I get it Friday" (109). The statement in fact compels Walter's return to the bureaucratic language and ritual of the Company. Soon after, Keyes reminds Walter, "Before you get on that boat, you'll have to hand to me the registry receipt for that statement. I've got to know I've got it" (109). Walter responds with a question about Lola: if she is not taken care of, Huff says, "you'll get no statement, and the case will come to trial, and all the rest of it" (110). Huff does not require a written promise from Keyes on that front—just his "solemn word" (110), reflecting Walter's gesturing toward a less official, more personal covenant. But Huff, ever the precision man, quickly slides back into the bureaucratic structure, assuring the reader that he finished the statement on Thursday afternoon and "sent it out by the orderly to be registered, and around five o'clock Keyes dropped by for the receipt" (111). The compulsive explication of the process involved in the confession recalls Walter's compulsive explication of the insurance industry itself, reflecting his deep entrenchment in the Company's bureaucratic logic. Further, Keyes needs the statement to insure the Company's good name, to arrange things so the Company does not have to pay, nor does it have to suffer the embarrassment of the trial of one of its own salesmen. Thus, the Company exerts control over Walter's desire by "registering" that desire's representation as if this confession process were a commodity transaction—with Walter effectively "selling" them the story of his transgressive desire. The extent of the Company's hold, the far-reaching nature of its systematic control, begins to reveal itself.

The confession also operates as a symbol of power between Huff and Keyes: Keyes must have it for the Company to survive the scandal; Walter uses this need to his advantage, one last gasp showing his ability to manipulate the Company, if nothing else. It is not until his post-confessional narrative that Walter realizes Keyes has won in spite of Walter's seeming freedom from the legal sanction: Keyes has planted Phyllis on the same boat as Walter. The Company rules the plot, after all. Walter has lost, trapped at sea with the lethal Phyllis. All he has left is her deathly sphere. He embraces it bodily, through the physical act of suicide. But further, the post-confessional narrative embraces it, embraces the gothic signification of Phyllis's red death robe, embraces that which eludes representation: the death itself, which cannot be told as the narrator dies in that embrace.

But is it Phyllis's sphere that Walter has entered in that deathly suicidal embrace? After all, it is the Company that has knowingly sent Walter onto the same boat as Phyllis, effectively engineering the couple's capture or death. Phyllis has shifted from being Walter's plant to being the Company's, as their virtual executioner. She operates unknowingly as a stand-in for the Company, which is effectively a stand-in for an all-consuming capitalist economy. Femininity so equated with death in the text, ends up forming a triangulated relationship with the stranglehold of business on Walter's desire. Both Phyllis and General Fidelity (the Company's name signifies its insistence on allegiance) provide Walter with opportunities to enact a family romance by betraying the patriarch, be it Mr. Nirdlinger or Company founder Norton (or Keyes). Trust in both instances is extended to Walter from the inside—via Lola, via Keyes. Walter is moved and disturbed by the trust (let us recall that Keyes's defense of Walter makes his "heart feel funny" [77]). The confession, demanded by General Fidelity/Keyes, is the effect of the long arm of the Company. The confession even yokes the Company to the beloved Lola as well, as Walter will not provide the document without a promise of Lola's safety, and he hopes that she will read it. Its readers then, as far as Walter is concerned, will be Keyes and Lola. He is writing it for them: they are the powerful interlocutors of whom Foucault speaks. Yet that confession, so invested in family dynamics, be they Company family or nuclear, is followed by another narrative, that cryptic last chapter.

Let us return, momentarily, to that last, post-confessional chapter. Huff's intended audience for these final pages is unclear; the interlocutor is presumably the general reader alone, but also Phyllis, who lurks over Walter's shoulder as he composes. And just as the discourse of affection (for Lola) and business lingo (for Keyes) infiltrate the language of the confession, Walter's responses to Phyllis seem to rule his language in this last chapter. It is not merely a contrast between the packaged, commodified confession versus the pure, unadulterated libido-ramblings of the last chapter. Reason, rationality, even the need to explain oneself, disappear: the last chapter is all about bare, primal anxiety, death wish, sickly desire. Phyllis is turned into an archetype and the two become doomed lovers with sharks (literal and figurative) swarming about them. Yet why does Walter, if he has so absorbed himself into this realm of deathly femininity, feel the need to document it, and for whom? The answer seems to lie not in the way that Walter has internalized the Phyllis function, but in the way he has internalized the juridical (and, by extension, Oedipal) function of his culture. Though Phyllis's lure has seeped into his language, thereby gothifying it, the impulse to confess—to speak even when the authority no longer requires it—reveals the extent of Walter's interpellation.

So has Walter eschewed Oedipal normalization, or been banished from it, or has he merely taken it within him, embodied it, and in fact become it? William Marling suggests that Walter's mistake was in failing to realize that the "emerging economy needed to limit [his brand of] aggressive rationality rather than to have insiders use what usually did not happen against it" (177). But rather, it seems Walter's error was in underestimating the extent to which he had absorbed, or "caught" the Company. Walter assumed he could beat it from the inside, not understanding that he was not inside the system; the system was inside him.

Once again we see that Phyllis, while appearing to be Walter's disease, is in fact his symptom of the larger Company pathology he has "caught." The disease is the Company he cannot beat because he has become it. Keyes knows that Walter cannot truly flee, and Phyllis unwittingly functions as the Company's hit man, the long arm of the Company reaching out to annihilate the stray. But Phyllis does not truly need to assassinate Walter; Walter recognizes what he carries within him and enters into death of his own volition. And just as Phyllis's femininity is at one with her deathliness but also with her "use-value," Walter's masculinity is defined through his entrenchment in the Company.

Neither Walter nor Phyllis can exit their respective gender systems, but for Phyllis, the death pact is an ecstatic communion with the system through which her femininity is defined and, if we accept her self-identification as Death, the system through which she defines herself. Conversely, for Walter, the suicide pact is a hysterical recognition of his own utter lack of agency. Ruled by Company logic, he has no choice but to play the role assigned to him: fall guy, Oedipus, Company casualty. The Company then is unveiled as Oedipal allegory, the family romance recapitulated, manipulating gender and desire for its own proliferation, just as in the Oedipal family model. The systems intermesh, interlock, and leave Walter with one position, white male cog whose body and function have been prescribed for him all along.

This lack of male agency amid larger social systems will prove a recurrent pattern within hardboiled fiction. While the weakness of the tough guy–as–sap in his interactions with the femme fatale is often broached, *Double Indemnity* demonstrates the extent to which that femme fatale is merely a symbol of larger and deeply oppressive societal structures that imprison both genders in tyrannically binary models. These binary models leave the tough guy stripped of individual agency; they forbid him from pursuing precisely what his untethered body seems to crave: a fluidity of gender identification and sexuality.

Knight Without Armor

In the novels of Raymond Chandler, coincidentally a one-time hugely successful adapter of Cain (as co-screenwriter of the film version of *Double Indemnity*), we encounter a similar play between unsanctioned desires and restrictive gender demands. The basic narrative structures apply: a first-person white male narrator moves through Los Angeles, confronting femmes fatales and criminal depravity. Like Walter Huff, Philip Marlowe, despite his self-employment, is primarily a "petty-bourgeois [entrepreneur]."[42] But while Huff is a murderer and a fraud, Chandler's Marlowe is of course the fabled "knight" of hardboiled fiction, a man with ideals that, although perhaps antiquated, continue to rule his behavior.

Philip Marlowe can be seen as an appealing figure for many American working- or middle-class male readers—both for his populist class resentment (*The Big Sleep* in particular bristles with Marlowe's distaste for the rich) and his individualist rhetoric. Marlowe is positioned explicitly against any system—juridical or baldly capitalistic. Ostensibly a "deductor" as a detective, he is, however, not a slave to the System of Knowledge and its seeming valorization of logic and reason. Instead, Marlowe lives by what he considers his own "code," his moral ideology, and he gets no "kick" from violating it through the familiar generic vehicle of transgression: a heterosexual liaison with the femme fatale.

Nevertheless, we can locate a "hysterical" Marlowe. His hysteria, however, is of a very different register than Walter Huff's. Marlowe does not carry any Company within him as Huff does, nor does he embrace libidinal urges so openly and completely. For Marlowe, incorporating otherness into himself is a surreptitious process, offering anxiety and often pleasure—pleasure that is redoubled when followed by self-righteous or guilty expulsion of that otherness. Fred Pfeil notes that the hardboiled detective derives pleasure from his weeding out of corruption, but that he also savors "precisely the opposite pleasure, that of yielding to and immersing oneself in the very morass that must finally be resisted and tamed" (113).[43] This contradiction, which takes far more variegated forms than the use of violence Pfeil references, fuels Marlowe's narratives and opens textual gaps that remain unsutured.

Slavoj Žižek persuasively distinguishes the hardboiled detective from the "classical" detective (i.e., Sherlock Holmes, Dupin) through the differences in their relation to the criminal acts. Žižek sees the classical detective as erecting and maintaining a distance from the crime, not allowing himself to get "mixed up" in the crime's "libidinal circuit" (60).[44] This distancing is achieved in part through his willingness to be paid for his efforts. But the hardboiled detective, with his sense of ethical and moral urgency, loses the "'exocentric' position" (62) of the outsider or analyst, and inevitably becomes drawn in or even implicated. While Žižek presents this absorption as morally painful to the detective, one cannot ignore an accompanying plea-sure that cannot be entirely concealed by the vigilant Marlowe's narration.

Indeed, unlike Walter Huff, Marlowe offers no confession, and he speaks to no authoritative interlocutor figure, other than the reader. But he, like Huff, cannot tell the reader everything; the narrative is always partial, always contains holes. Falling into the margins in Marlowe's hysterical text is an open expression of illicit pleasure, found in revelations about the unsteadi-ness or fragmentation of gender constructs and of subjectivity, which are often the same thing for Marlowe, the latter constituted only through a rigid binarization of the former, as we will see.

I Fall to Pieces:
Philip Marlowe's Consciousness

> "I heard you were hard-boiled," Toad said slowly, his eyes cool and
> watchful.
> "You heard wrong. I'm a very sensitive guy. I go all to pieces over nothing."
>
> —Raymond Chandler, *The Little Sister* (1949)

Philip Marlowe's relationship to his own masculinity, his own self-conscious view of his hardboiled role, is continually fraught. In order to uncover the particular construction of masculinity we find in Marlowe, I will turn to *Farewell, My Lovely* (1940) as a case study of sorts. In this, Chandler's sec-ond Marlowe novel, a series of telling interactions occur between Marlowe and an alcoholic female informant, Jessie Florian. Through these interac-tions we can see the different register of hysteria with which we are con-fronted, and its particular relationship to gender dynamics. Specifically, Marlowe's dealings with Florian serve as a characteristic example of his un-ease over the (in)stability of a traditional gender binary. In *Double Indemnity,* the binary set forward by the text, if only to be called into question, is that of masculine/sap and feminine/femme fatale. With Marlowe, the founda-tional binary emerges as masculine/hermeticism and feminine/contagion.

As in *Double Indemnity,* the femme fatale designation within Chan-dler's novels is a troubled one. *Farewell, My Lovely's* Jessie Florian offers a compelling example: she functions in curious relation to the femme fatale figure. That is, she is never considered a femme fatale in Chandler criti-cism (most likely because she is not young, nor is she presented as desir-able), yet I want to show that the text is far from definitive about her femme fatale status. Although she diverges from the physical appearance of the traditional femme fatale (in ways far more extreme than *Double In-demnity's* Phyllis), the response she inspires is peculiarly akin to aspects of the common tough guy reaction to the femme fatale. This unexpected similarity exposes much of the gender confusion within the text. In particular, an odd ambivalence exists between Florian and Marlowe that helps us to ascertain the text's constructions of a distressed, overdetermined masculinity.

Let us begin by noting that Jessie Florian physically disgusts Marlowe. She literally causes him to become "sick at [his] stomach" (34).[45] The question emerges, What about her so nauseates the seasoned detective? One of the first things Marlowe notices about Florian is that she is "blowsy" and "thick" of body, with large toes made "obvious in a pair of man's slippers of scuffed brown leather" (26). Marlowe refers to these slippers several times during their conversation, as if they keep protruding intrusively into his line of vision. When Florian implies, for instance, that she may offer information in return for liquor, Marlowe notes, "Cunning eyes, steady attentive face. The feet in the man's slippers didn't move" (28). No feminine pronouns interrupt here to call attention to Florian's actual gender, and Marlowe seems unable to avoid watching her mannish accouterments. It is an interesting moment, too, because it is one of the few times during their interaction when Florian abandons a lively, light demeanor, filled with "tittering" and what Marlowe judges to be a "bogus heartiness" (27). Marlowe clearly sees the schoolgirl routine as disingenuous. This sudden shift to business then functions as a striptease of sorts, a moment when the performance, the "act," is dropped and Marlowe sees a force to be reckoned with beneath it. That these moments should occur in tandem with Marlowe's taking note of the masculine slippers seems telling, as the question of where Florian fits in a traditional gender binary is thrown into doubt: she is the "performing," dissembling woman and yet she also wears masculinity on her person and appears to be asserting a steely (masculine?) will, leaving Marlowe to wonder where to place her, into which gender camp. Likewise, Marlowe describes Florian's voice as "dragg[ing] itself out of her throat like a sick man getting out of bed" (26). Her androgynous first name further contributes to the gender ambivalence.

Throughout the interaction, Florian's masculine signifiers surface each time the gaiety curtain drops. We must consider whether Marlowe imagines that the "performance" is the femininity, concealing an internal masculinity that the slippers signify, or whether both gender constructs exist simultaneously in Florian (as with Phyllis in *Double Indemnity*), with the play between the two serving as the uncanny element that Marlowe finds so unnerving. He does not know where to place her, or where desire fits into the equation.

Tellingly, the feminine signifiers of giggling flirtiness that appear in relation to Florian do so when her desire for alcohol—a desire repulsive to Marlowe (no shrinking tippler himself)—emerges. And the feminine signifiers are decidedly threatening; the fear seems to be that even as the affectations stem from a desire to consume alcohol, that consuming might turn sexual— or so Marlowe seems to fear. When, apparently intoxicated by Marlowe's plying liquor, Florian makes a scene, drooling and laughing and eventually throwing the empty bottle at him, Marlowe surrenders his investigation of her, admitting, "It might have been an act, but I didn't care. Suddenly I had enough of the scene, too much of it, far too much of it" (35–6).

As Marlowe attempts his exit, the extended scene is played for gothic uncanniness. Marlowe describes Florian's eyes as having a "peculiar glassiness. A murderous glassiness" (33). As he heads out, he cannot resist throwing a "quick look back at her before I closed the door, then shut it, opened it again silently and looked again" (36). His eyes irresistibly drawn to her, he thinks he can, despite her closed eyes, detect "something gleam[ing] below the lids" (36). Similarly, earlier, when Florian eyes Marlowe's bottle, we have the castrating and sirenlike image of her "[s]eaweed colored eyes stay[ing] on the bottle. A coated tongue coiled on her lips" (28). It is a complicated image filled with Medusoid fears. The look threatens castration, as her desire for (alcohol) consumption seems to, yet he must meet it. He is torn between needing to leave and feeling unable to stop looking.

This exchange recalls Walter Huff's attraction to Phyllis's uncanny look, as discussed earlier. But while Huff is titillated and terrified by Phyllis's gaze, Marlowe is disgusted and unnerved by Florian's. There is no palpable desire, though there is clearly compulsion. The references to her "tongue and lips" (28), her reaching "hungrily" (29) for Marlowe's bottle, her referring to Marlowe as "Handsome," her coy warning to him ("No peekin'") when her robe swings open—these are all the expected femme fatale–isms, but Florian is no beautiful figure; she defies all aesthetic criteria for the femme fatale. Interestingly, the text's "true" femme fatale, Velma, later mirrors Florian's robe gap gesture when she, Marlowe notes, "crosse[s] her legs, a little carelessly" (124) during their first meeting, which also involves heavy drinking and references to the female tongue: Marlowe describes kissing Velma, and finding her mouth "half-open and burning and her tongue was a darting snake between her teeth" (135).[46] But with Florian, Marlowe experiences all the uneasiness and discomfort, without the accompanying desire. Marlowe's response is not only to be sickened with her, but with himself: "A lovely old woman. I liked being with her. I liked getting her drunk for my own sordid purposes. I was a swell guy. I enjoyed being me. You find almost anything under your hand in my business, but I was beginning to be a little sick at my stomach" (34). It is important to note, however, that Marlowe's kissing session with Velma also ends badly, with her husband spotting them together and the shamed Marlowe feeling "as cold as Finnegan's feet the day they buried him" (135).

The question is, How do we read Marlowe's reaction to her, and why does the episode include so many gender-skewed femme fatale–isms? William Luhr writes about the scene as it appears both in the text and in the film version, " . . . There is something extremely unpleasant about [the episode]. It points to what is not there: the likelihood of sexual attraction."[47] It seems Luhr is right in noting a kind of absent presence in the scene. But Luhr goes on to say that the unpleasantness in the scene emerges because of the possibility that "sexually attractive" Marlowe might have to make "aesthetic compromises" to play the part of a titillated male to Florian's would-be seductress; further, "the self-deception involved in [Florian's] presumption of her own sexual desirability" heightens the text's emphasis on the "comparable nature of [Velma's] unlikely and manipulative sexual involvements.[48]

A potential parallel between Marlowe and Velma is interesting, but the central problem with Luhr's contention is that it takes Marlowe to be reader-surrogate and reliable narrator here when the passage seems far more complex than a basic moral-ethical self-disgust or sexual distaste. Luhr appears to accept Marlowe's expressed desire for Velma uncomplicatedly, and his nausea over Florian as simple physical displeasure at her decrepitude. This acceptance is problematic for several reasons, not the least of which is the uncanny similarity between Marlowe's encounters with the two women.

Just as we saw the similarity in the Medusoid images, both encounters end with lingering anxiety for Marlowe. After being caught kissing Velma by her husband, Marlowe abruptly orders her not to go "shrill on me," and describes feeling "nasty, as if I had picked a poor man's pocket" (136). Marlowe's accompanying gesture of wiping off her lipstick mimics the dirtiness Marlowe feels after the Florian interview when Marlowe feels utterly contaminated, later telling Officer Nulty, "I have to go home and take a bath and gargle my throat and get my nails manicured" (39). Just when we think he's cracking wise, Nulty asks, "You ain't sick, are you?" and Marlowe responds, "Just dirty. . . . Very, very dirty" (39).

What makes Marlowe feel so "dirty" after the Florian episode? Is it merely a realization of the unpleasantries his job demands: plying an alcoholic with liquor to get information? It may appear so on the surface, but Marlowe has, at that point, already plied a concierge with alcohol to get information from him.[49] It seems to be more than a disgust at his job's dark side. He has been "touched" by something "unclean."[50] What then has Marlowe "caught" from Florian? Marlowe returns to Florian's obsessively (three times total). His last encounter with her repeats this strange repulsive eroticism, this same disturbing funhouse mirror version of a femme fatale seduction scene. Marlowe finds Florian in bed, locating her by following the sound of groaning. He greets her and in response she "work[s] her lips together slowly, rubb[ing] one over the other, then slid a tongue out and moistened them and worked her jaws" (113).

Again we have the oral images, snake-like, threatening, but without the accompanying conflicted desire on Marlowe's part. He is the target of the Medusa, but feels the potential castration without the expected attendant desire. As if trying to reassert a Medusa-gaze power, Florian "[s]crewed her eyes up and then snapped them open as if trying to get rid of a film over them" (113). Marlowe promises to get her alcohol but first tells her he has looked up the deed to her house in what turns out to be an important clue that ties the novel's dual narratives together. It is Marlowe's trump card and it works. Florian becomes "rigid under the bedclothes, like a wooden woman. Even her eyelids were frozen half down over the clogged iris of her eyes" (115). Marlowe has become Medusa here, turning Florian to stone with his discovery of her secret. It does not last, however. Instead, as Marlowe fiddles anxiously with his unlit cigarette, Florian "move[s] a hand under the bedclothes" (116). The vaguely sexual image is once again also a threat. Marlowe stares at her, running his hand "up and down the door frame. It felt slimy. Just touching it made me want to take a bath" (116). Female sexuality is figured again as threatening, repellent, unclean, and pervasive. The very walls are covered with it. Marlowe cannot light his cigarette, cannot feign a casual pose along the doorframe. He decides to leave, clearly unnerved, when Florian throws "the bedclothes aside and jerked upright with her eyes blazing. Something glittered in her right hand. A small revolver . . ." (116). The purpose of her wandering hand was to locate the weapon. She threatens Marlowe with it, and Marlowe "looked at the gun and the gun looked at me" (116), but he notices that the gun "looks" at him far more shakily. Marlowe takes a chance and suggests, "You and I could work together" (116). The shock of the proposition makes Florian lower the gun and Marlowe takes his quick exit, "slid[ing] though [the door] and beyond the opening" (117), like a snake. Marlowe does not suffer after this encounter as he did the previous one; there is the sense that he faced down Medusa and won, his look was steady while her gun was not. As a Western showdown, she blinked first. Thus, he is able to leave, having learned not to look back, despite the fact that, as he leaves, his "back felt queer. . . . The muscles crawled" (117). He resists, and leaves uncontaminated, or close to it. [51]

What we must ask here is whether Marlowe is not attracted to Jessie Florian because she is unattractive, or whether she is not attractive because Marlowe is *not attracted* to her. That is, does her grotesqueness inhere in her sexual availability? Although Marlowe can justify his refusal to pursue Velma because of her marital status (and later her murderousness), Mrs. Florian has no such inhibiting attachment (or clear criminality). She is touchable because she is unmarried and is not a virginal cop's daughter, as the novel's Girl

Friday Anne Riordan is. Therefore, she must be repellent, must be made "Other" for the gender binary in place to continue to operate. Marlowe's construction of masculinity depends on the feminine being "beyond the pale." His masculinity obtains in his refusal to contaminate himself, refusal to involve himself sexually with a woman. Masculine means a hermetically separated space constituted in opposition to the feminine. The feminine need not be evil—as we see with "good" women like Anne Riordan, or *The Long Goodbye*'s Linda Loring, or *The Lady in the Lake*'s Adrienne Fromsett, or *The High Window*'s Merle Davis, or *The Big Sleep*'s Mona Mars—but if the woman is not evil, she must be untouchable in some other way: a virgin, a wife, a girlfriend of another man. If she were touchable, then she would be a contaminant.

This fine line between the contaminating femme fatale and the potentially contaminating "good" woman is made clear in the similarity between two scenes. First, in Chandler's first novel, *The Big Sleep* (1939), Marlowe famously ejects femme fatale Carmen Sternwood from his bed, rebuffing her advances. After she leaves, he returns "to the bed and look[s] down at it. The imprint of her head was still in the pillow, of her small corrupt body still on the sheets. I put my empty glass down and tore the bed to pieces savagely."[52] Second, in *The Long Goodbye* (1953), Marlowe says farewell to Linda Loring after their highly romantic interlude and then returns to "the bedroom and pulled the bed to pieces and remade it. There was a long dark hair on one of the pillows."[53] Although the second instance is meant to be bittersweet and the first, repellent, the similarities between the two are intriguing. The act of the woman leaving Marlowe's domestic space, followed by his return to the bed she was once in, and taking apart the bed "to pieces" in each instance is curiously doubled. The main difference is the ordering: Marlowe sees the imprint of Carmen and then tears apart the bed, versus tearing apart the bed then seeing a hair on the pillow. The first is a contamination to which he can react, the second is one that remains despite his efforts to efface it. The line between femme fatale and "good girl" is difficult to maintain, indeed.

We see, through the Florian encounters and this blurring of femme fatale and "good girl," a textual unsettling of the femme fatale figure, which in turn upsets the gender binary, navigated through Marlowe's unexpected lack of desire. This unsettling reveals hardboiled masculinity's utter reliance on the femme fatale for its own existence. With Marlowe, we see not a mutually constitutive binary so much as a house-of-cards masculinity built through a ritual transformation of every "other" element into a contagion to be avoided. Moreover, Marlowe's notion of masculinity, so dependent on hermeticism, on remaining free from contagion, affords no place for a woman who can volley masculine and feminine signifiers, hence the physical attraction that would have been safe becomes positively lethal. Marlowe only manages to succeed because he wins the showdown, sees Florian's gun shaking, thereby disrupting the possibility of Florian indeed having the phallus. The gun shakes and the veil is lifted and Marlowe wins. He can then safely proposition her (suggesting, "You and I could work together" [116]), knowing that the sexual potential has been eradicated.

This pattern of gender upset is not limited to the play with the femme fatale figure, however. When Marlowe encounters a woman he terms a "hysteric," *The High Window*'s Merle Davis, the hysteria seems to spread to him, like a contagion. Again, Merle is no traditional femme fatale but is instead prim, frigid, and terrified of men. As her hypernervous demeanor is meant to reveal, Merle has been traumatized by an unwelcome advance from her employer. The experience has left her so frightened of men that her teeth rattle if men come too close. She is casually diagnosed by a doctor with whom Marlowe speaks as "obviously a neurotic. It's partly induced and partly deliberate. I mean to say that she really enjoys a lot of it. Even if she doesn't realize that she enjoys it."[54] Later, the doctor tells Marlowe, "She'll always be high on nerves and low on animal emotion. . . . She'd have made a perfect nun . . ." (1170). He then imagines for what would, to him, apparently be the grimmest fate possible for a woman: " . . . [S]he will probably turn out to be one of those acid-faced virgins that sit behind little desks in public libraries and stamp dates in books" (1170). Hence, Merle could hardly be further from the voracious Medusa femme fatale figure that Velma or Carmen Sternwood or Eileen Wade (*The Long Goodbye*) embodies, or Jessie Florian is reconstructed as, and she is seemingly safe due to her frigidity.

But Merle still functions as a contagion to Marlowe. In his eyes, her hysteria is visible all over her body in her "anemic" nostrils, her "unstable" chin, her "vague expression," and her "slightly oriental" eyes that make her appear as if her skin was "naturally so tight that it stretched her eyes out the corners" (990). Much like *The Big Sleep*'s Carmen Sternwood (who is similarly "orientalized"), Merle affects Marlowe in extreme, physical ways. But while the former inspires unaccountable rage, the latter inspires unaccountable anxiety, even hysteria. For example, upon learning that Merle is headed toward his apartment, Marlowe begins speaking inexplicably fast, assuring his building manager that "It's a business matter entirely" (1127), as if he harbors irrational fears about the manager suspecting a liaison—the mere suggestion of which seemingly terrifies Marlowe. He then spots his image in a mirror and finds "a stiff excited face in the glass" (1127). When she arrives, he becomes unnerved by certain convulsions in her face and neck, saying they were "enough to start anybody's nerves backfiring" (1128). Trying to speak to her casually, he loses all coordination and physical control: "[I] tried to blow a smoke ring, but didn't make it. A nerve in my cheek was trying to twang like a wire. I didn't like it" (1129). The twitch continues, and Marlowe later tries to rub his cheek hard "to quiet the nerve" (1130). Merle's hysteria has spread and she and Marlowe are curiously doubled. Merle's frigidity is far more potent than a femme fatale's "nymphomania" because Marlowe identifies with Merle and therefore runs the risk of feminization. But consider too that Merle rebuffs Marlowe's harmless bodily gestures, saying that she "never let[s] men touch [her]" (1000), revealing her fear of male contagion. The question becomes, who has infected whom here?

Either way, it is Marlowe who ends up playing doctor to Merle's hysterical patient, later curing her by concealing her idiosyncrasies with makeup and clothes and dropping her off in Wichita with her mother, leaving her wearing a "bungalow apron and rolling pie crust" (1174), suggesting that the cure for hysteria is domesticity and traditional female interpellation, a rigid gender identity utterly in place. But Marlowe does not bother to cure himself, merely sequestering the contagion instead. He does not submit to a likewise hetero-paternal male interpellation, resisting it at every turn. After all, his identity—the masculine half of the gender binary—depends not on his becoming a patriarch, but on hermetic self-sufficiency.

While Marlowe, in his interactions with Jessie Florian and Merle, ends up with a certain agentic power, beating off the contagion through a showdown and a domestication/claustration respectively, he does not always have such powers. In fact, Marlowe's hysterical reactions persistently stem from an awareness of a lack of power in a given situation, a sense of solitude and isolation in a situation filled with danger and the threat of violence. In such situations, he is helpless to change things. On the macro-level, his powerlessness wounds him; he is frustrated at his absorption into the very system he detests (he tells us at the end of *The Big Sleep*, for example, "I was a part of the nastiness now" [230]). On the micro-level, however, it is often powerlessness that evokes Marlowe's most rhapsodic discursive moments—but it is a powerlessness made physical, bodily, and achieved through violence or forcible drugging, and he is reticent, elusive about expressing the pleasure it incurs.

Although critics such as Fred Pfeil have noted in passing Marlowe's curious relation to his body, no critic has considered fully Marlowe's particularly complex self-embodiment, or the connections between Marlowe's reactions to physical violence or lapses of unconsciousness and gender or sexuality. By examining just these tensions, we can begin to limn the peculiarly Marlovian brand of masculinity.

Marlowe's Vapors and the Void

I have lived my life on the edge of nothing.

—Raymond Chandler, in a 1957 letter[55]

It has become one of hardboiled detective fiction's most popular points of parody: the moment when the detective is knocked unconscious by thugs, or by the femme fatale herself. The regularity with which it occurs in Chandler's texts has led to a trickle of critical attention. But what is not addressed with regard to these bouts with unconsciousness is their relation to the textual constructions of gender.[56] I want to argue that the ways these moments are conveyed have much to do with the text's construction of a "deviant" masculine pleasure.

A telling example occurs early on in *Farewell, My Lovely,* when Marlowe is knocked out; we learn much later that the assailant is the femme fatale, Velma. The blow ends a chapter, and the next chapter begins with the following passage:

> "Four minutes," the voice said. "Five, possibly six. They must have moved quick and quiet. He didn't even let out a yell."
>
> I opened my eyes and looked fuzzily at a cold star. I was lying on my back. I felt sick.
>
> The voice said: "It could have been a little longer. . . . They must have been in the brush, right where the car stopped. The guy scared easily. They must have thrown a small light in his face and he passed out—just from panic. The pansy." (63)

Marlowe continues to hear this voice, figuring out what has happened as the voice simultaneously notes his "unmanly" behavior. Then, suddenly, Marlowe identifies the voice, telling us, "It was my voice. I was talking to myself, coming out of it. I was trying to figure the thing out subconsciously" (63). Marlowe then proceeds to tell himself to "Shut up, you dimwit" (63). The moment, at first, seems merely a clever conceit to illustrate Marlowe's slow regaining of consciousness and to make the reader experience the same confusion Marlowe does. But it is far from the only time such dissociation occurs. In fact, it also emerges in moments of seeming consciousness. In *Farewell, My Lovely,* for instance, the dissociation is inspired not by a head trauma but by a combination of Scotch and a necking session with Velma, followed by a conversation with good girl Anne Riordan that ends with her wiping Velma's lipstick off his face, aware of his guilty tryst. Marlowe drives away from the Grayles's home and, having set up a late appointment with Velma, begins reflecting on Anne Riordan, whose romantic interest he continues to reject: "'There's a nice little girl,' I told myself out loud, in the car, 'for a guy that's interested in a nice little girl.' Nobody said anything. 'But I'm not,' I said. Nobody said anything to that either. 'Ten o'clock at the Belvedere Club,' I said. Somebody said, 'Phooey.' It sounded like my voice" (139–40).

Here, the dissociation is more playful, more ruminative. But it is a dissociation, a split nonetheless. And both instances seem tied up with masculine expectation. In the first instance, Marlowe judges himself a "pansy" to have let himself be sapped. In the second instance, Marlowe is wrestling over a potential heterosexual romance with an available woman, Anne. If we have any doubt as to the interpellative position Marlowe sees himself as rejecting in Anne, consider that as he speaks to her he notes a "beautifully painted panel truck" drive by, with the legend, "Bay City Infant Service" (138). Rather than pursue Anne, then, he engages in a cat and mouse flirtation with the married Velma, whom he also rejects twice. Despite his claim that he likes "smooth shiny girls, hardboiled and loaded with sin" (196), Marlowe rejects both the good girl and the "smooth shiny" one. Masculine expectation is circumvented and dissociation occurs.

Marlowe's moments of loss of consciousness are persistently connected to a feeling of nothingness, a void. In the above instances, the void is a space of splitting allowing him to judge himself as if he were both himself and an Other. Other times, however, it offers Marlowe, at the most basic level, a method of self-effacement in which he surrenders response and responsibility. Masculine expectation is seemingly a demand Marlowe cannot quite manage to embody, hence trauma comes, allowing him to split, to avoid responsibility, to disengage from the demands of interpellation.

But this fragmentation and powerlessness often takes on a dreamy, pleasurable feel, as romanticized diction pervades the text, and Marlowe's tight, controlled prose appears to loosen and stretch out languorously before one's eyes. Fred Pfeil, in his fleeting comment on the "scarcely concealed sensual pleasure encoded in Chandler's descriptions of passing out" (117), cites a telling example in a footnote. The passage comes from *Farewell, My Lovely* and reads as follows:

> I felt for the white stool and sat down and put my head down on the white table beside the milky globe which was now shining again softly. I stared at it sideways, my face on the table. The light fascinated me. Nice light, soft light.
> Behind me and around me there was nothing but silence.
> I think I went to sleep, just like that, with a bloody face on the table, and a thin beautiful devil with my gun in his hand watching me and smiling. (157; quoted in Pfeil, 164n)

The eroticism in this passage, unreferenced by Pfeil, is rather stunning, with Marlowe dreamily watching this "beautiful devil" as the man suggestively holds Marlowe's gun in his hand (his "delicate, lovely hand," Marlowe notes a few paragraphs earlier). The hazy, fantasy-laced feel in such scenes is generally accompanied by Marlowe's finally releasing his resistance to the drug, the violent blow, the flurry of punches and, in that release, finding pleasure in surrender. In *The Little Sister* (1949), this response reaches its most hyperbolic form, wherein we have pages and pages of unconscious and semiconscious Marlowe, repeatedly drugged and physically subdued, with him and the reader unsure about what is occurring around him. Marlowe describes a series of responses to the dose of potassium chloride beginning with active resistance (trying to walk, move), then turning to passive frustration expressed a bit headily, even breathlessly: "My heart beat fast and thick and I was having trouble opening my lungs. Like after being winded at football. You think your breath will never come back. Never, never, never."[57] Then come fantastical ruminations: "There was nothing but the carpet. How did I get down there? No use asking. It's a secret" (328). Marlowe proceeds to escape into complete unconsciousness with a darkly romantic expression of surrender and disappearing subjectivity: "A face swam towards me out of the darkness. I changed direction and started for the face. But it was too late in the afternoon. The sun was setting. It was getting dark rapidly. There was no face. There was no wall, no desk. Then there was no floor. There was nothing at all. I wasn't even there" (329). Self-effacement operates as the climax of a series of lush dissolves; nothingness functions as the dreamed-for height of sensate excess. The sequence continues for several pages, savoring every detail of Marlowe's attempts to rouse himself, to leave the premises, to determine what has happened in his unconsciousness—all while he is still hallucinating and semi-conscious at best. Realistic descriptions of the crime scene mix with rhapsodic observations of how the "air still had the aromatic perfume of overripe peaches" (330). The scene climaxes with Marlowe coming upon a mortally wounded man just as he himself is shot again with a syringe of dope. He is helpless to save the man, as he can barely stand, so instead he watches as

> [t]he rattle stopped. There was a long silence. Then there was a muted sigh, very quiet and indolent and without urgency. Another silence. Another still slower sigh, languid and peaceful as a summer breeze drifting past the nodding roses.
>
> Something happened to his face and behind his face, the indefinable thing that happens in that always baffling and inscrutable moment, the smoothing out, the going back over the years to the age of innocence. (332)

The scene reads, out of context, as a sexual interlude, filled with intense romantic or erotic voyeurism. It is among the most openly physical and sexual episodes in Marlowe's generally tightly controlled prose narration. It is Marlowe watching a man die as he himself teeters on the brink of unconsciousness. Death and sexuality, Marlowe's void and erotic pleasure, intermingle, with Marlowe in a comfortable position of forcible passivity, describing breathlessly events he cannot alter and for which he is therefore not responsible.

We might conclude then that Marlowe spends so much of his conscious life shoring up his male subjectivity that when he is unconscious and his subjectivity splits, it is actually sexually pleasurable because he is freed from the necessity of constantly restabilizing his gender binary of male hermeticism and female alterity. The feminization that Marlowe reads as contamination in his conscious life takes a different form in his unconscious or semi-conscious moments. There, Marlowe himself takes on femininity, experiences a traditionally feminine passivity—and therefore femininity becomes defined not through the risk of contagion but through Marlowe's pleasure in his passivity. Unconsciousness liberates him from his rigid polarization, allows him to become "feminized" in a way that does not "infect" him—or the infection is reconceptualized as pleasurable.

Then, for Marlowe, the gender binary's stability and his own subjectivity are mutually constitutive, but while his rigid binary does not allow him sexual pleasure in his conscious existence (the risk of contagion is too great), unconsciousness frees him from the binary and sexual pleasure comes through, unmediated and guiltless.

But these bouts of unconsciousness are only one way that we see Marlowe reckoning with his fraught male subjectivity. As with Walter Huff, gender confusion is often staged as hysteria, but with hysterical trauma disguised behind the professional dissimulation of the private eye.

High on Nerves: Hysteria and the Private Eye

Marlowe's threatened masculinity is revealed in moments that are quite connected to the moments of dissociation discussed above—that is, in moments wherein we find a telling emphasis on performance and disguise. The dissociation in fact often reappears in moments of uncanny imposture, yoking the two manifestations of Marlowe hysteria. In *The Lady in the Lake,* for instance, a woman (we later learn she is the killer) pulls a gun on Marlowe. Both are in gigolo Chris Lavery's house under suspicious circumstances: Marlowe is posing as a bill collector and the woman in question, Muriel Chess, is posing as a landlady. Both are simulating here, dissembling before each other's eyes. She tells Marlowe that she has come for simple rent collection purposes: "I just didn't want him to get too far behind in the rent" (108).[58] The text then reads: "A fellow with a kind of strained and unhappy voice said politely: 'How far behind is he?'" (108). The voice, despite the use of the third person here, is Marlowe's. It is as though part of him is on autopilot, while the rest of him can comment on, characterize the performance of the other part.

Throughout *The Lady in the Lake,* we see Marlowe referring to those around him—suspects, implicated parties, even his own client—as "performing" their responses. Muriel Chess, posing as the landlady, stamps her foot in frustration, and Marlowe notes, "That was all the scene lacked. That made it perfect" (112). He later tells her, when she poses as Mrs. Kingsley, "You do this character very well. . . . This confused innocence with an undertone of hardness and bitterness" (207).

Of course, Muriel Chess is performing in the most basic sense of the word; she is an impostor. But, to Marlowe, there are other "performances." Potential love interest Adrienne Fromsett raises her eyebrows in a way that, Marlowe determines, "look[s] artificial" (130). Marlowe's client, Kingsley, exhibits his "misery [with] a theatrical flavor, as real misery so often has" (124). Around all these controlled performances—genuine or feigned (Marlowe, as we see with the Kingsley example, equates them all)—Marlowe is remarkably uncontrolled. He even tells the cool Miss Fromsett, "I'd like to be smooth and distant and subtle about all this too. I'd like to play this sort of game just once the way somebody like you would like it to be played. But nobody will let me . . ." (197). He envies the contained, composed self-presentation that he is unable, despite his frequent tough talk, to project; indeed, many times, other characters inform Marlowe that his "tough guy act stinks" (*The High Window* 1005).

We might think of Marlowe as having a perpetual crisis of profession. If hysteria, during Charcot's heyday, was a preeminently visual, even theatrical "disorder," filled, as Tania Modleski notes, with "very complicated kinds of role-playing" that always "threatened to draw the doctors into a world of appearances, illusion and duplicity," then we can see Marlowe working in a similar dynamic.[59] His profession demands skill at reading and interpreting dissembling and deception at the same time as it requires him to dissemble and deceive. For every impostor or disguise Marlowe comes across, we find a mask he must don, a character he must take on in order to retrieve information, but also to avoid suspicion and exposure.

Liahna Babener notes that in Chandler's novels, "personal identity is portrayed as unstable and uncertain. In a society of second chances and new beginnings, people are not what they seem or who they used to be."[60] The important difference here is that Marlowe experiences the fragmentation without controlling it. When Marlowe does pose as someone else, it is fleeting, even comic (telling Carmen Sternwood his name is Doghouse Reilly; posing as a stereotypical gay man at a pornographic lending library). He cannot quite pull it off. We might think then of Marlowe as suffering from a blurring of boundaries, a fear that the performances he controls (disguising himself as a debt collector, an aesthete, etc.) exist side by side with the ones he seemingly cannot: his lapses into unconsciousness, his feelings of fragmentation and dissociation, his sudden expressions of fears of death.

Elaine Showalter notes that, since World War II, doctors have still balked at calling male patients hysterics, claiming they do not exhibit the theatricality, emotionalism, or vanity. In turn, "When men with hysterical symptoms are emotional or theatrical, psychiatrists hint that they must be homosexual. Freud argued that hysterical men were sexually passive. Wilhelm Reich described the male hysteric as characterized by 'feminine facial expression and feminine behavior.'"[61] Although it seems unclear here whether Showalter is pointing to or creating a conflation between perceived homosexuality, sexual passivity, and femininity, the point is provocative in relation to Marlowe. Marlowe's hysteria is feminizing according to a traditional gender binary of agency/passivity because his dissociations involve helplessness and a lack of agency. In turn, his fits of uncontrollable laughter (another periodic reoccurrence in these texts), or his talking to himself involve self-display of the kind the female hysteric was expected to "perform." The performances and the passivity then characterize Marlowe's hysteria as distinctly feminizing. And with Marlowe, as with Huff and many other hardboiled heroes, femininity is repeatedly connected to death, or the void.[62] But if feminization can point to the void, it can also hide the void through performance, the performance of self-control.

For Marlowe, as we have seen, pleasure comes in the void between performativity and an essential subjectivity that may, Marlowe fears, not even exist. If unconsciousness means unacknowledged pleasure, consciousness means the risk of hysteria, and thereby the risks of sexual involvement and female contamination. Significantly, his primary leisure activity—chess—is steeped in rules, logic. It is the activity he indulges in to soothe himself, to gain self-possession, and always within his home, the place he goes to regain composure, comfort, stability. Chess performs a crucial function for Marlowe, an interesting corollary to Walter Huff's immersion in the rules of the insurance industry. But while Huff's entrenchment is presented, ultimately, as a prison, Marlowe's reliance on chess is a protective device. Consider the end of *The High Window,* for instance, wherein Marlowe presents chess as a constitutive cure: "Beautiful cold remorseless chess, almost creepy in its silent implacability" (1177). Marlowe looks at his face in the mirror, and determines, "You and Capablanca" (1177), referring to the chess master. Chess helps Marlowe feign a subjectivity he continually doubts. It functions as the height of masculine hermeticism, filled with rigid rules and, as Marlowe plays it, an utterly solitary activity. Moreover, Marlowe's identification with the knight, as evidenced throughout *The Big Sleep,* further genders the act of chess playing. Playing assures Marlowe of a gender binary he finds constantly unraveling, to his horror and his pleasure both. The fact that Marlowe finds chess's implacability "creepy," however, and the fact that Chandler gives the terrifying Muriel Chess in *The Lady in the Lake* such a surname, hints that even chess's hermetic, masculine promise is highly dubious. If Marlowe cannot perform a coherent subjectivity, or ritualize it into existence through activities like his beloved chess, from where does it derive? Does it exist at all?

Marlowe's subjectivity then is consistently thrown into question through an array of threats: the femme fatale, his own illicit pleasure in dissociation, disruptions in the gender binary that is supposed to secure that subjectivity. Performances he witnesses and is professionally mandated to take on himself further point to the instability of self, and of the gender binary that secures the solidity of that self.

Crucially, then, as hysteric and doctor (to the hysteric, Merle Davis, to all those who perform for him), text and interpreter, Marlowe occupies both sides of his own gender binary: He is his own greatest fear, as occupying both sides of the binary threatens the binary's stability, the gender difference that constitutes it and that it constitutes. Hence, Marlowe's pleasure in unconsciousness, in a nothingness devoid of coherent subjectivity appears all the more fitting because such a state conceals the binary, explodes personal identity, creating a helpless, free-floating play. Marlowe's masculinity then turns out to derive from a volleying between both sides of the gender binary. Masculinity is the failure of the binary to operate as it should. Masculinity is both masculine and feminine by the binary's standards, as is femininity, as the femme fatale figures show. Gender is ultimately rendered potentially illusory, manipulable, performed, and punishing.

⸺⸺ ⸺⸺ ⸺⸺

If masculinity in these texts is partially defined by a fraught structure in the face of feminine chaos, these texts show femininity to be an inevitable masculine interlude. Masculinity seems to depend on this embrace and then rejection of femininity, despite a textual acknowledgment of a covert play between sides of the binary. It is a structure of return. For Marlowe, the return is to a hermetic individualism. For Huff, it is to a doomed recognition of the power of the corporate economy of which he is a tool and dupe.

In both Cain and Chandler, the textual trajectory involves moving from masculine structures (capitalist-bourgeois, or individual), through realms of gender play or blurring, then to a forced (and therefore dubious) reconsolidation of a binary in Chandler, and to a recognition of the power of capitalist-bourgeois hegemony in Cain wherein the feminine turns out to be a mere tool by which to trap Huff within that hegemony.

Let us then turn to the question of the appeal of the white male protagonist offered up by Cain and Chandler. Does the white male reader identify with Walter's attraction to an alternative structure and his helplessness in the midst of the Company? Does the white male reader identify with Marlowe as the individual, a lone figure facing rampant corruption, both deriving pleasure from, and then constraining, alterity?

In many ways, Marlowe is the quintessential reader-surrogate in that he immerses himself in deathly appealing alterity and yet retains a purity, a moral(istic) high ground, just as the reader is permitted. But Cain's text will not let the reader do so—the last chapter of *Double Indemnity* unseats a readerly interlocutor status/power and stains. In the end, in fact, both Marlowe and Huff implicate the reader through the hysterical nature of their texts, which bid a readerly interaction, a filling of gaps, an involvement that risks identification. And it is the possibility of such an intense identification with the tough guy that, as the next chapter reveals, proved such a threat as hard-boiled readership grew and as the notion of a white male loner treading into transgressive terrain came to be increasingly suspect.

CHAPTER THREE

"ANOTHER SOFT-VOICED BIG MAN I HAD STRANGELY LIKED"

Containing White Male Desire

"Every man has got five per cent of that in him, if he meets the one person that'll bring it out . . ."

—James M. Cain, *Serenade*

IT IS OVER 100 PAGES INTO JAMES CAIN'S 1937 NOVEL *SERENADE,* IN THE LAST quarter of the text, that the central plot twist is revealed. What makes this twist particularly unusual is that, although the text is a first-person narrative, the secret divulged is one that the narrator has concealed from the reader. The revelation occurs thusly, as the narrator, vagabond and opera singer John Howard Sharp, speaks with his Mexican wife, Juana, who has just met Sharp's former mentor:

"Who is these man?"
We were in the cab going down, and it was like the whisper you hear from a coiled rattlesnake.
"What man?"
"I think you know, yes."
"I don't even know what you're talking about."
"You have been with a man."
"I've been with plenty of men. I see men all day long. Do I have to stay with you all the time? What the hell *are* you talking about?"

"I no speak of man you see all day long. I speak of man you love. Who is these man?"

"Oh, I'm a fairy, is that it?"

"Yes."

"Well, thanks. I didn't know that."[1]

Sharp then describes feeling "cold and shrivelled inside" (191) in an unmistakable image of emasculation, or even castration, emphasized by the comparison between Juana's initial question and the whisper of a "coiled rattlesnake." To complete the Medusa association, Sharp relates, "I could feel her there looking at me, looking at me with those hard black eyes that seemed to bore through me" (191).

Sharp feels Juana's "naming" of him, her unveiling of him, on the bodily level. And throughout the novel, Sharp's homosexuality inheres insistently with the body—and with the body as disconnected from any intellectual or emotional control. Specifically, in Sharp's case, his voice betrays his desire, though not through what he *says* but through how his voice *sounds*. His singing voice aurally reflects his sexual orientation (or "leaning," as the text configures it) in spite of his efforts to conceal it. The male body thus constantly threatens to "betray" the male conscious mind, the two split from each other. The body speaks what the conscious mind seeks to keep forever hidden, much as in the white male hysteria discussed in chapter two: "what the body suffers, the mind needn't think."[2] It is his wife Juana who forces Sharp to make conscious what his body is enacting, both to himself and to the reader.

This first hint we have that something is "wrong" with John Howard Sharp occurs when he recounts serenading Juana, the prostitute who will become his wife, early on in the narrative—an event that succeeds in aborting their seemingly prescient sexual encounter: "I . . . started to sing. I don't know how far I got. What stopped me was the look on her face. . . . [I]t was the face at the window of every whorehouse in the world, and it was looking right through me" (95). Juana's ability to penetrate Sharp visually, as we saw in the above accusation scene, finds its originary moment here. She asks him to leave, without explaining what she has "seen." Later, in his bed, Sharp bemoans how he had "tried to serenade a lady that was eas[il]y serenaded, and I couldn't even get away with that." He then reflects, "When I closed my eyes I'd see her looking at me, seeing something in me. I didn't know what, and then I'd open them again and look at the fog. After a while it came to me that I was afraid of what she saw in me. There would be something horrible mixed up in it, and I didn't know what it was" (96). But of course Sharp does know what she sees in him, although he will not disclose it to the reader for nearly 100 pages. Sharp's voice betrays him, reveals what he attempts to conceal or even deny to himself. And it is the female who can distill it, who can hear what his body (his singing voice) says to her and who can, by looking at him, remind him of his own "emasculated" state. Her auditory gleaning and his visual interpretation commingle. She looks at him and hears; he sees her hearing, and feels unveiled, exposed.

Further, it is significant that it is Juana who can so easily see Sharp's "secret." As a Mexican woman who is explicitly presented as naïve and primitive, she carries the authenticity of an Other, apparently making her particularly skilled at "seeing" the otherness of John Howard Sharp—that is, his homosexual past. Sharp and Juana's first sexual encounter is figured as a moment of essential primitivism. It transpires when the two embark on a trip away from the city and into more remote parts of Mexico. They become stranded in a church during a storm. The rough conditions and sacral surroundings inspire Juana to make offerings of food at the altar. Sharp, seeing her kneel before the altar, naked and praying, comments, "She had been sliding back to the jungle ever since she took off that first shoe, coming out of Taxco, and now she was right in it" (121). It is at this point that Sharp rapes her. "Yes, it was rape," he tells the reader, "but only technical brother, only technical. Above the waist maybe she was worried about the *sacrilegio,* but from the waist down she wanted me, bad" (121). The narrative, far from having Sharp pay for this crime, only bears him out, as this rape is presented as the passionate beginning of their long, often-idealized romance. We never "hear" Juana's thoughts on the rape, and are left only with Sharp's assertion that her body, if not her will, "wanted it." But it is revealing that Sharp, so much a victim of his body, which seems to want what his mind rises up against, should value what Juana's body "speaks" to him over what she consciously resists.

This particular burst of sexual violence is driven by an encounter in which Juana listens to Sharp sing and then whispers, Medusa-like, in a "long hiss," that he sings, " . . . Just like the priest" (120). Sharp's head begins to "pound like it would split" as he recognizes that she is right: his voice "had the same wooden, dull quality that a priest's voice has, without one particle of life in it" (120). His voice lacks what Juana will later refer to as the "*toro*" of heterosexual passion. It is ostensibly the sight of Juana at her most primitive that drives him to rape, but it is also clearly an act of asserting with a vengeance his status as a straight, white male, conquering this non-white, "primitive" female who disputes his "masculinity" and heterosexual potency—two terms that are configured virtually synonymously in the text.

Alas, while being raped "proves" to Juana, temporarily, that Sharp is heterosexual, the body still threatens to disrupt and expose. Sharp's voice gains the "*toro*" it had lost for some time, but when Sharp's former mentor/lover Winston Hawes enters their lives, the voice threatens to revert to its former passionless, priestly tones. It is Juana herself who explicates the novel's philosophy of a connection between voice and sexuality: "these man who love other man, they can do much, very clever. But no one can sing. Have no *toro* in high voice, no *grrr* that frightens little *muchacha*, make heart beat fast. Sound like old woman, like cow, like priest" (192).[3] Male homosexuality is thus configured as powerless, sterile, or sexless. But this particular configuration is far from consistent, as the text also represents male homosexuality as all-powerful and omnipresent. This version of male homosexuality is embodied in the mesmerist-like figure of Winston Hawes, who stalks Sharp across the globe, leaving scores of young lovers in his wake.

The distinction operating in *Serenade* seems to be between the man "susceptible" to homosexuality and the "true" homosexual who bewitches the former. Sharp, then, can still be "saved," the text offers, through the healing power of Juana's earthy femininity. After Sharp has admitted his past to Juana (and the reader), Juana holds Sharp to her, strokes his hair, and then, "shove[s] a nipple" in his mouth, exhorting, in a moment of high pulp, "Eat. Eat much. Make big *toro!*" Sharp responds, "I know now, my whole life comes from there" (194). All physicality, all that is of the body derives from the maternal breast; for man to exit the endogamous Oedipal model for sexual pleasure is thus conceived of as unnatural.

Moreover, *Serenade* pointedly attempts to show that heterosexual passion with an "uncultured" woman promises an essential wholeness that homosexuality cannot provide. Sharp proceeds to stay in bed with Juana for two days in what can only be described as a mammoth breast cure until Sharp finally understands "what a woman could mean to a man. Before, she had been a pair of eyes, and a shape, something to get excited about. Now she seemed something to lean on, and draw something from, that nothing else could give me" (195). Sharp's heterosexual encounters until this particular experience with the hyper-essentialized Earth Mother Juana are thus presented as superficial. But it is interesting to note that the source of comparison is not Sharp's affair with Winston Hawes (an affair whose physical aspect the text elides) but any of Sharp's heterosexual experiences. It is as if to invoke a comparison or even contrast between heterosexual and homosexual love or sex is too dangerous. To put the two side by side would mean they are commensurate experiences, and the text will not allow such an option. They are not equivalences; they are illness and cure, or attempted cure, as we will see.

Cain's own articulation of *Serenade*'s contorted philosophy appears in a letter he wrote to H. L. Mencken: "The lamentable sounds that issue from a homo's throat when he tries to sing are a matter of personal observation. . . . But the theme demanded the next step, the unwarranted corollary that heavy workouts with a woman would bring out the stud horse high notes. Right there is where it goes facile and I suppose silly."[4] One can detect the strain in Cain's own admission. Cain claims to be able to "hear" homosexuality in a singing voice, to be able to detect homosexuality auditorially, but he cannot actually envision a "cure" for how the gay man can procure the high notes, muster the necessary *toro*. If an active sex life with a woman—not to mention a "foreign" woman—cannot do it, what can? It seems Cain is actually positing an essential gayness here, one that cannot be "expunged" or from which one cannot be cured.

Juana's breast cure, and the promise of normative sexuality it embodies, ultimately fails to save the couple. While we do not see subsequent evidence of Sharp engaging in homosexual relationships, he and Juana do not "live happily ever after." Instead, Cain's tendency toward fatalistic narratives clearly sets the path for Sharp's "weakness" to be lethal: Juana will end up murdering Winston Hawes, sending the two on the run and eventually driving them apart (Juana will return to prostitution and eventually be murdered, seemingly doomed to self-destructive heterosexual liaisons).

It certainly seems that Cain cannot imagine a sexual relationship in which his white male protagonist is not a victim. He constructs Winston Hawes as a femme fatale, dangerous and alluring, but he cannot truly envision a woman as the restorative alternative. There is no safe sexual encounter for the lone white male, no encounter that will allow him a consistent position of power and control. As such, Sharp's relationships place him in what the text views as the intolerable and yet somehow fated position of submissive partner. Juana and Hawes both dominate Sharp, can read him better than he can read himself. Hawes's power seems equal to Juana's, with her only leverage being the weight of heteronormative strictures behind her. Paul Skenazy writes, "Hawes activates Sharp's homosexual desires, which undermines the '*toro*' of his art (and, presumably, body) and distorts his 'natural' (which seems to mean dominating male) character. Homoerotic feeling is equated with tenderness, softness, and a debilitating emotional dependence . . ." (59). Sharp bears only a passing resemblance to Skenazy's model of male homosexuality in his dependent "addiction" to Hawes. Sharp's homoerotic feelings seem to be more about uncontrollability and submission than tenderness or softness, suggesting Skenazy is sliding from the text's construction of homosexual desire to concerns about the representation of a weakened masculinity.[5] Even more tellingly, Hawes's characterization resists Skenazy's model entirely as a figure not of softness but of hypnotic strength and will to power.

Hawes's characterization in the text is not limited to his dominant personality, however, but extends to his affiliation with refinement and the arts. If Juana embodies primitive femaleness and Oedipal heterosexuality (with the castratory threat implicit within it), then Hawes, as a world-class conductor, embodies high culture, configured as effeminate but deeply penetrating. Sharp confides,

> [Hawes] was like some woman that goes to concerts because they give her the right vibrations, or make her feel better, or have some other effect on her nitwit insides. All right, you may think it's cockeyed to compare him with somebody like that, but I'm telling you that in spite of all his technical skills, he was hell of a sight nearer to that fat poop than he ever was to Muck. That woman was in him, poodle dog, diamonds, limousine, conceit, cruelty and all, and don't let his public reputation fool you. She has a public too. (180) [6]

Homosexuality is allied both with uncontrollable physicality (as signified by the throat's sounds, the voice) and, in a more common hardboiled linkage, with high culture, which is gendered feminine. As with the foppish pornographer Arthur Gwynn Geiger in Chandler's *The Big Sleep,* or the dandified Joel Cairo in Dashiell Hammett's *The Maltese Falcon,* male homosexuality is conflated with exotic artifice, rarefied taste, and, in the case of Cain's Winston Hawes, extreme emotionalism and hard cruelty. Hawes is not, however, the sartorial dandy that Geiger and Cairo are (Hawes wears a "rough coat, flannel shirt and battered trousers" [184]) and Cain imbues Hawes with none of the weakness and physical fragility that characterizes typical hardboiled representations. As noted earlier, Hawes is a force with which to be reckoned, with a mesmerist's hold over Sharp, who admits that he once "depended on [Hawes] like a hophead depends on dope" (182). Sharp is then both physically addicted to Hawes and dazzled by his prowess as a conductor: "He had a live stick all right. . . . He threw it on you like a hypnotist, and you began to roll it out, and yet it was all under perfect control" (191). Hawes's high culture genius is at one with his hypnotic hold, which seems at one with his sexual lure, as the innuendo in Sharp's claim about his "live stick" suggests.

Paul Skenazy considers Cain's representation of Hawes as part of a tradition beginning with Lady Brett's sailor friends in Hemingway's *The Sun Also Rises* and continuing on in figures like Hammett's Joel Cairo and Lindsay Marriott in Chandler's *Farewell, My Lovely.* He argues that "the effeminate male is a creature of ridicule and scorn in the tough guy tradition. He is the soft-boiled man in a hard-boiled world: vulnerable, gutless, impractical; often a man of high culture characterized by his 'precious' taste" (55). But Skenazy's reading is problematic in its tendency to replicate Cain's own anxious belief that it is Hawes alone who is homosexual. In Skenazy's reading, male homosexuality is personified in the text either by Winston Hawes or by John Howard Sharp. He cannot reckon a male homosexuality containing both characterizations. Most often, this blind spot results in Skenazy favoring Hawes as the text's model of male homosexuality, suggesting Sharp is not "really" homosexual, merely vulnerable to Hawes's contagious sexuality. This reading is one with which Cain would probably agree: Hawes is the homosexual man, Sharp is merely susceptible to one specific man. Hawes is a menace because he brings out what is presented as Sharp's weakness; Hawes has the power to unleash the dormant 5 percent and the tool by which he does it is presented as cultural: his musical virtuosity.[7]

Then, Juana's femininity, presented as primal, elemental, natural (Juana is referred to most consistently as "she," not by her name), and Hawes's homosexual masculinity, affiliated with culture, modernity, and taste, both threaten to dominate Sharp and his brand of seemingly vulnerable, sexually ambivalent masculinity. Skenazy argues that the "primitive maternal church [Juana] heals and empowers; the sophisticated world of class and art—the addictive 'Papa' [Winston Hawes]—destroys and emasculates" (60). But, as noted, Juana consistently uses her powers to emasculate Sharp. Consider, for instance, the scene right after Juana has learned Sharp's secret. Juana answers the phone and it is Hawes asking for Sharp: "[Juana] gave a rasping laugh and put on the goddamdest imitation of Winston you ever saw, the walk, the stick, and all the rest of it so you almost thought he was in front of you. 'Yes, your sweetie, he waits at telephone, talk to him please'" (193). After her performance, Sharp runs into the bedroom, "flop[s] on the bed, pull[s] the pillow over [his] head" (193). She inspires not anger or violence in him but fear, shame. As Skenazy goes on to concede, "He depends on Juana yet fears her strength. She creates his potency, but clearly also has the emasculating power to destroy him, as she did Hawes, with her elemental female knowledge" (61). Indeed, when Sharp flees with Juana, all is not happily ever after: Sharp cannot sing for fear he will be identified (the fear that his voice would betray his sexuality becomes the fear that his voice will betray his identity *in toto*). He even fails to recognize his own voice on the radio. Joyce Carol Oates writes, "[I]f the conscious wish of *Serenade* is to be a man, free from homosexual weakness, then surely the unconscious wish is to destroy whatever threatens this weakness—obviously, the female who prevents the comfortable illicit relationship with the male lover, artist, musician, man of taste, of wealth, etc. Is it possible that Cain did not understand what he was doing in *Serenade?*"[8] While I would not go so far as to suggest Cain was unaware of his own text's twisty logic, the point is apt. After all, if Sharp's life is his singing voice, Juana "prevents" him from using it when the two must go into hiding. Further, the text presents her emasculating accusations as the source of Sharp's loss of confidence and of his self-doubt. And, while Hawes's influence resulted in Sharp's greatest singing triumphs, it crippled his sense of masculinity.

Then, women and gay men occupy a near-identical space in relation to the hero (whose sexuality seems to be up for grabs, winner take all)—both threats, both emotional, strong, passionate, and hypnotically powerful. Consider Juana, in the midst of an elaborate toreador performance, murdering Hawes as he plays the part of a bull. In this performance, Juana is not reclaiming Sharp's masculinity: she is asserting her own power, and all bow to her, Hawes included. Upon watching this spectacle, Sharp surrenders utterly to Juana: " . . . I tried to tell myself I had hooked up with a savage, that it was horrible. It was no use. I wanted to laugh, to cheer, and yell *Olé!* I knew I was looking at the most magnificent thing I had ever seen in my life" (203). She has "won" him with her glorious performance, her riveting display of power.

Of particular note, however, is the fact that male homosexuality is configured in *Serenade* as a weakness all men have. "Every man has got five percent of that in him," Sharp tells his wife, "if he meets the one person that'll bring it out, and I did, that's all" (194). The text constructs masculinity in part through homosexual desire, which is destructive, and in part through heterosexual desire, which is also destructive. The only added danger of the former is that it is more shameful in the public eye and invades the body, seizing control of it. This construction functions through the logic of contamination and contagion (what lies dormant is unleashed) and also the logic of inevitability—an inevitability erupting from within the dangerously uncontrollable male body and male psyche. As Sharp relates, "A voice is a physical thing and if you've got one, it's like any other physical thing. It's in you, and it's got to come out" (220).[9]

⸻ ⸻ ⸻

Cain's *Serenade* teases out several strains that will preoccupy hardboiled fiction for the next two decades. First, as pursued in chapter two's discussion of male hysteria, we see the anxious relation of the hardboiled male to his own body, the sense that his body (and, potentially, its desires) can or will betray him. Second, we see the fear of feminization or emasculation, as reflected in *Serenade* and many hardboiled novels in representations of both a high culture gay man and a primitive, castratory yet maternal (or, castratory *because* maternal) woman—femmes fatales both. Third, we witness contamination fears (as we saw with Philip Marlowe's hermeticism) plaguing both the tough guy and, as we will see, the hardboiled writer himself, wary of the dangers of effeminacy implicit in literary pursuits. Last, we see hints of the larger contamination fears that will characterize particularly Cold War America's relationship with hardboiled or pulp popular fiction. The last development reaches paranoiac heights in the 1950s when it mingles with post–World War II anxiety over gender roles, homosexual panic, and Cold War hysteria.

Dangerous Identifications

In 1949, Gershon Legman, known at that time primarily as a humorist, published a contentious little pamphlet that eventually would become a small book entitled, *Love and Death: A Study in Censorship* (1963).[10] In chapters titled "Institutionalized Lynch," "Not For Children," "Avators [sic] of the Bitch," and "Open Season on Women," Legman attempts to expose the entanglement of sexuality with violence in literature and popular culture at the expense of what he sees as healthy expressions of sexual love. His most common targets are crime magazines and crime novels. Consider a sampling of Legman's baroque prose, of which we can hear echoes in past and present rhetoric bemoaning Hollywood or computer game violence: "In the midst of death, love is no part of our dream. Our imaginations stuffed with murder, we are too moral for sex. . . . [O]ur multi-millions of 'mystery' readers *prefer* their transvalued pattern—empty of sex, reeking with sadism—within the boundaries of which, as it would seem, no one dares to attack them."[11]

Legman's particular source of disgust is what he sees as sexualized violence in mass form: comic books, radio horror shows, televised sports, crime films, tabloids, and pulp fiction. The fact that these media garner immense audiences seems to be at the root of the disturbance for Legman, who calls such apparently passive consumers the "trapped millions" (27). In discussing the sadistic dangers of comic books, however, Legman reveals the latent message he fears the unthinking masses unknowingly receive: first, anti-Semitism via Superman's swastika-like "S" and the Flash's thunderbolt ("a swastika is two thunderbolts crossing" [42], Legman notes). But also, in collaboration with that creeping fascism, Legman detects an "undercurrent of homosexuality and sado-masochism" (42).

Legman is prepared for readerly surprise at this allegation, admitting, "The homosexual element lies somewhat deeper [than the brutality]" (42). This component needs to be ferreted out, and that is part of his project. He goes on to say that in comic books the homosexual undercurrent lies not, "at least, not importantly," in the

> obvious faggotry of men kissing one another and saying 'I love you,' and then flying off through space against orgasm backgrounds of red and purple, not in the tranvestist [sic] scenes in every kind of comic-book . . . not in the long-haired western killers with tight pants. . . . Neither is it in the explicitly Samurai subservience of the inevitable little-boy helpers . . . nor in the fainting adulation of thick necks, ham fists, and well-filled jockstraps. . . . It is not even in the two comic-book companies staffed entirely by homosexuals and operating out of our most phalliform skyscraper. (42–43)

One can feel the creeping McCarthyist logic here in Legman's anxious conspiracy theory. Clearly, male homosexuality is everywhere in comic books, and it is the purposeful project of companies overrun by homosexuals to infiltrate young minds with such "faggotry." But let us return to what Legman is leading up to here, the covert homosexuality that is far more insidious than the costumes and body-worship: "The really important homosexuality of the Superman theme . . . is in the lynching pattern itself, in the weak and fearful righteousness with which it achieves its wrong" (43). Legman claims that the child (gendered male by Legman) reading the average crime comic will identify with the criminal and therefore "consummate his Oedipan dream of strength" (43); but with "Superman, the Supersleuths, the Supercops," there is no such fruitful identification. Instead, the child will "align [himself] always on the side of law, authority, the father and accept their power passively from a bearded above" (43). With no competition for the Mother, development is perverted, Legman argues, noting, "Like Wild Bill Hickok, our own homosexual hero out thar where men were men—with his long silk stockings and his Lesbian side-kick, Calamity Jane—they are too unvirile to throw off fear, and kill as criminals" (43).

Legman's concern is that normative development will not be achieved and heterosexual assimilation will not occur. Instead, we will have a nation of homosexual men hiding behind the mask of government, exerting order without strength, the Law without an essential masculinity. The danger is one of identification. If, as Diana Fuss puts it, identification is the "detour through the other that defines a self," then Legman finds such a detour to be the ultimate risk of contamination.[12] Much like Philip Wylie's "momism" fears that were to emerge at the same time, Legman's anxieties are pop Freudian: What if young boys begin to identify with these weak pulp heroes? Will they never take up their appropriate patriarchal role? What will happen to the family? Here, we detect once again the anxiety that surrounds the figure of the marginal white man in post–World War II America: loners like Philip Marlowe, unmarried and childless drifters like Frank Chambers (*The Postman Always Rings Twice*)—how can one be sure of them? Who are these men who are not fathers, not husbands, not domestic patriarchs, and not company men? It may at first seem ironic that such ostensibly "tough" figures as these would pose a threat to masculine identification, but the resonances of a loner white man in America undergo a significant change from 1934 to 1952. The marginal man of the Depression, the glamorous neurotics of 40s noir occupy an increasingly uncomfortable position in post-war America with its compulsory models of appropriate masculine function. The meaning of representing or identifying with a white man standing outside the white nuclear family romance and company family romance is rewritten. Cold War polarities, post–World War II gender panics, rising consumerism (thus the rise of corporate models over a valorization of the individual) rendered the lone white male increasingly suspect.

Legman then represents a growing strain of public frenzy over the content of mass market pulp fiction and what it might be "telling" readers, consciously or unconsciously. He burrows through the hardboiled canon, asserting a pattern of sexualized violence, and violent sex at the expense of "healthy" sexuality—which, for Legman, means heteronormative sexuality, a kind of heterosexual grand passion between a willing and non-threatening woman and a virile man free of any homosocial involvement. Legman blames hardboiled architect Dashiell Hammett for perpetuating a pattern imitated by scores of followers: "[a] combination of coitus and killing—the essence of the Marquis de Sade's lethography" (65). In turn, James M. Cain horrifies Legman for his couplings of "homicidal females and meacock males" (66). Sexuality in these pairings is "strictly of a background nature," with violence taking the foreground. All sexuality in Cain's novels, according to Legman, is located in his breast references. When it comes to the film adaptations, this "breast fetishism [sic]" is all that remains, and even that is conveyed only visually, by "sixty-foot billboards displaying Miss Lana Turner's bosom" (66).[13]

But Legman reserves his greatest disgust for Raymond Chandler. According to Legman, the writer barely conceals a "repugnance" (68) for sexuality, by which Legman once again seems to mean his own brand of normative sexuality. Lurking behind the endless parade of "lecherous" (69) woman characters from whom Chandler's hero Philip Marlowe repeatedly withdraws is a repressed homosexuality. Legman quotes Chandler himself as saying, in his famed "The Simple Art of Murder" essay, "I do not care much about [the detective's] private life; he is neither a eunuch nor a satyr; I think he might seduce a duchess and I am quite sure he would not spoil a virgin."[14] Legman reads Chandler's claim as spurious, claiming no "sexual intercourse takes place. His women are all strictly flaming bitches, killers or corpses" (69).[15]

Let us be clear: no feminist agenda lies behind Legman's seeming critique of a Chandlerian misogyny as "anti-female necrophilia" (70). Instead, Legman uses what he sees as Marlowe's disgust for women as evidence for Marlowe's homosexuality, which in turn evinces the danger of his popularity in mass market pulp. By way of illustration, he sets a particularly ghoulish description of a dead woman in *The Lady in the Lake* alongside the luminous portrait of a male character, Red Norgaard, in *Farewell, My Lovely.* The glowing words Chandler/Marlowe offers for Red is lucid evidence to Legman, who notes a sadistic edge to the infatuation: "no matter how 'strangely' Chandler's detective, Marlowe, moons over these big men, they are always beating him up" (70). (In fact, Red does not beat Marlowe up but instead helps him.) Legman goes on to remind us that Marlowe shares a name with another "more famous Marlowe, who died avowing 'That all thei that love not Tobacco & Boies were fooles'" (70). Indeed, Legman asserts, in a phrasing that enraged Chandler when he read it, "Chandler's Marlowe is clearly homosexual—a butterfly as the Chinese say, dreaming he is a man" (70). His libidinal pleasure deriving from masochistic interactions with men far stronger than he, Marlowe is thus a butterfly on a wheel, spinning at the hands of brutish and gorgeous thugs. Legman shudders to think of readerly identification with this impotent figure.

In his reading, then, Legman presumes a series of links between a diegetic absence of sexual activity with women, admiration for a man, homosexuality, sadomasochism, and an utter lack of masculinity. A homosexual man is not a man; masculinity remains a dreamed-for ideal. Marlowe is all perverse lack. As Legman later claims, via Freud's "Psychogenesis of a Case of Homosexuality," "The parallel between homosexuality in men and frigidity in women is worth exploring. In both of them the dynamic is fear" (78). It is of course quite interesting that Legman parallels male homosexuality with female frigidity, instead of with female homosexuality. The suggestion seems to be that male homosexuality is founded on a complete lack of desire, a sexlessness (recall *Serenade*'s anxious analogy of the homosexual to the priest). All failure to engage in normative heterosexuality, for whatever reason, is quarantined as "Other."

At the root of Legman's argument, ultimately, is a fear that readers will identify with a character Legman sees as insufficiently male. One cannot emphasize enough the extent to which, with the 1940s and early 1950s rise in the paperback market, public fears focused around perceived dangers in pulp novels, and in the idea of mass readership in general. As discussed in chapter one, in 1952 and 1953 Senator Joseph McCarthy and the U.S. Congress conducted extensive and repressive investigations into the content of paperback novels, of which hardboiled fiction comprised the largest part. The House Select Committee on Current Pornographic Materials determined that, "some of the most offensive infractions of the moral code were found to be contained in low-cost, paper-bound publications known as 'pocket-size books' [which have] degenerated into media for the dissemination of artful appeals to sensuality, immorality, filth, perversion, and degeneracy."[16] This outcry reached a particular intensity in the Cold War era, as it coincided with the rapid growth of the paperback market, thereby swelling the readership and, presumably, increasing the threat of contamination such texts were believed to embody. Further, the fear and desire of the Other that drives the hardboiled novel coalesces in the 1950s with the large-scale Cold War containment anxiety over threats to—and within—American borders (see chapter one). In a "containment culture," to borrow Alan Nadel's term, what was once the threat of immorality becomes a larger, national threat against the era's dominant conception of the American way of life.[17]

Legman, among others, expresses a dread of "catching something" from these novels: catching homosexuality, a role out of the Oedipal relations, a role not socially prescribed and therefore deeply dangerous. Presumably, heterosexual sex affirms a host of ideals: normalcy, health, masculinity, Westernness, Americanness. The hardboiled hero's non-involvement in conventional romances, the marriage convention, fatherhood all become dubious. Moreover, any emotional connection to another man is suspect.

The year after Legman's small pamphlet was published, U. S. Representative Arthur Lewis Miller of Nebraska said the following on the floor of the 81st Congress:

> I would like to strip the fetid, stinking flesh off of this skeleton of homosexuality and tell my colleagues of the House some of the facts of nature. I cannot expose all the putrid facts as it would offend the sensibilities of some of you. It will be necessary to skirt some of the edges, and I use certain Latin terms to describe some of these individuals. Make no mistake several thousand, according to police records, are now employed by the Federal Government.[18]

Notice the language of disease Miller invokes—"fetid," "stinking," "putrid"—and the rhetorical language of clinical distance: he will not "expose all," he will "skirt some of the edges," he will use Latin terms.[19] Miller then advances what becomes the persistent rhetorical link in the decade to come, the link between homosexuality and the Soviet threat:

> I sometimes wonder how many of these homosexuals have had a part in shaping our foreign policy. . . . It is a known fact that homosexuality goes back to the Orientals, lon[g] before the time of Confucius; that the Russians are strong believers in homosexuality, and that those same people are able to get into the State Department and get somebody in their embrace, and once they are in their embrace, fearing blackmail, will make them go to any extent. (4527–4528)

Alterity fears conflate, and far sides of a series of binaries reconstitute, into one common enemy: a homosexual Communist from the East.

Write Like a Man

> The man in the black shirt and yellow scarf was sneering at me over the New Republic. "You ought to lay off that fluff and get your teeth into
> . something solid, like a pulp magazine," I told him, just to be friendly.
> I went on out. Behind me somebody said: "Hollywood's full of them."
>
> —Raymond Chandler, *The High Window* (1942)

In 1949, when the initial Gershon Legman publication appeared, Raymond Chandler received a copy in the mail from Legman himself. Chandler referred to it as a "strange little brochure," and it evidently caused him enough concern that he puzzled over it in a letter to James Sandoe, designating it "substantially a bitter and possibly envious attacks [sic] on all kinds of murder mystery, crime books, realistic sexy writing cum murder."[20] He also refers to a "nasty" letter he received from Legman himself that apparently accused Chandler of being a "homosexualist."[21] J. K. Van Dover, in relating the interaction, suggests that Chandler was sufficiently bothered by the charges that it is "probably not coincidental that Marlowe's non-abstinence is graphically proven—twice—in *The Long Goodbye*," Chandler's next novel.[22]

One of the ironies of this episode is that, in a mode of thinking not unlike Legman's theory of all-gay comic book staffs conspiring in phallic skyscrapers, Chandler himself, on more than one occasion in his letters, offered quite like-minded theories about the literary establishment, estimating, for instance, that 75 percent of American book reviewers are homosexuals.[23] Chandler was also prone to frame attacks on reviewers with charges of effeminacy, calling them "primping second guessers who call themselves critics."[24] The implication is that critics are not tough enough, not up to the task of reading or critiquing hardboiled literature. Johanna Smith, in discussing this strain in Chandler's letters, turns to "The Simple Art of Murder" and notes a similar dynamic when Chandler defends Dashiell Hammett by terming Hammett's derogators "flustered old ladies—of both sexes (or no sex)."[25] The remark bristles with the same kind of hostility Legman exhibits toward "homosexualists" and "frigid women." As Smith perceptively notes, "By thus conflating wrong-headed critical judgments with effeminacy, Chandler makes writing Hammett-like novels seem a guarantee of masculinity."[26] The surest claim to masculinity a writer can make is to write tough, hardboiled prose. Only those lacking masculinity or gender identification at all will fail to appreciate such writing.

Perhaps, then, Legman and Chandler are not so incompatible as Legman would make it seem. Both seem to be laboring under very pressing fears about threatened masculinity. For Chandler, the elite literary establishment, which by and large dismissed him, can be disregarded as a feminizing power one should avoid. Clearly, anxiety about the literary status or non-status of his work is then a central part of his attack. But beyond this anxiety itself, I would like to consider the telling vehicle Chandler offers it: feminization, effeminacy, homosexuality.

For Legman, homosexuality, rather circuitously, threatens normative Oedipal development, the family romance, and by extension a bourgeois nuclear family structure. Further, homosexuality's threat inheres not in some prospect of a titillating, exoticized gay subculture, as other contemporary polemics emphasized, but rather in its potential infiltration into real or symbolic positions of law and order, its ability to conceal a violent cult of quivering sameness behind the accoutrements of a stable hegemony.

Chandler, of course, finds his Marlowe an honorable figure in dishonorable times, but the threat of effeminacy is always lurking, both for Marlowe as a man who is neither married nor particularly sexually involved with women, and for Chandler himself as a writer, a man of literary pursuits. Hence, as Legman gay-baits Chandler, Chandler gay-baits the literary establishment. Legman fears mass culture infestation; but what Chandler manifestly fears—lack of acceptance, ghettoization of detective fiction—appears to conceal another fear that emerges through the way he characterizes his critics or attackers as effeminate or as homosexual. Anxiety over masculinity becomes utterly entangled with fears of charges of homosexuality, the two strains impossible to unfurl in Chandler's rhetoric.

But if Van Dover is right in seeing a link between Chandler's agitation at Legman's charges and detective Philip Marlowe's increased heterosexual activity in *The Long Goodbye* published four years later, then how do we read the intensity of male friendship in that same text? It would seem that Chandler is walking into a trap by portraying *two* highly emotional and conflicted male friendships in that text: that of Marlowe and popular historical romance writer Roger Wade, and that of Marlowe and the alcoholic and ruminative mystery man Terry Lennox. As Chandler wrote in regard to Legman's charges, "[Y]ou can certainly dismiss the remarks of Mr. G. Legman, since Mr. Legman seems to me to belong to that rather numerous class of American neurotics which cannot conceive of a close friendship between a couple of men as other than homosexual."[27] Naming Legman a neurotic to disarm him seems telling unto itself—a feminizing gesture suggesting Legman is both unstable and shut out from codes of masculine camaraderie. Chandler's suggestion that Legman sees a threat in any relationship between men is mitigated by his fraught response and his anxious distancing of himself from the very suggestion of a homoerotic aspect in those same relationships. Legman's criticism seems to sting because Chandler in part abides by the same theory of homosexuality as threat and masculinity as only as real as one's last heterosexual conquest.

Legman's small pamphlet and the book that followed are largely forgotten, but a like-minded piece has proven far more influential in Chandler criticism, Michael Mason's 1976 article, "Deadlier Than the Male." After its publication in the *Times Literary Supplement,* the article sparked a slow stream of criticism focusing on a repressed homosexuality in Chandler's novels. Mason's piece, ostensibly a review of the publication of Chandler's 1946 screenplay for *The Blue Dahlia,* puts forward what he sees as a curious gender divide in Chandler's novels. Specifically, his "murderesses are sadistically brutal in proportion to the degree of sexual arousal they produce in Marlowe," but there is a "compensating quality in certain male characters, an appeal and gentleness just where evil could be expected to concentrate itself."[28] Mason then points to certain "sexually anomalous traits" among Chandler's characters, such as the men's slippers worn by sleazy informant Jesse Florian (see discussion in chapter two). Although Mason never directly states that Marlowe or Chandler is gay, he slides into that interpretation from a claim disputing Marlowe's masculinity. That is, he maintains that Marlowe is "strikingly short of maleness, even in some of his most familiar aspects" (1147). These familiar aspects include the "celebrated backchat" Marlowe participates in, almost always with men (particularly powerful men); what Mason sees as Marlowe's misogyny; the "fastidious" manner with which he maintains his household; and the fact that it is a man, Terry Lennox (*The Long Goodbye*), who brings out Marlowe's greatest "human-heartedness" (1147). Finally, Mason determines that, as the novels proceed, Chandler "brings his secret concerns more into the centre of the fictions. *The Long Goodbye* actually contains a conversation about homosexuality—a circumstance sufficiently suggestive to put in question Chandler's lack of self-awareness about these matters" (1147). Note that Mason never directly terms Marlowe gay. Instead, he sets up a case for Marlowe's effeminacy and for his homosociality, both of which are presented as unnatural and a sign of male lack. According to Mason, these "darker . . . obsessive recurrences" startled Chandler himself, deriving from some unconscious place within the author. Mason goes on to suggest that *Playback,* Chandler's last novel, demonstrates Chandler "recoiling from the point his preoccupation had led him to" (1147). There, Marlowe is almost unrecognizable in his "new propensity for aggression and casual lust" (1147).[29] Further, Mason notes by way of criticism that the dialogue between the hero and his love interest in Chandler's screenplay for *The Blue Dahlia* is written in a strangely "uniform style that bridges the difference in sex" (1147). Mason's comments expose an intense dependence on binarized gender relations that surely do not originate in him but characterize larger social expectations—expectations for the genre or for gender representations on an even larger scale.

Then, Mason's argument betrays much implicit anxiety about the hard-boiled protagonist: what would it mean if tough guy prototype Philip Marlowe did not abide by traditional or expected gender and sexual binaries? What if all this time we had been reading Philip Marlowe novels and not known what we were *really* reading? What if mass reading audiences were absorbing these "darker . . . obsessive recurrences" without even knowing it? It is as if Mason feels duped, betrayed by Philip Marlowe, femme fatale.[30]

In his book *Something More Than Night* (1985), Peter Wolfe carries this line of criticism further, ultimately rejecting Legman and Mason's broadest claims about Chandler's own sexuality, but still participating in their psychologizing gestures: "Chandler probably had mild homosexual leanings. . . . He approached homosexuality . . . intellectually rather than instinctively, if the joys of straight sex sometimes incurred penalties, then from the drawbacks of gay sex might be teased out some pleasure."[31] Wolfe refers to the Marlowe of *Farewell, My Lovely* as a "dazed, bisexual boy-adventurer" (152), and argues that *The Long Goodbye* "displays the full range of Chandler's sexual ambivalence. And the ambivalence cuts deeply. The attention given in the book to types and degrees of male bonding is matched by a reductive attitude toward women" (210). Legman, Mason, and, to a lesser degree, Wolfe reveal concern that gender play and sexual fluidity might seep through the tough guy persona. Instead of pushing this transgressive potential, the reflex is to decry these novels' misogyny or to close off further discussion by summarily naming Chandler or Marlowe homosexual—and hastily attributing all gender and sexual subversion to the hidden orientation.

In the end, this critical strain, often full of insights about Chandler's gender play, runs the risk of representing its proponents as so unnerved at what they find or fear finding that they must set up a distancing and delimiting gesture that names Marlowe and/or Chandler as a repressed homosexual and then ceases further investigation as if such a pursuit would risk contamination. Surely these critics are not as threatened by gender play as is the hermetic Marlowe himself (he may savor it from afar, but he will not indulge in it). Yet they end up re-enacting precisely the same contamination fears and containment efforts that hardboiled writers articulated, celebrated, and suffered. Like Cain's John Howard Sharp (*Serenade*), it is as if they either fear readers may read these texts unawares and have that "five per cent" brought out, as seems the case with Gershon Legman, or they feel a compelling need to alert readers to a half-concealed homoeroticism, lest they not limn it on their own. By attributing the sexual and gender anxieties of these texts solely to a hidden homosexuality in either author or character (or both), such criticism deflects the threat these anxieties—and their subversive pleasures—pose. By seeing suggestions of homosexuality in Marlowe as only evidence of Chandler's own personal desires, the larger social questions they inspire can be contained.[32]

Hardboiled Desire and Gender Sleight of Hand

> "I like small close-built men," I said. "They never seem to be afraid of anything. Come and see me some time."
> "I might at that, Jack."
>
> —Raymond Chandler, *The High Window*

As we saw in chapter two's discussion of Philip Marlowe's lapses into unconsciousness, the detective frequently embodies a white male fear of fugitive desires, of experiencing desires that are unsanctioned. These desires are not only sexual but also desires for less rigid gender roles, for less rigid definitions of what it means to be a man. As might be Gershon Legman's worst fear, it would seem that readers identified with Marlowe not in spite of his disarming disassociations or strange interludes with "soft voiced" men but *because* of those aspects. In other words, the white man alone in urban space moves through World War II and the Cold War era still refusing a normative patriarchal role—secretly savoring gender indeterminacy and more free-floating, less normative definitions of desire, masculine desire, male desire at a time when compulsory models of patriarchal male heterosexuality were being enforced at all turns, when any deviation was not just a threat to the community but to the country or the "free world."

To pursue this argument, I want to begin by looking at *Farewell, My Lovely* (1940), the Chandler text that exhibits most openly both this gender play and this gender anxiety. While predating the Cold War, it is the text that most horrifies Cold War gender cop Gershon Legman and was in fact in active paperback circulation throughout the late forties and early fifties. In particular, I want to look at the encounter that inspired so much of the anxious critical reception outlined above: the encounter between Marlowe and Red Norgaard.

Marlowe describes Red as a "big redheaded roughneck in dirty sneakers and tarry pants and what was left of a torn blue sailor's jersey and a streak of block down the side of his face" (245). At the time, Marlowe is searching for a way to board gambler Laird Brunette's boat, so when Red "bumps into [him] casually" (245), Marlowe is willing to take a chance despite the fact that Red "looked too big. He had three inches on me and thirty pounds" (245). Red is illuminated—literally, backlit—as if he were a performer, a movie star, with the "light . . . dim and mostly behind him" (245). Initially, Marlowe is dismissive of Red's offers of a boat-for-hire, even telling Red to "Go darn your shirt. . . . Your belly is sticking out" (245), to which Red responds, perhaps suggestively, "Could be worse. . . . The gat's kind of bulgy under the light suit at that" (245). Red is implying that Marlowe's gun is keeping him from being allowed on the boat, but the twin references to physical excess, bodily protrusions, continues, as Marlowe asks, "What pulls your nose into it?" (245). Red then backs off. It is at this point that Marlowe softens, describing Red as "smil[ing] a slow tired smile. His voice was soft, dreamy, so delicate for a big man that it was startling. It made me think of another soft-voiced big man I had strangely liked" (245).

It is the coexistence of Red's brute size and his delicate voice (not wailing, not shrill, as both the femme fatale and the "Girl Friday" in the novel tend toward) that soothes Marlowe here, that sends him into a memory association. But who is the other "soft-voiced big man" to whom Marlowe refers? Although it is never stated, the referent seems to be the hulkish character Moose Malloy, whose size is repeatedly referenced, and whose voice is described often in such terms: "deep soft voice" (5), "[he] purred softly, like four tigers after dinner" (5), "his deep sad voice" (6), "he said gently" (6), or, in a strong echo of what we find here, "He spoke almost dreamily, as if he was all by himself, out in the woods, picking johnny-jump-ups" (8).

But while Marlowe responds with charmed fear to Moose, whom he admires for his sentimentality and loyal love for his old flame Velma, he remains physically intimidated by him. Marlowe responds quite differently to Red. The difference seems to be figured in terms of immediate intimacy. With Moose, the sense of physical threat is figured humorously; Moose grabs Marlowe's shoulder and Marlowe, having felt the clamp-like grip once before, "trie[s] to dodge him but he was fast as a cat. He began to chew my muscles up some more with his iron fingers" (6). Conversely, the threat Marlowe feels when he first sees Red seems harder to name, and not comic at all. It has the feel of vague menace, but also of predatory seduction: "[Red] looked thoughtfully this way and that. He had me angled into a corner of the shelter on the float. We seemed to be more or less alone" (246). Moreover, there is a feeling of illicitness as "People in gay clothes and gay faces went past us and got into the taxi. I waited for them to pass" (246). When Red propositions Marlowe, offering him a ride to the boat for a small fee, even smaller if Marlowe "come[s] back with friends" (246), Marlowe responds with sudden coldness, "'I don't have any friends,' I said, and walked away. He didn't try to stop me" (246). Marlowe therefore asserts social isolation in the face of an offer, much as he does with the "Girl Friday" of the text when she offers her companionship. It is a retreat into solitude: the white man alone in urban space must remain alone. The disavowal and retreat, however, also suggests a feeling of disaffection and a fear of being yoked with—or seen as part of—a transgressive group.

The scene continues as Marlowe wanders the pier, but Red soon enough sidles up beside him as the aura of a pick-up continues.[33] The way in which Marlowe describes the reappearance is most compelling: "A large blueness that smelled of tar took shape beside me. 'No got the dough—or just tight with it?' the gentle voice asked in my ear" (246). Red is figured as a shape, a presence, a disembodied voice, but this one soft and sweet, not shrill and wailing. And Marlowe responds with a surveying look filled with pleasure: "I looked at him again. He had the eyes you never see, that you only read about. Violet eyes. Almost purple. Eyes like a girl, a lovely girl. His skin was as soft as silk. Lightly reddened, but it would never tan. It was too delicate" (246–47). It is the way in which we would expect a hero to describe a heroine, filled with longing. Images of softness, delicacy, diaphanous unreality abound. Further, the central allure of the femme fatale of the later Chandler novel, *The Long Goodbye,* is characterized by her similarly haunting violet eyes. Critics attempting to read Marlowe as gay—from Legman to Michael Mason—point to this scene as evidence. But these critics miss the intriguing dance of gender that so dazzles Marlowe here. It is not just that Marlowe finds Red attractive. It is *what* he finds so attractive: Red's delicacy, his feminine allure, not a conventionally masculine handsomeness.

The passage continues: "He was bigger than Hemingway [Marlowe's in-joke nickname for a cop who has roughed him up] and younger, by many years. He was not as big as Moose Malloy, but he looked very fast on his feet. His hair was that shade of red that glints with gold. But except for his eyes he had a plain farmer face, with no stagy kind of handsomeness" (247). Red is both glamorous and authentic, the femme fatale in terms of desirability and mystery but without the sense of threatening masquerade or artifice. He is genuine. As such, Marlowe's hysterical fear of performativity (i.e., his responses to Muriel Chess's disguises in *The Lady in the Lake*, Carmen's eyes closing like curtains in *The Big Sleep*, Orfamay's masquerade in *The Little Sister*), so often associated with a negative femininity in these texts, does not emerge. In a sense, then, Marlowe rewrites stereotypical notions of femininity, detaching gender from biology and broadening its meaning. Red's "femininity"—his softness, his delicacy—appeals to Marlowe and seems unmitigated—in fact, enhanced—by his largeness, his strength.

As it continues, Marlowe and Red's interaction is increasingly infused with barely articulated or even unspoken currents of emotional intensity. Red gains Marlowe's trust by revealing himself, and in a way that shows his similarity to Marlowe himself:

> "I was on the cops once. They broke me."
> "Why tell me?"
> He looked surprised. "It's true."
> "You must be leveling."
> He smiled faintly. (247)

Like Marlowe, Red worked previously in law enforcement (Marlowe once worked for the district attorney). Further, his frankness, without pose or hints of performance, impresses Marlowe deeply: Red is substantial and authentic, in stark opposition to the surface glitter of the femme fatale. But the identification does not transform the encounter into a typical male friendship. Instead, the mix of ethereal romance and illicit seduction continues. Marlowe says to Red cryptically, "I've met a man once who could take you" (247)—seemingly a reference to Moose Malloy, but the comment comes suddenly and Red responds, "I wish there was more" (248). In turn, when Marlowe gives Red money for a boat ride onto an illegal gambling ship, the exchange continues to suggest a hustling pick-up as the men surreptitiously pass the money to each other. Then, with the money in hand, Red "fade[s] into the hot darkness outside the doors" (248). The encounter throbs with implications for Marlowe as the interactions with Red are steeped in sensual language and suggestive exchanges. As William Marling points out, the narrative transmutes into a "realm of pure emotional and sensory intensities" (233).

When Marlowe, conscious of men following him, slips discreetly onto the boat, the landscape is described darkly and romantically: "Once more the lights of Bay City became something distantly luminous beyond the rise and fall of alien waves. Once more the garish lights of the *Royal Crown* slid off to one side, the ship seeming to preen itself like a fashion model on a revolving platform" (251). The contrast set up between the soft reflecting lights and the gaudy boat lights echoes Marlowe's persistent placing of Red in a category of the authentic and beautiful and mysterious, while the femme fatale or Velma or criminal category bristles with performance, artifice, pose, as emblematized here by the preening fashion model.

The vision slides into Marlowe's startling comment, which seems to come out of nowhere: "'I'm scared,' I said suddenly. 'I'm scared stiff'" (251). There is little to prepare the reader for Marlowe's admission. Any self-reflection he has offered up until this time has been reserved for confidences to the reader, not another character, suggesting an interesting identification between the reader and Red himself. Marlowe continues, as Red turns and stares at him, "I'm afraid of death and despair. . . . Of dark water and drowned men's faces and skulls with empty eyesockets. I'm afraid of dying, of being nothing, of not finding a man named [gambler] Brunette" (251). Fear of the void overwhelms the passage and one is not sure how to take it. As if standing in further for the reader, Red pauses as if uncertain of Marlowe's gravity, then laughs, "You had me going for a minute. You sure give yourself a pep talk" (251). But the interaction is deeply meaningful as it is the closest Marlowe ever comes to confiding to another person in any of his novels. Red offers something no one else does. And Marlowe is sufficiently comfortable, even after Red's laughter, to share with Red all his concerns about his case. Marlowe informs the reader, in a remark that seems almost a parody of the way the hero speaks about a femme fatale: "I told him about it. I told him a great deal more than I intended to. It must have been his eyes" (251).

The dream-like feel continues as Red moves his boat up to the *Montecito,* and Marlowe's description is intensely physical, dankly erotic: "We sidled up to the greasy plates of the hull as coyly as a hotel dick getting set to ease a hustler out of his lobby" (255). The choice of simile is provocative, as is the one that follows soon after, as Marlowe and Red prepare to enter the *Montecito:* "The wet air was as cold as the ashes of love" (255). As they begin to disembark, "Red leaned close to me and his breath tickled my ear, 'She rides too high. Come a good blow and she'd wave her screws in the air. We got to climb those plates just the same'" (255). When the two part, Red refuses money for the return trip, saying, "'I think you're scared.' He took hold of my hand. His was strong, hard, warm and slightly sticky. 'I know you're scared,' he whispered" (257). The touching hands of two men, while not remarked upon by Marlowe, is a gesture of physical intimacy that feels rather stunning in the tough guy context. And, once again Marlowe's fear, his nerves are erotically pleasurable; here they are paired with his admiration and physical esteem for Red, for his largeness and his largesse. Marlowe tells Red he'll "get over" his fear, "[o]ne way or another," and Red "turn[s] away from me with a curious look I couldn't read in that light" (257). Red repeatedly offers Marlowe help, but Marlowe continues to refuse, finally saying, "[E]ither I do it alone or I don't do it" (258). His final words to Marlowe before they part are, "That open loading port . . . That might buy you something. Use it" (258). And Marlowe goes it alone once again. As significant as his encounter with Red has been, in the end the figure remains a solitary one by necessity. He has no partner, cannot have a partner.

The return trip with Red takes up little narrative space, but the whole episode and the fact that Red waits for Marlowe and brings him safely back to land are clearly quite meaningful to Marlowe, as he will return home and reflect on it at length. Later that night, Marlowe lies on his bed and the "four walls of the room seemed to hold the throb of a boat, the still air seemed to drip with fog and rustle with sea wind. I smelled the rank sour smell of a disused hold" (272). One can feel the signifying power of that "disused hold" as the site of Marlowe's shut-off emotional and sexual center, the hold to which Red has given Marlowe access. Fittingly, Marlowe's thoughts then take him to "the giant with the red hair and the violet eyes, who was probably the nicest man I had ever met" (272). Then, "I stopped thinking. Lights moved behind my closed lids. I was lost in space. I was a gilt-edged sap come back from a vain adventure. I was a hundred dollar package of dynamite that went off with a noise like a pawnbroker looking at a dollar watch" (272). This reverie recalls Marlowe's lapse of consciousness as discussed in chapter two and cues us to read the lapse as deeply pleasurable, even masturbatory. In turn, the images are of power leashed and unleashed, harnessed and released, a canny symbol of Marlowe's encounter with Red, which revealed to Marlowe things about himself and his own pleasures, but from which he ultimately retreated.

Peter Wolfe, in his psychoanalysis of Chandler via this episode, determines that "Norgaard's bigness, his absence, and his association with male authority all stir in Chandler the excitement originally called up by the missing father" (54)—a reading that misses the feminine significations accorded Red. It is important to emphasize the extent to which Marlowe's reverie, the intensity of his emotional interlude with Red, the attraction he feels toward him, derives not from Red's masculine physicality, his impressive strength and virility. Instead, the primary lure is the entanglement of masculine and feminine signifiers. In the last chapter, we considered Marlowe's lapses into unconsciousness as acutely pleasurable surrender into disappearing subjectivity.[34] In this case, Marlowe is also in large measure surrendering control: Red is engineering the action, is literally navigating the lonely streets for Marlowe, and Marlowe finds that experience soothing—not so much as passive damsel but as a partner who can both recede and step forward at his choosing. Likewise, we may note how Marlowe and Red take turns at playing the femme fatale role: Red is mysterious with a powerful physical presence that draws Marlowe; in turn, Marlowe is secretive, seeking help but remaining enigmatic about the details of the case for quite a while, resisting Red's efforts to know more. Both hold secrets from the other in femme fatale fashion. It is a dance. And while in chapter two we considered Marlowe's lapses into unconsciousness as sexually pleasurable because he is freed from the necessity of constantly restabilizing gender binaries, here the sexual pleasure derives from the constant, moodily romantic alternation between binary positions as well as the intermingling of the binary characteristics within single subjectivities: an option Red embodies and enacts for Marlowe.[35]

Hassell Simpson presents a compelling reading of this pleasurable ambivalence. Although ultimately rejecting readings of Marlowe as definitively gay, Simpson offers that Marlowe's more suggestive encounters "[allow] him to give ironical expression to his admiration for another man without having to examine or express what that admiration might mean" (47). Simpson determines that "in representing Marlowe without apology or explanation as a man of mingled sexual impulses, Chandler tells us clearly that he fully understood the often contradictory attractions and repulsions felt and displayed by his narrator and alter ego. Whether he intended it or not (I think he did), he maintained his protagonist's public masculinity—and his own—unshaken to the end, at a time when doing otherwise would have alienated many potential readers" (47). How successful Chandler was, given Legman's attacks and the threat to the paperback industry at large, might be called into question, but Simpson's conclusion elucidates the strictures that so bound the white male figure, noting that the "yearning but undemonstrative detective finds no outlet for his most powerful emotions. Strong and handsome younger men may bump him or even hold his hand, beautiful women may kiss him or ask to be kissed, but Marlowe cannot open himself to others by initiating intimate intact in such ways . . ." (41).

Then, we can see the danger that Gershon Legman and others sensed in these textual wrinkles amid the rigid traditional binaries that generally rule both Chandler and hardboiled fiction in general. The fear derives from the potential that the man alone, the tough guy, might in fact participate in gender play or gender dissolution, that this figure of seemingly unimpeachable and hardboiled masculinity might in fact engage in less contained or binary-rigid circuits of identification and desire. A man already alarmingly unfettered by paternal or household roles might in fact threaten the very binaries that rule Cold War America, that constitute Cold War America. The seeming apex of tough masculinity might at the same time embody gender disintegration or a pleasurably tangled network of sexuality and homosociality, of eroticism and intimacy that is not constituted through male/female at all. If these gender binaries are disabled, who is to say how secure any of them are, be they gay/straight, black/white, Eastern/Western, capitalist/communist, American/Soviet?

As we have seen, Gershon Legman, writing in the late forties, fears contagion, desires containment of "dangerous" identifications. But how different is Michael Mason, writing nearly thirty years later, who seems upset at the unconscious beneath the "acceptable" and generic attributes of Chandler (what if we're catching something unawares, while we think we're enjoying these texts?). It is the same anxiety we see in James Cain's *Serenade:* What if something dormant within us were to face the one catalyst that can unleash it? Mason and Wolfe are sent into mini-homosexual panics by these texts' occasional and deeply mitigated refusals to abide by patriarchal heteronormative structures. In so doing, they impose the same structures on Marlowe that Legman does, that 40s–50s American bourgeois social dictates do. Desire is only hetero-procreative family-focused and is dependent on female submission. This is not to suggest that Marlowe or Chandler actually offer a definitive deconstruction or destruction of gender or sex binaries—only that a fear that they *might* inspires an intense anxiety that curiously mirrors the texts' own reactions to the subversive potential it unfurls: we must contain that which has been let loose.

Alan Nadel, in his book *Containment Culture,* suggests a similarity between the narrative of the closet, as laid out by Eve Kosofsky Sedgwick, and the narrative of containment, noting, "In distributing the potentials for domination and submission, allegiance and disaffection, proliferation and self-containment, loyalty and subversion—all of which require clear, legible boundaries between Other and Same—the narrative of the American cold war takes the same form as the narratives that contain gender roles" (29). George Kennan, the American charge d'affaires who first set out the containment strategy, certainly demonstrates this conflation. Nadel notes that Kennan "recommend[s] Hemingwayesque masculinity" in the face of Soviet threats (31). Further, Kennan's writings rely heavily on constructions of Russia as a femme fatale figure, an Eastern exotic who does not abide by the rules of (masculine) logic. Hardboiled texts follow the same narrative structures, by and large, suggesting that the threat of the feminine and/or feminization be met with hermetic self-containment (Chandler, Hammett) or containing violence (Spillane, who kills Commies, male or female).

But, like his frontier precursor, the tough guy is not merely facing the dangers of feminization or emasculation. Central to the frontier hero's reckoning with the "uncivilized" territory is his function as a patroller of borders, containing the encroachment of always-threatening racial and/or ethnic Others. Likewise, for the tough guy, the burgeoning ethnic diversity of his environs and of urban space more generally offers a lurking danger that is yoked tightly to gender (the femme fatale, after all, is both female and "exoticized" or even racialized) and to his anxieties about his own whiteness, his own racial prerogatives. Just as he expresses an urgent need to shore up his masculinity in the face of feminization, the tough guy must assert his whiteness—but an effective assertion of whiteness means, paradoxically, that he must make that whiteness invisible. He must work to present his white body as the unmarked one: raceless, transparent, universal.

CHAPTER FOUR

THE WOMAN IN WHITE

Race-ing and Erace-ing in Cain and Chandler

". . . [O]n the back of each card there is a blank space. And on blank spaces, or even on written ones, there is sometimes invisible writing."

—Raymond Chandler, *Farewell, My Lovely*

IN JUNE 1998, *THE NEW YORKER* MAGAZINE PUBLISHED NEW EXCERPTS FROM Beat writer Jack Kerouac's journals. One excerpt, written in August 1949, recounts a night Kerouac spent walking through Denver's "Negrotown." Later appearing in shortened form in *On the Road,* the excerpt serves as a (more dewy-eyed) Norman Maileresque vision of what Kerouac perceives as the more earthily beguiling world of blacks, Mexicans, or, as Kerouac writes, "even a Jap." Andrew Ross uses the passage, in its *On the Road* context, as an embarrassing example of 1950s white bourgeois glamorization of minority culture, which it surely is.[1] But what makes the writing so compelling is its self-conscious awareness of white (bourgeois) (male) self-loathing. Likewise, while attempting to anatomize the appeal of "minority culture," the excerpt serves instead as an unconscious or half-conscious articulation of the construction of whiteness at Kerouac's historical moment:

> . . . [T]hat night my dream of glory turned gray, because I saw that the best the "white world" had to offer was not enough ecstasy for me, not enough life, joy kicks, music; not enough night. . . . I wished I was Negro, a Denver Mexican, or even a Jap, anything but a white man disillusioned by the best of his own "white world." (And all my life I had white ambitions!).[2]

What begins here as a "White Negro"–style rumination on the primitive exotic allure of the Other transmutes, as Kerouac proceeds, into the race-ing of what are traditionally presented as universal or at least class-bound values. For Kerouac, whiteness is drab, lifeless, and inherently false as opposed to the "true-minded" life of the Negroes. Kerouac offers well-worn expressions of "black authenticity," but he is also able to turn his eyes to the accompanying project: the universalization of whiteness.

Holding onto whiteness as a subject is as slippery for him as it has been for race theorists, up against centuries of the universalizing of whiteness. As Richard Dyer points out in his work on whiteness, "any instance of white representation is always immediately something more specific—[e.g., the film] *Brief Encounter* is not about white people, it is about English middle-class people" (46).[3] For Kerouac, likewise, whiteness is less a constructed racial prerogative than a set of class attitudes. His yearning reveals its steepage in class quickly, showing the extent to which Kerouac yokes whiteness with bourgeoisness. Whiteness slides seamlessly into middle-classness, and middle-class values of conformity, economic success, propriety. This slippage becomes apparent when Kerouac continues his narrative by describing how he runs into a softball game, noting

> [T]he strange young heroes, of all kinds, white, colored, Mexican, Indian . . . performing with utter seriousness. They were just sandlot kids in uniform, while I, in my college days, with my "white ambitions," had to be a professional-type athlete, I hated myself thinking of it. Never in my life had I been innocent enough to play ball this way before all the families and girls of the neighborhood—no, I had to go and be a college punk, playing before coeds in stadiums, and join fraternities, and wear sports jackets instead of Levi's and sweatshirts. (56)

Whiteness is equated with bourgeois institutions, like college sports and fraternities, and uniforms (the sports jacket); but whiteness is also world-weary here, in contrast with the naïve, faintly primitive (and presumably ambitionless, to Kerouac's eyes) ballplayers. But interestingly, the group of sandlot kids are a mélange of "*white,* colored, Mexican, Indian." Bodily color is disconnected from a metaphoric racial designation by Kerouac, as the white kids in that sandlot do not harbor "white ambitions." Whiteness is not about physical signifiers here (though it is in part about sartorial signifiers like clothing). Instead, it is an expression of class, even *is* class. For Kerouac, figurative whiteness means an investment in bourgeois advancement. Physical whiteness may or may not be attached. Of course, whether those "colored" kids can also be burdened with "white ambitions" remains to be seen.

Whiteness, for Kerouac, is not just generically bourgeois, but is also academic, and deeply conformist. He writes of walking to the house he had "spent my $1000 on for nothing, where my sister and brother-in-law were sitting worrying about money and work and insurance and security and all that, in the white-tiled kitchen" (55–56). Whiteness means a bourgeois life of money, savings, nine-to-five days, job security, while blackness means simple pleasures, an equation that recalls Gertrude Stein's "Melanctha" and its references to the uncomplicated beauty of "sunny Negro laughter."

Although embarrassingly stereotype-ridden, Kerouac's Cold War–era musings stand as significant history in their attempt to specify and particularize what is so ritually made to seem universal, transparent. It is, in fact, the contrived invisibility of whiteness that is precisely the source of its power.

In chapter two, I investigated the ways in which gender and sexuality identifications are constant sources of anxiety for the male characters of James M. Cain and Raymond Chandler, anxieties both written on the body and in the margins of the texts. But deeply implicated with this dread over threats to heterosexual maleness are concerns about racial designations, another way bodies are marked.

In this chapter, I examine the way the manipulation of race—particularly whiteness—in hardboiled fiction both solidifies and further unsettles the status of the urban white male. In doing so, I want to problematize the notion that these texts are merely historically racist, a charge that, however accurate, generally serves only to shut down discussion or further analysis. It is my contention that by looking at how these texts, or their protagonists, attempt to fix a stable and powerful whiteness by racializing others, at the same time as they obsessively present whiteness as racelessness, we can learn much about the era's racial anxieties.

In the last twenty years, race theorists have increasingly anatomized the construction of American whiteness—or *blanchitude,* as Sylvia Wynter terms it in her pioneering 1979 article, "Sambos and Minstrels."[4] Toni Morrison, Robyn Wiegman, Harryette Mullen, David Roediger, and Eric Lott, among others, have demonstrated the importance of investigating the relationship between whiteness and blackness in American culture—specifically, the consolidation of an American whiteness through a conceptual dependence on the creation of an Othered blackness.[5] This consolidation is repeatedly veiled behind the persistent recapitulation of whiteness as the norm. As George Lipsitz writes, "As the unmarked category against which difference is constructed, whiteness never has to speak its name."[6]

Likewise, in the realm of film theory, Richard Dyer has importantly illustrated the theoretical imperative of making whiteness visible, marked, to show the specificity and constructedness of that which has been strategically staged as essential. As Dyer points out, the "property of whiteness, to be everything and nothing, is the source of its representational power."[7] It is therefore crucial to expose whiteness's undergirding, its constantly bolstered beams and supports, in order to understand its construction and how its construction has worked to demonize and dominate.

We find, however, that when we turn this investigative lens to hardboiled fiction we do not locate a calmly self-assured representation of whiteness, secure in its hegemonic invisibility; instead, we see a persistent, crippling dread from within these white male protagonists over the precariousness of their whiteness, and what it would mean for its construction to be revealed.

Los Angeles: White Lights, Big City

I used to like this town.

—Raymond Chandler, *The Little Sister*

As figures who walk on social margins, on the perimeter of the white bourgeois patriarchal hegemony, hardboiled protagonists are situated repeatedly among the racially or ethnically abject. As discussed in chapter one, the narrative structure of a white man moving through the spaces of "the Other" betrays hardboiled literature's relationship to the Western and to frontier literature of the previous century. As Frankie Y. Bailey writes, focusing on the detective in particular,

> Like the woodsman to whom he traces his antecedents, the tough guy private eye . . . is a man who lives on the edge of society, holding himself aloof from its seductions. The Negroes he encounters on the streets of the city are like the Indians the woodsman encountered in the forest. Sometimes they are friendly. Sometimes they are an obstacle to his quest.[8] (49)

But when critics address the racial binaries that preoccupy the hardboiled protagonist and his ancestors, they tend to neglect the race-ing of the tough guy himself except through the lens of what he is *not: not* black, *not* Mexican, *not* Asian. What the tough guy *is* is white, and how that whiteness is constituted is our project here.

In their focus on Los Angeles and its environs, Cain and Chandler's texts offer an atmosphere replete with racial tensions, particularly white fears of growing Mexican, Chinese, Japanese, and black populations. These texts are then responding to the tensions arising from the increasing ethnic diversity in Southern California in the 1930s and 40s. This ethnic diversity existed side-by-side with harsh segregationary policies, particularly in terms of housing, that were designed to keep non-white groups enclaved from white Californians.[9] Cain and Chandler's texts reflect white anxiety over the growth of these enclaves in two ways. First, these texts seek to perpetuate and maintain the illusion of whiteness as a universal, as an invisible, raceless norm. Second, these texts show the ways in which white America racializes all those of non-white ethnic backgrounds. Ethnic diversity transmutes into a *racial* binary of white and Other, white and black, white and Mexican. And, tellingly, the white male protagonist of Chandler and Cain is often the sole character—or, the sole *male* character—who falls on the white side of the binary.

The conflation of a variety of ethnic groups into the blanket category of Other characterizes the atmosphere of 1930s and 40s Los Angeles. The atmosphere reached a particularly volatile flashpoint in the early 1940s: in 1942, the infamous Sleepy Lagoon murder case—a case that demonstrated in excess the extent of police brutality committed against Chicano youths—dominated headlines and, the following summer, the notorious anti-Mexican Zoot Suit riots tore through the city. In a characteristic comment of the era, the head of the Foreign Relations Bureau of the Los Angles sheriff's office, in his report to the jury of the Sleepy Lagoon case, offered that "the Chicano was an Indian, that the Indian was an Oriental, and that the Oriental had an utter disregard for life."[10]

Bethany Ogden points out that the hardboiled story tends to "take place in large, urban, multiracial cities," yet the hardboiled detective "describes a world in which he is the sole 'normal' person," his normalcy assured by his white male heterosexuality.[11] But unlike other urban settings, Los Angeles in the 30s and 40s presents a marked difference in ethnic landscape—even from, for instance, New York City. Robert Fogelson notes,

> Unlike most eastern and midwestern metropolises, which were divided between native Americans and European immigrants, Los Angeles was divided between an overwhelming native white majority and a sizable colored minority. Nowhere on the Pacific coast . . . was there so diverse a mixture of racial groups, so visible a contrast and so pronounced a separation among people, in the 1920s.[12]

William Marling argues that *Double Indemnity* exemplifies Cain's new awareness of Los Angeles's exceptionalist status in terms of ethnic population, an awareness missing from *The Postman Always Rings Twice,* in which the "Other" is Greek. He argues that *Double Indemnity's* Walter Huff is Cain's "first protagonist who operates in a California context rather than in a national one. Part of this context is a new racial hierarchy, with Greeks no longer at the bottom" (179). Marling's primary evidence for this reading is that Huff "patronizes the Chinese . . . and employs a Filipino houseboy who 'beats Clark Gable' when it comes to clothes" and that, hierarchically speaking, a European American character (the poor graduate student and one-time suspect Beniamino Sachetti) "rank[s] over Asian immigrants" (179).

But the ease with which Huff interacts with various ethnic groups (conveniently, they are predominantly service workers) says less about Cain's efforts to ethnographize Los Angeles than about the difference between Walter Huff, middle-class insurance salesman, and Frank Chambers, a hobo. Whiteness is far more secure in *Double Indemnity* (perhaps so secure Marling cannot even "see" it) than in *The Postman Always Rings Twice;* therefore, the hierarchy is presented as solid, and minorities are servants, not threats. The difference is a class one: Huff is white-collar, and the Nirdlingers are a family of industry (oil, in particular). In contrast, *The Postman Always Rings Twice's* protagonist, Frank Chambers, is a tramp and both he and his adulterous lover Cora Papadakis work *for* the immigrant, Greek American Nick Papadakis.

In *The Wages of Whiteness: Race and the Making of the American Working Class,* David Roediger explores how nineteenth-century white laborers clung to and helped create images of a powerful whiteness, affording them both a (largely phantom) privilege their working-class status denied them and a space of projection onto which they could transpose anxieties about their own abjection, stereotypes imposed upon themselves by those in power. In particular, Roediger considers the efforts working-class whites made to distance themselves from comparisons with African American slaves in antebellum America. Emphasizing the servitude of white workers, who were often themselves under indenture or impressment, Roediger argues that it was "difficult to draw fast lines between any idealized free white worker and a pitied or scorned servile black worker."[13]

It is perhaps too easy to consider the Depression-era context of Cain's *The Postman Always Rings Twice* in light of this particular form of racialized anxiety. Obviously, Americans of all ethnic backgrounds suffered (though to different degrees) under economic hardship, thus a somewhat "equalizing" poverty threatened to blur racial demarcations, which, as we have seen, were particularly firm in Los Angeles. But, as George Lipsitz reminds us, minority populations were hit hardest not just on the economic front but also on the relief and recovery front: the Federal Housing Act of 1934 sanctioned discrimination and both the Wagner Act and the Social Security Act excluded farm and domestic workers from coverage, "effectively denying those disproportionately minority sectors of the work force protections and benefits routinely afforded whites."[14] These discriminatory measures, however, were not enough to assure many working-class white Americans that the distinctions between "us" and "them" were sufficiently firm. In particular, for many white working-class males during the Depression, the perception was that minorities were enjoying the most relief and that white women were enjoying a disproportionate number of jobs.[15] Then, I want to consider how Cain's novel illustrates the ways 1930s joblessness precipitates a threat to an explicitly white working-class masculinity.

Warren Susman, borrowing from Frederick J. Hoffman, famously articulated a Depression-era social and literary type he termed the "marginal men." As "[f]orced wanderers . . . vagabonds . . . [and] tramps," these men lack any social place, any communal role. Indeed, the marginal man has "no commitments and no culture."[16] Susman claims that although similar figures in other periods were driven by ideological concerns to reject society, the marginal men of the thirties lack any ideological commitment and are characterized in large part by predilections for alcohol and violence. Susman attaches no specific race to the marginal man type, but the novelists he cites (Nelson Algren, Jack Conroy, and Edward Dahlberg) present marginal men who are white; the silent presumption seems to be that these marginal men are significant because, *although white,* they have become abject. Lacking the social structures of employment, family, household, and property ownership, these men have fallen into the margins and, as such, their masculinity seems to reside not in father/husband/employee functions but in their ability to express physical power through violence and sheer survival.

It is with these tensions in mind that I want to approach James Cain's *The Postman Always Rings Twice.* Cain's novel, I hope to show, exposes the paradox of the marginal man seeking assurance of masculinity although exiled from the society that defines it, and seeking assurance of whiteness, although exiled into the abject space supposedly reserved for racial Others.

"I'm Just as White as You Are":
Whiteness as Speech Act

In James M. Cain's paradigmatic hardboiled tale *The Postman Always Rings Twice,* the doomed lovers Frank and Cora first come together in an exchange alarmingly charged with racial anxieties and studded with the word "white." Whiteness is so fetishized in the scene that it is surprising that no critics have considered the episode (or the novel as a whole) through this lens. Repeated incantationally, the word "white" comes to take on erotic meaning for the adulterous couple. Frank intuits quickly Cora's sensitivity about a racial significance to her marriage to the Greek immigrant Nick Papadakis. After eating the enchiladas she makes him, he comments, "Well, you people sure know how to make them."[17] The exchange continues:

"What do you mean, you people?"

"Why, you and Mr. Papadakis . . ."

"That's not what you meant. . . . You think I'm Mex. . . . Yes, you do. You're not the first one. Well, get this. I'm just as white as you are, see? I may have dark hair and look a little that way, but I'm just as white as you are. You want to get along good around here, you won't forget that."

"Why, you don't look Mex."

"I'm telling you. I'm just as white as you are." (6–7)

Despite the fact that Papadakis is Greek, Cora's fear is that she is mistaken for Mexican, that the combination of her enchilada expertise, her black hair, and her feeling that she "look[s] a little that way" points dangerously in that direction—a direction more dangerous than Greekness, given Southern California's charged history of Mexican-Anglo relations, which were reaching ugly proportions in the early 1930s.[18] In a few sentences, Cora conflates and racializes ethnicities, clustering them on one side of a rigid binary: white and Other.[19] And in so doing, she responds to Frank's seemingly innocuous compliment by repeating three times, "I'm just as white as you are."

What of this repetition? Cora's anxious reiteration smacks of overcompensation, as if repeating it will make what is false become true. If Cora need give the information three times in four sentences, it calls into question the assertion's reliability. Clearly, Cora is not so confident in the reliability or believability of her claim—the fact of her whiteness. Even Frank's affirmation, "Why, you don't look Mex," does not assure her. In turn, Frank plainly realizes she is not confident and perpetuates it to increase her vulnerability. His saying she does not *look* Mexican is not the same as saying, "I know you're not Mex," or, even better from Cora's viewpoint, "You're white." Not *looking* is not the same as not *being,* and evidently Cora thinks she may even "look a little that way." Visuality both *is* and *should not be* a signifier for race.

Frank quickly picks up on Cora's anxiety and adopts a familiar strategy to ease her anxiety: derogation of the feared identificatory group:

"No, you don't look even a little bit Mex. Those Mexican women, they all got big hips and bum legs and breasts up under their chin and yellow skin and hair that looks like it had bacon fat on it. You don't look like that. You're small, and got nice white skin, and your hair is soft and curly, even if it is black. Only thing you've got that's Mex is your teeth. They all got white teeth, you've got to hand that to them." (7)[20]

Cora's physical appearance is complimented through Frank's rhetorical distinctions between a stereotypical "Mex" woman's body and Cora's. But Frank relies on *visual* cultural stereotypes to distinguish her, though she has just presented visuality as an unreliable racial signifier. In actuality, however, it is not visuality that assures whiteness here, nor even the *verbal* insistence of visual whiteness; it is Frank's speech, the speech of a "white man." Frank's words serve as a curious blazon to Cora's physical attributes, but more significantly they stand as a reassurance of her whiteness, or in fact the verbal creation of Cora's whiteness. Sylvia Wynter asserts, "the value of white being needs to be constantly realized, recognized, attained by the social act of exchange with the relative non-value of black being" (153). Here, Cora's whiteness is solidified through a systematic derogation of "Mexness."

Of course, the more substantial threat Cora would seem to face is to be mistaken for Greek, given her husband's ethnicity and their shared last name, Papadakis. In this exchange, Cora insists to Frank that her maiden name is Smith, but she does not reference Greekness specifically, only Mexicanness. As suggested earlier, behind this substitution lie white Southern Californian anxieties about the rise in Mexican immigration.[21] After all, Cora, subsequent to telling Frank her maiden name, adds, "What's more, I don't even come from around here. I come from Iowa" (7)—the Midwestern designation seemingly further assuring her white pedigree. The question lingers, does Cora fear being mistaken for Greek or Mexican? It seems for Cora they are one and the same thing, all under the umbrella heading "not white."

Frank confides to the reader what he has intuited from this exchange, "It wasn't those enchiladas . . . it wasn't having black hair. It was being married to that Greek that made her feel she wasn't white, and she was even afraid I would begin calling her Mrs. Papadakis" (7). He rejects the seeming Mexican indicators, and any indicators on Cora's person, as the source of her racial anxiety. Instead, he pinpoints her marriage, which is figured as interracial, as miscegenation, to the degree that Cora urges Frank to call her by her first name so as not to validate illocutionarily her status as "Greek," or wife of an Other. Speech is again of utmost importance in her assertion of whiteness. If she is called Cora, she can forget her feeling of non-whiteness, her anxiety about how she is racially perceived. Likewise, Frank's determination that it is her relationship with Nick that makes her feel less than white also serves to assure Frank himself of her whiteness, makes his desire not desire for the Other but desire for one co-opted by the Other.

Speech then operates as a "race-ing" instrument in *The Postman Always Rings Twice.*[22] Sometimes it is successful and sometimes it is not, but it is performative in the sense that Cora attempts to erase any visible or semiotic indicators of non-whiteness through the act of repeatedly announcing a racial identity for herself. Frank's verbal agreement gives weight to her performance, grants it an integrity that helps the racialization take hold. As Robyn Wiegman articulates, "the construction of race is predicated on its obsessive performance."[23]

What, then, is happening with the unspoken, seemingly assured identity in this anxious performance: the white *male?* What does Cora's need to establish her white femaleness have to do with white maleness? Cora requires Frank to shore up her whiteness, but why does his perception of her race carry such weight here? Even the potential for a racial anxiety of his own is made utterly invisible. The question needs asking: Does Frank have any anxiety over his own whiteness as a "marginal man," someone who is an active part of neither capitalist industry nor a family romance? Cora tells Frank that he physically signifies as white; that is his power to Cora. Unlike Cora, Frank's bodily prison is not a questionable racial makeup but the pangs of illicit desire; he never expresses anxiety over his racial status. From where does his security derive? The implication seems to be, in part, that white men—of any class—have the power to assure white women of their (dubious) whiteness.

Masculinity in this text is then configured through whiteness, and vice versa. Frank's whiteness at first takes the form of his freedom, his mobility, his transient lifestyle. While one measure of whiteness, as Kerouac's diary excerpt shows, seems a commitment to bourgeois respectability and institutional conformity, another brand of whiteness is the liberty to move at one's will, with responsibility only to oneself and one's desires, with a "white" security in always being able to find someone willing to help or hire oneself. As such, it is a particularly white *male* construction, exemplifying male prerogatives to move relatively safely through spaces, to find labor when one needs it, to live free of racial or gender discrimination.

It is the maleness implicit in this brand of whiteness that dooms Frank's initial attempts, during their aborted elopement, to introduce Cora to the whiteness embodied in his hobo lifestyle. She cannot endure one afternoon of the marginal man experience. When Cora, after the couple's exoneration for the murder of Nick, attempts to domesticate their once-outlaw relationship, it is equally problematic. She has effectively introduced class climbing and ambition into their shared conception of whiteness, and aimless Frank's assured masculinity is at last called into question. Specifically, Cora announces that Frank's beloved road "don't lead anywhere but to the hash house. The hash house for me, and some job like it for you. A lousy parking lot job, where you wear a smock. I'd cry if I saw you in a smock, Frank" (16). Cora emasculates Frank's brand of whiteness for him by dressing it in a smock. She rhetorically casts the smock as a degrading spectacle that will inspire her pity for Frank rather than her desire. Cora's discursive invocation of a smock also yokes Frank to the novel's other significant service uniform: Cora's white nurse's uniform she wears while working in the kitchen. Cora's suggestion is that Frank will be no better than Cora herself—a woman, and a racially questionable one—if he ends up in a smock.

Richard Dyer writes about the white man's constant risk of his "masculinity 'tainting' his whiteness or his whiteness emasculating him."[24] As such, Cora paints as feminizing and degrading precisely what Frank views as freedom: "[D]o you think I'm going to let you wear a smock, with Service Auto Parts printed on the back, Thank-U Call Again, while [Nick] has four suits and a dozen silk shirts? Isn't that business half mine?" (16–17). Class, gender, and race commingle in images that corrupt Frank's conception of white masculine freedom on the road, his shoulders hard from run-ins with railroad detectives. Cora bluntly contrasts Nick and Frank: Nick wears the plush uniform of the successful businessman, while Frank is doomed to wear the generic and even feminizing smock of the service employee. By putting Frank in a smock rhetorically, she is not just feminizing him, she is "race-ing" him as non-white, because in this text, femininity and non-white go hand in hand. Further, she paints him as "less white" or, more pointedly, less skilled at the performance of whiteness than Nick, who wears the suits of (white) success.

Then, *The Postman Always Rings Twice* defines whiteness in two ways: first, through a masculine freedom that is ultimately rejected, and next, through imprisonment, however willing, in domestic bourgeois trappings. Frank and Cora's status as laborers, and especially laborers married to and/or working for an Other, in 1930s California, severely mitigates claims to whiteness. Although Frank compensates in part through a hardboiled masculine freedom, Cora cannot do so. Instead, she calls into question the masculinity of his freedom, showing him another way to achieve whiteness, one that will allow him a woman but not impose the smock on him: specifically, installation into bourgeois family/business. Shut out from Frank's whiteness-through-freedom, Cora forces them both into the other route: whiteness through bourgeoisness.

It is thus the entrance of the (questionably) white female that disrupts Frank's hold on his whiteness, weakening it through emasculating rhetoric and the stirring-up of class and racial resentment by an unfavorable comparison to Nick's success. As such, Cora eventually brings out in Frank a desire for white bourgeois respectability: the two try to create an enterprising nuclear family. Specifically, after murdering their employer and the family's patriarchal head (conveniently before Nick can make good on his stated desire to impregnate Cora), the couple expands the restaurant, adding a beer garden and making a string of improvements. Directly prior to Cora's accidental death, she learns she and Frank are to have a child, seemingly providing the final step in their simulation of a bourgeois family. With Cora's death and Frank's (wrongful) incarceration for her death, we can see that their attempts were doomed from the start. The couple has evidently paid the price for their illicit passions—passions that signified their prohibition from middle-class structures. This prohibition is signaled in the text's repeated use of animal imagery to describe Frank and particularly Cora. Likewise, their sexual episodes defy all notions of staid bourgeois behavior. Their "savage" erotic talk consists notoriously of Cora's cries of "Bite me! Bite me!" with Frank sinking his teeth "into her lips so deep [he] could feel the blood spurt into [his] mouth" (11). Sexual preludes brim over with bestial violence: "I . . . swung my fist up against her leg so hard it nearly knocked her over. 'How do you get that way?' she was snarling like a cougar. I liked her like that. 'How are you, Cora?' 'Lousy.' From then on, I began to smell her again" (13).

The oft-discussed "primitive" sexuality of Frank and Cora is thus at odds with the structure of whiteness to which Cora, and eventually Frank, aspire. As the couple's love is legitimized, bourgeois whiteness emerges as the dreamed-for ideal, and it is defined through entrepreneurial drive, domestic rituals, and familial and business responsibility. Cora tells Frank, "I want to work to be something, that's all. But you can't do it with love. . . . Anyway, a woman can't" (16). To gain the white bourgeois lifestyle, however, Cora must animalize herself. Specifically, to get the life she wants, Cora believes she must murder her husband. This act of "depravity" is precisely that which prevents her entrance into those white bourgeois structures, that which turns her into a focus of law enforcement scrutiny, that which casts her into a roadside attraction as a murderer who got away with it.

When the restaurant business begins to turn a profit and the potential of marriage and family looms, the couple's sexual violence disappears from the text and more sentimental or romantic language takes its place, as when Cora speaks to Frank of "Lovely [kisses], Frank. Not drunken kisses. Kisses with dreams in them. Kisses that come from life, not death" (110). This yearning for "pure" love suggests Cora and Frank have learned to surrender "primitive" bodily desires for each other. In its place, they adopt a more respectable mode of consumption—bourgeois consumerism. That is, through installing themselves as striving owners of a service business, they can participate in an acceptable kind of consumption: the selling of commodities, the consumption of bourgeois ideals.

> *"From what we see around here . . . a real White-Man has very little chance for help"*
>
> —*New York resident in a 1936 letter to President Franklin Roosevelt*

Sylvia Wynter discusses the efforts of slavery-era proletariat Southern whites to seek equality with rich whites through "their claim to equally exercise forms of mastery over the Black"; as such, we see a pattern emerge in which the "bourgeoisie projects its own bourgeois model as Norm, so that it can be internalized by the proletariat who then vindicate their claim to equality within the context of the bourgeois universe of signification."[25] Later in this chapter, we will see that Philip Marlowe's slippery class status makes his role in such a dynamic difficult to determine, but Frank and Cora's class status is much more unequivocally established. Frank is a hobo, and Cora is a hash slinger yearning to own her own business in pure American dream fashion. Their working-class position raises the stakes in their need to forge an indisputable claim to whiteness.

Wynter writes of the white "anxiety of falling into the socially stigmatized," configured as "negro"; to avoid this fall, one imitates the established norm, "inscrib[ing] on one's psyche the marks of repression, repress[ing] all that the place of the Norm stigmatizes as its non-negation" (152). Most crucially, the "absolute privilege of the caste position compensates for the relative non-privilege of the class position. The lower the class position, the more absolute is the anxiety that the caste position should be retained and recognized as absolute" (153).

If we view Frank and Cora through the lens of their clinging to caste prerogatives, Nick Papadakis's role in this forging of whiteness cannot be underestimated. In terms of speech, Nick is referred to in Frank's narration far more frequently as "the Greek" than by name—a designation both depersonalizing and "racializing."[26] Nick is likewise both feminized and made cartoonish by both Frank and Cora. He is soft, not hard; he drinks sweet wine that disgusts Frank. He postures and primps in his fancy suits, and pouts when Frank's idea for the restaurant proves surprisingly successful.

Frank's characterization of Nick as simultaneously a feminized dandy and a pouty child reaches a telling peak in the scene when Nick returns from the hospital after his "accident" (Frank and Cora's failed attempt to murder him). The accident received newspaper attention as an oddity, and Nick includes the articles in his scrapbook, which he displays for Frank proudly. The scrapbook advertises Nick's American assimilation process and includes his naturalization certificate, his wedding certificate, and his license to do business in Los Angeles County. Over his naturalization certificate Nick has affixed American flags and a picture of an eagle, and over a photo of himself in the Greek Army, Greek flags and yet another eagle (35). Nick's scrapbook essentially is a claim to bourgeois whiteness as the text defines it: he is the business owner, the patriarchal household head, the homeowner, and the proven American, as his naturalization certificate attests. Nick in fact comes closer to earning bourgeois white status than the "officially white" Frank. Nick has a wife and a business, where Frank has neither. Nick even has evidence of his military history, bolstering up the masculinity Frank attempts to deny him: as Nick shows Frank the scrapbook, Frank condescendingly offers suggestions, all the while confiding to the reader that Nick is a "dumb cluck" (36). Moreover, this immigrant man relies on the work of two employees, both of whom are purportedly white, but who work *for him*. As such, Nick's scrapbook is a testimony of his fulfillment of a series of requirements for bourgeois whiteness—requirements Frank significantly lacks. It seems that Frank's (perhaps unconscious) awareness of this lack motivates his distaste for the scrapbook, which he finds ridiculous and childlike. It is telling that Frank likens Nick's documentation of his accident and his sudden sartorial elegance to a "wop that opens a drug store," gets "that thing that says Pharmacist" and suddenly dons a "gray suit, with black edges on the vest, and is so important he can't even take time to mix the pills, and wouldn't touch a chocolate ice-cream soda. This Greek was all dressed up for the same reason" (36). The Greek is the Wop is the Mex—all occupying the other side of the binary but all threatening to adopt a greater claim to white bourgeois life than the supposed "white man," Frank.

Of course, it is worth noting that Nick's *marriage* license occupies a featured space in his scrapbook. Nick partially justifies a claim to (or assurance of) his own whiteness through his marriage to Cora. Cora in fact, despite her own racial anxieties, serves as a whitening agent for both Nick and Frank. Frank is made to feel whiter for helping her feel white, is more confidently white thanks to her need for his whiteness, her use of his whiteness.

In this way, Cora authenticates male whiteness and seeks white validation. We thus have a virtual merry-go-round of white validation. Nick and Cora's own means of validation are even similar: both seek it through speech. Nick repeatedly asserts,"[Cora] is my little white bird. She is my little white dove" (8). Cora's reaction to Nick's designation is one of disgust, at least insofar as she can use it to outrage Frank. She asks Frank privately,

> "God, do I look like a little white bird?"
> "To me, you look more like a hell cat."
> "You know, don't you. That's one thing about you. I don't have to fool you all the time. And you're clean. You're not greasy. Frank, do you have any idea what that means? You're not greasy. . . . No man can know what that means to a woman. To have to be around somebody that's greasy and makes you sick at the stomach when he touches you." (15)

"Little white bird" and "little white dove," pet names it seems Cora would covet as assertions of whiteness, turn out to be precisely what she rejects in favor of Frank's "hell cat" designation. Though she will later assert that she is not truly a hell cat but must "turn hell cat to get out of a mess" (16), Cora is excited by Frank's rejection of Nick's quaint and pure pet name in favor of the sexual and wild "hell cat." She acknowledges that she looks nothing like a white bird, and that acknowledgment is geared toward showing how ignorant Nick is of her true self, both interior and exterior. But it seems the designations are less important than who delivers them—illocutionary acts depend on the speaker's authority, after all. If it were Frank, not the non-white Nick, who called her a white bird, her response might be quite different, may be one of pleasure. After all, Cora openly expresses pleasure in Frank's "whiteness." If Cora feels her marriage to Nick has "darkened" her racial status, then a liaison with Frank would help "whiten" it. As Harryette Mullen writes about the act of racial passing, "A Person becomes adeptly white when he or she acquires a partner whose white credentials are unquestionable and produces perceptibly white (not 'mulatto' or 'mixed') offspring."[27] Cora seems to be creating a miscegenation scenario, warning Frank, "I can't have no greasy Greek child, Frank" (38). At the same time, Cora refers to Frank's "cleanness" in a highly racialized manner, comparing him favorably to Nick's greasiness, which makes her "sick at the stomach when he touches [her]" (15)—a canny parallel to Frank's nausea of desire upon smelling Cora's body at the beginning of their relationship. Further, Cora types herself and encourages Frank to type her as non-white, as animalistic at the same time as asserting Frank's whiteness, which is deeply implicated in masculinity for Cora: "[Y]ou're hard all over. Big and tall and hard. And your hair is light. You're not a little soft greasy guy with black kinky hair that he puts bay rum on every night" (16).

Whiteness is hardness for Cora—a bodily hardness, however, only insomuch as bodily hardness stands in for the hardness of ambition. Cora is heightening the erotics for Frank and herself, but is also attempting to persuade Frank to help her out of her doomed situation. She shores up his masculinity through emphasizing his whiteness, his lightness.

David Roediger, in discussing W. E. B. DuBois's *Black Reconstruction,* notes the importance of DuBois's idea that "the pleasures of whiteness could function as a 'wage' for white workers. That is, status and privileges conferred by race could be used to make up for alienating and exploitative class relationships, North and South. White workers could, and did, define and accept their class positions by fashioning identities as 'not slaves' and as 'not Blacks'" (13). Roediger, in limning the importance of *Black Reconstruction,* continues: "White labor does not just receive and resist racist ideas but embraces, adopts and, at times, murderously acts upon those ideas. The problem is not just that the white working class is at critical junctures manipulated into racism, but that it comes to think of itself and its interests as white" (12). And Frank and Cora, in assuring each other of their whiteness, are actually justifying their own murder plot, in fact are using the "whiteness" talk to goad themselves on. It is not just a matter of how Cora can be white and married to a non-white, but how either Frank or Cora can be white if they *work for* a non-white.

Then, what we see in *The Postman Always Rings Twice* is a proletariat whiteness that fails to cohere when the definition of whiteness is perceived by its characters again and again as deriving from bourgeois normativity, from middle-class desires acted upon through middle-class means. While Cora's whiteness is ever precarious due to her gender, her miscegenation potential, her ability to animalize herself, Frank's whiteness is at risk, too. His conception of his hard white freedom as a hobo is exposed as either feminized (he will inevitably end up in a smock working for the Man), or illusory because it eschews bourgeois interpellation, eschews interpellation into the definition of white man as husband, father, property-owner, and provider.

As with *Double Indemnity*, we find the white man as trapped victim of a system larger than him and at odds with his body, his bodily desires—a system that encourages his consumption desires but then punishes them, a system that teases him with a white solidity then shows whiteness to be a class prerogative to which he has no access.

"The Streets Were Dark with Something More than Night": Black and White in Chandler

Turning to the works of Raymond Chandler, class and whiteness occupy far more enigmatic positions. Philip Marlowe's class status is fairly difficult to pinpoint due to his roving status between echelons.[28] Moreover, the Marlowe novels do not offer the explicit foregrounding of whiteness as we find in *The Postman Always Rings Twice*. Instead, what we find far more readily is a fixation with racial Others, with non-whites. And this fixation serves, typically, as a mask behind which whiteness anxiously attempts to consolidate itself.

Chandler's personal attitudes toward minorities are well documented and betray the white racism of his day. Frankie Y. Bailey points to a July 1949 letter Chandler wrote in which he bemoans "some damn editor [who] made me white-wash four or five niggers" in his short story "Pick-Up on Noon Street."[29] Likewise, responding to a woman writing to him about his stereotypical Jewish characters in *The High Window* (1942), Chandler wrote back, "The Jew is a type and I like types" (47).

But we need not go to Chandler's own letters, when his novels themselves bear similar attitudes. The presence of minority groups is typically used as a barometer of urban decline. "Blacks had moved in, whites had moved out, and the old neighborhoods were sliding downward into slums—neglected slums" (48), Marlowe notes in *Farewell, My Lovely*, one of the most common texts to which critics turn in demonstrating either Marlowe or Chandler's racism. Edward Thorpe exemplifies this criticism in noting, "In 1940, when the novel was written, Chandler was more or less in accord with his reactionary readers. Negroes . . . represented not only the deterioration associated with poverty but demoralization, degeneration, depravity too" (quoted in Bailey, 48).

But what we find in the Philip Marlowe novels is also more complicated than a basic equation of non-whiteness and degeneration. Marlowe often exhibits a self-consciousness of his own racial stereotyping, as evidenced by his amused shock when an African American chauffeur quotes T. S. Eliot to him in *The Long Goodbye*. Characters routinely criticize Marlowe for his racism, such as *The Long Goodbye*'s Chilean houseboy, Candy, who will not accept Marlowe's slurs. The foregrounding of Marlowe's racism, however, does not necessarily lead to Marlowe's revision or correction of it. Instead, we often find his self-conscious racism matched by a redoubled stereotype, as when a Jewish character in *The Little Sister* points out Marlowe's anti-Semitism at the same time as he displays "a generous hand on which a canary yellow diamond looked like an amber traffic light" (292–3). The episode is typical of Marlowe's combination of reactionary bigotry and a playful awareness of bigotry, Chandler's stereotyping and matching self-consciousness of the stereotype. It is a dynamic that speaks to the ambiguous point in history to which these texts belong. Marlowe is conscious of the flaws or limits of his stereotypes as he lives and works in an increasingly diverse population, but he also serves a model of hasty retreat (Marlowe's move from downtown apartments to a rental home in the Hollywood Hills is classic white flight) from that diversifying population, which seems a threat to his white male self-conception.

Marlowe's anxious racism often gives way, however, to a class camaraderie forged with those of other ethnicities, or symbols thereof. Frankie Y. Bailey points to Marlowe's series of interactions with a stone jockey on the wealthy estate of his corrupt client in *The High Window*. Marlowe seeks "solidarity" with the statue as a fellow victim of the wealthy, and Bailey reads this impulse as Marlowe "see[ing] himself as having more in common with the underclasses than with those who pay him for his services" (50). But class can also be a divider, as we saw in the intersections of class and race in *The Postman Always Rings Twice*. Indeed, Marlowe's efforts to distinguish himself morally from upper-class greed, middle-class hypocrisy, and lower-class depravity can be read as attempts to mark him as classless. Likewise, his racial stereotyping of various minority groups serves to brand his whiteness as racelessness, a great power in texts obsessed with what "race" might mean. These efforts at an invisible and potent whiteness, however, repeatedly come up against Marlowe's strained sense of his own white masculinity. As we see by looking more closely at the texts, race and gender identifications continue to inform and complicate each other.

Pierrot: Racial Crossovers in Chandler

The very first line of Chandler's *Farewell, My Lovely* is Marlowe's pronouncement, "It was one of the mixed blocks over on Central Avenue, the blocks that are not yet all Negro" (3). Marlowe has found himself in this neighborhood to track down a (presumably) Greek man named Dimitrios Aleidis. Just as in *The Postman Always Rings Twice,* Greek ethnicity occupies both a liminal space between white and black, a "mixed" space, and the same space as blackness, as Mexicanness, as any "category" against which whiteness is forged. We are then in a domain of contested whiteness from the novel's outset, on a mixed block in pursuit of a man of questionable whiteness.

It is a fitting opening to a novel haunted by racial ambiguity. The first scene, as we will see, concerns racial crossing of the most explicit kind: characters of one race entering, as minorities, the space of another race. Marlowe, in his pursuit of the Greek man, observes a hulking white ex-convict named Moose Malloy. Looking for his old flame, Malloy rather forcibly recruits Marlowe to accompany him to the place his flame once worked: a bar called Florian's that has, during Malloy's prison term, become a "dinge joint" (6). Malloy goes on to wreak havoc, spewing racial epithets and even committing murder in his single-minded effort to find out what has happened to his former girlfriend.

As a few critics have suggested, the race-baiting Malloy is, at the same time, given mixed racial identification. Although Malloy is apparently white (he is never explicitly described as white, only "pale"), cultural indicators and stereotypical characteristics hint at other possibilities. He is first described as looking like a "hunky immigrant" (3). His flashy attire, replete with colored feathers in his hat and golf balls for buttons on his jacket, hints at connections to Zoot Suit culture (typically associated with young Mexican men in Los Angeles at this time).[30] Moreover, his physicality is described in the primitivizing terms of racist rhetoric: "He would always need a shave. He had curly black hair and heavy eyebrows that almost met over his thick nose" (4). Further, Marlowe offers a simile to describe him that associates Moose with blackness amid, or even preying on, whiteness: "he looked about as inconspicuous as a tarantula on a slice of angel food" (4). Of course, the contrast between this subtle "race-ing" and the racist, dehumanizing way the text treats, for example, a "brown youth" whom Malloy throws onto the sidewalk, is staggering. The "brown youth" is likened to sounding "like a cornered rat" and is referred to, seven times in a single paragraph, as "it." On the other hand, Malloy, the perpetrator of this violent action and several murders, is given amiable narration by Marlowe, who comes to admire Malloy's torch-bearing bravado. Malloy then appears to occupy an acceptable space between white and Other, and it is a space that accords him the child-like, unsocialized innocence of the Noble Savage.

When we confront another character in *Farewell, My Lovely* who also occupies an ambiguous racial position, however, the "race-ing" is far more threatening, and the difference is deeply implicated with gender. Hyper-masculine Moose is not threatening in the way the other raced character, Velma, is as the novel's contaminating femme fatale. Moreover, her race-ing is part and parcel of her dangerous feminine masquerade, not a sign of pre-social, old-fashioned naïveté.

To begin considering the different race-ings, let us look to Marlowe's invocation of *Othello* at the ending of *Farewell, My Lovely*. At this point, both Velma and Moose are dead. Marlowe, a romantic at heart, is attempting to persuade a police detective that Velma killed herself in order to save her society husband, Lewin Lockridge Grayle, the pain of a murder trial. In so doing, Marlowe refers to Grayle as an "old man who had loved not wisely, but too well" (292). Such an analogy conjoins Velma with Desdemona, and Grayle with Othello, seemingly effacing racial difference from the equation. But in actuality, the narrative sets up other versions of *Othello,* including one that reverses genders: that is, Grayle is more Desdemona, Velma more Othello. After all, it is Velma who takes her own life. It is Velma who is, as we will see, yoked with blackness. And it is Velma who has risen in status and won her husband through metaphorically pouring honey in his ear. Moreover, Moose Malloy is an Othello figure as well, a warrior of sorts, driven by jealousy and passion, even killing in his rage. What we find when we attend to these rotating associations with Othello and Desdemona is that the variations are more than playful allusions but actually point to the text's quiet but turbulent obsession with race and racial indeterminacy.

Moose and Velma's racial indeterminacy, in fact, is set up in this first scene, beginning with Moose's subtle race-ing, but continuing with Velma's. When Malloy and Marlowe enter the black-owned bar, the scene is pure imperialist gothic, with Marlowe noting, "There was a sudden silence as heavy as a water-logged boat. Eyes looked at us, chestnut colored eyes, set in faces that ranged from gray to deep black. Heads turned slowly and the eyes in them glistened and stared in the dead alien silence of another race" (7). This description, which feels lifted from Kipling or H. Rider Haggard, is not mitigated by Marlowe's vague efforts at pointing out the irony that police stations and the big newspapers do not care about the murders of black men. After all, Marlowe's main reaction to Malloy's violence against several of the men at Florian's, from the bouncer to the owner, is faint bemusement and an occasional concern for his own well-being in the face of Malloy's hair-trigger temper.

The locale and its inhabitants are primarily a dash of danger to set the plot in motion, but the black bartenders, manager, and patrons also serve two clear purposes other than a touch of pseudo-realist exoticism. First, the scene introduces Malloy's violent pursuit with victims that readers are presumably to find fairly disposable; cued by Marlowe's bemused spectatorship, readers are discouraged from judging Moose a villain for his nonchalant murder of the bar's manager. This casual racism, so characteristic of the hardboiled genre, is often cited by critics, but without reference toward its constitutive function in terms of *whiteness*.[31] That constitutive function leads us to the second purpose of this scene: the episode serves to show the dangerous degeneration of Malloy's old flame, Velma. This degeneration potentially originated with her association with the primitive Moose, even as Marlowe seems to find a "white" nobility in Malloy's torch love. While Velma, we eventually learn, has moved to the height of society as the wife of the wealthy Lewin Lockridge Grayle, the fact that the place where she once sang is now a "dinge joint" links Velma with the bar's "racialized" degeneration. As Malloy laments, "There ain't nothing left of the joint . . ." (11).

Velma's past thus operates in two ways. First, the shift of Florian's from a white to a "Negro" bar (with no ensuing name change) signifies a basic civic and quality-of-life deterioration in Marlowe's universe.[32] The fact that the place with which Velma is associated has "degenerated" hints at a corresponding degeneration in Velma. Second, that the point of origin to which Malloy returns to look for Velma is a "Negro joint" raises unconscious suggestions about Velma's race. Malloy's murderous rage escalates with each assertion that Florian's is a *black* bar; Malloy cannot bear to hear it, seemingly reading it as a vague insinuation about Velma. The employees and patrons' assertion of the bar's "blackness" feels like an assertion of Velma's race; their co-optation of Florian's feels like a co-optation of Velma.

Indeed, Velma's whiteness is very much in question in the text; she is a shape-shifter whose principle threat inheres in her questionable racial status, as, potentially, does her lure. When Marlowe himself gets his first glimpse of Velma, it is via a publicity photograph proffered by the dubious and threatening informant Jessie Florian (see the discussion of Jessie Florian's questionable gender status in chapter two). Marlowe describes the headshot as different from the other photos in Florian's stash, which are characterized primarily by "pleasant dullness" or "vicious" looks (32). Rather, Velma's photo is "much nicer," showing a girl in a "Pierrot costume from the waist up," complete with the conical white hat. Marlowe notes, the "face was in profile but the visible eye seemed to have gaiety in it. I wouldn't say the face was lovely and unspoiled, I'm not that good at faces. But it was pretty. People had been nice to that face, or nice enough for their circle." Marlowe adds, however, "it was a very ordinary face and its prettiness was strictly assembly line." The photo is signed, "Always yours—Velma Valento" (34).

Like Marlowe, readers connect this Pierrot image with Velma through the majority of the novel. It is not until the final pages that readers learn this photo is *not* Velma. And when the photo is revealed as a fake, it is a back-handed revelation. Marlowe's Girl Friday, Anne Riordan, holds up a picture of the genuine Velma and the Pierrot photo and comments, "[T]hese two photos are not of the same woman," and Marlowe responds, "No" (285). It turns out that the two mysteries of the novel—Where is Velma? Who stole Mrs. Grayle's jewels?—are shown to be one and the same: Velma *is* Mrs. Grayle. For the plot to unfold suspensefully, the photo *needs* to be of another woman, otherwise Marlowe would immediately recognize society woman Mrs. Lewin Lockridge Grayle as Velma and the seemingly unconnected mysteries would reveal their interconnection. Of course, there is no reason for readers or Marlowe ever to see a photo purported to be Velma. Why does the photo appear at all?

The photo functions as a red herring, to be sure; but it also functions significantly as a sentimental marker of lost love to Marlowe, with its eventual exposure seeming a cruel hoax. Marlowe makes efforts to keep the photo, and refers to it repeatedly as the Pierrot photo or Pierrot girl, possibly indicating his sneaking suspicions that it is not Velma, but also repeatedly calling attention to the costume the woman in it wears: that of a Pierrot clown. When Marlowe is shown a picture of Mrs. Grayle for the first time, he responds viscerally, calling her a "blonde to make a bishop kick a hole in a stained glass window" (93); but, more significantly, he notes she is wearing "street clothes that looked black and white" (93), an odd inclusion, given that it is presumably a black and white photo. The detail, however, links the color scheme with the Pierrot clown who, like a harlequin, traditionally dons black and white. Crucially, a Pierrot clown is characterized both by the black and white attire, and also by whitened or "floured" skin.[33] The Pierrot association then demonstrates that Velma or the Velma "sign" is awash not only in black signifiers but white ones as well—and not the supposed "invisible" signifiers of whiteness, but conspicuous and artificial ones (*whitened,* not white), as we will see.

Folded into this dual racing is the fact that, in the novel's present, Velma is a full-blown society woman facing occasional blackmailers who learn of her jaded past as a gin joint singer. Velma's transformation is the classic story of a working-class girl climbing her way to the top, the stuff of scores of Joan Crawford and Barbara Stanwyck movies of the 20s and 30s. But the class rise in *Farewell, My Lovely* is significant in that it is given distinct racial conno-tations—of racial ambiguity and racial passing. How does class get folded into race? And what does that mean for Marlowe?

Velma is the femme fatale as shape-shifter. As Marlowe will later tell Anne, "She must have had a little hideout where she could change her clothes and appearance. After all she lived in peril, like the sailors" (284). There is a sense, as with Eileen Wade of *The Long Goodbye*, that Velma has no essential self (even her real name remains a mystery). Marlowe notes, after speaking with her on the phone, "She hung up, leaving me with a curious feeling of having talked to somebody that didn't exist" (271). Velma, torch singer, society hostess, is a consummate performer—and one of her performances is whiteness, so much so that it is whiteness fading into blankness, non-existence. This is not to suggest that Velma is not, by the text's standards, white. Instead, Velma's indeterminacy highlights the construction of whiteness, taking the seeming universal and revealing it to be a performance.

And it is a performance with a costume. Like the Pierrot garb of the phantom Velma (is she any less "Velma" than Velma herself?), Mrs. Lewin Lockridge Grayle is characterized by her attire, particularly her white fox fur cloak. Both times Velma actually materializes in the text, this cloak plays a part. In Marlowe's first meeting with her, Velma describes the cloak in order to explain how the exotic Fei Tsui jade she was wearing would have been concealed by its elaborate white fox fur. Significantly, Velma paints such a powerful and evocative picture that Marlowe appears able to visualize her in the cloak, remarking, "I bet you looked a dream" (129). The second time Marlowe meets Velma (they meet only twice), she actually wears the cloak: "She stood there half smiling, in the highnecked white fox evening cloak she had told me about. Emerald pendants hung from her ears and almost buried themselves in the soft white fur" (277). Then, just as the faux Velma is characterized by her Pierrot costume, the "true" Velma is characterized by her animal covering, her white drag. The drag is only heightened by her gold hair described as "gleaming" (127). Indeed, Velma herself is described as "gleaming" (126). Malloy's Velma is a redhead, suggesting that at least the gold is a dye job, if not both the red and gold. Velma then is imbued with a "gleaming" falseness, a shiny artifice calling into question any deeper authenticity.

Marlowe relays Velma's coda after her escape from the Los Angeles police: "One night a Baltimore detective with a camera eye as rare as a pink zebra wandered into a night club and listened to the band and looked at a handsome black-haired, black-browed torcher who could sing as if she meant it" (289). The simile of the pink zebra repeats the fox fur association of Velma with artificiality and animality. Further, like Pierrot, white becomes black— or black becomes white becomes black. Velma has moved from white to black, from platinum to brunette, from society woman to torch singer. Velma of the "black" nightclub becomes Mrs. Grayle of the white fox and whiter mansion, who then becomes a raven-haired lounge singer. Though there is no reason to assume that the nightclub is a black one, the association to Florian's still emerges, as that is the other place we associate with Velma's performing. Further, we learn that the detective "must have smelled marihuana because she was smoking it, but he didn't pay attention then. She was sitting in front of a triple mirror, studying the roots of her hair and eyebrows. They were her own eyebrows" (289). Stereotypic associations abound: black torchers with stirringly emotive singing ("who could sing as if she meant it") and off-stage drug (especially marijuana) habits, and the term "black-browed," which blurs the line between eyebrows, and one's "brow," or forehead. Moreover, the detective sees Velma studying the roots of her hair and brows in the mirror and, Marlowe tells us, "They were her own eyebrows" (289), implying her hair is naturally black, but also that everything but her brows is a mask, always a mask.

Velma does not pass for white when she becomes Mrs. Grayle; she can pass for anything, with no essential racial identity of her own. In doing so, she calls into question the very idea of race. Velma's danger then inheres in her ability to separate whiteness from the body, from "nature" itself. She unsettles because she cannot be clearly raced, but also because she seems to be able to control her own race-ing, to "pass" as she sees fit—an ability that threatens the universality, essence, and hegemonic power of whiteness itself by showing its construction, its manipulation, its own manufacture of an othered blackness.

It is not an unusual occurrence within hardboiled texts (or films) to find the femme fatale racialized or exoticized. *The Big Sleep*'s Carmen Sternwood, for example, is repeatedly "orientalized," conjoined to the Chinoiserie that surrounds her in her friend Geiger's apartment, an association encouraged by her predilection for jade earrings. But Velma's case is unusual in the way her racialization functions to expose whiteness as a drag, and one that she can maneuver at will. Her drag makes conspicuous that which is supposed to remain invisible—whiteness—and thus turns out to be her doom. By merely changing her hair from (platinum) white to black, she enacts precisely the dangerously easy move between racial signification that her narrative has highlighted. As Marlowe points out, "[T]he way [Velma] hid was pretty obvious once it was found out" (289).

But what is Marlowe's reaction to Velma's subversions? Does he feel that his whiteness is in jeopardy? Or that his interactions with Velma constitute some kind of forbidden miscegenation? Not exactly. After all, Marlowe romanticizes Velma's final acts of violence quite self-consciously, offering his theory that Velma killed herself upon capture to "give a break to the only man who had ever really given her one" (292)—that is, her husband, whom, Marlowe argues, was then saved the public humiliation of a trial. Marlowe's theory is dismissed by Detective Randall, who retorts, "That's just sentimental." Marlowe's response is, "Sure. It sounded like that when I said it. Probably all a mistake anyway" (292). But the presumption here is that Marlowe at least half-believes in this maudlin, recuperative view of Velma.

Of course, it is "safe" for the hermetic Marlowe to romanticize Velma. He has safely avoided sexual contact with her, and such contact's inherent taint. Marlowe's whiteness thus remains intact. After his sole clinch with Velma, he is disgusted with himself primarily because her husband witnessed their kiss. Afterwards (as discussed in chapter two in terms of his resistance to romantic commitment), Marlowe stands by his car and watches, trance-like, as a "man from [a] panel truck that said Bay City Infant Service came out of the side door of the house dressed in a uniform so white and stiff and gleaming that it made me feel clean just to look at it" (139). Marlowe is assured of his whiteness, configured as purity despite the questionable encounter. The image of cleanliness assuages him; speculating that the man had "just changed a diaper," he recognizes that one may deal in uncleanness yet remain pure. A shadow of doubt comes only in the use of the word "gleaming" to describe the Infant Service uniform. Let us recall that "gleaming" is also the word used (twice) to describe Velma and her (fake) blonde hair, throwing its purity in doubt. This scare, however, seems to put the fear of the Other into Marlowe, as he does not see Velma again until the end of the novel and, when he does, he dodges resuming any sexual contact with her.

In *The Big Sleep,* the alterity embodied by Carmen Sternwood and others taint Marlowe, who recognizes at the novel's end that he is "part of the nastiness now" (230). But in *Farewell, My Lovely,* Marlowe emerges safely from his encounter with Velma. He resists her, and therefore he can also sentimentalize her. Her exposure of whiteness's construction remains separate for Marlowe because he can type it as a solely class-climbing tale; Velma exposed not the lie of whiteness but the grim realities of class imposture and the price one pays for it, according to Marlowe's conventionalization—"A girl who started in the gutter became the wife of a multimillionaire" (281), as Marlowe frames it. Marlowe fails—or chooses not—to recognize the interconnections between race and class, between racial fictions and imposture and class climbing. This blind eye conveniently allows him to avoid a consideration of his own whiteness, a whiteness in doubt not the least because of his ambiguous class status.

One last, lingering note: at the moment of Velma's dissembling, when she has just shot her old flame Moose and is about to flee, Marlowe describes her eyes as "a dead gray, like half-frozen water" (282). Trapped between the two binary poles of black and white, she becomes a lifeless gray, and in this space, she kills. This shape-shifting, and its murderous stasis, is not just about racial ambiguity, however; it is always already about gender and sexuality, too. Built into the femme fatale is a threat that both embodies racial indeterminacy, and derives from racial fears—and the threats go right to the quavering heart of white male subjectivity. The racial threat Velma represents lingers for Marlowe and even his efforts to romanticize her as her story (via

Othello) do not dilute the power of her transformations. While Marlowe remains untainted in that he never fully succumbs to Velma, the narrative itself shows pressure at its seams: he is haunted by her mutability, and what it might mean.

Gendered White

> I was a blank man. I had no face, no meaning, no personality, hardly a name.
>
> —Raymond Chandler, *The Little Sister*

In *Farewell, My Lovely*, then, Marlowe forcefully narrates Velma into a traditional, even canonical parable of romantic sacrifice and doomed class ascent. And this intense effort reveals how urgently he needs to frame the shifting Velma into a narrative stripped of "race." This need suggests the linkage between Marlowe's anxiety over whiteness and his gender structure of masculine hermeticism and feminine contagion, as outlined in chapter two. When the non-white person with whom he comes into contact is male, Marlowe can either teasingly antagonize him or occasionally develop a rapport, but when the non-white person is female, she represents a decided threat he must avoid.

Although Chandler's texts are filled with minor non-white *male* characters, if usually of the parking lot attendant or servant variety, there are extremely few non-white women, even in what we may consider parallel servant roles to the non-white males who operate as chauffeurs and "houseboys." But we must consider the potential exception of Dolores Gonzales, the highly sexualized movie actress of *The Little Sister*. Marlowe is physically attracted to her but is repelled by what he sees as her sexual availability, by the fact that she "looked almost as hard to get as a haircut" (259). Not insignificantly, Dolores is also curiously raced. We eventually learn that her purported Mexicanness is a fraud. Prior to that revelation, her Mexicanness is all gesture, calling Marlowe "*amigo*" and dropping the occasional Spanish phrase. While her neck and later her throat are described as "brown," her scalp is "white as snow" (259). Marlowe refers to her once ironically as the "All-American Gardenia" (335). She is, however, presented in harsh femme fatale terms as a virtual cannibal: "The next thing I know I had her in my lap and she was trying to bite a piece off my tongue" (262) and "I got out a handkerchief and scrubbed the lipstick over my face. It looked exactly the color of blood, fresh blood" (263).

Echoes of Cora Papadakis in *The Postman Always Rings Twice* abound in this representation of Dolores, in the violent sexuality and the connection to

Mexicanness. But Dolores occupies the opposite position in both cases. Cora urges her lover Frank to bite her, while Dolores does the biting. Cora furiously denies being "Mex," although she admits to looking "a little that way" (6). Dolores, contrarily, co-opts a Mexican persona for her movie career. These differences serve to make Dolores far more dangerous than Cora, as Dolores's acts are infused with a threatening masquerade and menacing sexual agency. After it is revealed Dolores is not Mexican at all, but another white Midwesterner (like Cora), Marlowe confronts her, "The only thing Mexican about you is a few words and careful way of talking that's supposed to give the impression of a person speaking a language they had to learn" (409). Because she cannot truly hide the fact that she is not Mexican from the vigilant Marlowe, the threat the masquerade poses is minor. Her deadliness inheres instead in her rapaciously sexual femininity. Marlowe relays, "[S]he was exquisite, she was dark, she was deadly" (413)—indeed, she is "[r]eeking with sex. Utterly beyond the moral laws of this or any other world I could imagine" (414). Marlowe stunningly allows Dolores to be murdered and notes coolly that on her corpse one could see "the dim ghost of a provocative smile" (416). The harsh attitude toward Dolores does not emerge in Marlowe's interactions with all femmes fatales, or even the far deadlier ones (Eileen Wade and Muriel Chess do far greater damage). The combination of her sexual boldness and her racial masquerade appear to send Marlowe over the edge. She is white and yet still behaves this way? For Marlowe, *whiteness* is something Dolores may have, but is not something she exudes. A full-blown, conspicuous whiteness resides in another, safer character in *The Little Sister.*

That is, the place in Chandler we find the most open delectation of whiteness, along with a very compelling admittance of its illusory quality, is with the character of the movie star Mavis Weld. It seems appropriate that the exemplar of whiteness would be a film actress. *The Little Sister* is a text eager to poke holes in the artifice of Hollywood, and Mavis serves as a desirable emblem of that artifice. Richard Dyer has importantly linked whiteness with cinematic, particularly Hollywood, illusion. Tracing developments in film technologies, he shows how "interactions of film stock, lighting and make-up illustrate the assumption of the white face" (91). Moreover, Dyer locates the development, originating primarily in Victorian representation, of what he terms the "glow of the white woman" as constructed in media, from cinema to advertising to television.[34] While Dyer looks at the lighting of silent stars Lillian Gish and Mary Pickford to show its role in whitening these actresses until they mirror angel iconography, whiteness also evokes high glamour in Hollywood films of the 30s and 40s. And Mavis Weld certainly partakes of this representation process.

Midway through *The Little Sister,* Marlowe visits Mavis's soundstage and watches from behind a screen as a scene is shot that simulates a jaunt on a yacht deck. He spots Mavis resplendent in a white sharkskin swimsuit. In his initial meeting with Mavis in her apartment, Marlowe made no reference to her whiteness. In contrast, in this scene, after watching her performance before the cameras, Marlowe comments, "the pale glow of her skin in the light seemed to fill the [dressing] room" (313). The whiteness is so bright as to have a material weight all its own that pervades the space with its white glow. Inexplicably, Marlowe, while talking with her, touches her palm with his fingertip. She draws away and Marlowe says, "I used to do that to girls when I was a kid" (313). Mavis replies, "I know . . . It makes me feel very young and innocent and kind of naughty. And I'm far from being young and innocent anymore" (313). Marlowe has accepted the whiteness as a kind of purity and his pressure on the skin seems to be a way of assuring it, the satisfying return of whiteness after the momentary reddening, darkening. Before he leaves her, he watches her "one hand on her knee cap, squeezing it" (314), and Marlowe fixates on the image, finding it hard to leave.

When Marlowe next sees Mavis, it is under troubled circumstances: she is about to confess to murder. He describes her face as "not chalk-white because the light was not white" (366). The curious reference to the lighting is what interests me here. Without the appropriate lighting, Mavis is not white—not "chalk-white," at least. What kind of white is she? And how substantive or meaningful is whiteness if lighting can create or remove it? As they talk, Mavis is enigmatic, distressed, and Marlowe notes her "mouth [is] edged with white" (367). Soon, the lips look "bluish," as Mavis becomes faint. He revives her with brandy, and the blue look disappears. As she begins to recover her demeanor, she "gave her head a toss and swung the soft loose hair around her cheeks and watched me to see how hard that hit me" (369). Performance, via Mavis's constant acting, posing, simulating, permeates her every action—and Marlowe is riveted by the display. He comments, "All the whiteness had gone now. Her cheeks were a little flushed. But behind her eyes things watched and waited" (369). We can see here Marlowe's fixation on Mavis's skin color as a barometer for the genuineness or artifice of her actions, words, feelings. The paler, the more fragile, the more natural, the more to be trusted. Color means performance, even the performance of calculated seduction. As he finally begins to push past the performance and get to the truth, her confession, she "put her hand down on her knee and spread the fingers out, studying the nails" (370), in an echo of the gesture that so enraptured Marlowe before. She then bites her knuckle as she confesses while showing him her white-handled automatic.

The painful confession process goes on for several pages as Marlowe pieces together what has happened. Pitying Mavis, Marlowe takes her hand, turns it over, and "open[s] the fingers out. They were stiff and resisted. I opened them out one by one. I smoothed the palm of her hand" (374). Marlowe offers to try to help Mavis. She tells him she cannot make him an accessory to her crimes, but he persists. She bites her lip "cruelly" and Marlowe proceeds to go over to her and "[touch] her cheek with a fingertip. I pressed it hard and watched the white spot turn red" (377).

What do we make of this strange ritual of flesh pressing? It seems to be Marlowe's obsessive efforts to test the materialness of Mavis's whiteness, the truth of it, the illusoriness of it. Touching her skin becomes a way to authenticate her whiteness through contrast with the blood beneath. It also forces a blush on Mavis, which is perhaps meant as a sign of feminine humility. Moreover, the act brings blood up to the skin, materiality in the face of hollow illusion: Is Mavis a woman to be trusted, or a femme fatale shapeshifter like Velma, like Dolores? Racial crossings mix once again with Marlowe's rigid gender binary. Although Mavis's whiteness is not, Marlowe seems to discern, a drag like Velma's, it is in fact not material enough. At the end of the novel, Mavis evaporates for him; his feelings for her aside, he anticipates that a relationship with her would fail: "I could sit in the dark with her and hold hands, but for how long? In a little while she will drift off into a haze of glamour and expensive clothes and froth and unreality and muted sex. She won't be a real person any more. Just a voice from a sound track, a face on a screen" (414).

Marlowe comes dangerously close here to exposing the illusion of whiteness, but what emerges instead is the illusion of *female* whiteness. Even when a woman *is* white, like Dolores, she is not white. Even when a woman *embodies* whiteness, like Mavis, she is not white because she is not even real. The cleavage of whiteness from femininity is complete, but what happens when whiteness is made visible again, this time in the form of a white *man*?

The Whiteness of Terry Lennox

The physical attributes that most consistently characterize Marlowe's glamorous, Gatsbyesque friend Terry Lennox in *The Long Goodbye* are his prematurely white hair and his scarred face. Both physical features will prove crucial to the text's configuration of Lennox's racial crossover from white to Mexican, paralleled with his crossover from hero to villain. As critics have often observed, Lennox is a highly romanticized figure for Marlowe and their relationship has periodically been read as homoerotic. But Lennox's character has never been discussed through the lens of whiteness, odd given the text's obsession with fixing his race at the same time as disguising it.

Readers are repeatedly given reference, from his first introduction in the text, to Lennox's prematurely "bone white" hair, a clash with his "young-looking face" (419). Lennox, though in his thirties, is referred to by Marlowe as "the white-haired *boy*" (emphasis added, 420) before Marlowe learns his name. Along with the shocking white hair, Lennox is characterized by the "plastic job" that has left the damaged right side of his face "frozen and whitish and seamed with thin fine scars. The skin had a glossy look along the scars" (421). Despite these seemingly freakish attributes—or because of them—Lennox is presented as dissolute but dashing. I would point here to the particular emphasis on whiteness in terms of what Richard Dyer would call "hue" and "skin."[35] In other words, Terry is considered white; there is no suggestion otherwise (indeed, he is English, upping the stakes of his Anglo-Saxon whiteness). But more than that, he is literally tinted white. The hair is preternaturally white, excessively so. The skin is grafted and shiny, calling attention to his whiteness. The plastic surgery scars freeze the hue, and the hue has even become so intensely white that the skin, as Marlowe points out, is capable of turning "so pale that the long thin scars hardly showed." Terry's white hue is in fact so extreme that, according to Marlowe, his eyes appear, stunningly, "like holes poked in a snowbank" (424). His clothes further assure whiteness. Unlike Velma's costumey white wrap, Terry sinks naturally into his "oyster white raincoat and gloves and no hat and his white hair . . . as smooth as bird's breast" (431). The white clothes highlight his whiteness: like a chameleon, he disappears into them. Marlowe even fetishishtically notes Terry running "a finger down the side of his good cheek hard enough to leave a red streak" (441), further dramatizing the whiteness through fleeting contrast, and echoing Marlowe's pressing of Mavis's flesh to assure its whiteness, its materiality.

At the novel's end, when the presumed-dead Terry returns, he is in disguise as a Latin American. During their encounter, we do not know at which point Marlowe realizes the man before him is Terry Lennox (just as Marlowe's discovery of Dolores's non-Mexicanness and Velma's society identity occur in the margins of the texts). All we know is that Marlowe first describes him as "a well-dressed Mexican or Suramericano of some sort" (726–27). Marlowe's description does not belie any knowledge of imposture: "He sat by the open window smoking a *brown* cigarette that smelled strong. He was tall and very slender, and very elegant, with a neat *dark* mustache and *dark* hair, rather longer than we wear it, and a *fawn*-colored suit of some loosely woven material" (emphasis added, 726). The telling "we" ("longer than *we* wear it") reveals the extent to which the reader is proscribed as white and is yoked with Marlowe in opposition to this man. The description proffers an elegance that may be designed as a clue to Terry's identity. More crucially, the color references pile up: brown, dark, dark and fawn (vs. oyster) colored. All the whiteness of Terry has been turned to brown. If he advertised his whiteness on his body and clothes before, he has now replaced it with brownness. But the drag does not work, as we will see.

Curiously, the first major hint to the reader of Lennox's identity comes when Marlowe notes feminizing attributes: "He smelled of perfume as he went by. His eyebrows were awfully dainty too. But he probably wasn't as dainty as he looked because there were knife scars on both sides of his face" (727). Why is Terry (or Señor Maioranos, as he suggestively calls himself here) given feminine attributes, along with the clue about the (masculinized) scars? It would seem to correlate with a Chandlerian emphasis on the female shape-shifter. Like Velma Grayle, or *The Lady in the Lake*'s Muriel Chess, there is a pattern of the woman who "passes" as someone else. Femininity brings a threat of deception, is equated with disguise, dissembling, identity fragmentation. But why does this equation attach itself to Terry? Is he the femme fatale?

Marlowe will not accept Terry's/Señor Maioranos's deceptive tale. The two bluff and play around, Marlowe finally showing his cards, and Terry then removing the disguise by "[taking] the dark glasses off. Nobody can change the color of a man's eyes" (730). No matter the efforts at disguise, there can be no complete concealment of whiteness for the light-eyed. Only the thin covering provided by his green sunglasses hold this tenuous camouflage in place.[36] Marlowe then proceeds to lay out the cosmetic work that enabled the racial passing:

> They had done a wonderful job on him in Mexico. And why not? Their doctors, technicians, hospitals, painters, architects, are as good as ours. Sometimes a little better. . . . They couldn't make Terry's face perfect, but they had done plenty. They had even changed his nose, taken out some bone and made it look flatter, less Nordic. They couldn't eliminate every trace of a scar, so they had put a couple on the other side of his face too. Knife scars are not uncommon in Latin countries. (730–1)

Lennox's procedures are rendered explicitly an attempt at de- and re-racialization. Terry is made un-white, and then made Latin. But all the cosmetic work, all the cultural signifiers, fail to fool Marlowe. Why is it that Marlowe can see through the pass?

When Marlowe begins to shame and irritate Lennox by pointing out his weaknesses and moral turpitude, Terry reveals an "uneven flush on his face under the deep tan. The scars showed up against it" (73). Marlowe is capable of forcing Terry to reveal his whiteness of hue and ethnicity—and in a much more satisfying way than raising Mavis Weld's blood to the surface. It takes far less effort to stir Terry's conscience. And once again the lifting of the mask is paired with a wave of femininity: as Terry pulls a lighter out, Marlowe "got a whiff of perfume from him" (733). When Marlowe brings Terry nearly to tears by refusing to resume their friendship and revealing his disgust in Terry's deceit, Terry strangely tries to assert his manhood, "I was in the Commandos, bud. They don't take you if you're just a piece of fluff. I got sadly hurt and it wasn't any fun with those Nazi doctors. It did something to me" (734). Terry is simultaneously attempting to shore up his masculinity in Marlowe's eyes and offer an excuse for his own moral lapses. Marlowe returns with more jabs at Lennox's masculinity, tinged also with assertions of Terry's lack, his nothingness: "I'm not judging you. I never did. It's just that you're not here any more. You're long gone. You've got nice clothes and perfume and you're as elegant as a fifty-dollar whore" (734). Terry responds "almost desperately" to Marlowe's feminizing attack:

> "That's just an act," he said almost desperately.
> "You get a kick out of it, don't you?"
> His mouth dropped in a sour smile. He shrugged an expressive energetic Latin shrug.
> "Of course. An act is all there is. There isn't anything else. In here—" he tapped his chest with the lighter—"there isn't anything." (734)

Lennox is dubbing himself as the void-like figure so associated with the femme fatale, like Velma Grayle, who leaves Marlowe "with a curious feeling of having talked to somebody that didn't exist" (271). Lennox is materially *white* for Marlowe in a way Dolores or Mavis Weld are not, but at the same time, he is both physically feminized and simultaneously shown to be morally empty. In other words, Terry Lennox *is* the femme fatale and Marlowe has just barely eluded contamination. The real threat here is not the femme fatale as racial Other but the femme fatale as male. As such Marlowe would prefer to keep Terry non-white, would prefer to buy the disguise rather than deal with the ramifications of a male femme fatale. A male femme fatale summons up the ultimate danger: the destruction of the hermetic gender binary by which Marlowe functions, where the threat is female and the male must remain isolated from such a threat. Hence it is of no small import that Marlowe bids goodbye not to "Terry" but to the "Mexican man" before him: "So long, Señor Maioranos" (734).

⸺⸺ ⸺⸺ ⸺⸺

Midway through Raymond Chandler's *The Long Goodbye*, readers come across what may be seen as a throwaway moment, a little "color" thrown in as Marlowe waits for his appointment with a potential client. As he sits in a hotel bar, Marlowe looks through the plate-glass wall into the pool area and watches, with a complicated voyeuristic pleasure, a girl in a white sharkskin bathing suit (the same kind of überwhite suit Mavis Weld wears in *The Little Sister*) as she dives into the pool and then joins a male friend sitting poolside.

Critics often point to the following description as evidence of Marlowe's (or Chandler's) misogyny: "She opened her mouth like a firebucket and laughed. That terminated my interest in her. I couldn't hear the laugh but the hole in her face when she unzipped her teeth was all I needed" (489). It is important, however, to consider this moment's context, and its relevance to whiteness. In a text where whiteness has been so insistently associated with Marlowe's friend Terry Lennox and his shock of white hair, the fascination Marlowe has for this woman in white takes on added meanings. After all, the woman in the bathing cap is in effect white-headed and white-garbed, much like Terry Lennox is in his oyster suit. Of interest here is not just the whiteness of the scene itself, but Marlowe's emphasis on it, which mirrors Cora's repeated reiterations of the word "white" in *The Postman Always Rings Twice*. Indeed, Marlowe uses the word "white" multiple times in the paragraph, to describe the "white sharkskin suit," the "white helmet" of a bathing cap, the "small white table," the man's "white drill pants," and that white flesh between the suit and the tanned leg of the girl. Moreover, observe the sensual way Marlowe speaks about this latter body part: "I watched the band of white that showed between the tan of her thighs and the suit. I watched it carnally" (488–89). The contrast, the teasing "true" white beneath the costume of the suit and the artifice of the tan, is the locus of desire here.

The pleasure is disrupted when, after the girl removes the cap and shakes her "bleach job loose," she begins to laugh. Marlowe cannot even hear the laugh, but "the hole in the face when she unzipped her teeth was all I needed" (489). The *vagina dentata* image is clear, but consider the gesture directly preceding the laugh: the man has patted the girl's thigh. The potential of sexual exchange between the two as evinced by the intimate thigh tap (how different is it from Marlowe's flesh pressing with Mavis Weld's hand?) disgusts Marlowe, opens the door to a sexuality no longer masturbatory, hermetic, voyeuristic, and solitary—his sexuality. Instead, her open mouth shows her desire: consuming, voracious, and a testament to how all the whiteness she wears and all the whiteness her tan *almost* covers can disintegrate into a soundless open maw of hunger, of Otherness made cannibalistic. Whiteness is no guarantee of purity; the threat of sexuality, of female appetite or feminine disguise, can still contaminate.

Whiteness Visible

For Philip Marlowe, then, whiteness is potentially authentic in "white" men, but may be an illusion, construction, or performance in "white" women—a masquerade that is at one with the feminine masquerade more generally. Male whiteness is no guarantee of hermeticism, but is a defensive position against the threat of the Other. Female whiteness is a mask, a trick. Even morally sound white woman Anne Riordan in *Farewell, My Lovely* presents a white female trap: into domesticity, luring Marlowe into *paterfamilias*.

For Cain's characters, too, whiteness has different meanings for men and women. Male whiteness is intertwined with physical masculinity, Frank exiling Nick Papadakis to ethnic femininity at every turn. Two options exist within the structure of male whiteness: first, hobo freedom, which runs the risk of feminization at the hands of an employer or, worse yet, an immigrant employer; second, the normative father/husband/businessman role, much like the one Marlowe associates with Anne Riordan. The second option is not necessarily feminizing in Cain (though it is in Chandler), but it is blocked heavily by bodily desires and class immobility. Likewise, female whiteness is entrenched in *The Postman Always Rings Twice* with class ascension, with success. Cora embraces alterity, the hellcat role, to achieve her chance at the American dream, but it is precisely that alterity that dooms her: she is narratively punished for her bodily passions, for her dreams of class ascent. For Cain, then, whiteness is but a self-destructive weapon by which the working class divides itself and dooms itself. Whiteness is up for grabs without power, and is guaranteed through power, but lacks any materiality, any meaning; it is an illusion one can wear successfully with the cloak of power, financial and social. Whiteness is a class prerogative in Cain—no less slippery in Chandler where whiteness is a trick of gender, a pasteboard front women may use, suggesting, dangerously, that it is a pasteboard front no matter who uses it. Marlowe can only cling to racial stereotypes and laments about racial degeneration to assure himself of a whiteness that does not seem truly to exist.

Interestingly, however—and perhaps crucially—what we find in the cases of Cain and Chandler is that any threat posed by the anxious and deeply mitigated consolidation of whiteness and of masculinity disappears when the texts moved to the screen. Sexually complex Philip Marlowe, as embodied by impeccably tough Humphrey Bogart and reconfigured by Howard Hawks's signature gender stylings, becomes far less of a threat, far more of an icon of white masculine potency. Cain's working-class adulterers no longer need bemoan their lack of racial prerogative amid intensifying and threatening racial diversity. Whiteness is assured by Hollywood's silvery gaze. Anxiety over race or gender privileges fades in the face of the impeccable power of the studios, cinema's glowing celluloid promise, the stars and the myth-making apparatus so firmly in place.

"NOTHING YOU CAN'T FIX"

Hardboiled Fiction's Hollywood Makeover

"But pictures and books are different, naturally."
—Raymond Chandler in a letter to Dale Warren[1]

The Woman in White: Redux

The first image of the famed 1946 film version of James M. Cain's *The Postman Always Rings Twice* is of a hand-painted sign reading "Man Wanted." When hobo Frank Chambers (John Garfield) takes the position to which the sign refers, lured in by the site of the luscious Cora (Lana Turner), he burns the sign. A man was wanted, and now he is there to do the job: eliminate the weak older man and sexually overpower the young wife. Of course, the question of who has ensnared whom—a question fundamental to much of film noir—persists through the entire film. Is the sign "Man Wanted" an expression of lack begging fulfillment, or is it a siren song? Is the tough vagabond Frank bringing a masculine promise to the Twin Oaks Tavern, or is he leaving behind the freedom of the road to be trapped in a doomed and dooming domesticity?

The Postman Always Rings Twice is often dismissed by cineastes as too "big studio-slick" to be truly hardboiled, or truly film noir—the categorization applied to the majority of hardboiled adaptations. Aside from adopting the novel's fatalistic narrative, the film actually uses few of the conventions that would later be associated with noir: *chiaroscuro* lighting, seedy (and often cheap) sets, unusual camera angles, and urban milieus. The smutty grit of the novel, with its violent sex between lovers so enflamed with shameful desire that they actually vomit, is replaced by sparkling white sets, immaculately coifed stars, and romantic clinches. Foster Hirsch writes that the novel was "emasculated in its screen adaptation, made by the wrong studio (tinselly MGM), and miscast in two of its roles (Lana Turner too poised and glamorous for Cora, Cecil Kellaway far too refined for Cora's dimwitted and gross husband)."[2]

For Hirsch to term the adaptation an emasculation irresistibly suggests fears that a male-gendered novel has been stripped of its masculine potency when re-fashioned by Hollywood. The film version of *The Postman Always Rings Twice* is in fact often described as having just as many elements of a "woman's picture" or melodrama as a crime movie or film noir, from its focus on domestic spaces to its emphasis on a "double bind."[3] The changes the film makes are then repeatedly named as feminizations by critics, the hard, lean maleness of the novel transformed into a bloated, glossy love story. Many of its adaptive choices, however, have more to do with ducking the censors: violent sexuality transmutes necessarily into the more discreet conventions of romance. More important, despite Hirsch's suggestion that the film is an emasculation of Cain's tough novel, the film actually offers far more assured and inviolable models of whiteness and white masculinity than the novel affords. The hard and brittle edges of the novel's rendering of white maleness are made so slick as to appear seamless and impermeable within the film.

These kinds of sleek conversions of the more frayed and tangled edges of hardboiled novels—and the success of such conversions—will be the subject of this chapter. The goal is to pursue what happens to the knotty difficulties of Cain and Chandler's bristling and quivering protagonists when they are embodied in Hollywood stars like John Garfield and Humphrey Bogart and when their more renegade desires must pass through the cogs of an immensely powerful and profitable industry.

Such a study is crucial, as while the film adaptations of Cain and Chandler have been the focus of intense film scholarship, that scholarship generally focuses on everything but their relationship to their source texts. *The Postman Always Rings Twice* offers a prime example: its rendering of whiteness and its managing of the novel's open wrestling with crossings of race, gender, and class have received scant critical attention. One of the film's most telling strategies in constituting whiteness is ironically one of the film's most talked-about characteristics. That is, when moviegoers recall the film, they inevitably refer to the delicious irony in costuming the carnal and criminal Cora in all white. Throughout the film, Lana Turner is dressed in white from head to toe, her matching hair a resplendent platinum. In only two scenes does she don a different color. In these scenes—returning from her mother's funeral and contemplating suicide—she wears all black. In the film's terms, Cora then embodies a contradiction, a walking binary, and it is a flip of tradition in that her white costumes are linked to her moments of sexual availability, while her black ones indicate sobriety and distance. (The binary is further emphasized by the use of a literal reversal: the white turban Turner wears in several scenes is an inversion of the black turban she wears after her mother's death). Most critics have pointed to the choice of white clothing for Turner as a canny joke, a sight gag, given the character's transgressive nature. It is as if the filmmakers are winking at the audience: don't let the white garb fool you; she's no angel.

Tay Garnett, the film's director, has recounted a different purpose, though one just as invested in the iconography of whiteness-as-purity, "At that time there was a great problem of getting a story with that much sex past the censors. We figured that dressing Lana in white somehow made everything she did seem less sensuous. It was also attractive as hell. And it somehow took the stigma off everything she did."[4] The untouchability of the color white coalesces with the often skimpy quality of the white clothing, creating a tantalizing combination of reserve and availability. In this way, the audience is encouraged to mirror Frank's initial reaction to Cora: She is not mine to take, yet I must have her. Consider the film's most famous sequence. Frank (Garfield) sits on a stool in the diner, considering Nick's offer of a job. The camera focuses on Frank in a medium shot and we hear the sound of an object rolling. Frank looks down offscreen and then there is a cut to a shot of the linoleum floor. A white tube of lipstick rolls into frame. The camera traces the path of the tube, moving backward across the floor, which is shot through with sunny light prisms. The camera stops as it reaches a pair of white open-toe sandals. Tilting up, the camera reveals a pair of legs, beginning with the ankles and moving up to just above the knees.[5] There is a cut to a close medium shot of Frank looking down and offscreen (presumably at the legs) and then slowly raising his gaze upward, with a stupefied expression. His gaze and the camera's are aligned. There is a cut to a full shot of Lana Turner, standing in the doorway. She wears a white turban, white halter top, and tight white shorts, a white compact in her hand. Frank picks up the lipstick tube and, as he does, the sun through the blinds creates shadows across his back, in a subtle version of the common noir symbolism of slats and prison bars. He asks her if she has dropped the tube and she looks down at him, smiles condescendingly, and says, "Yes, thank you," holding out her hand as she looks at herself in the compact mirror. She does not move toward him or the tube. Frank, feeling the insolence, does not move either. She must walk over and take it from him, which she does. Coolly, she applies the lipstick in front of him then saunters away, the camera seemingly as agog as Frank with the shot of her curvaceous figure exiting, closing the white kitchen door behind her.

But what I want to point to here is not merely the fairly generic symbolism of whiteness and female sexual purity or ironic sinfulness. In fact, I find it rather startling that so many critics have looked to this scene without ever considering its racial connotations. This neglect suggests both a failure to connect the film to its racially obsessed source text and the invisibility, once again, of the construction of whiteness. After all, the novel's introduction of Cora is of a woman terrified that she appears "Mex," asserting violently to Frank, "I'm just as white as you are" (7). The film's famous introduction of the all-in-white Cora offers a compelling example of its strategy in addressing the textual anxiety over threatened whiteness—a strategy that proffers *visual* evidence over the fervent rhetorical assertions of the text. Who could look up at the screen and see the glowing Turner and still question her whiteness? The uniquely visual power of film—what Mary Ann Doane terms the "ultimate epistemological guarantee" (229)—to render obsolete the concerns with which the novels wrestle proves one of the enduring strategies of the hardboiled adaptations.

Richard Dyer traces a recurrent Western representation of "[i]dealised white women . . . bathed in and permeated by light. It streams through them and falls on to them from above. In short, they glow" (122); he adds that blonde hair and white clothing also serve to heighten the "glow" of the white woman (124). Dyer sees this representation as dominating the Victorian era and that era's racial upheavals (decline of imperialism, the U.S. Civil War). But the long history of idealized images of white women that, Dyer shows, reaches grand heights in film due to the power of cinematic lighting, suggests much about the representation of Turner in *The Postman Always Rings Twice.*[6] As discussed in chapter four, the novel emerges from a historical context of 1930s Los Angeles, overripe with ethnic conflict, particularly between Anglos and Mexicans. Amid this atmosphere, cinematic portrayals of idealized white femininity take on added resonance. Mary Anne Doane importantly suggests, in relation to *Imitation of Life* (1959), that the film's racial drama is "cured" by the delegation of the "representation of racial identity" to the white woman—once again, Lana Turner. Doane writes, "[W]hiteness becomes most visible, takes form, in relation to the figure of the white woman. . . . When a white patriarchal culture requires a symbol of racial purity to organize and control its relations with blacks . . . the white woman represents whiteness itself, as racial identity and as *the* stake of a semiotics of power" (244). The perpetual embodiment of white femininity in Hollywood cinema makes the white woman the perfect carrier for whiteness; she *already* is all-body, all the better to signify what should remain invisible and thus utterly assured on the white male: his whiteness. In this way, *The Postman Always Rings Twice* affirms a stable white masculinity through the whiteness of Cora. In so doing, the film palliates the text's anxieties

about the racial status of Cora, while also underlining its very need to eliminate the racial fears of the Cora of the novel. She cannot be questionably
white because she must signify whiteness for the white male(s) around her.
Then, instead of the novel's questionably white woman seeking to whiten
herself through ambition, class-climbing, and a relationship with a "whiter"
man, the film presents the white woman *extraordinaire*—the femme fatale
whitewashed, turned into a sexualized Victorian angel.

The film's "deracination" of the novel's anxieties over whiteness takes
non-visual forms as well. The novel's couple, Nick and Cora Papadakis, become Nick and Cora Smith (in the book, Smith is Cora's maiden name), and
Nick's thick Greek accent is replaced by the vaguely anglicized patter of Aus-
tralian actor Cecil Kellaway. As such, all the book's intimations of miscegenation in Cora and Nick's marriage are removed. But it is the *visual*
consolidation of whiteness that stands out so startlingly. The notion that
Cora looks "Mex" could hardly be less imaginable with this vision of the
gilded Lana. There is, however, the sense that the film protests too much.
Turner's hair is not naturally platinum, of course, as her early films attest.
Further, there is an element of hyperbolic parody in the excessive whiteness
of her visage, highlighted by a scene when she and Frank hitchhike and
Cora's white traveling suit becomes increasingly dirtied despite her attempts
to brush off the stains of road dust. Turner's unimpeachable whiteness suggests the extent to which the anxieties that drive the novel are not simply
erased in the film, but are also turned back upon themselves. If Cora fears
being read as Mexican in the novel, she is embodied as an almost-parody of
white femininity in the film. She is whiteness as Hollywood spectacle.

But what do we then make of Frank's "less white" status in the film
through the casting of Garfield? Garfield's casting flies in the face of the
book's presentation of Frank as, according to Cora, the pinnacle of
white(male)ness: "[Y]ou're hard all over. Big and tall and hard. And your
hair is light. You're not a little soft greasy guy with black kinky hair that
he puts bay rum on every night" (16). Garfield in fact is dark-haired, and
not particularly tall. The actor himself, né Jacob Julius Garfinkle, was Jewish American, the son of a clothes-presser on New York's Lower East Side.
Throughout his career, Garfield was frequently cast in "ethnic" (a Mexican
general in *Juarez*) and/or working-class roles. One might argue that the
film savors the forbidden image of the sparkling white Turner in the arms
of a not-entirely-"white"-looking Garfield, but I would offer a more basic
explanation: the Hollywood female lead must be white; the male lead's
"race," as long as he is not "not-white," is irrelevant. Golden Age Hollywood glamour is characterized by silvery images of actresses in satiny white
gowns and sets—in particular during the 1930s platinum hair craze,
sparked by sex symbol Jean Harlow's mane. Casting Lana Turner, whose

platinum hair in the film mirrors Harlow's to a tee, cements the film's commitment to this model of Hollywood femininity. Hence, the novel's questionably white figure is given the full Hollywood treatment, made over into the silver-tinted white goddess, Lana Turner. Turner is a willful choice, utterly miscast as a woman who "wasn't any raving beauty" (*The Postman Always Rings Twice*, 4).[7]

The Postman Always Rings Twice thus both "cleans up" its source text and quells much of that source text's anxieties, while also offering particularly visual cues that point reflexively at its own slick ablutions and containment. This adaptive process is one that, I will show, characterizes several of the Cain- and Chandler-based films that proved so popular and enduring.

Gone Hollywood

"They gave me a [screen] test. It was all right in the face. But they talk, now. The pictures, I mean. And when I began to talk, up there on the screen, they knew me for what I was."

—James M. Cain, *The Postman Always Rings Twice*

A substantial gap of time exists between the publication of these hardboiled novels—particularly those of James M. Cain—and their film adaptations. The film rights for *The Postman Always Rings Twice* were purchased in 1934, yet the film was not produced until 1946. Rights for 1934's *Double Indemnity* were snapped up by Hollywood in 1936, yet that film was not made until 1944. This gap is true to a lesser extent with Raymond Chandler, whose *The Big Sleep* (1939) experienced a lull of seven years between publication and production. The reason for these intervals is most often attributed to the rise of the Production Code.

In 1934, the Motion Picture Producers and Distributors of America, under the leadership of its president, Will Hays, authorized the Production Code Administration to enforce its four-year-old code of standards for motion picture content.[8] Written by a Jesuit priest and the editor of *Motion Picture Herald,* who was also a well-known Catholic, the Code imposed on the industry a series of "moral" standards, including prohibitions against profanity, "impure love," and portrayals of miscegenation. In turn, the Code dictated that adultery "as a subject should be avoided" when possible, but if necessary to the story, then it "must not be explicitly treated, or justified, or presented attractively."[9] Further, movies "shall not infer that low forms of sex relationship are the accepted or common thing." The ideological stance was such that the "sanctity of the institution of marriage and the home shall be upheld."[10] Further, crimes were to be treated with great care and their portrayal should not allow for viewer sympathy with the wrongdoers.[11]

Given this atmosphere, it should come as no surprise that Cain's tales of adulterous couples engaging in rough sex and getting away (or nearly getting away) with murder did not reach the silver screen in the 1930s. John Huston's adaptation of Dashiell Hammett's *The Maltese Falcon* (1941) snuck in just before a new impetus for avoiding hardboiled subject matter emerged: the U.S. involvement in World War II. As the country entered the war, pressures on Hollywood to avoid stories or scripts offering bleak views of American institutions such as the police and the justice system contributed to the further suspension of hardboiled adaptations. As Frank Krutnik notes, "There is evidence that the studios were warned off making films like *The Maltese Falcon* which ran counter to the wartime project of 'cultural mobilisation'" (36).

During the war, two Chandler novels did make it to the silver screen, but in quite contorted condition. The central mysteries of each novel were plucked out and adapted for serials. In 1942, *The Falcon Takes Over,* an adaptation of *Farewell, My Lovely,* and *Time to Kill,* an adaptation of *The High Window,* were released. *The Falcon Takes Over* used the Chandler plot as a vehicle for the RKO "Falcon" detective series. Likewise, *Time to Kill* adapted the Chandler story for its Mike Shayne series. It was not until 1944's *Murder, My Sweet* (another adaptation of Chandler's *Farewell, My Lovely*) that a Chandler novel was used as more than source material for other vehicles. It was also the first cinematic evocation of Philip Marlowe, as interpreted by former song and dance man Dick Powell.

The timing of *Murder, My Sweet*'s production was no coincidence. It was not until the mid-forties that a greater laxity emerged in terms of the Code atmosphere. Richard Schickel notes that the "movie industry's acquiescence in censorship was a function of its lust for middle-class respectability, which it had more or less achieved by the mid-1940s, when its super-patriotic war work had brought it into close, mutually admiring relationship with Washington" (20).[12] Studios and eager filmmakers quickly took advantage of the more tolerant atmosphere, beginning production on a number of crime films.

As the war drew to its close these adaptations came fast and furious, although in highly bowdlerized forms. *Murder, My Sweet* and *Double Indemnity* were released in 1944, and *The Big Sleep* and *The Postman Always Rings Twice* in 1946. Film versions of Chandler's *Lady in the Lake* (1946) and *The High Window* (filmed as *The Brasher Doubloon* in 1947), Cain's *Mildred Pierce* (1945) and *Serenade* (1956) all made their way to the big screen. As noted earlier, the majority of these films would eventually be categorized by film scholars as penultimate examples of film noir. Paul Schrader, in his seminal 1972 article, "Notes on Film Noir," articulates the relationship between hardboiled fiction and noir: "When the movies of the Forties turned to the American 'tough' moral understrata, the hard-boiled school was waiting with preset conventions of heroes, minor characters, plots, dialogue and themes . . . the hard-boiled writers had a style made to order for film noir."[13]

It is important to note that film noir was not a term used by the film-makers in question (they generally considered themselves to be shooting crime films or melodramas). Instead, after its initial coinage by French critic Nino Frank in 1946, the term began to flourish within cinema studies in the 1950s, particularly among French scholars. The most influential critical text in this era was Raymond Borde and Étienne Chaumeton's *Panorama du film noir américain* (1955). Within film theory, noir remains a divisive term, however. An influential 1974 article by Janey Place and Lowell Peterson characterized it as dominated by "moods of claustrophobia, paranoia, despair and nihilism" expressed visually through low-key lighting, the withholding of establishing shots, night-for-night lighting, "claustrophobic framing," and a mise-en-scène "designed to unsettle, jar, and disorient the viewer in correlation with the disorientation felt by the noir heroes."[14] Despite this and multiple other attempts at classification, debate over what characteristics films noirs share persist. Further, scholars continue debating whether noir is a genre, a historical period, a film cycle, or a visual style, along with disagreements over the start and end dates of noir and which films can be categorized as noir.[15]

Perhaps due in large part to these tendentious debates, Chandler and Cain adaptations are frequently absorbed into discussions of film genre, history, and style, diverting the important concerns that the films raise in relation to their source texts.[16] Although many critics do consider the relationship between hardboiled novels and the ensuing noir adaptations, the tone is frequently dismissive of the novels—Cain's in particular—as lesser pulp; or, in the case of Chandler's *The Big Sleep,* the source novel is invoked primarily to assert its plot holes and convolutions, which the film then adopts. An exception is Frank Krutnik's *In a Lonely Street: Film Noir, Genre, Masculinity* (1991), which devotes a chapter to the hardboiled origins of film noir. Krutnik, however, confines his discussion to the chapter rather than connecting it to his discussion of the films themselves. Within the chapter, he offers a brief history of hardboiled fiction, offering a case of the mutual affinity between Hollywood films and these crime novels. William Luhr's *Raymond Chandler and Film* attempts a fuller discussion of the relationship between text and film, but Luhr's focus leans heavily on production history and a recounting of Chandler's Hollywood experiences rather than critical analysis.

Then, a systematic examination of the choices these films make in regard to the novels from which they emerge is still missing. While such a project is beyond my scope here, I do wish to propose several inroads. This discussion aims to reveal that the white male figure at the center of this book transforms in telling ways in the shift to a visual, far more profit-driven, immensely popular medium. The urban white male of the novels appears to prove a genuine threat within the motion picture industry. To make his way to the screen—a move that increases his audience exponentially—he must undergo a true Hollywood makeover.

Femme Fatale, Homme Fatal, Romans Fatals

When we look at the Cain and Chandler adaptations through the lens set up in this book thus far, we can see that, in part, they are expurgations of many of the tensions and ambiguities that emanate from the texts. As we saw with *The Postman Always Rings Twice,* the narrativized racial tensions of the novels disappear from the films' diegesis. Likewise, the femme fatale's destabilizing or hystericizing power, even as a projection of the white male hero's anxieties, is severely limited. Further, the homoerotic charges and gender play are parsimoniously rendered or completely occluded.

But these films do in fact reflect ambivalence about the white male figure at the center of their source texts. While seeking in some measure to normalize the figure and install him in a familial and/or heteronormative structure, the films also reveal a covert pleasure in transgression that mirrors the texts' comparable pleasure.

Central to these contradictory gestures is the relocation these films orchestrate with regard to the origin of danger within the source texts. Rather than working obsessively to contain the threat of the femme fatale, these films contain the threat of the renegade white male, overrun by fugitive desires—homoerotic desires, desires for submissive positionality, desires for racial or ethnic identifications. The notion of a white male figure prowling the urban landscape without wife or children, without familial ties or male friends, without a boss, a company, a community position is profoundly disturbing to World War II and Cold War films. That is, while within the narrative the femme fatale serves as the motivator and principle threat, the adaptive choices the films make reflect a pressing need to "normalize" and interpellate the white male protagonist. But, much like the tough guy who savors the dark pleasures of the lethal vamp before destroying her, the films enact a schizophrenic pattern of pleasure and containment with regard to the tough guy and, specifically, the novels that foreground him.

The novels then serve as the femme fatale for the adaptation process. The films must remain hermetically sealed from their threat. Janey Place writes about the femme fatale, "The ideological operation of the myth (the absolute necessity of controlling the strong, sexual woman) is thus achieved by first demonstrating her dangerous power and its frightening results, then destroying it."[17] Likewise, if, as we have shown, Cain and Chandler novels offer partly veiled expressions of fugitive desires and a refusal to enter into patriarchal or juridical structures, the films must find ways to protect themselves from such desires, or at least from openly expressing them. Further, as Place asserts, part of the femme fatale's danger lies in her ambition and her freedom of movement (46). Likewise, the tough guy's lack of any ties or affiliations make the white male loner a renegade in need of containment. The femme fatale is contained, by and large, through her destruction or imprisonment; the hardboiled hero is contained in these films through his immediate or eventual repositioning safely within traditional patriarchal structures. The white male loner must be reinscribed into traditional modes of masculinity—modes defined through patriarchy, the Law.

Contain and Subvert:
Film Noir's Smuggling Ring

Each of the adaptations discussed here turn their source novels into a narrative more conducive to producing an interpellated masculinity. The narratives become infused with family romances that reinstall the loner hero into patriarchal structures that allot him a firm position free of transgressive contagion. Further, the novels' racial anxieties are entirely evacuated from the latent content of the films, with non-white characters "made white" in the film, and with racially or ethnically mixed settings occluded (*Murder, My Sweet* recasts the African American bar of the novel as a white working-class milieu). But, as we saw with *The Postman Always Rings Twice*, the films often find ways of expressing these same anxieties through visual means—in *Postman*'s case, through the too-white representation of the novel's femme fatale.

Narratively, the films protect themselves from the contaminating effects of this white male loner—a figure who can contaminate with his outlaw desires and committed isolation—but not without offering primarily visual trespassing into more dangerous territory along the way. *Murder, My Sweet* director Edward Dmytryk has suggested that the Production Code contributed to the visual power of film noir because it forced filmmakers to convey illicit plots and themes "deviously," such as through lighting, framing, and camera movement.[18] Contemporary filmmaker Martin Scorsese similarly notes that noir's B-film directors became film "'smugglers' who subverted preconditioned expectations regarding film production, style, and content."[19] While the films I am looking at here—*Murder, My Sweet, Double Indemnity,* and *The Big Sleep*—with their big stars and big studios, are not "B-films," we can discern a significant amount of smuggling. I conceive of the smuggling operating in these films as primarily a stylistic or visual twist that shakes the film out of its slick, orderly narrative, that suggests hidden fetishes and tensions at work in its evocation of hardboiled masculinity.

By way of example, I want to consider a moment of what I would characterize as "smuggling" in Dmytryk's *Murder, My Sweet*. The film is known in large part for its much-vaunted expressionistic dream sequences that seek to approximate Philip Marlowe's point of view: his unconscious terrors become the viewer's. For instance, when, in his drugged state, Marlowe hallucinates smoke, smoke effects are simultaneously superimposed across the screen obstructing the viewer's vision. This melding of the viewer's perception with Marlowe's is enhanced by the highly influential use of voiceover in the film. Dick Powell's Marlowe narrates the story in flashback, often in language taken directly from the book. The fact that the visual expressionistic effects emerge when Marlowe is drugged or knocked unconscious suggests an interesting imposition of a weakened, vulnerable subjectivity onto the viewer him/herself. Viewers are thus encouraged or forced to identify more with Marlowe's out-of-control, hysterical mode than with his controlled, tough-talking one.

To J. P. Telotte, however, the importance of this effect in establishing film noir's interests in subjectivity and challenges to traditional perspective is mitigated. Referring in particular to the smoke effect noted above, Telotte asserts, "While such scenes let us see as Marlowe supposedly does, though, we also, if illogically, see *him,* for he remains the central focus of the frame, even as we seem placed in his motivating point of view."[20] Telotte surmises, "[T]his peculiar combination of subjective and objective vantages in the same field of vision points to *Murder, My Sweet*'s peculiar strategy: its effort to evoke but control subjectivity, to deploy it but without the disturbing sense of effacement that might follow and point up the limitations on our cinematic seeing."[21]

Telotte misses, however, what we may consider a far more unusual instance of experimentation with subjectivity. The film actually offers a still-more subversive bit of perspective trickery. And the viewer's identification is not with Marlowe at all, but with the alcoholic would-be informant, Jessie Florian. In the scene, Marlowe has come to Florian to secure information about Velma, his client's missing girlfriend. Florian goes into her bedroom to locate a picture of Velma and Marlowe spots her surreptitiously hiding one photo before she emerges with a large stack for Marlowe to peruse. The scene continues via alternating medium shots of the blowsy, boozing Florian chattering away, and Marlowe feigning to look at the photos while, the viewer intuits, biding time to get into the bedroom and see what Florian was hiding. The two are seated across from each other. Then, the crosscutting between the two ceases and the camera momentarily stays with Florian, drinking and talking, her eyelids drooping with pleasure. The viewer can see the open door of the bedroom behind her chair. Suddenly, the music ceases its random piano melody and the keys pound to a dramatic halt, cueing the viewer to be alarmed. Florian looks across from her and her eyes pop. The camera pulls back to a long medium shot that reveals Marlowe's empty chair. Florian turns around and looks at the bedroom behind her. She rises and stumbles over, the camera following, and she, and the viewer, finds Marlowe with a photo in his hand and intoning angrily, "Why did you hide this picture of Velma?"

This scene is unusual for two reasons. First, throughout the rest of the film, viewer perspective has been repeatedly allied with Marlowe, both as the interlocutor of his voiceover narration and as the viewer whose field of vision has always been equivalent to Marlowe's (i.e., when he is knocked out, the mise-en-scène becomes black, too). In this scene, however, the viewer shares *Florian's* vision. She fails to see Marlowe get up and walk over and enter the bedroom and so does the viewer, who is permitted to realize what Marlowe has done only after Florian has. Second, there is a subjective element to this occlusion. The viewer *should* actually see Marlowe walk behind Florian, as the entrance to her bedroom is quite visible in the shot. The viewer does not, defying spatial logic. This blockage suggests that the viewer is experiencing Florian's drunken lack of awareness, but to such an extent that the viewer can see no more of what goes on behind Florian than Florian does, despite a camera placement that gives the viewer full visual access to the background, to Florian's blind spot. The seemingly objective mise-en-scène—a mise-en-scène that, were it to lean toward any subjective viewpoint, would surely be Marlowe's—is proven severely limited, manipulated, and even more impaired than the pathetic Jessie Florian's perspective.

There are several points I want to make about this curious moment. First, the sudden, if fleeting jarred identification with a character other than Marlowe highlights the extent to which in the novels and in the film the reader/viewer is so tenaciously aligned with the detective that the alignment becomes invisible.[22] With this moment, however—the only moment like it in the film—the viewer is forced suddenly into an awareness of the perspective alignment: the fleeting and rare *mis*alignment makes conspicuous the relentlessness association between Marlowe and the viewer.

From a more thematic perspective, this moment carries another significance. As mentioned above, in identifying with Marlowe, the viewer is forced to identify with a persistently weakened, vulnerable subjectivity. But further, throughout the film, Marlowe's subjectivity in fact is linked with images of blindness or partial vision. The first time we see Marlowe, he is blindfolded, and he remains this way throughout the frame narrative.[23] Significantly, this blindness is not present in the book; the film chooses to add it, intensifying Marlowe's vulnerability. This literal blindness is matched by the blindness of Marlowe's unconscious states (he is knocked out four times in the film).

As with many private detective films, Marlowe must negotiate much of the film with partial knowledge or misinformation, while others conspire around him. It is then important that, in the scene with Jessie Florian, Marlowe does see her attempts at concealing information and it is *Florian*—and the viewer—whose vision is occluded. Although the viewer is a step ahead of Florian in knowing that Marlowe has seen her conceal the photo, Florian is a step ahead of the viewer in that she spots Marlowe's disappearance from the chair a split second before the viewer. In both cases, however, the viewer is *not* focalized through Marlowe and instead is more closely focalized through Florian. This alignment suggests that the viewer is identified with whomever is the most visually impaired and vulnerable in the scene—in this case, the tipsy Florian. In turn, since, as mentioned earlier, this scene is virtually the only time in the film when the viewer is separated from Marlowe's perspective, it suggests a meaningful connection between Florian and Marlowe. All other characters are a step ahead of Marlowe, but not Jessie Florian—at least not consistently.[24] Then, we have a situation where Marlowe's subjectivity is scarcely more intact than the besotted Florian, and the viewer's guide or double through the mystery is either fraught and purblind or drunk and incoherent. The power of any viewer's gaze to dominate carries no weight here, and the film forces its audience to account for both the inherent instability of the white urban male hero and their own visual competence. The ability to retain a coherent and vigilant subjectivity is thrown into question.

This instability works as part of the film's ongoing celebration of unconsciousness; *Murder, My Sweet* devotes long stretches to Marlowe's drugged nightmares and unconscious states, finding pleasure in partial vision and bodily vulnerability. Far from seeking to heal or shore up Marlowe's masculinity through a restoration of male agency and power, the film actually seems to fetishize this bodily helplessness and even impotence, making it the leit motif of the film. This vision actually accords with Chandler's Marlowe, who expresses the most ethereal pleasures in the novels when he is knocked unconscious. As noted in chapter two, repeatedly in the novels, Marlowe's semiconscious states upon being drugged are filled with lush images and a clear, even romanticized pleasure in the experience. The pleasure seems connected to the complete subjection, nothingness, the black pit that can terrify but also promise a sensual passivity that, for the hermetic and tightly wound Marlowe, appears deeply appealing.

We then have a model of the "smuggling-in" of both reflexive critique and covert pleasures. Of course, it becomes crucial that these films not enjoy these pleasures too much. The persistent strategy instead seems to be to contort and inoculate the white male figure diegetically, while savoring his transgressive milieu stylistically.

Having set up the means by which smuggling can occur, I now want to focus on three primary ways that this containment/subversion process operates: the defatalization of the femme fatale, the admixture of the family romance or family structures into the narrative, and the infusion and valuation of male relationships. To pursue these strategies, I will consider the three famed adaptations that followed fast upon each other in 1944–1946: *Murder, My Sweet, Double Indemnity,* and *The Big Sleep.*

Femme Fatale

In a typical rendering of the role of the femme fatale in film noir, Foster Hirsch writes, " . . . all of noir's fatal women seem to move in a dreamlike landscape. They are projections of male fears and fantasies that seem merely to be simulating human action. These women are acted in a remote, compressed, semi-abstract style . . . to embody their dreamlike otherness, the actresses who impersonate them perform in a cryptic stylized manner, sleepwalking through masculine nightmares" (157). He argues that the ultimate femme fatale is Barbara Stanwyck's Phyllis Dietrichson in *Double Indemnity,* whom he claims is a "grotesque in woman's clothing, a character conceived by men who hate and fear strong women" (152).

The debate over whether the femme fatale is merely a misogynist projection of male fears of female agency, or whether she represents a profound power that is of use value for feminist theory has been brewing for over twenty years, triggered in large part by Janey Place's 1978 article, "Women in Film Noir." Place argues that noir offers "women [who] are active, not static symbols, are intelligent and powerful, if destructively so, and derive power, not weakness, from their sexuality" (35). Elizabeth Cowie, in line with Place's argument, offers that these films "afforded women roles which are active, adventurous and driven by sexual desire."[25] She goes on to suggest that female as well as male viewers can savor the "fantasy of the woman's dangerous sexuality," a fantasy whose "pleasures lie precisely in its forbiddenness" (136).

Frank Krutnik offers a perspective that correlates interestingly with what I have been presenting as the conflicting impulses of these films. He writes of the femme fatale as a "woman as a kind of hydraulic 'fuck machine' [that] clearly establishes her exclusion from the masculine regime of language" (42–43). But, Krutnik adds, this "forceful visualization also made it less easy to accomplish such an authoritarianism of the male voice" (43). The visual power of the femme fatale and the dominance of her image in each film may carry more potency than all the male-centered, male-identified, and male-narrated stories that sought to contain her.

But when one considers the Chandler and Cain noirs—with which all these critics concern themselves in part—*in concert with their source texts,* the debate takes on quite a different cast. We find that the femme fatale actually loses much of her potential power in the translation from novel to film, even if her visual presence leaves a lasting imprint on the films in question. Instead, as I have already begun to suggest, a new femme fatale is reborn in the guise of the white male protagonist, whose threat seems to require far more containment than the traditional "fatal woman."

First, let us consider how the femmes fatales of the novels are—as in Chester Himes's genre-busting romans policiers, which we will explore in chapter six—distinctly "defatalized" in these film adaptations. This process occurs in two primary ways: through the "making ordinary" of the enigmatic, nearly supernaturally evil Gothic femme fatale, or through the transformation of the femme fatale into a conventional romantic love interest.

Case Study A: The Iron Maiden

When critics invoke the ultimate femmes fatales of film noir, they inevitably include Barbara Stanwyck's icy portrayal of Phyllis Dietrichson in Billy Wilder's *Double Indemnity,* scripted by Wilder and, in an interesting quirk of fate, Raymond Chandler.[26] When one considers Stanwyck's portrayal in concert with the Phyllis of the book, however, we see a fundamental conventionalization of the novel's femme fatale. The novel's mass murderess and death cultist transmutes into Barbara Stanwyck's icy gold-digger. Instead of stepdaughter Lola coming upon Phyllis standing before her mirror in her horrific death garb—red silk gown, white Kabuki face, dagger in hand—Lola merely spots Phyllis smugly modeling a mourning hat.[27] Instead of a Phyllis who, we learn late in the novel, has killed a string of others, including three children, before she meets insurance salesman Walter Huff, the film's Phyllis has killed only once before (her current husband's first wife), for explicit financial gain. She operates primarily as a generic amoral woman with no conscience.

Further, although the extent of her sincerity is never proven, the film's Phyllis does appear to "soften" dramatically in her final scene. She shoots Walter, wounding him, and yet cannot manage to "finish him off." Her arm falls, the gun going limp in her hand. Walter sardonically asks her if she could not go through with it because she is in love with him. She responds, her coldness melting into tears and tenderness, "No, I never loved you, Walter. Not you or anybody else. I'm rotten to the heart. I used you just as you said. It's all you ever meant to me. Until a minute ago. When I couldn't fire that second shot. I never thought that could happen to me." Walter retorts, "Sorry. I'm not buying," to which Phyllis replies, "I'm not asking you to buy. Just hold me close." They embrace and then we see a look of shock and horror on Phyllis's face as she presumably feels his gun pressed against her. He says, "Goodbye, baby," before shooting her.

In several ways, this rendering is the polar opposite of the couple's last moments together in the book. In Cain's version, as discussed in chapter two, Walter helplessly follows the sanguinary Phyllis into a grisly suicide pact, the image of her in her red shroud virtually staining the novel's closing lines. In the film, as we have seen, Phyllis turns softboiled at the end, and Walter coolly finishes her off. Significantly, these shifts allow for a far more containable femme fatale. The almost supernaturally evil Phyllis Nirdlinger holds a death grip on the novel's Walter Huff; he spends the novel fighting what proves to be his unassailable fate, to follow her into death.[28] Fred Mac-Murray's Walter Neff does not survive the film, but he dies having successfully expunged Phyllis's far more generically mercenary threat—and possibly having even "cured" her of her lethality by eliciting her love. As such, the taint of the femme fatale is lifted, leaving the last scene to a masculinist interaction between Walter and claims investigator Barton Keyes, two men who care for each other with a gravity and meaning that Walter and Phyllis never manage.

All of this is not to suggest that we cannot detect some distinct smuggling at work in *Double Indemnity*'s rendering of its femme fatale. That smuggling takes the form of kitsch and parody. Specifically, I am speaking of what may at first appear a minor element: the conspicuous and ostentatious blonde-banged wig Stanwyck wears in the film. While seemingly a mere costume choice, consider that this wig dominates popular memory of the film. Director Billy Wilder in fact admitted that the wig choice was calculated: "I wanted her to look as sleazy as possible."[29] As Wilder biographer Ed Sikov relays, "Since she would be playing a siren from Southern California—the kind who wears perfume from Ensenada—Stanwyck's hair needed to radiate on celluloid as intensely platinum-blonde as possible. So a wig was produced in a shade verging on pure white" (203). The wig—so iconographic now that recapturing its initial eccentricity is difficult—prompted one studio executive to snort, "We hire Barbara Stanwyck and here we get George Washington" (quoted in Sikov, 203).

Richard Schickel relays that Wilder worried over the wig, wondering, "Was it just a bit too much, a tad over the top?"—a question that, as Schickel reminds us, "devotees of the film still debate as earnestly as Wilder did. . . ."[30] James Naremore takes the point further, writing that, compared with Cain's Phyllis, the "character portrayed by Barbara Stanwyck is much more blatantly provocative and visibly artificial; her ankle bracelet, her lacquered lipstick, her sunglasses, and above all her chromium hair give her a cheaply manufactured and metallic look"[31]—Phyllis is "so bad that she seems like modernity and kitsch incarnate" (89). In other words, Phyllis embodies such a falseness, such artifice that she points to her role as the projection, or better still, a manufactured product, of male fantasies and fears.

She is fashioned outrageously as the spider woman ne plus ultra, whose overt and flamboyant lethality points reflexively to her status as a male construct. For Naremore, she embodies the fears of modernity, consumer plasticity. But she also embodies specific male fears of the powerful woman who will move men like chess pieces to gain what she desires. Further, the suddenness with which she reforms at the end highlights the fantasy of the evil woman cowed into feminizing love by the man who is now so tough that he can kill without pause or remorse. Walter has become (or was all along) precisely what he says about her: "No nerves. Not a tear. Not even a blink of the eye." Phyllis's wig, like her fetishized and gaudy ankle bracelet, her mask-like face, calls attention to its own condition as a fantasy. Of course, by placing Phyllis, in part, in quotation marks, her power is diminished and the film can easily discard her in favor of what it seems to see as a more compelling relationship, one safely in the masculine realm, a point to which I will return.

Case Study B: The Inoculated Beauty

An analogous kind of conventionalization operates in Howard Hawks's famed adaptation of *The Big Sleep*. The film serves as a process by which the potential femme fatale is turned into, or tamed into, a romantic love interest. Vivian Sternwood, cold, deceitful, and thrice married in the novel, is reconfigured, in the form of Lauren Bacall, as a once-married banter-partner for Humphrey Bogart's Marlowe. As she proves her fealty to the detective, Vivian undergoes a reformation from spoiled rich girl to able romantic partner.

As I will discuss later, Humphrey Bogart's star power overwhelms the characterization of Marlowe, much as the Bogart-Bacall dynamic overtakes the film. The parry-banter-clinch dynamic is, in large part, transplanted from the couple's previous pairing, Hawks's adaptation of Ernest Hemingway's hardboiled *To Have and Have Not*. An earlier edit of *The Big Sleep*, released in 1998, shows the conscious effort of the final version to enhance the romance between the couple. Scenes were added to capitalize on their off-screen relationship and Bacall's growing star power, which the studio wanted to nourish with care.[32]

The film adds a romantic arc to the narrative—an arc that is characteristic of Hawks's repeated motif of tough men and efficient women—that effectively becomes, one might argue, the primary plot and raison d'étre in the film's last hour. In the novel, Vivian Sternwood shares a (duplicitous) kiss with Marlowe, but her main function in the text is to divert Marlowe from the truth: Her sister, Carmen, has killed Vivian's (third) husband. Marlowe's main sexual and romantic attraction in the novel is the gangster Eddie Mars's eminently faithful wife, Mona, whom Marlowe meets only once. Her loyalty to her husband and her reserve attract Marlowe hopelessly, and when he manages a kiss from her, the fact that her "lips were like ice" (*The Big Sleep*, 198) carries an erotic charge. In the film, Mona appears on screen only a few moments. Bacall's Vivian replaces her role in the scene, and, as the film progresses, she shifts from a manipulative sparrer to a devoted partner, verbally matching Marlowe but implicitly serving him through her actions (in the climatic final shoot-out he prescribes her movements like a film director). To underline the reformation, Bogart's Marlowe charts her progress along the way, saying things like, in reference to Mona Mars's loyalty, "I wonder if you'd do what she did for a man," and later, after she acquits herself calmly in a tough spot, "You looked good, awful good." And consider the film's famous final exchange (an invention of screenwriters William Faulkner, Leigh Brackett, and Jules Furthman). Vivian says to Marlowe, "You've forgotten one thing. Me." He says, "What's wrong with you?" Vivian replies with a smile, "Nothing you can't fix."

On the most obvious level, this adaptive choice speaks to the rather pragmatic desire to fabricate a Bogart-Bacall romance within an essentially romance-free mystery. That desire, however, replicates Howard Hawks's recurring romantic configuration, one that Hollywood celebrated throughout the era: the narrative transformation of the cool, sometimes insolent heroine into a devoted and yet proficient and savvy partner who can serve the hero in his adventures (*cf.* Hawks's *Only Angels Have Wings, To Have and Have Not*, and, to a lesser extent, *His Girl Friday, The Thing,* and *Rio Bravo*). Brian Gallagher sketches Vivian's role in the film: " . . . Vivian is a type of citizen-soldier's ideal mate, containing a complementary degree of toughness, realism, and unabashed sexuality, without being, like [her] psychotic [sister] Carmen, naturally treacherous or murderous. And she is also willing [to] be subservient and compliant, circumstances permitting" (152).[33] Gallagher suggests, in this way, Vivian is made into the "type of woman whom many servicemen might expect, were they sufficiently realistic, to encounter on their return home" (152). I would counter this charge in part, as it seems Gallagher overstates Vivian's "unabashed sexuality." As noted earlier, the film significantly transforms the multiply married Vivian of the novel (which also references a supposed promiscuity on her part) to a once-married Vivian of the film.[34] But what is significant here, regardless of the degree of Vivian's sexual availability, is that any spider woman attributes the novel accords her are redistributed elsewhere, specifically on the mentally unstable thumb sucker, Carmen Sternwood. Even Carmen (played memorably by Martha Vickers) is permitted to pose little threat, disappearing from the entire second half of the film. Further, in the novel, Carmen is a murderess, while in the film, her guilt is transferred to another, male character, gangster Eddie Mars, further deflating her potential danger. Carmen's instability is thus made relatively innocuous, while Vivian's treachery is turned into easily repaired insolence. In the film, Vivian evokes no threat at all, merely a sexy challenge.

A telling instance that points to the film's earnest efforts to defatalize Vivian comes when one considers the pre-release edit of *The Big Sleep*. During an early scene between Marlowe and Vivian, Vivian wears a hat with an elaborate, admittedly odd veil that cuts across her face. When the film was doctored to accent the Bogart-Bacall relationship, the scene was reshot with a different outfit entirely—one that, probably not coincidentally, echoes Bacall's outfit through much of *To Have and Have Not*. Significantly, the veil is gone entirely.[35] Mary Ann Doane devotes a chapter of her book *Femmes Fatales* to veils, using Marlene Dietrich's characters as her primary examples. In particular, she notes how Dietrich's veils can work as "marks of a dangerous deception or duplicity attached to the feminine" (49); and "[u]sually, the placement of the veil over a woman's face works to localize and hence contain dissimulation, to keep it from contaminating the male subject" (75). The veil serves as an erotic screen and as a reminder of the essential unknowability of the femme fatale. The elimination of Vivian's veiled hat in favor of a perky beret points to the film's ritual stripping of the deathly erotic shadings of the femme fatale.

While one might find the film's refusal to demonize its female characters laudable, along with its offering of a more influential role in the plot for a woman, it is crucial to note that these revisions offer a domestication of the femme fatale that is just as much a function of masculine solidification as the destruction of the femme fatale in the typical hardboiled rendering. In fact, all of this defatalization echoes *The Big Sleep*'s larger ideological thrust. Brian Gallagher notes that the film's Marlowe is a "very sexual creature, willing to take his pleasures . . . where he finds them, which in this film is almost everywhere" (147). David Thomson takes this point further, calling Hawks's film a "seemingly infinite realization of male fantasies."[36] From the female cabbie to the luscious bookstore clerk to the casino waitresses and the counterwoman at a diner, these women offer themselves up to Bogart's Marlowe, who responds, to varying degrees, in kind. As Michael Walker writes, "This is pure Hawksian fantasy."[37] Recall the film's last line, Vivian's disciple-like assurance to Marlowe that what is "wrong" with her is "Nothing [he] can't fix." Instead of a Marlowe surrounded by deceitful femmes fatales, he is surrounded by one mischievous deviant (Carmen Sternwood) whom he easily contains, and scores of women eager to be seduced, saved, or "fixed" by his restorative powers.

Both a cause and effect of the defatalization is the hypermasculine rendering of Marlowe as played by Humphrey Bogart.[38] Bogart's iconographic status tends to result in a bleeding together of his actually quite distinct portrayals as a hard and cruel Sam Spade (*The Maltese Falcon*), a tough and honorable Harry

Morgan (*To Have and Have Not*), a savvy Rick whose conscience rises to the exigencies of the time (*Casablanca*), and a wisecracking knightly Philip Marlowe, moving through the mean streets to weed out corruption and save damsels in distress.[39] As such, it is difficult to distill the cultural memory of Marlowe from that of Bogart and his gallery of characters. But Bogart's Spade accords tightly with Hammett's detective, teetering perilously on the brink of psychosis, particularly when he batters a young gunsel. Contrarily, Bogart's Marlowe remains in control of himself and the situations in which he finds himself. This Marlowe bears minimal relation to the detective of Chandler's novels. As we have seen, while Chandler's Marlowe is a man of honor and a wielder of wisecracks, he is also a man who plays chess by himself rather than engaging in relationships with others, a man who seals himself away from perceived sexual contamination, a man who can be driven to dissolution and hysteria.

Bogart's Marlowe (or, Hawks's) does not disintegrate as the novel's Marlowe does. He does not find himself laughing inexplicably upon killing a thug in self-defense, as the novel's Marlowe does. He does not tear his bed to pieces because the unstable Carmen Sternwood has been in it, as the novel's Marlowe does. Instead, Bogart's Marlowe acquits himself with cool efficiency in one instance after the next. No femme fatale has a chance with this model of concretized virility; conveniently, no femme fatale interferes with the film's narrative.

It is then in this excessively intact masculinity and in the constant reaction of female characters to Marlowe that *The Big Sleep* centralizes almost to the point of parody a potent heterosexual appeal and virility within its masculinity model. Indeed, his masculinity and heterosexual appeal are deeply entangled: when Marlowe appears, rather unaccountably, to be pretending to be gay, the transformation involves effeminate stereotyping, including a lisp, but, as Brian Gallagher interestingly notes, "It is a measure of the film's audacity, its heterosexual audacity, that it allows Bogart (whose slight lisp might already be considered of a suspicious nature sexually) to parody himself—and still remain unquestionably and completely heterosexual" (155–56). Perhaps this hypermasculinity and hyperheterosexuality protests too much and hints at a smuggled-in pleasure in its own over-the-top quality, but it seems more a case of hardboiled bravado: Marlowe has been "fixed" by this film, his sexual ambiguities and hermetic isolation is renovated and given a new face, that of the confident and game Humphrey Bogart.

Family Affair

It is a common assertion to suggest, as Frank Krutnik does, that film noir, and the hardboiled fiction from which it derives, express a distrust and criticism of "communal and familiar bonding" (36). This view has been put forth most influentially by Sylvia Harvey in her essay on the role of family in film noir in E. Ann Kaplan's classic 1978 collection, *Women in Film Noir*. Harvey sees in noir a critique of the traditional family structure and marriage, as well as the role of women within these repressive institutions. The critique takes various forms, including the representation of a corrupted or sterile family, the portrayal of a "kind of anti-family," such as the outlaw couple, or in the conspicuous absence of any family model. Harvey concludes, "The absence or disfigurement of the family both calls attention to is own lack and its own deformity and may be seen to encourage the consideration of alternative institutions for the reproduction of social life" (33).[40] Much like the insistence that the femme fatale exudes a lingering power in spite of her annihilation in these films, Harvey writes that, "Despite the ritual punishment of acts of transgression, the vitality with which these acts are endowed produces an excess of meaning which cannot finally be contained. Narrative resolutions cannot recuperate their subversive significance" (33).

Harvey's assertion of a sweeping anti-family rhetoric at the heart of noir, however, remains problematic in relation to the films discussed here, particularly when, once again, one considers their relations to their source texts.[41] In fact, her point does seem apt in regards to the novels (consider the hopelessly corrupt Sternwood family at the heart of Chandler's *The Big Sleep*) but less so in the films that emerge from them. It is my contention that conventional family models—models very influenced, like much of film noir, by psychoanalysis—play a far different role in the films than in the Cain and Chandler novels. The family structure that is critiqued in the novels becomes a means of normalizing the male protagonist in the films.

As noted throughout this book, one of the primary characteristics of the white urban male figure that is the focus of this study is his bachelor status, his childlessness, his complete lack of any familial connection. Philip Marlowe, Frank Chambers, Walter Huff—these men are neither heads of their own families, nor sons in their father's domain.[42] As Chandler himself wrote in a letter to Maurice Guinness a month before his death,

> . . . a fellow of Marlowe's type shouldn't get married, because he is a lonely man, a poor man, a dangerous man, and yet a sympathetic man, and somehow none of this goes with marriage. I think he will always have a fairly shabby office, a lonely house, a number of affairs, but no permanent connection. . . . It seems to me that that is his destiny—possibly not the best destiny in the world, but it belongs to him. No one will ever beat him, because by his nature he is unbeatable. No one will ever make him rich, because he is destined to be poor. But somehow, I think he would not have it otherwise, and therefore I feel that your idea that he should be married, even to a very nice

girl, is quite out of character. I see him always in a lonely street, in lonely rooms, puzzled but never quite defeated. . . . [43]

For Chandler, Marlowe's lack of familial or marital ties is a central attribute and, significantly, one of the sources of his nobility, his shabby knight dignity, bearing out Harvey's point that families may corrupt, not redeem. Likewise, the unconnectedness of Cain's Walter Huff and Frank Chambers helps constitute their existential solitariness; family ties would only distract the novels' lean, fate-obsessed narrative drive. When Cain does deal with families, in his novels *Mildred Pierce* or *The Butterfly,* familial bonds are shown as inherently or, in the latter case, literally incestuous.

Families then exist only as tainted structures the loner white male may trespass, or whose boundaries he might patrol for a fee. But the film adaptations, although not "giving" these characters families of their own, certainly seek to install these men more firmly in family romances and marital inevitabilities.

In the novel *The Big Sleep,* the wealthy Sternwood family is rotten to its core, riddled with sexual sins and corrupted by wealth gained from raping the land for oil. At the novel's end, Marlowe famously feels like he too is "part of the nastiness now" (230) for having aided such a family and concealed their crimes. But Marlowe's involvement with the family in the film version proves far more recuperative. His robust romance with the daughter whom he reforms by his mere presence repositions his role in a family as its greatest hope for a healthy new generation. As such, as Brian Gallagher points out, Marlowe adopts several cleansing roles in the Sternwood family. He plays the role of "son" for General Sternwood, "father" for the arrested Carmen and, by film's end, "husband" for Vivian (146).

Edward Dmytryk's *Murder, My Sweet* offers a more extreme instance of wedging the family into these narratives. The film not only emphasizes but actually imports a family romance into its story. In the source novel, Chandler's *Farewell, My Lovely,* Marlowe's girl Friday, Anne Riordan, is the daughter of a former police chief famed for his probity. She helps Marlowe solve the case surrounding the wealthy Grayle family. In the film, Anne Riordan becomes Anne Grayle,[44] the stepdaughter of the femme fatale, Helen Grayle, and daughter of aging millionaire Lewin Lockridge Grayle. By making Anne Riordan the daughter of Mr. Grayle, Jonathan Buchsbaum argues, the novel's social critique is defanged. In the novel, Riordan's deceased father had been the sole honest member of a dirty police force. In losing this detail in the film version, we also lose the contrast between Marlowe's "integrity" and the "small-time corruption of a small-town police force." Buchsbaum adds, "Thus, there is no world in the film independent of Marlowe's connection to a single family, and the one independent character from the book has been added to the family."[45]

But still more significant is the fact that the revision of the Riordan character initiates a family romance narrative that is not present in the book. In fact, it replicates (and gives a happy ending to) the family romance at the heart of another novel, Cain's *Double Indemnity*. The romance occurs thusly: Marlowe is tempted by the "mother," Helen Grayle; the daughter, Anne, admits to being "more than . . . fond" of her father and hating her (step)mother. These dynamics are played out in the triangulated blocking of the scene in which all four characters occupy the Grayle living room. Repeatedly in the scene, the four characters are positioned in two overlaid triangles emphasized by the frame composition, which places Anne at the apex of one triangle and Helen Grayle at the apex of another, with Marlowe and Mr. Grayle occupying the bases of both. In the end, both parents are killed and the two "children" end up in a romantic clinch happy ending, presumably on the road to producing a family of their own.

James Maxfield connects the family romance model to Marlowe's temporary blindness in the film, suggesting that Marlowe's desire for Helen Grayle (which, I think, he overstates) is "essentially Oedipal."[46] Maxfield points out that by having Mr. Grayle murder his deceitful wife, the film suggests that both of the "'children' [Marlowe and Anne] seem to realize that they aren't strong enough to stand up to the desired or hated mother and that only the father possesses sufficient authority to do so" (42). Maxfield does not note, however, the fact that this plot point is an invention of the film. Mr. Grayle is not even present at the novel's climactic shoot-out, nor is Anne. Instead, Helen murders her ex-boyfriend Moose Malloy and escapes. We eventually learn that she kills herself upon being captured three months later. The film then effectively grafts a family romance dynamic onto the film—a dynamic that importantly solidifies the final pairing off of Anne and Marlowe.

In Chandler's version, Marlowe is attracted to but deeply resists the domestic pull of Anne and a potential involvement with her. The novel's end leaves the question of any future relationship between the two. The next-to-last chapter abruptly closes with Anne Riordan insisting to Marlowe, "I'd like to be kissed, damn you!" (288). We never hear his response—verbal or physical. The last chapter is devoted to Marlowe's self-consciously romantic recounting of the Grayles' sad end.

In closing with a romantic clinch between Marlowe and Anne, the film offers the promise of a "healthy" family free of the painful Oedipal desires that so occupy it earlier in the film. Marlowe and Anne's pairing suggests a fresh start, and importantly installs the wayward Marlowe into acceptable social institutions: heterosexual romantic love and, presumably, marriage. The family romance is unfolded as a device to bring together a more perfect union, and to save Marlowe from his life of lonely danger.

In contrast to *Murder, My Sweet* and *The Big Sleep,* however, *Double Indemnity* actually downplays the novel's flirtation with a family romance narrative. The novel features Walter Huff falling in love with Lola, the daughter of the man he kills and the stepdaughter of his partner in crime, Phyllis. In Cain's version, however, Walter realizes that there can be no place for him in a traditional bourgeois family structure; he is too tainted to risk involvement with the pure Lola. The film, while retaining Walter's tender feelings for Lola, never suggests that Walter has actually fallen in love with her—and it appears that the reason for this occlusion is the same as the novel's reason for having Walter step away from Lola. That is, as Ed Sikov relates, screenwriters Wilder and Chandler felt that Lola "must remain uncorrupted, could not afford to get too close to an older killer, the man with whom her stepmother had already had an affair, the man who broke her own father's neck" (204).

Therefore, the film avoids even temporary interludes with the taboo of Lola becoming involved with Walter. As such, the effect is to make Walter seem softer, kinder: he takes care of her out of guilt and some untapped goodness, not out of romantic love. Of course, this shift tellingly duplicates a basic nuclear family model in which Walter plays the paternal role in regard to Lola, taking over for her father, whom he has killed. Still, however, the film sharply limits Lola's role in favor of time spent on the film's couples—Walter and Phyllis, but, with even more intensity, Walter and Barton Keyes.

Men Among Men

"[T]he guy you were looking for was too close. Right across the desk from you."

—Walter Neff (Fred MacMurray) to Barton Keyes (Edward G. Robinson) in Billy Wilder's *Double Indemnity* (1944)

Indeed, what I want to focus on here is the relationship that, in many ways, takes precedence over any other relationship in *Double Indemnity:* that of insurance salesman Walter Neff (Fred MacMurray) and claims investigator Barton Keyes (Edward G. Robinson). In the novel, it is a friendly gamesmanship. In the film, the pair's bond is given far more attention and emotional charge. Lifelong bachelor Keyes, whose one romantic engagement ended when he "investigated" his fiancée and found her to be filled with secrets, is the *über* claims man who can "sense" a phony claim—an intuition that Keyes metaphorizes as the "little man" inside him who tells him whom to suspect and whom to trust.

The suggestion is that male-female relationships can be (are) inherently lethal and masochistic, while male-male relationships are characterized by intense bonds of mutual respect and emotional investment. When Walter betrays his relationship with Keyes by "cheating" the Company with which Keyes so clearly identifies, he must pay with his life, but both his choice to confess (in the book, he confesses only as part of a deal negotiated with the Company) and to whom he does confess—Keyes—suggest the extent to which Walter admires Keyes. In fact, Walter is caught for his crimes only because he bothers to return to the insurance office and spend hours confessing before attempting an escape.

Keyes serves, in part, as the Father against whom Walter has transgressed. But their interactions are also given a distinct romantic cast. Romantic conventions, in fact, dominate their exchanges: their affectionate banter, the running joke the two share about Walter lighting the always-matchless Keyes's cigars, their implicit trust in each other—to a fault in Keyes's case. The cigar lighting obviously works as a bit of comedic flourish turned poignant when the act is reversed: Keyes lights a match for the dying Walter as the film's last gesture (although it is still Walter's match).[47] The repeated interaction (it occurs upwards of five times in the film), however, is also significant in terms of Hollywood signification, which imbues cigarette lighting and smoking with sexual activity. *The Big Sleep* celebrates this signification in its opening credits, which show a male silhouette lighting a female silhouette's cigarette. Then, each smoking silhouette places a cigarette in an ashtray, suggesting the end of foreplay and the shift to sexual consummation. (This Hollywood tradition reaches its pinnacle in *Now, Voyager,* in which Paul Henreid famously lights two cigarettes in his mouth before gallantly handing one to Bette Davis.) In *Double Indemnity*'s riff on the tradition, Walter "plays" the man and the diminutive Keyes "plays" the woman. James Maxfield writes that

> Although [Keyes] probably doesn't consciously recognize the fact (and the authors of the script may not have either), Keyes has a deep homosexual attachment to Walter Neff. Keyes's feelings are symbolically revealed in the motif of his requiring Walter to light his cigars for him. . . . Keyes's dependency on Neff to strike the matches to light his cigars—and to enable him to derive his satisfaction of being able to smoke them—reveals his subconscious desire to have the younger man satisfy him sexually. (32)

Maxfield's suggestion that Billy Wilder and Raymond Chandler may not be aware of Keyes's attachment to Walter is for the most part belied by Billy Wilder's intimation, quoted a few pages earlier by Maxfield, that he conceived of the film as a "love story between the two men and a sexual involvement with the woman" (29).

We can see this foregrounding of the Neff/Keyes relationship as, curiously, both a means by which the destructive power of the femme fatale is limited (she does not enthrall Walter to the degree that Walter can forego his relationship with Keyes) and by which the import of males (as configured as rational, logical, and essentially moral actors—with Walter merely slipping momentarily and Keyes invulnerable to such slippage) is valued and validated. Further, by greatly increasing Walter's attachment to Keyes in the adaptation process, the urban white male figure is installed far more firmly within a juridical, patriarchal structure. Less the potential gender/Company outlaw as he is through much of the book, the film's Walter is entrenched deeply in a masculinist and capitalist hegemony. His transgression becomes far more directed at, and circumscribed by, this economy. Much like the importing of the family romance in *Murder, My Sweet* in order to install the loner male into a disciplined structure, Walter's potential renegade status is lessened both by the defatalization of Phyllis (his attraction to her loses its hysterical and potential radical tincture) and the inscription of a Walter-Keyes relationship that ties Walter to the Company and ascribes all Walter's motives to his relationship to it.

But the Walter-Keyes relationship also suggests a significant degree of smuggled transgression. The relationship between the men is shown as far more meaningful than a relationship with the exogamous woman—a woman whose function is shown in large part to be of value primarily for the effects her actions have on the relationship between men (*cf. Gilda*). Further, deepening the relationship between Walter and Keyes magnifies the extent to which the femme fatale exists only in her effect on the men. Further, and even more interesting, the relationship recasts Walter in the role of femme fatale to Keyes's sap, throwing the traditional gendered femme fatale/sap binary into confusion. That is, Keyes repeatedly defends Walter and protects him from suspicions while Walter hides his guilt. The dying Walter tells Keyes, "Know why you couldn't figure this one, Keyes? I'll tell you. Because the guy you were looking for was too close. Right across the desk from you." In other words, Keyes's personal feelings for Walter clouded his rational judgment. Keyes responds, like the still-besotted lover, "Closer than that, Walter," to which Walter responds with his usual acerbic rejoinder suddenly turned poignant, "Love you, too." It is the film's last line.

In contrast, in *The Big Sleep*, relationships between men offer neither the warmth nor the emotional intensity that they seem to offer in *Double Indemnity*. Instead, the valorization of the Hawksian heterosexual romance absorbs all the hardboiled sentiment, which can be managed in part because of the hypermasculine rendering of Marlowe that Bogart offers and in part because of Vivian/Bacall's defatalization, as noted earlier. The film explicitly "smuggles" in suggestions of homosexuality—but to a different end. In the novel, murder victim and pornographer Arthur Gwynn Geiger is explicitly termed a "fag" (100). Production Code dictates would forbid a direct characterization of Geiger as homosexual, and as such the film uses the "code" Chandler also uses: the intensely Orientalized décor of Geiger's home and the unclarified presence of Geiger's male lover Carol Lundgren (referred to only as his assistant). Brian Gallagher notes that the film retains events from the novel—Lundgren's laying out of Geiger's body in a candlelit bedroom, his revenge murder of Brody—that make little sense without the existence of the relationship.

Annette Kuhn interestingly argues that Hawks is not merely tossing around homophobic stereotypes for "color," but that the film itself is working through a complex relationship with these transgressive desires. The mise-en-scène, she argues, "embod[ies] in distorted form elements displaced from, and unspoken and unspeakable within, the narrative" (94).[48] In the film, Marlowe returns repeatedly and often inexplicably to Geiger's home, a point Kuhn addresses: "Not only is this the site of Geiger's murder and of various other activities transgressive of institutional law, its mise-en-scène also constitutes a symptomatic representation of sexualities which, transgressing the law of patriarchy, are not consciously speakable in the text" (94). Kuhn's point is that, "The trouble, the disturbance, at the heart of *The Big Sleep* is its symptomatic articulation of the threat posed to the law of patriarchy by the feminine" (95). Kuhn's analysis, then, rests heavily on a notion of "smuggling." The film's complicated relationship to homosexual desire— a relationship of both disgust and fascination, of violence and obsessive attraction—plays out on two levels, with the narrative level seeking to mock or contain the same desires that lushly suffuse the film's visual aesthetic.

On a like note, Michael Walker suggests that the film's fundamental question is whether Marlowe is able to "purge himself of his obsession with the noir world and commit himself to Vivian as heroine."[49] Then, we can in fact consider Marlowe as the one who needs reformation on the text's "unconscious level." If, as Deborah Thomas offers, "film noir is most obviously about the blockage of men's emotions and the structuring of their sexuality by conventional norms of gender (toughness, ambition) and class (respectability, middle-class marriage)," then Vivian may need Marlowe to "fix" her, but Marlowe needs her as well; he needs her heteronormative, familial promise to save him from the dark fringes of the film's narrative.[50] In the novel, Marlowe's attraction to the untouchable and faithful Mona Mars poses no threat to his hermetic distance from the ties of heterosexual and patriarchal systems. Further, the novel can indulge safely in the detective's suggestive appreciation of other men: the noble Harry Jones who dies rather than exposing his no-good girlfriend to danger, the appealing gray-suited gangster Eddie Mars with whom Marlowe savors bantering. In the film's diegesis room is made only for a quick expression of praise for Jones, and Eddie Mars is turned into the villain and primary murderer. The tighter system of the film indulges in unarticulated expressions of Marlowe's more fugitive desires, through his perpetual return to Geiger's, as Kuhn points out, his excessive brutality with Geiger's gay lover, the dream-like quality of the mise-en-scène. But it is the film's narrative drive that seeks to draw Marlowe to Vivian as much as to draw Vivian to Marlowe. The two end up together with a promise of mutual reformation and interpellation, though not without a lingering doubt. After all, the film's last moment involves Marlowe and Vivian trapped in Geiger's house, surrounded by gangsters, waiting for the police. Sirens sound that should promise rescue, but Hawks lets the camera linger on the couple as they exchange anxious, wordless glances.

> *I was sitting in the empty theater. The curtain was down and projected on it dimly I could see the action. But already some of the actors were getting vague and unreal.*

> —Raymond Chandler, *The Little Sister*

Humphrey Bogart's physical mannerisms or tics—his famed baring of his upper gum, his leaning posture, his lisp—are often catalogued and discussed. Their deployment across films and characters attest to his status as a star whose persona, within a limited range, remained consistent through most of his post-celebrity performances. But one such tic plays a conspicuous role in his portrayal of Marlowe and operates as a key undercurrent in *The Big Sleep*. The tic in question is Bogart's rubbing of his earlobe.[51] It occurs generally in Marlowe's moments of reflection. As such, it often appears at scenes' ends, with Marlowe attempting to piece together recent events and is often followed by a snapping of fingers. It is significant, however, that this tic occurs not occasionally or regularly but in nearly every scene and in almost fetishistic fashion. It calls attention to his body. It makes *thinking* physical; cerebral activity is made bodily and visible. It is the counterpoint or corollary, in many ways, to Carmen's thumb manipulation in the novel and film: Carmen repeatedly bites her thumb, with Marlowe eventually insisting she stop. The thumb biting, in the novel in particular, disturbs Marlowe with its *vagina dentata* threat, or its suggestion of a female phallus. The film then gives Marlowe a gesture of his own to counter hers.[52] I think, however, that there is a residual effect to Bogart's "physical thinking"—one that would have probably not been felt by the film's original viewers. This tic now is absorbed into the tics that announce the tic-heavy actor's presence: the ear rubbing announces "Bogart," and asserts his gallery of tough characters. Marlowe disappears from the equation with each Bogartian gesture. Then, in a way filmmakers could never have intended, the instabilities of Marlowe's masculinity are effaced through this repeated advertisement of Bogart's impeccable record of unmitigated American masculinity. This yoking of Bogart with Marlowe eventually fixes the once-threatening lone urban white male as an eminently safe nostalgia icon suggesting a phantasmal time when "men were men," and tough white guys moved through the city with all the assurance their race and gender status accords, a status that, through the gauze of nostalgia, seems endless.

Then, the mid-forties film renderings of this figure find a use value in calcifying a surface counterfeit of the tough guy, an icon with increasingly faint connection to its original. Later noir, however, reflects a different choice in containing this "homme fatal." After this spate of films there would be another decade or more of noir, including more Cain and Chandler adaptations. But one can detect a distinct shift in the hard-boiled hero of noir in its later years. Paul Schrader articulates it by nam-ing the period of noir from 1949 to 1953 as that of "psychotic action and suicidal impulse. The noir hero, seemingly under the weight of ten years of despair, started to go bananas" (59). Citing films like *White Heat, Gun Crazy, In A Lonely Place* (with Bogart as an emotionally unstable screen-writer), *The Big Heat,* and especially the Spillane adaptation, *Kiss Me Deadly,* Schrader argues that the "psychotic killer" under the glass or on the margins of earlier noir now becomes the hero. Then, noir disappears. The urban white male loner has little place in films of the mid- to late-fifties. Schrader postulates that the "rise of McCarthy and Eisenhower demonstrated [that] Americans were eager to see a more bourgeois view of themselves. Crime had to move to the suburbs. The criminal had to move to the suburbs. The criminal put on a gray flannel suit and the foot-sore cop was replaced by the 'mobile unit' careering down the expressway. Any attempt at social criticism had to be cloaked in ludicrous affirma-tions of the American way of life" (61). While it seems Schrader's strokes are too broad here, neglecting as they do some of the compelling trends of the era, such as the rebellious teen films or the socially relevant pulp of B-genius Samuel Fuller, his point is apt. Where does the urban white male protagonist go as the fifties continue? Even while his presence leaves film in large part, it remains in pulp, but in different guises. Mickey Spillane's sociopathic detective Mike Hammer becomes the era's most widely consumed representation of the tough private eye, his sales dwarf-ing those of Chandler even at the latter's height of popularity. From 1947 to 1953, Spillane was the best-selling author in the country, and "almost single-handedly established a mass readership for the American paperback industry" (Naremore, 293 n. 9; 151). The author's popularity persisted—as evidenced by a successful television series, *Mickey Spillane's Mike Ham-mer,* from 1957–1960—even as the author ceased writing for ten years upon a religious conversion.[53] But the racist, misogynist, and jingoist Hammer is not the only "revision" of the tough guy of lore. The white male patrolling the mean streets does in fact receive sustained attention of a different kind in the systematic revision that another, perhaps unlikely novelist offers it.

The novelist is Chester Himes, known through the late forties and early fifties as a social protest writer but famed now in large part for his string of violently deconstructive riffs on the white masculinity endemic to hard-boiled fiction. Beginning in 1957, Himes slowly dismantled the universalist assumptions at the root of the hardboiled hero's compulsive insistence on white masculinity, and he would continue for twelve years, until the night-mare cityscape of his novels reached an apocalyptic standstill.

CHAPTER SIX

"The Strict Domain of Whitey"

Chester Himes's Coup

CHESTER HIMES'S 1959 CRIME NOVEL *RUN MAN RUN* CHARTS A BOOK-LONG chase between white New York City police detective Matt Walker and black porter Jimmy Johnson, an eyewitness to Walker's murder of two other porters. [1] Walker exhibits the familiar characteristics of hardboiled detectives like Mike Hammer, whose name his echoes. Hard-drinking, angry, embittered and quick to violence, Walker is the white man alone in urban space presented both from his own perspective (to which readers are accustomed) and, far more fully and exceptionally, from the perspective of the black men he terrorizes. He is seen, not just seeing. He is "othered" rather than merely navigating the foreign space of those whom he "others." The novel begins from Walker's viewpoint and in the conventional, clipped hardboiled style: "Here it was the twenty-eighth of December and he still wasn't sober. In fact he was drunker than ever" (7).[2] But within a few sentences, the subjective viewpoint shifts and readers are given Walker from the outside: "His lean hawk-shaped face had turned blood-red in the icy wind. His pale blue eyes looked buck wild. He made a terrifying picture, cursing the empty air" (7).

That it is so remarkable to see a white male character like Walker represented from the outside is a testament to the extent of hardboiled fiction's inherent whiteness and the affinity between narratorial perspective and the white male protagonist. It is a stunning shift in generic expectation when the narration in *Run Man Run* repeatedly melds into the perspectives of its black characters. While Himes's use of third-person narration enables a more elastic perspective spectrum than, for instance, Chandler's first-person narratives, the difference is not merely one of viewpoint. *Run Man Run* offers Walker's basic physical presence through a traditional omniscience, yet the physical description is not generic or objective but is instead infused with subjective interpretation, portraying Walker as a fiend characterized by diabolism and animalism.[3] In other words, he is represented as hardboiled readers might expect black characters to be. In fact, the phrase "buck wild" to describe his eyes rings faintly of ironic commentary on racist "black buck" imagery. The characterization persists when another physical description of Walker is offered through the eyes of the porter Fat Sam: "Covertly Fat Sam studied his face. Bright red spots burned on the high cheekbones and the lick of hair hung down like a curled horn. He couldn't make out whether the white man's eyes were blue or gray; they had a reddish tinge and glowed like live coals" (7).[4] The image of whiteness presented here is rife with diabolical connotations, from the fire references to the horn imagery. Moreover, the fact of his whiteness is insistently highlighted in the same curious way one sees in Raymond Chandler: through an emphasis on Walker's *redness*.

As discussed in chapter four, the blush, or the redness on white skin when pressure is applied, can serve as a visual assertion of whiteness, signifying precisely what is momentarily absent: whiteness. The red spots on Walker's cheeks mark him throughout the novel, but always when he is seen by another character, and seen as a threat. Jimmy likens Walker, upon first sight, to the Phantom of the Opera with his "*flushed,* taut, skeletonized face" (emphasis added, 30). The Phantom figure is typically characterized by whiteness, not a flush, but the flush seems to be precisely what underlines the skeletal appearance, what illuminates the whiteness, asserting it through contrasts, as we saw in chapter four's discussion of Philip Marlowe repeatedly pressing the flesh on the women he encounters, as if "testing" their whiteness. Later, Jimmy will describe Walker's "hard white jaws" as "wheat stalks on a snow-covered field" (30)—an image of ineluctable whiteness rivaled only by Raymond Chandler's description of Terry Lennox's eyes as "holes poked in a snowbank" (*The Long Goodbye,* 424). The physical whiteness of Walker, moreover, is presented as a distinct barometer of Walker's internal evil—the more dangerous he is at a given moment, the more the red flush points to his whiteness. An equivalence emerges between whiteness and evil that signifies powerfully on hardboiled fiction's comparable equivalence of blackness with degeneration or depravity.

The self-consciousness of Himes's play with the hardboiled genre and its white male protagonist emerges early in the text when the porter Fat Sam, soon to be Walker's first victim, begins referring to the police detective as "Master Holmes." The jolting juxtaposition of the famously urbane and intellectual literary detective with the drunken, brutish Walker functions as Himes's riff on detective fiction's permutations and the fissure between the literary detective and his real-life counterpart. But if Walker is the reality of the white urban detective, it is a reality Fat Sam still finds anachronistic. He laughs heartily at Walker when the detective insists (mistakenly, it turns out) that his car has been stolen. Walker blames the porters for the theft and Sam cannot contain his amusement:

> "Here you is, a detective like Sherlock Holmes, pride of the New York City police force, and you've gone and got so full of holiday cheer you've let some punk steal your car. Haw-haw-haw! So you set out and light on the first colored man you see. Haw-haw-haw! Find the nigger and you've got the thief. . . . Now chief, that crap's gone out of style with the flapper girl. It's time to slow down chief. You'll find yourself the last of the rednecks." (15)

Fat Sam's curious mix of Uncle Tomisms (calling him "Chief") and mockery (calling him a redneck in a class gibe) strike Walker at his very core. The text blends rapidly into Walker's enraged perspective: "Fat Sam's laughter had authority. It touched the white man [Walker] on the raw. He stared at Fat Sam's big yellow teeth and broke out with frustrated rage. Instead of scaring these Negroes they were laughing at him" (15). This laughter, the white man cannot bear. His dominion is not only challenged but utterly refused, and the laughter becomes emasculating. Fat Sam's reaction threatens the genre, the archetype of the urban white male, the power position of the white male in any interaction with an appointed Other; he names them all as outdated (hardboiled fiction originates in the 1920s, precisely the era to which Sam refers). Fat Sam is not playing by the rules on which these structures depend. Walker proceeds to take out a gun, and "To Fat Sam it looked as big as a frontier colt" (15), a winking reference to the hardboiled detective's generic predecessor: the Wild West or frontier hero.

Walker's subsequent shooting of Sam is awash in images of over-the-top whiteness. As Fat Sam falls, a container of "[t]hick, cold, three-day-old turkey gravy poured over his kinky head as he landed, curled up like a fetus, between a five-gallon can of whipping cream and three wooden crates of iceberg lettuce" (17). The food images are both white and white-bread, indicative of the racial politics of the restaurant where these black porters work, serving pseudo-homemade food to white patrons. Fat Sam dies amid the congealed, bilious, overwhelmingly white food made for white consumption, murdered by this figure referred to through these first few chapters only as the "white man"—nameless in the same way so many black characters remain nameless in hardboiled fiction ("the colored garage attendant," "the Negro"). In a sense, it is murder by whiteness. In turn, Walker proceeds to vomit after killing Sam, as if he had consumed the very food surrounding his victim—or the victim himself—and then expelled it, suggesting cannibalism. Himes, ever eager to drive an image over the top, has Walker feeling "spent" and thinking that a "couple of glasses of milk was what he needed" (18).

Hegemonic white masculinity, so threatened by Fat Sam's dismissive laughter, continues to fight for supremacy in the text. Walker stalks another black porter, Jimmy Johnson, seeking to eliminate the only living witness to his crime. Johnson hides until he can no longer tolerate hiding and decides to confront Walker and take his chances. Walker and Jimmy Johnson's battle culminates in a Wild West–style duel. At this stage, the relationship between the two men comes to resemble a more traditional masculine competition: that of the gunfight between the good man/bad man or white hat/black hat.

And, as befits the Western duel convention, a woman functions as the totem between the two men. Prior to the climactic dual, racial divides have intersected with gender binaries: the white detective Walker has become involved with Johnson's girlfriend, Linda Lou. In a reverse of Othello and Desdemona, it is the white man here who serves as the bewitcher, with Linda feeling "as though he were casting a spell over her" (129). While the black men in the text focus on Walker's skin color, Linda Lou, who is also black, fetishizes Walker's blonde hair. For her, Walker's whiteness and blondness equal innocence. In this way, Himes foregrounds the deeply ingrained cultural significations that equate whiteness with goodness and purity: "He looked so fresh and boyish in that atmosphere of crime and sex. He smelled of outdoors. She visualized him with a sweetheart somewhere. She'd be a nice girl who thought of marrying him. She'd rumple his shiny blond hair and caress him" (127). Linda Lou is seduced by Walker's whiteness, showing that the bond of race does not extend across genders in Himes's text. The black woman betrays her black man when the lure of white masculine power arises. Her attraction to Jimmy heightens the minute he straightens his hair in a bid to compete with Walker's white allure. In Himes's play with the hardboiled white protagonist, the villainy resides in the white man, and betrayal in the black woman, the easy dupe of the power of white masculinity.[5]

Himes's manipulation of the iconic white male detective effectively exposes the latent and manifest racism, violence, and paranoia that drive the figure, that in fact constitute him. Like Philip Marlowe and his melancholy ruminations on Los Angeles, Matt Walker notices how Harlem's encroachment has altered the neighborhood of his City College days: "Colored people were moving in and it was getting noisy. Already Harlem had taken over the other side of the street. This side, toward the river, was still white, but there was nothing to stop the colored people from walking across the street" (111). Walker's racial anxieties are complicated, however, as he then bemoans, "Poor colored people, soon they'd have to live on riverboats" (111). Walker quickly shifts again, however, to note the rise in Puerto Ricans, "crowding out the Germans and the French . . . who'd gotten there first. It was like a dark cloud moving over Manhattan" (111). He finally surmises, chillingly, "These poor colored people; they had a hard life, he thought. They'd be better off dead, if they only knew it. Hitler had the right idea" (112). Himes reveals how quickly sympathy slides into a more deeply seated fascism, and how tightly intertwined the feelings of racial pity and racial violence may be. Walker is completely unaware of his own racism, even denies it, cannot fathom how he has absorbed or been created by it. He is a product of a whiteness embedded so deep, made so invisible that he cannot see it, nor will the genre he represents allow it to be seen.

Then, the black servants who compose the barely-there background of white hardboiled texts dominate Himes's, placing readers in a position normally occluded from them: that of the black men who must live beside these white male loners. Himes's coup here is not just a demonization of the white tough guy, however. Instead, Himes offers something a bit more surprising: hints that the white tough guy is a dupe of a larger system—unnamed but *there*—that has created within him a sense of his own measureless entitlement and dominion.[6] Walker is a man stunned by his own racist aggression, wondering aloud to the porter he is about to kill, "I never had nothing against colored people. I don't know what made me think like that—suspecting you porters [of stealing my car]. I guess I must have just picked it up" (22). As Stephen Milliken suggests, "What menaces Jimmy . . . is not one sick young man in a privileged position [Walker], but the national psychosis of racism, fully exposed" (257). In this way, Himes unveils the racist violence of the tough guy at the same time as suggesting the larger social systems that perpetuate and depend on this racist violence, though precisely what those systems are remains murky, manifested only as an ominous hidden hand.

As discussed throughout this book, the tough guy occupied an idiosyncratic place in nuclear family–obsessed post–World War II America. He instigates anxiety as he does not fulfill the roles expected of a white male at that time: he is not a family head in a bourgeois setting in a time when masculinity is defined through one's role as patriarch and/or as the Organization Man or the archetypal man in the gray flannel suit. The lack of a familial or company role positions the tough guy dangerously close to the category of "Other." One way to diminish this threat is to create racial categories of alterity through a constructed "difference" from oneself. In this way, the white tough guy refuses marginality and asserts the primacy of the lone white male. And that process frequently takes the form of stripping black characters of their humanity, or, as is so frequently the case in hardboiled texts, stripping black male characters of their masculinity.

As we saw in chapter four, the treatment of black men in white hardboiled fiction has historically been dominated by fear and anxiety, echoing larger social perceptions of black masculinity held by white male America— i.e., black males are threats requiring violent suppression. Robyn Wiegman

(1995), among others, has provided an extensive recounting of this bloody history.[7] While these white male anxieties are deeply rooted in American culture, manifesting themselves historically in lynchings and race riots, they also appear in more subtle forms, such as narrative emasculations of black male characters, from the docility of Uncle Tom to the passivity of bowing servants and easily frightened porters in Hollywood film. As Wiegman relates, "In aligning representations of black men with the constructed position of women, dominant discourses routinely neutralized black male images, exchanging potential claims for patriarchal inclusion for a structurally passive or literally castrated realm of sexual objectification and denigration."[8] If, in hardboiled fiction, to be a black man is to be a weak servant or symbol of degeneration existing only to be beaten, Himes's intervention is to affirm an occluded black male subjectivity during a time in U.S. history when a sweeping civil rights movement was attesting to the change and tumult black leaders could inspire. This intervention becomes problematic in the slippery space between configuring emasculation as the ultimate punishment of black male subjectivity and configuring feminization as the greatest punishment of all; emasculation slides into feminization, suggesting that the only thing worse than being put in the position of a castrated man is being put in the position of a black woman.

"I Just Made the Faces Black": Himes and Noir Noir

In his autobiography, Chester Himes writes of the advice he received from the French editor who recruited him to write detective novels: "Read . . . Raymond Chandler. Read Dashiell Hammett. . . . You know how to do it. Read *The Maltese Falcon*."[9] Himes was already quite familiar with Hammett and Chandler, having read them while in prison, particularly in the legendary pulp magazine *Black Mask*.[10] When he sat down to write the first in his crime series, *For Love of Imabelle*, Himes recalled, "I became hysterical thinking about the wild, incredible story I was writing. . . . And I thought I was writing realism. It never occurred to me that I was writing absurdity. Realism and absurdity are so similar in the lives of American blacks one can not [sic] tell the differences" (*My Life of Absurdity*, 109). Thus, Himes articulates the expressionistic, darkly humorous style he adopted for his crime novels: a pastiche of hardboiled realism, cartoonish surrealism, and absurdist violence.[11]

In 1953, Himes relocated from America to Paris, where he lived and wrote for many years. This shift to expatriate life was accompanied, significantly, by a shift in Himes's writing. Already known as the author of a string of scathing "social protest" novels such as *If He Hollers Let Him Go* and *Lonely Crusade*, the expatriated Himes was commissioned by Série Noire editor Marcel Duhamel to write a series of nine police thrillers published in France, and only secondarily in America. Set in Harlem, all but one (*Run Man Run*) of these so-named romans policiers featured a police detective duo named Grave Digger Jones and Coffin Ed Johnson.[12] Himes's success with French readers far eclipsed his minor status in America: he was awarded the illustrious French literary prize, the Grand Prix de Littérature Policière, for his first detective novel, *La Reine des Pommes* (1958), published in 1957 in America as *For Love of Imabelle* (and later as *Rage in Harlem*).

Although Himes was writing these novels in distant France, they presented a simmering and often explosive portrait of 50s and 60s Harlem, U.S.A.[13] Moreover, they featured the first significant inroads by an African American author into the overwhelmingly white world of hardboiled fiction.[14] Entering the arena of hardboiled fiction, which is so dominated by— in fact, defined by—the central figure of the urban white man, Himes begins his confrontation with the genre's racism not only through his creation of black detective heroes but by supplanting the constantly shifting terrain of the traditional white hardboiled hero. In its place, he sets his novels entirely within the black neighborhood that served only as a temporary exotic interlude in Chandler, Hammett, or Spillane.

Himes would later write that when he finished *For Love of Imabelle* he realized it was not a detective story but, he writes, "Maybe . . . an unconscious protest against soul brothers always being considered as victims of racism, a protest against racism itself excusing all their sins and major faults" (*My Life of Absurdity*, 111). This awareness inundates Himes's detective novels, which "protest" with perhaps even more rigor than his social protest novels because they serve as over-the-top but cut-to-the-bone exposés of an American literary tradition that celebrates American white maleness through the marginalization and vilification of appointed Others.

Himes famously wrote that he too was a tourist in Harlem, having never lived there for any length of time, but that "The Harlem of my books was never meant to be real; I never called it real; I just wanted to take it away from the white man if only in my books" (*My Life of Absurdity*, 126). Thus, choosing to write these Harlem detective novels is a radical act for Himes, an act of literary theft with political resonance. He not only attempts to reclaim Harlem, liberating it from tales of racial exoticism or black authenticity, but he also infiltrates a tremendously popular but overwhelmingly white genre—hardboiled fiction—and shakes it to its white core. If, as Edward Margolies suggests, "For Himes, the genre is the message,"[15] then Himes's use of hardboiled conventions to present a vision of black masculinity takes on added resonance, for, as we have seen, hardboiled fiction is a historically racist tradition with a long history of taking great pains to ignore, diminish, or stereotype black men.

As discussed in chapter one, hardboiled fiction's racist roots extend back to its connection to like-minded frontier or cowboy traditions in which the white man navigates the wilderness, fighting off threats posed by the Other. It should then come as no surprise that the endlessly revisionary Himes should riff on Western allusions in small and large ways, through self-conscious references to Matt Walker's frontier colt (*Run Man Run*) or having a character refer to his detective-heroes Coffin Ed and Grave Digger as "those damned Wild West gunmen."[16] Robert Crooks traces a transformation of the Western and frontier novels to contemporary urban spaces, arguing for a shift in frontier ideology from the idea of the "far side of the frontier" to the Others collected and contained in urban centers, like Los Angeles, "where population densities and the size of minoritized communities threatened individualist ideologies, since the collective experience of exploitation lends itself to collective resistance or rebellion" (178). As such, the "other side of the frontier" has shifted from "enemy territory" to be conquered to "pockets of racial intrusion, hence corruption and social disease to be policed and contained—insofar as the 'others' threaten to cross the line" (178). The word "contained" is apt. The hardboiled protagonist consistently exhibits horror at the increase of minorities in the cities he navigates, as with Philip Marlowe, as with Himes's Matt Walker. But Himes's main innovation is his repositioning of the hardboiled consciousness. No longer narrated from the perspective of the marginal white man moving between "pockets of racial intrusion," his novels force the reader to reckon with, amid all the expected hardboiled lingo and motifs, the perspective of both black law enforcement and black criminals. The lines of containment are no longer warning signs of the exotic and imminent dangers of the Other; instead, the lines are prison bars of socioeconomic privation, viewed from within the cell itself.

Himes would later call his crime novels mere recapitulations of the hardboiled formula wherein he "just ma[de] the faces black, that's all" (quoted in Milliken, 251).[17] But that process of making the faces black is more than a minor riff on a genre. It in fact overturns the genre, exposing its very whiteness. By "making the faces black" Himes calls attention to hardboiled fiction's dependence on othered racial groups, calls attention to its very whiteness, making visible what had been invisible, what had been presumed, exposing the racist structures that do not just emerge in the hardboiled tradition but that, in large part, constitute it.

One of Himes's most stunning twists is his shift from starkly pseudorealist (James M. Cain, Horace McCoy, Jim Thompson) or cynical-romantic tones (Chandler, arguably Hammett) of certain hardboiled texts to an often slapstick, baroquely violent, and grand guignol style. This generic shift is about more than style, however. Himes critiques Chandler and other hardboiled writers and the white privilege of their protagonists through a hyperbolic and expressionistic portrait of black masculinity—particularly that of his detective protagonists—dramatized to absurdist ends. The hardboiled tradition's containment of black masculinity through the marginalization, emasculation, or minstrelization of black male characters is turned on its head by Himes, who infuses the hardboiled style with a pair of fierce black authorities (the police detectives Grave Digger and Coffin Ed) and a gallery of aggressive black male grifters, thugs, and gamblers.

As such, I would like to proceed through a discussion of Himes's intervention by asking the question, What does Himes accomplish by "making the faces black"? The answer to a question that seems to be about genre reveals itself more fully to be about historical constructions of race and gender. That is, I want to pursue how Himes's "making the faces black" gesture responds to an anxiety, given voice in hardboiled fiction, over racial and gender alterity. The particular anxiety to which Himes responds is a fear and suppression of black heterosexual masculinity. The hyperbolic response often treads on women and gay men in order to fight that suppression, thereby recapitulating white hardboiled structures in surprising ways.

The Containment of Black Masculinity

"It is a fantastic, masculine work. . . . American male writers don't produce manly books. Himes's autobiography is that of a man."

—John Williams on Himes's autobiography,
The Quality of Hurt (1971)

Critical attention to Chester Himes has generally taken two paths: considerations of how Himes alters (or *whether* he alters) the genres of hardboiled or detective fiction, or considerations of Himes's status and difficulties as an African American writer in post-war America and Europe. In other words, genre or biography tend to dominate the discussion. While biographic and especially generic concerns obviously matter, I want to use them as inroads into areas of Himes's work less discussed, less interrogated. Himes's intervention goes beyond his forefather role in black detective fiction and his revisionary position within the white hardboiled tradition. Himes is not simply tweaking or updating a genre but is working through large paradigms of race and gender. Specifically, Himes does important damage to the white male figure who controlled so many of the texts—literary, cinematic, cultural—of this period, although not without ancillary casualties, as we will see. These texts confront the figure of the tough guy and respond to that figure through various, and often troubling in their own right, configurations of masculinity, male heterosexuality, and violence.

In order to probe these interventions, I will approach Himes's romans policiers, produced through the late fifties and into the sixties, through what at first might seem an abstruse connection: Himes's relation to the Cold War principle of containment. The term "containment" originates with the famous "long telegram" that American chargé d'affaires in Moscow George Kennan composed in 1946. In it, Kennan suggests that the perceived Soviet threat can be managed if "contained" within a specific sphere of influence. The following year, Kennan, writing under the name "Mr. X," outlined the containment strategy in an article for *Foreign Affairs* entitled, "The Sources of Soviet Conduct." In particular, he advocates "long-term, patient but firm and vigilant containment of Russian expansive tendencies."[18] One might hear echoes of the shoring up of masculinity in Kennan's insistence that "such a policy has nothing to do with outward histrionics: with threats or blustering or superfluous gestures of outward toughness." The United States must "remain at all times cool and collected."[19] Hysteria must be avoided in favor of cold control, in a canny alignment with the gender crises we have located in the hardboiled texts leading up to the Cold War.

Recently, critics such as Andrew Ross (1989) and Elaine Tyler May (1988) have worked with Kennan's influential writings and shown the extent to which we can locate recapitulations of the foreign policy strategy of containment within 50s domestic culture.[20]

In his parsing of the "long telegram," Andrew Ross delineates two meanings of containment: the Cold War military efforts to restrain Soviet expansionism (a meaning Kennan disavowed) and what Kennan says he was attempting to advocate, the internal "political containment of a political threat" (quoted in Ross, 46). Ross clarifies the distinction, observing, "The first speaks to a threat outside of the social body, a threat that therefore has to be excluded, or isolated in quarantine, and kept at bay from the domestic body. The second meaning of containment, which speaks to the domestic contents of the social body, concerns a threat internal to the host which must then be neutralized by being fully absorbed and thereby neutralized" (46). In the latter meaning, Ross points out, we find hints of the Red Scare to come. All told, Ross demonstrates the extent to which containment was always already domestic, in Kennan's explication as well as in the culture of hysteria that embraced—or sprung from—it.

Likewise, Elaine Tyler May contends that containment is the central ideological apparatus through which 1950s America operated, writing, "More than merely a metaphor for the cold war on the homefront, containment aptly describes the way in which public policy, personal behavior, and even political values were focused on the home" (14). According to May, atomic anxiety, the long-term effects of the Depression, and post-war fears about gender role dissolution led to an intensity of focus on the role of domestic life as a potential panacea. While women suffered in their restrictive role in the home, men suffered too—most inconspicuously from a loss of individuality or agency as so-called Organization Men in the "mass, impersonal white collar world" (21). Home, May contends, provided these men with a space in which they might have autonomy and even dominion: "Where . . . could a man still feel powerful and prove his manhood without risking the loss of security? In a home where he held the authority, with a wife who would remain subordinate" (88).

May's argument, however, relies heavily on a study whose participants were entirely white (and chiefly Protestant and middle class). But, she insists, "[B]lacks as well as whites participate in the same postwar demographic trends" (13)—i.e., baby boom, rising marriage rates, lower divorce rates. Although May gestures toward statistics that emphasize these demographic trends among African Americans, her analysis of domestic containment relies almost exclusively on the testimony of white bourgeois survey respondents and white bourgeois culture, from ads created by and for white bourgeois consumers to predominantly white bourgeois publications (i.e., *Ladies Home Journal*), and to other scientific studies centered on white bourgeois respondents, such as the Kinsey Report.[21]

My aim here is not to criticize May's sample, but to extend still further her investigation into the containment trope beyond the self-contained population of which she makes use. It is precisely the ease with which one can carve out the population of white bourgeois families for assessment that points to the extent to which this population's containment strategies were successful. What do these containment strategies mean for one of the groups so anxiously cordoned off? I want to stretch her use of containment through a consideration of the way the 1950s hardboiled texts of Chester Himes might be responding to containment: the containment of black masculinity in post-war, Civil Rights–era America.

In this vein, I offer that Himes was confronting what he saw as the "containment" of black masculinity in the 1950s through his romans policiers, both through his choice of genre and his revisions within that genre. Within hardboiled fiction, the white man confronts internal threats in the urban space, threats that are narratively quarantined, crushed, or effectively neutered through devices of plot and characterization or through representational diminishment. Himes sees the black man as the primary internal threat in both the genre and in America more largely. What is particularly interesting here is the degree of marginality the urban white male of hardboiled fiction (and film noir) occupies in a fifties culture that views white masculinity almost entirely through the figure of the family head, the patriarch.[22] The marginality of the tough guy figure within the new post-war culture, of course, is merely symbolic, while the containment of non-whites was deeply institutionalized. At the same time as gathering civil rights efforts were begining to show results, such as with the desegregation of the U.S. armed forces in 1948, other brands of institutional racism were actively buffered from reform. Consider the quiet and insidious policies of the Federal Housing Administration, which, in the late 1940s until 1968, participated with great vigor in restrictive covenants and a practice of drawing red lines on maps to "identify the boundaries of changing or mixed neighborhoods" and green lines around suburban areas.[23] Home loans were doled out according to these red and green lines, resulting in the flourishing of white suburbia and the fomentation of urban ghettoes for ethnic minorities.[24] These modes of containment of minority populations dominated the era, and the atmosphere of racial oppression was a key factor in Himes's move to Europe. From this distant perch, he wrote his series of novels that sought to strike back at the quintessential white urban genre of hardboiled fiction— the genre that had so insistently, so anxiously shored up white masculinity through the ritual emasculation of non-white men.

Himes writes in his autobiography,

> To describe a black man, the blackness of his skin, black sexual organs, black shanks, the thickness of his lips, the aphrod[i]siacal texture of his kinky hair, alongside the white breasts, pink nipples, white thighs and silky pubic hair of a white woman, no matter how seriously intended, is unavoidably pornographic in American society. Given the American background, the bare colors create a pornography of the mind. Just to put a black man into a white woman's bed is to suggest an orgy. (*The Quality of Hurt,* 285)

Himes is referring specifically to his challenges in writing *The End of a Primitive,* a novel focusing on a relationship between a black man and a white woman, but his foregrounding a black male physicality and sexuality points to a representational absence Himes is eager to redress. Interestingly, however, Himes goes on to discuss how his aim with *The End of a Primitive* is to expose the white American perception of "the American black" as an ignorant "idiot"; it becomes instantly clear what Himes means by "the American black": black American *men.* He goes on to say, "Obviously and unavoidably, the American black man is the most neurotic, complicated, schizophrenic, unanalyzed, anthropologically advanced specim[e]n of mankind in the history of the world. The American black is a new race of man; the only new race of man to come into being in modern time" (*The Quality of Hurt,* 285). The slippage in each sentence between "American black" and "American black man" is quite significant. The black *man* in America is Himes's focus, his abiding concern. Further, as the description of the sexual encounter between the black man and white woman above underlines, it is in fact the American black *heterosexual* man who forms Himes's locus—not just in *The End of a Primitive,* but, as will become apparent, in his revision of the hardboiled hero as well.

Willfried Feuser writes that Himes's concern with black protest is "matched only by his concern with black heterosexuality."[25] But in fact the two are deeply connected for Himes. Black protest comes about by and for black heterosexuality—or, to be more precise, black *male* heterosexuality. Feuser might well have merely quoted Himes himself, who wrote in his introduction to *Black on Black:* "These writings are admittedly chauvinistic. You will conclude if you read them that BLACK PROTEST and BLACK HETEROSEXUALITY are my two chief obsessions."[26] For Himes, the two projects are profoundly linked to each other and to black masculinity.

Indeed, Himes constructs a potent black masculinity in a genre and era that denies it. The means by which he achieves this masculinity are various. He approaches a genre that offers only caricatures of black Americans and constructs a hardboiled universe with black characters at the center, with whites afforded only peripheral presences, if presences at all. He offers his revision on the hardboiled protagonist through his characterizations of the tough black police detectives Coffin Ed and Grave Digger, both legendary and feared within Harlem. In turn, he invests Coffin Ed and Grave Digger with none of the destabilizing gender ambiguity that emerges as hysteria in Chandler or Cain's protagonists (though Himes's cops, especially Coffin Ed, become more hysterical as the series continues, as we will see). Lastly, Himes defatalizes the gender-threatening femme fatale, by making her a source of humor, a locus of abuse, or a caricature.

"Hard, Harlem Characters": Revising the Genre

"Lay off for your own good. That boy spells trouble."
"What of it? Trouble is our business."

—Chester Himes, *Blind Man with a Pistol* (1969)

To trace Himes's response to literary and cultural containments of black masculinity, I want to consider first how Himes moves black male characters from representations peripheral and stereotypical (as icons of degeneration or service industry employees) to the center, revamping the genre's white core. To this end, I will consider a scene already discussed in chapter four, the opening chapter of Chandler's *Farewell, My Lovely* (1940), situated alongside what I offer is Himes's deconstructive twist on Chandler and the hardboiled tradition in his second roman policier, *The Real Cool Killers* (1958).

As noted in chapter four, *Farewell, My Lovely* is one of the most common texts to which critics turn in arguing for Chandler's racism, due largely to its opening set piece in a black-managed and -patronized bar. This opening scene has proven deeply influential to the detective genre.[27] An interview in which Himes recalls 1940s Los Angeles indicates that he was in fact familiar with the scene in question: "Some of Raymond Chandler's crap out there, he writes in *Farewell, My Lovely*, he has this joker ride abut in the Central Avenue section. Some of that's very authentic—it was like that. A black man in Los Angeles, he was a servant" (*Conversations with Chester Himes*, 54–55).

Farewell, My Lovely's opening scene in Florian's bar, then, seems very much on Himes's mind when he begins *The Real Cool Killers* with an episode that distinctly recalls it. The novel, which features a youth gang called the Real Cool Moslems, centers around Coffin Ed and Grave Digger's attempts to solve the murder of a white man on Harlem streets. It begins, like *Farewell, My Lovely*, with a white man in an all-black bar. But while Chandler's Moose Malloy barrels into Florian's in what is presented as knightly pursuit of his woman, Himes's white man—who is called "the Greek," in an echo both of Marlowe's client at the start of *Farewell, My Lovely* and of the murder victim in Cain's *The Postman Always Rings Twice*—is savoring the Harlem nightlife, watching women dancing with "cynical amusement."[28] He is explicitly presented as the "only white person present" (5) and is described, like Malloy, as physically large. Suddenly, a black patron announces dangerously, "Ah feels like cutting me some white mother-raper's throat" (6). The patron then pulls out a knife and accuses the white man of "trying to diddle my little gals" (6). At the time, this threat seems unprovoked, but much later we find out that this white man is actually a predator who has been luring teenage black girls with money and then beating them with a bull whip.

In *Farewell, My Lovely*, the white man in the black space dominates all whom he encounters. The white man in *The Real Cool Killers*, however, ends up running for his life. First, the knifeman threatens him, then, a drug-addled young man on the street begins chasing him, accusing him, in play, of being involved with his wife. Soon after, the Real Cool Moslems street gang, in their Arab disguises, begin chasing him, too. Eventually, the white man is murdered by, we learn in the novel's last pages, a young black girl who was one of his victims and feared that her friend, coincidentally Coffin Ed's rebellious daughter, would be next.

So what can we make of the differences between the two similar scenes? Chandler's stylized violence, with its descriptions of black men with hands the "size and color of a large eggplant" (9), revels in the sheer power of the white man to command the space of the Other. Like a one-man imperialist invasion, the white Moose Malloy dominates all the tough black men in his path, breaking a bouncer's belt "like a piece of butcher's string" (9) and hurling the large man across the room smack into the baseboard. In contrast,

Himes takes his racialized violence and pushes it to absurdist ends, exposing its roots in white male phantasy. In his version, the black bartender does not roll his eyes in minstrel-fashion and hide but instead, seeing a high roller white customer threatened, pulls out a fireman's ax and cuts off the arm of the threatening knifeman at the elbow. As Himes writes it, "The severed arm in its coat sleeve, still clutching the knife, sailed through the air, sprinkling the nearby spectators with drops of blood, landed on the linoleum tile floor, and skidded beneath the table of the booth" (8). Clearly, the white man is no longer knight but degenerate predator. More crucially, however, the black men in Himes's version physically dominate the scene, not as exotics but as active agents in the violence. It is not a reversal, with Himes merely ennobling his black characters or transferring power from the white man to the black men. Instead, the black characters respond in a variety of ways, not one programmatic one—the bartender exhibiting cut-throat business savvy, the angry patron exhibiting unchecked hostility, the crowd exhibiting horror, amusement, disgust. The scene refuses the dynamic of dominator/dominated, and instead offers an infusion of bodily force and masculine presence, for better or worse, for motivated or random violence.

The hardboiled protagonists of Chandler or Hammett or Cain cannot conceive of a black male potency that could not be crushed by the appropriate white male. Black masculinity, when it is even granted, is a strawman set up to be knocked down by the white male, the Moose Malloy. Far more commonly in hardboiled fiction, however, black masculinity is not conferred representation at all. To imagine black masculinity is to imagine black humanity, which is inconceivable. Or, in Himes's terms, to imagine black masculinity is to imagine a black phallus, which would explode the genre entire. Then, for Himes, to subvert the genre, or the figure of the white male in the urban space, is not only a matter of "making the faces black"; it is not only a matter of Himes exposing a universal whiteness and foregrounding blackness. Himes's hardboiled intervention is also about gender. He is not just making the faces black; he is making blackness masculine.

"We're the Men": Grave Digger Jones and Coffin Ed Johnson and the Re-Race-ing of Masculinity

"It's the white men on the force who commit the pointless brutality," Coffin Ed grated.
"Digger and me ain't trying to play tough."
"We are tough," Grave Digger said.

—Chester Himes, *Cotton Comes to Harlem* (1965)

The first introduction of the detective heroes Coffin Ed Johnson and Grave Digger Jones occurs fifty-two pages into Himes's first *roman policier*, *For*

Love of Imabelle, and the physical description, aside from Coffin Ed's soon-to-be-scarred face, varies very little in the ensuing seven novels: "Both were tall, loose-jointed, sloppily dressed, ordinary-looking dark brown colored men. But there was nothing ordinary about their pistols. They carried specially made long-barreled, nickel-plated, .38-calibre revolvers, and at the moment they had them in their hands" (2). Coffin Ed and Grave Digger rule the streets of Harlem on the strength of their custom-made Wild West–style guns, and through these two figures, Himes forges a space for an agentic, potent black man in the hardboiled novel, even to the point of parody or self-conscious absurdism.

According to Stephen Soitos, Himes's detective fiction follows the generic conventions of the hardboiled tradition in that it is characterized by "violence, uneven handling of gender, and a cynical attitude concerning corruption and class" (142). Certainly, Coffin Ed and Grave Digger do resemble the hardboiled protagonist of yore in their connections to Wild West sheriff tradition. The novels' fetishization of guns echoes the phallic obsessions with weaponry we find in Spillane, among others. Likewise, Coffin Ed and Grave Digger's violent reactions to criminals or suspects (mitigated only by their larger concerns for common folk) echo the hostility found in many a hardboiled dick. And, of course, Himes's novels are saturated with the misogyny built into the genre, where women are either sirens or saints.

But, as Soitos argues, Himes does "create something different" (142). Formally, Himes rejects the common use of first-person narrator for which Chandler, Cain, and scores of others opted. In addition, as Soitos notes, Himes transforms the detective figure from a lone white male working outside the system to two black men with families working for the Law (144). Readers are no longer following a lone man, but two partners, bound by professional and personal loyalties. It is a striking difference. Whereas Marlowe or Cain's Walter Huff or Frank Chambers have no confidantes, no friends in whom to confide (the reader comes closet to filling that function), Himes offers two men working in concert and often opening up to each other. The loner has become a pair of bonded loners, isolated from the community in many ways, but not from each other. While Cain and Chandler's first-person narratives position the reader as confidante and even interlocutor, Himes's choice of third-person narration means the reader is rarely privy to the direct personal testimony of his heroes, save through "overhearing" the feelings one of the men expresses to the other. The confidante role the reader assumes in Cain and Chandler is filled by the partner in Himes. As Coffin Ed and Grave Digger rarely indulge in non-professional conversations of any length, even these moments are scarce.[29] As such, the reader is at a more distanced relation from Coffin Ed and Grave Digger, often no closer than s/he is to the criminals. (Himes in fact often brings the reader closer to the criminals, and devotes more pages to their experiences.) This distance allows the reader a safe detachment from both criminals and cops, both the supposed bad guys and the supposed good. Moral codes erected with comparative assurance in Chandler become eminently more complex for the reader. The "knight" wandering the "mean streets" has become diffuse and the codes by which he lived are exposed as facile and naïve given the complexities that multiple viewpoints reveal.

So the loner becomes a duo and the reader's role shifts. But still further, Coffin Ed and Grave Digger are not fatherless bachelors like Marlowe or Walter Huff or Frank Chambers. They are family men with wives and children in Queens, giving them, as Stephen Soitos points out, "a social history most hardboiled loner detectives do not possess" (144). The social history is fitting, given Himes's efforts to give narrative space to representations of a black American community so occluded in other texts. All told, however, little attention is paid to the detectives' families.[30] While Coffin Ed and Grave Digger are placed within more conventional domestic situations, readers are given little access to that domesticity. We spend far more time in Marlowe's breakfast nook or Walter Huff's Los Feliz apartment than in Coffin Ed and Grave Digger's Queens environs.

A last crucial distinction is that, unlike hardboiled icon Philip Marlowe, Coffin Ed and Grave Digger are not ennobled. In *For Love of Imabelle,* the narrator tells us, "They took their tribute, like all real cops, from the established underworld" (59), which would be unimaginable in Chandler, who rarely even allows Marlowe to accept earned money. Of course, this reference, in the first of the series, is never repeated in the later novels—in fact, in *Blind Man with a Pistol,* the narrator claims, "they hadn't taken a dime in bribes" (97). But the refusal to beknight his heroes, who often hurt witnesses, brutalize women, and even (accidentally) shoot innocent bystanders, seems important to Himes: he will not sanctify these men, and in fact the texts seem eager to present a Harlem so oppressed and cordoned off as a wasteland that moral grace has been made impossible by dire social conditions: "Blind mouths eating their own guts. Stick in a hand and draw back a nub. That is Harlem" (*For Love of Imabelle,* 111).

However limited their agency may be by Harlem's blight, the source of Coffin Ed and Grave Digger's power is clear; it operates on fear and intimidation, as "Folks in Harlem believe that Grave Digger Jones and Coffin Ed Johnson would shoot a man stone dead for not standing straight in a line" (52).[31] Grave Digger and Coffin Ed had to be "tough to work in Harlem. Colored folks didn't respect colored cops. But they respected big shiny pistols and sudden death. It was said in Harlem that Coffin Ed's pistol would kill a rock and Grave Digger's would bury it" (59). In fact, Coffin Ed and Grave Digger wear their phalluses in their holsters, knowing their guns must be visible, conspicuous, for them to have any respect or control in the community. The spectacle, and the ritual, are entirely necessary: their incantations of "Straighten up!" and "Count off!" ensure a temporary order in the midst of crimes or potential crimes. The white hardboiled hero is not feared and has limited agency; he lacks a public role or shuns it. He is in the margins of his white world. Coffin Ed and Grave Digger are not. They are legends. But their status is far from secure and they are not viewed as heroes, merely as threats, dangerous conduits between the Harlemites and the white police/law.

Agency is configured in Himes as the power to make people move, to control situations. In his Harlem, one achieves this agency through a threatening display of masculinity, and through not just the promise of masculine force, but the evidence of it. Coffin Ed and Grave Digger's power differs from that of the series of gangsters and gamblers who achieve fame in Harlem, such as *Cotton Comes to Harlem*'s Johnny Perry, whose car inspires a frenzy of awe in neighborhood children. Coffin Ed and Grave Digger are not admired for their power, nor is the civic purpose behind it valued. Their power to intimidate is a tool used to impose an order neither respected nor generally desired—thus, the difficult position in which Coffin Ed and Grave Digger find themselves. Feared and yet not particularly respected, the two cops are viewed by Harlemites as Others despite any claims to brotherhood. Likewise, Coffin Ed and Grave Digger are far from integrated into the predominantly white and racist police force. The fellow white policemen, however, do see Coffin Ed and Grave Digger as useful subaltern figures: "The white cops looked at Grave Digger and Coffin Ed with the envious awe usually reserved for a lion tamer with a cage of big cats."[32]

Manthia Diawara writes that Himes focuses attention on the "way of life that has been imposed on black people through social injustice, and that needs to be exposed to the light" (263). Himes in effect uses hardboiled motifs, or noir, as Diawara puts it, in order to illuminate the hand-to-mouth reality of black urban life. Diawara is perhaps too quick to lay aside Himes's reveling in the stylization of sex and violence, the hum and purr of hardboiled speak. But his central contention that Himes "uses the conventions of the genre to subvert its main tenet: that blackness is a fall from whiteness" (263) proves crucial. Diawara's argument attends to how black filmmakers use noir to alter the "relation between light and dark on the screen as a metaphor for making black people and their cultures visible" (263), but the point is apt in relation to Himes's novels. No longer will black characters be mere signposts of a Fall, of a neighborhood lost, or a character's lapse from innocence. That is not to say, however, that Himes is not interested in portraying Harlem as the inevitable and deeply distressing result of socioeconomic collapse, although the cause here, the hidden hand, is not internal

moral failure or racial inferiority. The cause is the white hegemony determined to suppress and isolate the black community.

What needs to be taken into account, however, is the extent to which the
radicality of Himes's move, the insistence on visibility and a potent social criticism, is mitigated by rampant misogyny and homophobia that reveals an insistent need to vivify and calcify a black heterosexual masculinity through
displays of violence against gay men and against women. This dynamic is what
threatens to yoke Himes closely to the same tradition he so actively critiques.

Whither Imabelle?
The Castration of the Femme Fatale

> Her skirt had hiked up to her sky-blue nylon panties, exposing a
> smooth brown sheen of legs above her stockings. The violent exertion
> had opened her pores and a strong compelling odor of woman and per-
> fume came up from her like scented steam.
>
> —Chester Himes, *Run Man Run* (1959)

In his article on novelist Walter Mosley and his detective hero Easy Rawlins,
Roger Berger discusses Rawlins's often violent sexual encounters (including
the rape of his wife) through the lens of stereotypes of rapacious black male
sexuality. He cites bell hooks on the subject: "The portrait of black masculinity . . . perpetually constructs black men as 'failures' who are psycho-
logically 'fucked up,' dangerous, violent sex maniacs whose insanity is
informed by their inability to fulfill their phallocentric masculine destiny in
a racist context."[33] Berger's point is that Mosley ends up recapitulating white
tough guy detective fiction dynamics, revealing what remains "latent" in
Raymond Chandler; specifically, a "relentless misogyny coupled with an inability or unwillingness to question the underlying 'law' of white patriarchal
society" (288). Berger cites hooks's point that "black men who embrace patriarchal masculinity, phallocentrism, and sexism . . . do not threaten or
challenge white domination . . . but reinscribe it."[34]

When we consider this point in relation to Chester Himes, it is illumi-
nating yet problematic. Almost completely absent from white hardboiled fiction (far more so than black men), black women appear prominently in
Himes's novels. By and large, however, only two kinds of women recur:
vamps and survivor-victims. While this bifurcation of female characters is
quite in keeping with prior hardboiled fiction, one might expect the revisionary Himes to overhaul these generic expectations as he does others, rather
than merely transpose the familiar white female stereotypes onto his black
women characters. What is a striking revision is the lack of a "true" femme
fatale in these texts. Although Himes's novels all offer sexually attractive and

enticing female characters—for whom men will often go to great lengths—these women lack the power of the femme fatale to unsettle, destabilize, and disempower male characters. The femme fatale is in effect defatalized.

This defatalization begins with Himes's very first novel in the series: *For Love of Imabelle*. The description of Imabelle, the siren at the center of the mystery, maintains the hardboiled tradition: "She was a cushioned-lipped, hot-bodied, banana-skin chick with the speckled-brown eyes of a teaser and the high-arched, ball-bearing hips of a natural-born amante" (6). While Imabelle is a classic spiderwoman in that she maneuvers the men around her, playing them off each other to best advantage, Imabelle's effect on men is quite different. She may have a hypnotic allure in the eyes of her sap, Jackson, but Imabelle embodies no uncanny threat or lure, no power to match that of those grand machinators we find in *Double Indemnity* or *Farewell, My Lovely*.[35] The difference is often quite subtle, as in scenes such as the one in which Imabelle must sway Jackson, who knows she has betrayed him, from hurting her. The text reads, "[She] looked at his face and *read him like a book*. She ran the tip of her red tongue slowly across her full, cushiony, sensuous lips, making them wet-red, and looked him straight in the eyes with her own glassy, speckled bedroom-eyes" (emphasis added, 114). Allowing the reader the perspective of the femme fatale would have been unthinkable in Chandler or Cain. Witnessing her calculation ("[she] read him like a book") defuses her power. The spell is broken. Compare the Imabelle episode with Walter Huff's interactions with Phyllis in *Double Indemnity*, first near the beginning of the novel: "[I] put my arm around her, pull[ed] her face up against mine, and kiss[ed] her on the mouth hard. I was trembling like a leaf. She gave it a cold stare, and then she closed her eyes, pulled me to her, and kissed back" (13). And then, at the novel's end: "She smiled then, the sweetest, saddest smile you ever saw. I thought of the five patients, the three little children, Mrs. Nirdlinger, Nirdlinger, and myself. It didn't seem possible that anybody that could be as nice as she was when she wanted to be, could have done those things" (113). Huff has gained no more insight into Phyllis, is still just as mystified and chilled by her at the end of the narrative as he is at the beginning. She is unfathomable to him and he follows her to death.

But it is not merely the new access to the woman's perspective that, perhaps counter-intuitively, limits the power of the would-be femme fatale in Himes—after all, that access is in large part the result of the move from first-person to third-person omniscient narration. More fully, Himes's female characters do not seem to exert any narrative control, do not seem to inspire any crippling hysteria nor the agency that such a power would afford them. Instead, they tend to inspire violence, which, however evincing a male hysteria, proves quite successful in crushing their own agency in any situation.

Although liberating in the sense that female characters are no longer mere projections or vessels of male anxiety, these women unfortunately also inspire the same kind of violent treatment that traditional femmes fatales inspire, but without the accompanying power to subvert or deflect it, as we will see.

In its most generically typical manifestation, violence against women in Himes's hardboiled novels demonstrates masculine loyalty.[36] Grave Digger assaults Imabelle in order to avenge the injury done to his partner, even though Imabelle was not the actual cause of Coffin Ed's wounds. Interestingly, Grave Digger's assault on Imabelle emerges not from any physical threat she presents, nor any smug or taunting words from Imabelle, but from her flirtatious self-presentation. He sees her sitting "quietly with crossed legs showing six inches of creamy yellow thighs, as she contemplated her red-lacquered fingernails" (144). Seeing Grave Digger, she gives him a "bedroom look" and "hitche[s] her red skirt higher, exposing more of her creamy yellow thighs." Grave Digger responds,

> "Well, bless my big flat feet. . . . Baby-o, I got news for you."
> She gave him her pearly smile of promise of pleasant things to come.
> He slapped her with such savage violence it spun her out of the chair to land in a grotesque splay-legged posture on her belly on the floor, the red dress hiked so high it showed the black nylon panties she wore.
> "And that ain't all," he said. (144)

The scene continues with Grave Digger standing over Imabelle "in a blind rage" (155), contemplating his partner in the hospital. He is wearing Coffin Ed's pistol and actually has it in his hand without even remembering how it ended up there; "it was all he could do to keep from blowing off some chunks of her fancy yellow pratt" (155). One could easily read Grave Digger's violent reaction as hysterical, as an analogue to Philip Marlowe's tearing up of his bed after the femme fatale has been in it in *The Big Sleep*. But the narration here is fully aligned with Grave Digger, enjoining the reader to see Grave Digger's actions as justified and noble. In turn, Grave Digger's violence serves to dominate and humiliate, unlike what we find in Marlowe.[37] The narration lingers over Imabelle's prone figure, her red cheek, her skirt thrown up, her "mouth a mangled scar in a face gone bulldog ugly" (156).

Imabelle's abasement is savored by the narration, even as Grave Digger, far from enjoying the spectacle or his own power, is consciously out of control, his body moving "jerkily as he holstered the pistol. His tall, lank frame mov[ing] erratically like a puppet on strings" (155). Imabelle does not hold the strings to the puppet; her visage is merely a catalyst, not a carrier of power, just as Mary Anne Doane defines the femme fatale (2). But although the femme fatale is that which needs to be evacuated in traditional noir narratives, Imabelle and her counterparts do not pose enough threat to warrant such a desperate execution. They are effectively diminished through humiliation or brutality. Moreover, the femme fatale is typically characterized by the epistemological crisis she inspires: she is a mystery who compels unraveling. Himes's women are not confounding mysteries. Their motives are generally transparent and their "bad behavior" quite explicable, and often their only means for survival. I am by no means suggesting some kind of nascent feminist impulse in Chandler or Cain versus a crude misogyny in Himes. I want to show instead that part of the conferral of a spectacular black masculinity in these texts is an accompanying diminution of female power and a use of female humiliation to shore up that masculinity. In other words, we have a different version of the same effort found in white hardboiled fiction, where shoring up masculinity occurs at the perpetual expense of women, either through demonization or humiliation.

Further, in Himes's rendering, the male-male relationship supercedes all others, and inspires the most emotional responses. When Walter Huff shudders and cries over Phyllis in *Double Indemnity*, we can presume it is her lethal lure that inspires it. But when Grave Digger reacts to Imabelle so violently in the above scene, it is Coffin Ed's violation that seems to be the true source of his anger, with Imabelle as a symbol of the brutal criminal subculture that surrounds both men. As mentioned earlier, however, it is important to remember that Imabelle serves as a symbol despite the fact that she is actually not responsible for Coffin Ed's scarring. Later, Grave Digger will kill the man responsible for his partner's injury, but it is a moment of far less potency: "Grave Digger said, 'For you, Ed,' took dead aim with Coffin Ed's pistol held in his left hand, and shot the dying killer through the staring left eye" (179). It has often been remarked upon that, in Bram Stoker's *Dracula* (1897), the narration slathers over Lucy Westenra's death for pages, while dispatching the Count in a neat sentence. Likewise, Grave Digger's revenge murder feels terse compared with his attenuated abuse of Imabelle.

We must also note that Imabelle's sexual invitation infuriates Grave Digger, seems a threat to his control of the situation. He must humiliate her. At the end of the novel, Grave Digger tells the district attorney to let Imabelle go because, "Ed and I will square accounts. We'll catch her uptown some day with her pants down" (189). The choice of the "pants down" idiom is appropriate given that the vehicle of humiliation seems to be an exposure. But it is not just Grave Digger's need to humiliate women in this particular way. Throughout the series (twice in *Blind Man with a Pistol* alone), women are seen in the humiliating position of their skirts flown in the air, their upper thighs or pubic area exposed, having been hit or pushed to the floor by men, particularly Coffin Ed and Grave Digger. Is the sight also meant to titillate readers in its expression of potency? The suggestion seems to be that the spectacle of female genitalia, far from inspiring a crippling castratory fear, actually "unveils" and therefore disempowers the woman.[38] Further, Stephen Milliken points out, "The function of these women . . . is, quite simply, to be desired and to be frightened. They offer literary thrills that have obvious and direct affiliations with the realms of sex and sadism" (250). And female fear is decidedly sexualized, as when *Cotton Comes to Harlem's* glamorous beauty Iris comes upon Deke, her boyfriend, restrained by gunmen, and "Nausea came up in her like the waves of the ocean and she gritted her teeth to keep from fainting. Her terror was so intense it became sexual—and she had an orgasm. All her life she had searched for kicks, but this was the kick she never wanted" (142).[39] Iris is puritanically punished for her independent, pleasure-seeking lifestyle. But more acutely, her fear is sexualized, suggesting that female fright is pleasurable to women, is sexually fulfilling, desired.

The question remains, what drives Himes's treatment of black female characters in a text so eager to redress generic containments of black male characters? The answer seems in part to lie in just that attempt to foreground a black masculinity. Built into Himes's unleashing of black masculinity is a construction of that masculinity as dominant, dominating, heteronormative, and unimpeachably black. Coffin Ed and Grave Digger, after all, are described as "almost as dark as the night."[40] Moreover, these episodes featuring violence against black women repeatedly occur with women who are "light-skinned," or termed "yellow." The scenes of violence seem designed to reassert blackness, maleness, heterosexuality through a ritual containment of light-skinned blacks, of women, and of gay men (a point to which I will return). Himes's revisionary role in the hardboiled tradition then limits itself to instituting a secure black hetero-masculinity invulnerable to any "weaknesses" or "feminizations"—whether of gender, skin color, or sexual orientation.

The persistent yoking of sexual attractiveness and light skin is far from Himes's invention, and is reflective of very real social conditions favoring light-skinned black men and women. It is not Himes who is asserting that light-skinned black women are more desirable; he is rehearsing the cultural beauty standards of the day.[41] But the link these texts offer between *morality* and skin color among women is more alarming. As Robert Skinner notes, "The archetypal Himes woman is a seductive, curvy, amoral sexpot with very light skin. . . . At worst she may be a murderess but at best she will be a liar, a cheat, or a faithless lover."[42] The police lieutenant in *For Love of Imabelle* calls Imabelle "penitentiary bait," thinking to himself, "It's these high yellow bitches like her that cause these black boys to commit so many crimes" (157). Such a blame-laying of particularly black male violence on light-skinned black women recurs through the novels and goes a long way to explaining Grave Digger's harsh treatment of Imabelle in comparison with the black man actually responsible for his partner's injuries. With Imabelle, he believes he has located the impetus and the source.

A parallel emerges in the narrative treatment of the character of Iris in *Cotton Comes to Harlem*. Although she is presented more positively than Imabelle, with an emphasis on her hardscrabble survival skills, Iris is the requisite "high yellow" moll, and is treated as such. Initially, when Grave Digger and Coffin Ed suspect that Iris tipped off her criminal boyfriend on the phone, Grave Digger

> slap[s] her with such a sudden violence she caromed off the center table and went sprawling on her hands and knees; her dress hiked up showing black lace pants above the creamy yellow skin of her thighs.
>
> Coffin Ed came up and stood over her, the skin of his face jumping like a snake's belly over fire. "You're so goddamned cute—" (28)

Again, the narrative offers up the ritual humiliation of the skirt flying up and the skin exposed, with the added suggestion of the genitalia nearly revealed, concealed only by lace. But Iris, unlike Imabelle, fights back and hits Coffin Ed, inducing him nearly to strangle her before Grave Digger restrains him: "Grave Digger stood looking down at [Iris and Coffin Ed] . . . thinking, *Now we're in for it;* then thinking bitterly, *These half-white bitches*" (29). The narrative grants Iris the awareness that the anger she incites is about a desire to dominate, and that such a desire can take a sexually violent form. She later tells Coffin Ed, "If I could only rape you, you dirty bastard" (124).

But what of Iris's skin? Her "yellowness" becomes one of the vehicles by which Coffin Ed and Grave Digger humiliate her. Her pride in her appearance, and her refusal to align herself with the black community are punished; the detectives, supposedly for the purposes of the investigation, force her to don the guise of a "black woman." Grave Digger tells her, "Make yourself into a black woman and don't ask any questions" (125). Grave Digger and Coffin Ed even buy her the clothes to fit the part, going to Blumstein's Department Store, buying a dress, dark tan lisle stockings, a white plastic handbag, gilt sandals, and a hand mirror. Also, at Rose Murphy's House of Beauty they purchase "some quick-action black skin dye and some make-up for a black woman and a dark-haired wig" (122). Iris then prepares herself and appears looking like a "fly black woman in a cheap red dress" (125). Grave Digger warns her, "Watch your language and act dignified. . . . You're a churchwoman named Lotus Green and you hope to go back to Africa" (125). When Iris's friend Billie sets eyes on her, she sees only a "woman who looked too black to be real, dressed like a housemaid on her afternoon off" (130). When she realizes it is Iris, she says Iris looks like the "last of the Topsys" (130). At Billie's mirror, Iris begins "frantically rubbing her face to see if the black would come off. Yellow skin appeared. Reassured, she became less frantic" (130–31).

Part of Iris's humiliation derives from the class status she is bid to take on in her masquerade. She appears as a housemaid when she is actually a well-appointed lady of leisure. But also implicit in the costuming of Iris is the belief that to "pass" as a churchwoman, she must have darker skin. We see a familiar association between dark-skinned black women and noble victimage, and light-skinned black women and duplicity. Such a divide does not emerge in the characterization of black men, although dark-skinned black men, beginning with *For Love of Imabelle*'s Jackson, tend to be dupes or naifs.

We are seeing a different but analogous representation of women than we find in the hardboiled texts of Chandler and Cain. In Himes, light-skinned women are insistently the cause of violence and purveyors of duplicity. Like the male hysteria that femmes fatales inspire in Cain and Chandler, Himes's "yellow" women (and some of the dark-skinned women as well) inspire textually sanctioned violence and suffer textual humiliation by having their skirts lifted up over their heads, by having them experience pratfalls, by having their wigs torn off or clothing ripped salaciously. They do not successfully destabilize masculine assurance, and their humiliation actually serves to assure masculine potency, even if that potency, in the case of Coffin Ed especially, is presented as hair-trigger and uncontrolled. What emerges is a parallel race and gender bias in Himes: the Other who needs to be killed or exiled in white hardboiled fiction has been replaced by the "high yellow woman" who needs to be humiliated, her sexuality punished, her body violated for titillation and control.

While less assiduous a strategy than Himes's deployment of humiliated vixens, the treatment of gay men in these texts performs a similar function. Coffin Ed and Grave Digger's attitude toward gay men is articulated at one point as that of distanced tolerance: "[Coffin Ed and Grave Digger] had no use for pansies, but as long as they didn't hurt anyone, pansies could pansy all they pleased. They weren't arbiters of sex habits. There was no accounting for the sexual tastes of people. Just don't let anyone get hurt" (*Blind Man with a Pistol,* 29). This highly mitigated assertion of tolerance is certainly more than one expects from Philip Marlowe or a Cain character. But, by and large, as Stephen Soitos notes, Himes "reserves his most vitriolic attacks for black gay men . . . fall[ing] back on the traditional hardboiled convention of a masculine viewpoint that links hatred of homosexuality and sadistic mistreatment of beautiful women and presents it as status quo, acceptable behavior" (58). The difference between the white hardboiled treatment of homosexuality, as discussed in chapter three, and what we find in Himes is compelling, however. The tense homophobia of Philip Marlowe and Dashiell Hammett's Sam Spade, their hysterical and often violent reactions to gay men is firmly echoed in Himes, but in Himes it is conjoined with an unexpected exoticism—unexpected because it seems to mimic rather cogently the exoticist treatment of black settings so prevalent in white hard-boiled fiction.[43]

Let us consider briefly Himes's presentation of a Harlem gay club in *All Shot Up* (1960). Perhaps no less sensationalist than any of Himes's over-the-top nightclub scenes, the spectacle still smacks of an exoticism more typically found in Van Vechten–style portraits of 1920s black decadence or primitivism:

> The usual Saturday night crowd was gathered, bitching young men wearing peacock clothes with bright-colored caps, blue and silver and gold and purple, perched atop greasy curls straight from the barbershops at $7 a treatment. And the big, strong, rough-looking men who made life wonderful for them. But there was not a woman present.
>
> Coffin Ed was not a moralist. But their cliquish quality of freezing up on an outsider grated on his nerves. (27)

Coffin Ed attempts to secure information from the crowd, reminding them, "We're all colored folks together" (27). But the only response is a lone soft giggling and silence. The attempt at racial solidarity fails, the implication being that for these patrons, sexual orientation trumps race. Coffin Ed breaks down the wall of silence only by beating up patrons until he receives the information he needs.

Similarly, in *Blind Man with a Pistol,* the narrative offers a description of a white man watching "the sissies frolic about the lunch counter in the Theresa building" (15). Allowing for a certain amount of narrative immersion into the perspective of the white man, the description still rings sharply of exoticism:

> Their eyes looked naked, brazen, debased, unashamed; they had the greedy look of a sick gourmet. . . . Their voices trilled, their bodies moved, their eyes rolled, they twisted their lips suggestively. . . . Their motions were wanton, indecent, suggestive of an orgy taking place in their minds. The hot Harlem night had brought down their love. (15)

Both episodes interestingly echo Hemingway's depiction of Lady Brett's gay friends at the *bal musette* in *The Sun Also Rises.* Coffin Ed's annoyance at the "freezing up" of a group of gay men recalls Jake Barnes's unnerved and complicated disgust at the "clique" surrounding Brett. The in-group exclusion from which both men are forbidden couples with an exoticization smacking of hardboiled anxiety over feared identification with a fellow marginal group. In other words, anxiety over a perceived ravenous sexuality is strangely coupled with a feeling of marginality over the lack of inclusion in the group, over the insularity of the group being surveyed from the outside.

In his fascinating reading of Hemingway's *bal musette* scene, Ira Elliott suggests that Jake's response derives less from disgust at "homosexual behavior" than anxiety over the implied "gender-crossing"—the "rupture between a culturally-determined signifier (the male body) and signified (the female gender)."[44] For Jake, his "sexual inadequacy and the homosexual gender transgression are therefore conjoined: neither can properly signify 'masculinity'" (82). While Coffin Ed and Grave Digger are not so wounded, their masculinity seemingly iron-clad, there does seem to be a similar anxiety over being aligned with gay men. In a case involving the murder of a white gay man in Harlem, Coffin Ed bemoans,

> "Too bad there ain't a mother-raping law against these freaks."
> "Now, now, Ed, be tolerant. People call us freaks." The grafted skin on Coffin Ed's face began to twitch.
> "Yeah, but not sex freaks."
> "Hell, Ed, it ain't our business to worry about social morals," Grave Digger said placatingly, easing up on his friend. He knew folks called him a black Frankenstein, and he felt guilty because of it. If he hadn't been trying so hard to play tough the hoodlum would never had a chance to throw the acid into Coffin Ed's face.
> "Leave 'em dead." (*Blind Man with a Pistol,* 108)

Coffin Ed's fear as a figure marginalized for his race (within the police force and in the country at large), for his job as cop (within police-hating Harlem), and for his wounded face, is that he will be grouped with another marginality: homosexuals. For Grave Digger, at least for the moment, solidarity can be located in marginality and the term "freak" can be a leveling gesture, but for the scarred Coffin Ed, distance is not just desired but required.

Such fears reach their peak and their most traditionally hardboiled in the last of Himes's series, *Blind Man with a Pistol* (1969). Coffin Ed's treatment of a young black gay man, John Babson, replicates Sam Spade's excessively and uncontrollably rough treatment of the gunsel Wilmer in Hammett's *The Maltese Falcon* and Philip Marlowe's of the young hood Carol Lundgren in Chandler's *The Big Sleep.* Babson, like the maligned "high yellow" femmes fatales, is light skinned, and exotically featured: "His eyes had a slight Mongolian slant, giving his face a bitsa look, a bit of African, a bit of Nordic, a bit of Oriental" (86). Coffin Ed makes an excuse to go back to Babson's apartment after the official and fruitless questioning has ended. Coffin Ed proceeds to beat Babson, supposedly for information. When Babson insists sneeringly that he is as "clean as a minister's dick," Coffin Ed responds,

"That's too mother raping bad" (91). Then Coffin Ed becomes hysterical: his "burn-scarred face twitching like a Frankenstein version of *the jerk,* as he moved in with his long nickel-plated, head-whipping pistol swinging in his hand. 'Your ass pays for it'" (91). Coffin Ed's bodily reaction is crucial, exhibiting a lack of physical control that ruptures the cool facade of unquestioned masculine authority. Moreover, his reference to his swinging gun and Babson's "ass" bristles with suggestions of rape and humiliation.

Lastly, gay men in these texts are often presented as exhibiting a frank emotionalism that Coffin Ed and Grave Digger find embarrassing and seemingly emasculating. When a gay bartender begins hysterically laughing ("Emotions exploded") as an expression of grief over the loss of his lover, the white detective "cursed" and Grave Digger "banged the meat edge of his hand against the steering wheel. The muscles in Coffin Ed's face jumped like salt on a fresh wound as he reached across the back of the seat and double-snapped the bartender with his left hand" (51). Once again, Coffin Ed's body reacts spastically, uncontrollably to these gay men when they fail to submit to his demands and reject his authority, and when they merely express emotions. Both gestures are seen as dangerous, potentially emasculating, and powerfully unsettling.

Then, although Himes's femmes fatales are not fatal, are not powerful catalysts of male terror, we still witness male hysteria in Himes, as we see in Coffin Ed's responses to these gay characters. Consider the similarity between Coffin Ed's reaction to John Babson and the scene in *The Heat's On* when Coffin Ed, mistakenly believing that Grave Digger has been murdered by white hoodlums, assaults a young black female witness. As with Grave Digger's beating of Imabelle, the motive for the violence is presumably homosocial loyalty—the desire to avenge the wounding of a partner. Coffin Ed strips the witness and cuts a shallow line across her throat, presumably to inspire her to talk. But the act is clearly more than a police tactic: "[Coffin Ed] knew that he had gone beyond the line . . . he knew that what he was doing was unforgivable. But he didn't want any more lies. She lay rigid, looking at him with hate and fear. 'Next time I'll cut to the bone,' he said."[45]

In chapter two, I considered how hardboiled texts operate through a structure of white male hysteria in the face of femininity or threats to a traditional gender binary. The hysteria emerges through seemingly inexplicable bodily reactions, such as Walter Huff's uncontrollable wailing, or Philip Marlowe's losses of consciousness. These hysterical reactions reappear in peculiar ways in Himes's romans policiers. The site of the bodily hysteria resides, with increasing intensity as the series continues, in Coffin Ed's facial scars and, beginning with *Cotton Comes to Harlem,* Grave Digger's neck. In the first novel in the series, *For Love of Imabelle,* Coffin Ed is hideously scarred when acid is thrown at him by a criminal. This scarring proves the first and most consistent point of distinction between the two cops. Outwardly, Coffin Ed is scarred and inwardly, he is transformed. Coffin Ed becomes the more dangerous man, the one with the hair-trigger temper and itchy trigger finger. Grave Digger often has to restrain him from his more excessive acts of violence, which go so far as shooting a young man who throws water at him (he mistakes it for acid, underlining the traumatic effect of his initial injury). But the major difference between the two men— the wound from which Coffin Ed suffers—begins to dissolve when, in a later novel, Grave Digger too is wounded, shot in the neck. His throat wound sparks more threatening behavior and the two men become more difficult to differentiate. In fact, their scars both pulsate, virtually come alive when danger is imminent: "The skin on Coffin Ed's face was jumping with a life of its own and Grave Digger felt his collar choking as his neck swelled" (*Cotton Comes to Harlem*, 93).

The bodily response is just not some sixth sense but is implicated in the structure of hysteria also found in Cain and Chandler. As with other hardboiled heroes, Coffin Ed's and Grave Digger's bodily responses, radiating from their wounds, is the outward display of inner hysteria, and is a symptom of feeling out of control. Consider how the wounds are both stereotypically masculine and feminine simultaneously. First, they are essentially "war wounds," indicating courageous survival yet signifying the trauma of the event that caused them.[46] Likewise, the wounds themselves carry feminine significations, such as the equation of scars with female genitalia, and old associations between the neck and the entrance to the womb. Less obscurely, the wounds also point to a feminine weakness as they signal the men's fright in the face of danger.[47]

The difference between Coffin Ed and Grave Digger's hysteria and that of the white tough guys derives most plainly from the respective relationships to femininity. Coffin Ed and Grave Digger are rarely responding to a femme fatale or a perceived gender instability in these hysterical moments of rage or fright. In fact, these moments are driven instead by frustration, personal humiliation, or the threat of violence from other men. For instance, in *Cotton Comes to Harlem,* the potential femme fatale, Iris, spurs this brand of hysteria, with Coffin Ed and Grave Digger exhibiting neck-bulging, scarhopping anxiety in response to her antics. This hysteria, however, emerges not because she is an object of desire or an obvious physical threat. Instead, she provokes them in minor ways, such as tipping off her hoodlum boyfriend or withholding information. Their furious response seems less about her potency as a dangerous beauty than about her positioning as a stumbling block in their investigation, and the fact that the stumbling block is one of "*[t]hese half-white bitches*" (29), as Grave Digger refers to Iris after the incident. Not only is their work being occluded, but occluded by just the kind of woman who inspires so much violence, sinking so many black men into lives of crime.

But these are not the only occasions for hysterical reactions. Other times, the hysteria emerges from strictly personal and hurtful slights, such as the striking moment in *The Crazy Kill* when a criminal tells Coffin Ed that his scarred face resembles that of Frankenstein's creature. Coffin Ed becomes enraged. After Grave Digger restrains him and calms him, Coffin Ed "le[ave]s the room without uttering a word, st[ands] for a moment in the corridor and crie[s]." [48] Not long after, in the midst of a conversation about the case, Grave Digger tells Coffin Ed, "What you need is to get good and drunk one time," to which Coffin Ed responds by rubbing his scarred face and saying "in a muffled voice," "And that ain't no lie" (110). Release is what is required, and the hysterical symptoms signal emotions that are bursting through, that can no longer be kept in check. The containment of black male emotions and rage proves oppressive, resulting in a hysteria that spreads through the body and overtakes it.

In a sense, however, this dynamic is precisely what we find in Cain and Chandler, with the only difference being that the hysteria is not *triangulated through* a woman. In Himes, the projection of the femme fatale, the apex of the triangle, disappears and we have a direct correspondence between male fears over threats to masculinity and bodily hysteria. The common denominator in these instances appears to be feelings of impotence. The detectives' work is frustrated, their appearances mocked, their community disintegrates before their eyes, these "high yellow women" instigate crimes and distance themselves from other black Americans, their agency is limited. As we see in *The Heat's On,* when Coffin Ed attempts to avenge the shooting of his partner, the hysteria is propelled by feelings of helplessness: "Coffin Ed was in a crying rage, caught up in an impotent self-tormenting fury that gave to his slightly disfigured face a look of ineffable danger. . . . Tears were seeping from his eyes and catching in the fine scar ridges between the patches of grated skin on his face as though his very skin was crying" (101). The body speaks in this case, and speaks volumes. A combination of masculine loyalty and fear of impotence, fear of an inability to exact vengeance is also coupled with a fear of public ridicule. Coffin Ed remembers Grave Digger's revenge-murder of the man who scarred him with acid, a thought that leads Coffin Ed to "th[ink] of the effect [of Grave Digger's death] on the Harlem gunslingers. He knew if he backed down now, he'd never live it down" (127). Public status is then one of Coffin Ed's major fears, one of the primary causes of his hysterical reaction: he would not be able to "live it down" in the eyes of the community. An unwritten code of masculinity and the importance of its public display drive Coffin Ed.

It is also important to consider that these moments of hysteria occur with increasing frequency and intensity as the series goes on. The question begs, is the detectives' growing psychic estrangement a necessary result of their long immersion in crime or of the constant demands of masculine spectacle? Their increasing instability is surely a testament to changing times, to the transition from the late 50s civil rights era to the late 60s Black Power and Nation of Islam movements. But we find an analogue in more generic concerns. If these novels speak to the containment of black masculinity but rely on a traditionally white genre and a politically limited positioning (as police officers) for the heroes, perhaps the series reaches its own limits. It cannot contain these men or the community of Harlem thereby represented. The genre is overstuffed by Himes and explodes.

"Them Doctor Toms": Black Cops as Heroes

"What hurts me most about this business is the attitude of the public towards cops like me and Digger. Folks just don't want to believe that what we're trying to do is make a decent peaceful city for people to live in. . . ."

—Chester Himes, *The Heat's On* (1966)

Peter J. Rabinowitz, in his influential article "Chandler Comes to Harlem: Racial Politics in the Thrillers of Chester Himes," offers a most compelling argument for how Himes's hardboiled novels transformed the genre. Rabinowitz's central contention is one of ideological difference between Chandler and Himes, a difference that reflects a racial divide. He argues that in Chandler's novels, there is no tidy resolution because the evil that set the plot in motion cannot be expunged. As opposed to an Agatha Christie tale of the lone disturbed murderer who is expelled from the community at the novel's end, Chandler's perpetrators are part of the order itself, and in fact, "from Chandler's perspective . . . order was not *interrupted* by evil, but was itself the very source of evil."[49] Marlowe's heroism then derives from his loner position, a position of purity through isolation. But, Rabinowitz argues, "What the novels obscure . . . is the question of under what conditions this brand of heroism is possible" (21), as in Himes's novels, "even though [Grave Digger and Coffin Ed] are caught up in a world of Chandlerian evil, Chandler heroism is not an option" (21). Their team status further emphasizes Himes's belief in the unavailability of the role of loner hero in the social conditions he wishes to evince. In the end, the Chandler formula must be refused because Coffin Ed and Grave Digger "do not have the luxury of the Marlowe option, of detaching themselves from the criminals and the victims among whom they work" (23). Coffin Ed and Grave Digger, although part of the Order as enforcers of the law, are aware of the bonds of blackness, loyalty to the Harlem community, to fellow black citizens—a loyalty by which Marlowe need not be hampered.[50]

Indeed, one of the byproducts of Himes's choice to make Coffin Ed and Grave Digger police detectives is their unusual position in relation to the Harlem community. To be marginal within Harlem is to be black yet still work for "the Law," the source of so much oppression for Harlemites. So Coffin Ed and Grave Digger are at once part of the community and also at odds with it. The question remains: Why make Coffin Ed and Grave Digger *police* detectives? The fact that Coffin Ed and Grave Digger rarely appear until well into each novel and generally occupy far less narrative space than his other characters reveals the extent to which Himes is more interested in his gallery of crooks, con men, and con victims.[51] But what would it mean for Coffin Ed and Grave Digger to be, for instance, private investigators, like Philip Marlowe, himself a former investigator for the district attorney? What does Himes gain through making them "the Law"?

Their role as cops situates Coffin Ed and Grave Digger in an interesting space between white and black, between Institutional (and corrupt) Order and the (often criminal) oppressed. They must negotiate between two worlds. As such, they often face conflicting loyalties, as when we see in their regret over all the Harlemites who lost money in the Back-to-Africa robbery: "Everyone has to believe in something; and the white people had left them nothing to believe in. But that didn't make a black man any less criminal than a white; and they had to find the criminals who hijacked the money, black or white" (*Cotton Comes to Harlem*, 26).

Many critics have weighed in on this curious positioning. Stephen Soitos links up the detectives's liminal role to what he terms double-conscious detection, a literary trope he traces from Pauline Hopkins and J. E. Bruce to Himes. The term "implies . . . the overriding consciousness of African American detective characters of both their position as blacks in America and their connection to trickster themes in black folklore" (150). In Himes, for example, "Coffin Ed and Grave Digger are double-conscious detectives in the sense that they themselves are trickster figures who bridge the white and black worlds, using both to their advantage" (150). Soitos then uses this reading to explain the widening chaos of the later novels, as "With Himes double-conscious detection becomes increasingly darker as the tricksters dupe fellow blacks and, in the end, themselves" (150). John M. Reilly, in turn, makes the claim that Himes's choice to make his heroes police detectives is a "commentary on the difficulties of moral survival in the community. The tough guys [Coffin Ed and Grave Digger] need the protection of police sanction, for were they private eyes inevitably they would offend the people who profit on Harlem's fundamental misery as much as they offend small time crooks."[52] Likewise, Robert Crooks points out that "[s]elf-policing of a community, even an oppressed one, is not necessarily complicitous with the oppressive order" (182), particularly when the crimes combated are ones that promulgate capitalist exploitation. Anxious about individualist impulses in Grave Digger and Coffin Ed, Crooks argues that it is "because of their need to resist the manifestations of individualist competition as criminal entrepreneurship that Himes's police detectives . . . work in their own communities" (182). Crooks adds that Coffin Ed and Grave Digger, as "insiders," cannot "mount any consistent resistance to white oppression. Rather . . . they seize opportunities where they arise, never working directly against the interests of the police department, but twisting situations and police procedures in such a way as to subvert them and turn them to the use of the Harlem community" (187).

Himes himself weighed in on his choice in a 1970 interview with Michel Fabre:

> MF: I had the feeling that in all your detective stories the real heroes are Coffin Ed and Grave Digger, even though they're cops.
>
> CH: Sure, that was my aim, to make the detectives the heroes.
>
> MF: Doesn't it create a strange situation, since they work for establishment?
>
> CH: They do, but they don't. Most genuine black detectives are reactionary, fascist-minded, and very unlikeable [sic]. I had to create a pair of characters the reader would like.
>
> MF: So you don't think they betray the black community?
>
> CH: Not the way I created them. This is what makes my creation unique. In real life, black detectives are commonplace in black neighborhoods, but they're brutal and reactionary. The interesting thing is that official law enforcement only moved into the black ghetto during this century. When black people were first free, and lived in ghettoes or in communities of their own, white policemen never went into those communities. black people had to create their own laws to protect themselves.
>
> MF: So you don't believe that Coffin Ed and Grave Digger are traitors to their race?
>
> CH: Not the way I've portrayed them.
>
> MF: So, Coffin Ed and Grave Digger could be said to represent the kind of detectives that should exist, living in the community, knowing the people, enforcing law, dealing humanely with everyone.
>
> CH: This is what I thought. I replaced a stereotype. I've taken two people who would be anti-black in real life, and made them sympathetic. (*Conversations with Chester Himes*, 85)[53]

This exchange is interesting for a variety of reasons. Himes explicitly states that Coffin Ed and Grave Digger are meant to be heroes, however, they are

not grittily realistic figures but fantasy figures fighting for justice that in actuality goes unrealized. In reality, nobody occupies this difficult position between poles. In fact, it seems Himes is saying no one could. He has created
a fictional structure that defies social realities as he sees them and thereby
comments on the oppressive absurdity of black life in a racist America.

In a sense, by making his black heroes cops, Himes is retaining, although
revising, the hardboiled hero's marginality.[54] To be marginal in Harlem is to
be aligned with the law. Coffin Ed and Grave Digger occupy a liminal space,
black yet Other, just as Marlowe or Frank Chambers are white yet Other.
But Himes confronts difficulties as the series continues and his racial politics as well as the racial politics of the day change. The position Coffin Ed
and Grave Digger occupy becomes increasingly untenable. Himes contains
Coffin Ed and Grave Digger by making them bound to authority, but
Himes's novels show the difficulty of keeping up the conceit. Much as Philip
Marlowe's anachronistic position in the late fifties world of *Playback* (1958)
feels forced and pained, Coffin Ed and Grave Digger are self-consciously ancient in *Blind Man with a Pistol*, bemoaning the youth of the day and their
anarchic violence. Moreover, the later novels in the series rely less and less on
hardboiled formulas or mystery structures; instead, they become increasingly
violent and absurd, with the crimes becoming less and less solvable and the
law proving more and more to be a panoptical star chamber—an unholy al-
liance of the white Syndicate, white politicians, and white society.

Edward Margolies writes that Coffin Ed and Grave Digger's position as
enforcers of a racist hegemony may "in part explain the excesses of violence they employ on persons (almost always black) whom they suspect of
wrongdoing. Are they directing their rage away from themselves for serving an oppressive society? Are they expressing subconscious hostility toward their own people? Must black cops be tougher on blacks than white
cops? Or is their brutality really justified?" (69). Margolies speculates that
Himes was unable to answer these questions himself, and thus stopped the
series. Margolies's argument is compelling, but his suggestion that Himes
could not answer the very problems his texts raised seems a bit overstated.
I would argue instead that Himes's later novels prove ultimately to demonstrate the limits of the hardboiled tropes, their collapse in the midst of social change, their anchoring in imperialist and patriarchal traditions that
glamorize and empower the figure of the lone white man who must confront the primitive horror of the Other. His series shows that, to a large extent, the hardboiled hero *needs* to be out of time or history. As Raymond
Chandler once noted, "The whole point is that the detective exist complete and unchanged by anything that happens" (quoted in Mason, 91).
Himes introduces contemporary political unrest into the genre, and the
genre shows the strain.

In the end, then, the race and gender tensions Himes critiques and indulges explode the genre, a genre that cannot maintain Himes's revisions nor the historical changes he seeks to reflect or feels bound to reflect. The last complete novel in the series, *Blind Man with a Pistol,* unravels before the reader's eyes, the purported mystery it offers never resolved. The generic structure cannot contain the mutations. The difficult role Himes uses to replace that of the white tough guy—the black police detective—results in an unstable position that proves impossible to sustain in the midst of the social change and revolutionary zeal Himes envisions or reacts against. Violence is no longer random but focused, directed toward political ends, no longer absurd for its own sake, but absurd to mirror a larger, quite real absurdity Himes felt. As Stephen Soitos writes,

> Himes redefined the use of violence in the detective novel tradition, using it not only for drama but as a weapon for political change. Himes's use of violence in his detective series starts off as a reflection of white and black culture out of control . . . by the late sixties he began to consider violence—that is, black violence as retribution for white racism—as the only legitimate response for black America . . . violence in his stories moved at this time from random comic horror to an overt radical means to political ends. (171)

Himes effectively creates or at least writs large a new tradition, setting the stage for Walter Mosley, Ishmael Reed, and others to follow, and his war against containments of black masculinity can be felt in scores of texts to come even as direct political commentary receded with the turbulent 60s and 70s.

But although Himes forged a space for blackness in a whitewashed genre, the white tough guy survives the lambasting and the genre overturn. Himes exposed the white tough guy to the limits of time and history, yet the figure so imprinted in hardboiled fiction endures, even thrives. The Othering whiteness of the hardboiled genre that Himes so fully laid bare becomes, through the lens of cultural nostalgia, invisible once again. Despite attempts in the 1970s (most notably Robert Altman's film version of *The Long Goodbye*) to strip the white tough guy of any of the gravitas he exudes in the popular white imagination, the white tough guy weathers repeated variations, reincarnations, gentle parodies. With each reemergence (in *Chinatown,* even in James Ellroy's less glamorous representations in his Los Angeles trilogy), he solidifies his status as a beloved nostalgia icon, a figure from an antiquated dream, a recurring white fantasy that persists still.

EPILOGUE¹

"Forget it, Jake. It's Chinatown."

WHILE A FUNDAMENTAL PLEASURE IN FILM SPECTATORSHIP CONSISTS OF viewer identification with the characters on the screen, Slavoj Žižek has suggested that what is so compelling about American film noir for today's audiences is not a viewer identification but precisely the opposite: a "kind of distance [that] is its very condition" (112). Although we may snicker at the dramatic moments in films like *Murder, My Sweet* (1944) and *Out of the Past* (1947), we are in fact fascinated by the imagined gaze of the film's original audience, the viewers whom we assume could still identify with what they saw onscreen, and who recognized that flickering world as their own. When we watch noir, Žižek claims, we are transfixed by the gaze of this "mythic 'naïve' spectator, the one who was 'still able to take it seriously,' in other words, the one who 'believes in it' for us, in place of us" (112). This dissonance, and the triangulated path of desire between today's irony-infused viewer and the imagined originary viewers, resonates equally when one considers the hardboiled novels from which these films so often derived—those tough, taut, and darkly rendered tales of lone detectives navigating violent urban streets. In the decades since their publication, the novels' stylized American idiom and lean, razor-sharp prose have been flattened out and burlesqued; the snap and purr of the dialogue now reads as a parody of itself, the original that we mistake for a copy.

This contemporary viewer or reader reaction suggests the extent to which these films and novels are products of their historical moments, but it also suggests much about the way the hardboiled tradition has been distorted and contorted for use in each ensuing era. In fact, as outlined in chapter five, we view the hardboiled hero now in large part through the Humphrey Bogart icon. His interpretations of Marlowe and of Sam Spade have combined with other, still-tauter models of white masculinity to create a hyper–tough guy who bears little relation to any individual film and even less so to the novels, not to mention the eras from which these texts derive. The Bogart icon persists because he accords with (and helps create) our nostalgic vision of the tough guy figure. The often hysterical and reactionary, fraught and fumbling figure of the novels is occluded in favor of the confident, controlled, sexually potent hero: a man recalling an imagined time when "men were still men."

However, another more recent text has come to occupy a key reference point in relation to the hardboiled tradition. Nearly five years after Chester Himes wrote his final, incendiary, genre-collapsing roman policier, over fifteen years after Chandler's last Marlowe novel, and forty years since Cain's *The Postman Always Rings Twice*, Roman Polanski's lush 1930s period film *Chinatown* appeared in theaters.

Fredric Jameson has characterized *Chinatown* as a "nostalgia film" that seems to take place in "an eternal '30s."[2] In particular, he uses *Chinatown* (and, more fully, Lawrence Kasdan's riff on Cain's *Double Indemnity, Body Heat* [1981]) as an example of postmodern pastiche, itself a "symptom of a society that has become incapable of dealing with time and history" (117). I agree with film scholars such as James Naremore and Michael Eaton who argue that Jameson overstates his case; his point is more apt with the comparatively hollow evocations offered by films like *Farewell, My Lovely* (1975) with Robert Mitchum as a heroic Marlowe, or the endless cable-made movies that adopt the supposed accoutrements of noir (snap-brim hats, the whiskey bottle in the desk drawer) without any of the thorny, historically entrenched tensions of the hardboiled novels and films from which they purportedly derive.[3] With *Chinatown*, however, the connection to the past seems considerably more complex, particularly its relation to the hardboiled tradition.

To pursue *Chinatown's* function in the more contemporary usages of the white male hardboiled hero, let us consider its emergence. First, it is crucial to note that the film came out one year after a significant attempt to deflate the hardboiled hero. Released in 1973, Robert Altman's sardonic updating of Raymond Chandler's *The Long Goodbye* cast a gimlet eye at the Philip Marlowe mystique. It is not within the scope of this project to examine the myriad stylistic, visual, and ideological differences between *The Long Goodbye* and *Chinatown*, nor is it my aim to bring the popular consumption of the white hardboiled hero up to date. Instead, I want to focus briefly on the rejection of one treatment of this figure and the embrace of another, virtually simultaneous approach. Specifically, Altman's film met with a great deal of critical venom for its iconoclastic take on Philip Marlowe and was considered a box office failure. *Chinatown*, however, was lauded by critics and audiences alike and was nominated for a string of Academy Awards. Further, *Chinatown* has taken a canonical position alongside *The Big Sleep* and *The Maltese Falcon* as ceaseless referent points within the noir genre.[4] What do these widely differing reactions say about the status of the white hardboiled hero?

Scores of critics, from James Naremore to John Cawelti (who saw *Chinatown* as truly iconoclastic) to the string of *Film Comment* contributors who attacked Altman's *The Long Goodbye* and offered ecstatic praise for Polanski's film, have debated the resurgence of what has come to be called "neo-noir."[5] These critics, however, tend to remain mired in genre concerns, and in lauding the so-called originals over the supposedly paltry successors. The more salient issue seems to be what considerations drive the choices these later evocations make and why certain representations linger in popular consciousness while others end up so much cultural detritus. What does *Chinatown* offer that *The Long Goodbye* does not?

Robert Altman approached filming Chandler's *The Long Goodbye* with the express purpose of demythologization. Reportedly referring on-set to the famed detective as "Rip Van Marlowe," the director asserted, "I think Marlowe's dead. I think *that* was 'the long goodbye.' I think it's a goodbye to that genre—a genre that I don't think is going to be acceptable any more."[6] The criticism came in large part from those who might be called Chandler "purists," but also from many other film critics and scholars. For instance, Paul Jensen argued in *Film Comment* that the film's "demythification of a relatively realistic character concept ends up offering an even less satisfying alternative."[7] In the same issue, Richard Jameson pointed out, "[I]f you're going to demonstrate the outdatedness and the fallaciousness of an artist's vision, you can't expect to be applauded—or to prove anything, for that matter—if you bash what you're criticizing out of shape and then point at it and say, Wow, that's some silly shape!"[8]

Leigh Brackett, who co-wrote the screenplay for *The Big Sleep* with William Faulkner and Jules Furthman, also co-authored Altman's *The Long Goodbye*. In an article that reads as a defensive response to the vociferous criticism of the liberties the film takes with its source material, Brackett writes, "Twenty-five years had gone by since *The Big Sleep*. In that quarter-century, legions of private eyes had been beaten up in innumerable alleys by armies of interchangeable hoods. Everything that was fresh and exciting about Philip Marlowe in the '40s had become cliché, outworn by imitation and overuse. The tough loner with the sardonic tongue and the cast-iron gut had become a caricature."[9]

Altman, in defending his vision, would say that offended critics were confusing Chandler's Marlowe with Bogart's more potent Marlowe, noting, "I see Marlowe the way Chandler saw him, a loser. But a *real* loser, not the fake winner that Chandler made out of him. A loser all the way" (quoted in Brackett, 28). Of course, as pointed out in chapter five, Bogart's co-optation of the Marlowe icon in popular memory seems to have affected the makers of this film as well. That is, while screenwriter Brackett asserts that the goal was to "strip" Marlowe of his "fake hero attributes," her characterization of Marlowe feels more like Bogart than Chandler's anxious, tainted loner: "Chandler's Marlowe always knew more than the cops. He could be beaten to a pulp, but he always came out on the top one way or another. By sheer force of personality, professional expertise, and gall, he always had an edge" (28). As the preceding chapters have amplified, Chandler's Marlowe suffers constant defeat, retreating, time and again, to his own isolation.

Regardless, Altman's demythologization is fervent. Everything limited or contained in Chandler's Marlowe—efficacy, sexual expression, knowledge—is adamantly refused in Altman's rendering. Altman directs Elliot Gould as a bumbling, mumbling Philip Marlowe whose constant refrain is, "It's okay with me." His chivalric ideals, vaguely expressed, mark him as anachronistic amid the yoga nudists, drugged hippies, caftan-wearing grifters and leisure-suited hoods around him. Abused and manipulated throughout, Gould's Marlowe ends up shooting his betraying friend Terry Lennox at the end—an invention of the film, not the novel. The look of the film is aggressively contemporary with no noir flourish; it is dominated by harsh fluorescents, muddy night scenes, clogged mises-en-scènes, and, of course, Altman's characteristic overlapping dialogue. (It is hard to imagine a dialogue style more distinct from the sparkling and snappy repartée of 40s noir.) Altman aims to topple the Marlowe legend but succeeds more in portraying a malignancy in 1970s, Watergate-era Los Angeles. All told, his film is based on a fundamental misunderstanding of the Marlowe figure, who was a self-professed anachronism even within his era, but also an anachronism characteristic of—and produced by—his era. Strip Marlowe of his context, and Marlowe evaporates. He is made static and therefore any critique of him is defanged. A pointed demythologization, for instance, might have been made by targeting the misogyny, or racism or homophobia at the heart of the tough guy figure (a project that has, in large part, been taken up by James Ellroy's novels). But Altman's choice to focus instead on the figure's anachronistic quality succeeds largely in making Marlowe seem quaint and a bit slow. Finally, in his murder of Terry Lennox, the film offers up an absurdist gloss that serves as a more astute critique of contemporary Dirty Harry vendetta impulses than anything relating to the hardboiled mythology.

The Long Goodbye's critical and commercial failure, however, probably says less about the film's muddied demystification efforts than the discomfort inherent in pulling such a historically specific figure out of his historic moment and expected milieu. In fact, the success of *Chinatown* suggests the degree to which audiences respond to a hardboiled rendering that telescopes the context that produced this figure, even if that telescoping configures a past less literal than reimagined.

A fevered critical debate has continued for over twenty years as to whether *Chinatown* celebrates or rewrites the noir tradition. John Cawelti has argued that *Chinatown* is a radical revision in which the "basic characteristics of a traditional genre" are exposed as the "embodiment of an inadequate and destructive myth."[10] Specifically, he sees *Chinatown's* demythologization as "setting the traditional model of the hard-boiled detective's quest for justice and integrity over and against Polanski's sense of a universe so steeped in ambiguity, corruption, and evil that such individualistic moral enterprises are doomed by their innocent naiveté to end in tragedy and self-destruction" (238). James Naremore, alternately, writes that *Chinatown* "inspires a sentimental fondness for old Hollywood, giving the 1930s a fascinating sleekness, intimacy, and plenitude. My own reaction to the ending of *Chinatown* is therefore a bit like Lionel Trilling's toward *Heart of Darkness:* I'm not sure whether to recoil, or to take subtle pleasure in the elegance of 'the horror'" (210).

I would like to suggest that one need not argue *Chinatown* as either a celebration or as a radical revision when it can clearly be seen as both. The film is perhaps most famous for the "My sister . . . My daughter" scene in which detective Jake Gittes brutally slaps seeming femme fatale Evelyn Mulwray into a confession he had not suspected—that she has been raped by, and had a daughter with, her father. Each slap emits a seemingly opposite truth: Is the young girl Evelyn's sister or her daughter? It is revealed that both sides of the binary are true, undercutting all convention, expectation, sense of coherent order. The scene suggests the pivot or lever by which the film operates. It is not either/or, but both.

Jake Gittes's Nose Bandage

Nearly forty-five minutes into *Chinatown* (1974), private eye Jake Gittes (Jack Nicholson) is threatened by two thugs, one of whom viciously jabs a knife up Gittes's nostril. For the next forty minutes—the entire middle third of the film—Gittes dons a large white bandage over his nose. Critics have pointed to the bandage as evidence of actor Jack Nicholson's commendable willingness to forego personal vanity for the veracity of his performance. The bandage does call attention to the actor's devotion to his craft, thereby thumbing a nose, if you will, at glamorous Hollywood conventions (while also, rather ironically, lauding the newer glamour of the method actor).[11] However, the bandage evokes much more within the context of the film itself and its half-nostalgic, half-iconoclastic vision of hardboiled novels and film noir. There is an obvious symbolism: the nose wound signifying the nosiness of detectives. The film openly cites this symbolism by having the thug (played by the film's director, Roman Polanski) say to Gittes before cutting his nose, "You're a very nosy little fellow, kitty cat, huh? You know what happens to nosy fellows? Huh? No? Wanna guess? Huh? No? They lose their noses." Further, one can imagine a displaced castration threat. After wounding him, the thug warns, "Next time you lose the whole thing. I cut it off and feed it to my goldfish. Understand?" The film then enacts a process by which the phallus is wounded, veiled, and gradually restored, the bandage significantly disappearing after Gittes's sexual congress with the beautiful Evelyn Mulwray (Faye Dunaway). Evelyn removes the bandage to clean his wound as he sits before her. The moment is ripe and sexual. She stares openly at the long gash on his nose and he responds by rising and meeting her gaze. As if in retaliation for being made vulnerable by the exposure, he points out a flaw in her eye, a bit of black amid the green of her iris. Their shared wounds propel them into an embrace, and from this point on, we see Jake's small cut, but no bandage. This scene marks the pivot after which Jake becomes more aggressive in his investigation; he moves from puzzled voyeur to active pursuer who pushes forward despite his always-partial knowledge.

What we see then is the hardboiled hero's manifest vulnerability—the unavoidable bandage to which all characters stare gapingly—healed. The exposure of his wounded state assures his masculinity rather than diminishes it. Likewise, his sexual conquest of the femme fatale, from which he rises unscathed and potent, proves he shares neither the hermeticism nor the contaminated state of Chandler or Cain's protagonists. This consolidation of white masculinity does not result, however, in the white hardboiled hero becoming an action hero or a Mike Hammer–like avenger. Instead, the consolidation is romanticized, given a dreamy, doomed eroticism. Jake is tougher, more resilient than Marlowe or any of Cain's heroes, but he still cannot fight the impenetrability of the woman, the racialized mysteries of the Other. The family romance has contorted to literal incest. Damsels cannot be saved because, as Marlowe exhorted, it is still no game for knights. This gloomy and romantic hardboiled mindset is given full expression, but with a more contained model of white masculinity to deliver it to us. As such, the film strips the traditions from which it emerges of their historical anxieties and smoothes over the messy contortions with a lush and mournful dream. When we see it, we long for the moody era it evokes, blind to its status as phantasy.

The bandage, then, has a significant metatextual purpose when one considers *Chinatown*'s larger function within (and in response to) the noir/hardboiled legacy. In contrast to the farcical, genre-bashing *The Long Goodbye*, *Chinatown* recuperates much of the glamour of the tradition, allowing for a degree of nostalgia and a certain haunted aesthetic. That is, gone are the styl-

ized jagged edges, expressionistic horrors, and intensely subjective narra-
tion/voiceovers of film noir and hardboiled fiction. Instead, *Chinatown* offers a classical, seamless vision: the past era is reconstituted with a creamy
smoothness, serving to alleviate, not exacerbate contemporary anxieties. The
hardboiled figure is imbued with a timeless luster and resilience he never had
before. The whole film has a burnished look, faded golds being polished as
we watch.

This recuperation, however, is strategically mitigated by the film's more
deconstructive work. Indeed, the bandage on Jake Gittes's nose then serves
as a canny metonym for the simultaneous anatomization/recuperation
process the film undertakes. The wounds the bandage conceals are inflicted
not only by the Vietnam- and Watergate-era cynicism that pervades the film
(the conspiracies of power spiral up and up) or the postmodern kitschifica-
tion of the genre, but by the film itself and its transformation of the hero
from the knightly Marlowe model to Gittes's slick, self-seeking businessman.
The film likewise deconstructs the casual racism of 1930s Los Angeles and
of the noir tradition through the spectacle of Gittes telling a dirty "China-
man" joke, unaware that highly respectable Evelyn Mulwray stands behind
him. Gittes is humiliated, but while the shame is primarily gender-based, the
"racial" basis of the joke cannot be ignored in a film that uses the urban
space of L.A.'s Chinatown as its central symbol. The exotic "orientalism"
that is put to use in noir from *The Maltese Falcon* and *The Big Sleep* on is
writ large in *Chinatown*—both exposed and yet curiously embraced. The
film's extensive use of Asian American characters as servants to the wealthy
Mulwray and Noah Cross (John Huston) is historically appropriate and
avoids traditional stereotyping. However, Anthony Easthope, among others,
has pointed out that the film "envisages Evelyn Mulwray as a mystified feminine other in association with the racial other of Chinese culture."[12] This exoticization's primary purpose, nonetheless, seems to be to critique the
hardboiled trope of the orientalized femme fatale and the binaries that compose the tradition, as Evelyn proves to be no vicious spiderwoman but a self-
sacrificing victim.

Further, in a larger sense, the film reveals the way white men like Gittes
use Chinatown as a symbol of the unknowable, the enigmatic, the Eastern.
Chinatown brutally exposes the extent to which orientalist stereotypes are
projections of urban white male fantasies and anxieties about the Other. Of
course, at the same time, the film's diegesis employs the same symbology. It
has no interest in a real, literal Chinatown, or in breaking down the binaries
that name Chinatown, or Woman, as the place of the Other. That is, the
film indulges in the oppositional structures that constitute the hardboiled
tradition at the same time as it critiques those structures. Likewise, its arch-
villain is an old white male patriarch and capitalist robber baron who rapes

the land and his daughter. At the same time, however, the film's perspective is explicitly that of the white male, of Jake Gittes himself.

Indeed, as the film progresses, the film's revisionary efforts recede and a certain amount of reconstructive healing occurs behind that bandage on Jake Gittes's nose. The traditional noir elements, initially so disjointed, begin to fall into place. Gittes is made more romantic, less glib, more invested. He begins to accord more fully with the nostalgic ideal, but a nostalgia the film feels it has earned with its earlier critique and its refusal to bow to traditional noir iconography.

The hardboiled detective's essential impotence, however, has seldom been so relentlessly dramatized than in the last scene of *Chinatown*. Trying to rescue her daughter from her father Noah Cross, Evelyn Mulwray is killed by the same police officer to whom Gittes is handcuffed. Evelyn's screaming daughter is spirited away into what Peter Biskind memorably refers to as Cross's "enveloping . . . vast paw."[13] The final image of the film is a crane shot, depicting Jake Gittes being helped along by his two partners, one on either side, as the trio makes its way down the street. The police are ordering the area cleared; bystanders, almost entirely Chinese Americans, are moving from the middle of the street to the sidewalks, making their way to the margins of the frame. As they do so, the white urban male, no longer alone and no longer self-sufficient but assisted by two other white urban men, must be commandeered in his journey down the city street, out of the literal Chinatown that served as such a canny symbol of Otherness throughout the film. The film's last lines are the police lieutenant's bark, "On the sidewalk! On the sidewalk! Get off the street! Get off the street!" Space is thus cleared for the crime scene but also for the wounded Jake, who recedes into the darkness as the credits roll. A question emerges: Is the command to "Get off the street" directed at the bystanders who are ordered to abandon the street, metaphorically, to the hardboiled hero? Or is the command directed at Jake himself, a figure to whom the streets no longer belong? *Chinatown* refuses an answer, but the last image suggests a figure banished both from the space of the Other (Chinatown) and the space of Power, emblematized by scion and villain Noah Cross and by the police whom, Evelyn tells Jake in her last words, Cross owns.

What could be a more telling representation of the fate of the hardboiled hero? Both romanticized and deflated, both given classical, epic resonance and laid bare as the weakened, impotent figure he fears himself to be. The image of impotence and banishment exposes the hysterical fear of the hardboiled male, while also still making use of the binary structures of

Self/Other, Male/Female, White/Non-White that so constitute him and the hardboiled tradition itself. The ambivalence is telling. The white tough guy speaks to audiences still; we seek him out, bolster him up, tear him down, and continue reinventing him. Out of his historical moment he becomes an icon of what was fearsome and beautiful about a reimagined era, a phantasy that we cannot relinquish, only revise, revamp, and calcify. The streets change, gender and sexuality significations shift, race relations advance, but the hardboiled hero who was such a product of his time is made static, stony, burnished and immutable.

APPENDIX
Toward a Hardboiled Genealogy

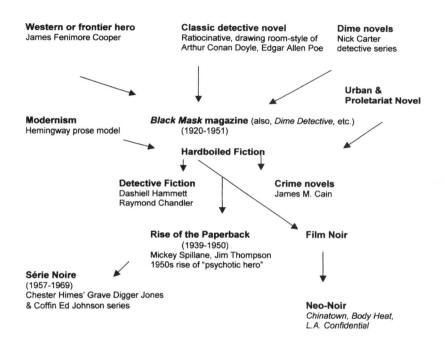

Western or frontier hero
James Fenimore Cooper

Classic detective novel
Ratiocinative, drawing room-style of
Arthur Conan Doyle, Edgar Allen Poe

Dime novels
Nick Carter
detective series

**Urban &
Proletariat Novel**

Modernism
Hemingway prose model

***Black Mask* magazine** (also, *Dime Detective,* etc.)
(1920-1951)

Hardboiled Fiction

Detective Fiction
Dashiell Hammett
Raymond Chandler

Crime novels
James M. Cain

Rise of the Paperback
(1939-1950)
Mickey Spillane, Jim Thompson
1950s rise of "psychotic hero"

Film Noir

Série Noire
(1957-1969)
Chester Himes' Grave Digger Jones
& Coffin Ed Johnson series

Neo-Noir
*Chinatown, Body Heat,
L.A. Confidential*

NOTES

Chapter One

1. State Department Information Program, *Proceedings of Permanent Subcommittee Investigation of the Senate Committee on Government Operations,* March 1953, 88.
2. State Department Information Program, 88.
3. Woody Haut, *Pulp Culture: Hardboiled Fiction and the Cold War* (London: Serpent's Tail, 1995), 3.
4. Compare, for instance, the fact that Mickey Spillane's best-selling novels have sold over forty million copies (Larry Landrum, *American Mystery and Detective Novels: A Reference Guide* [Westport, CT: Greenwood Press, 1999], 14), while Nathanael West had the misfortune to hear from his publisher that his novel *The Day of the Locust* (1939) had sold only twenty-two copies over two weeks of its first month in bookstores (Otto Friedrich, *City of Nets: A Portrait of Hollywood in the 1940s* [New York: Harper & Row, 1986], 11).
5. Liam Kennedy, "Black Noir: Race and Urban Space in Walter Mosley's Detective Fiction," in *Criminal Proceedings: The Contemporary American Crime Novel,* ed. Peter Messent (London: Pluto Press, 1997), 43.
6. Judith Butler, *Bodies That Matter: On the Discursive Limits of "Sex"* (New York: Routledge, 1993), 171.
7. Judith Butler, *Gender Trouble: Feminism and the Subversion of Identity* (New York: Routledge, 1990), 25.
8. Eric Lott, *Love and Theft: Blackface Minstrelsy and the American Working Class* (New York: Oxford University Press, 1993), 18.
9. Geoffrey O'Brien, *Hardboiled America: The Lurid Years of Paperbacks* (New York: Van Nostrand Reinhold, 1981), 77.
10. See Kaja Silverman, *Male Subjectivity at the Margins* (New York: Routledge, 1992).
11. Robert Sklar, *City Boys: Cagney, Bogart, Garfield* (Princeton, NJ: Princeton University Press, 1992), 9.
12. For Sklar, the city boy's recognizability allows for intense identification. Further, the shifts within the figure over time mirror larger social transitions, including changing views of the rebel in American culture. Indeed, the

oppressive scrutiny experienced by city boys like John Garfield and Humphrey Bogart's at the hands of the House Committee on Un-American Activities parallels the efforts of the House Select Committee on Current Pornographic Materials to monitor and control the paperback market and the potentially dangerous novels it made so easily available.

13. Director Robert Altman, in his film adaptation of Chandler's *The Long Goodbye,* will use Marlowe's inherent anachronistic qualities as the source of caustic satire, putting his Marlowe, still donning a suit and driving a vintage car, amid naked hippies, pervasive drugs and a counter-culture-infused Los Angeles setting.

14. This literary model is perhaps most famously articulated by Leslie Fiedler, but was rather prominently deconstructed by Nina Baym in her essay "Melodramas of Beset Manhood: How Theories of American Fiction Exclude Women Authors" (*American Quarterly* 33.2 [Summer 1981]: 123–139). Baym showed how this critical strain confers literary value in relation to a novel's accordance with a white male individualist hero seeking self-definition away from so-called feminizing society.

15. This sense of isolation and entrapment has led to a stream of criticism focusing on the existentialism of hardboiled fiction. Indeed, Albert Camus's *The Stranger* purportedly derives from James M. Cain's *The Postman Always Rings Twice.*

16. Jopi Nyman, *Men Alone: Masculinity, Individualism and Hard-Boiled Fiction* (Costerus New Series 111. Amsterdam: Rodopi, 1997), 3.

17. Nyman, 6–7.

18. For example, Philip Durham, *Down These Mean Streets a Man Must Go* (Chapel Hill: University of North Carolina Press, 1963); Herbert Ruhm, "Raymond Chandler: From Bloomsbury to the Jungle—and Beyond," ed. David Madden, *Tough Guy Writers of the Thirties* (Carbondale: Southern Illinois University Press, 1968), 171–185; John G. Cawleti, *Adventure, Mystery, and Romance* (Chicago: University of Chicago Press, 1976); Ernest Fontana "Chivalry and Modernity in Raymond Chandler's *The Big Sleep,*" *Western American Literature* 19.3 (1984): 179–86; William F. Nolan, *The Black Mask Boys.* New York: Morrow, 1985.

19. Ralph Willett, *Hard-Boiled Detective Fiction,* British Association for American Studies, *Pamphlets in American Studies* 23 (Halifax, England: Ryburn Book Productions, 1992), 8.

20. Mike Davis, *City of Quartz: Excavating the Future in Los Angeles* (New York: Random House, 1992), 37. Hereafter, this work is cited parenthetically in the text.

21. Liahna K. Babener, "Raymond Chandler's City of Lies," in *Los Angeles in Fiction: A Collection of Original Essays,* ed. David Fine (Albuquerque: University of New Mexico Press, 1984), 110

22. Later postmodern takes on Los Angeles, from Thomas Pynchon's *Crying of Lot 49* (1965) to Joan Didion's *Play It As It Lays* (1970), would take this notion of Los Angeles still further, as emblematic of either the collapse of, or the overwhelming and untraceable surfeit of, meaning.

23. David Fine, "Beginning in the Thirties: The Los Angeles Fiction of James M. Cain and Horace McCoy" in *Los Angeles in Fiction: A Collection of Original Essays,* ed. David Fine (Albuquerque: University of New Mexico Press, 1984), 51.

24. The two novels are *If He Hollers Let Him Go* (1943) and *Lonely Crusade* (1947). Mike Davis pointedly refers to the pair as "constitut[ing] a brilliant and disturbing analysis of the psychotic dynamics of racism in the land of sunshine" (43).

25. The popular conflation of crime and private eye variants is the reason why William Marling uses the term "roman noir" in his study of the relationship between Dashiell Hammett, Raymond Chandler, and James M. Cain and late 1920s–1930s technology, economics, design, and the media, noting "[l]iterary scholarship lacks a term for the complex of values that began in the mid-1920s and led to film noir" (*The American Roman Noir: Hammett, Cain, and Chandler* [Athens: University of Georgia Press, 1995], IX). Hereafter, this work is cited parenthetically in the text.

26. Tony Hilfer, *The Crime Novel: A Deviant Genre* (Austin: University of Texas Press, 1990), 8.

27. See especially Durham (1963), Cawelti (1976), Stephen Knight, *Form and Ideology in Crime Fiction* (Bloomington: Indiana University Press, 1980), Dennis Porter, *The Pursuit of Crime: Art and Ideology in Detective Fiction* (New Haven: Yale University Press, 1981), Hilfer (1990).

28. Raymond Chandler, "Introduction to 'The Simple Art of Murder,'" rpt. in *Later Novels and Other Writings* (New York: Library of America, 1995), 1016. Hereafter, this work is cited parenthetically in the text.

29. Porter, 169.

30. Robert Crooks, "From the Far Side of the Urban Frontier: The Detective Fiction of Chester Himes and Walter Mosley" in *Race-ing Representation: Voice, History and Sexuality,* eds. Kostas Myrsiades and Linda Myrsiades (Lanham, MD: Rowan and Littlefield, 1998), 177. Hereafter, this work is cited parenthetically in the text.

31. Richard Slotkin, "The Hard-Boiled Detective Story: From the Open Range to the Mean Streets" in *The Sleuth and the Scholar: Origins, Evolution, and Current Trends in Detective Fiction,* eds. Barbara A. Rader and Howard G. Zettler (Westport, CT: Greenwood Press, 1988), 97.

32. One cannot forget that future leftist Dashiell Hammett was himself a Pinkerton detective as a young man; Hammett later claimed he was once approached to murder a union leader.

33. It should be noted, as Tony Hilfer (1990) does, that hardboiled crime novels have received far less critical attention and genre analysis than hardboiled detective fiction.

34. Kennedy, 45.

35. Manthia Diawara, "Noir By Noirs: Toward a New Realism in Black Cinema" in *Shades of Noir,* ed. Joan Copjec (London: Verso, 1993), 263. Hereafter, this work is cited parenthetically in the text.

36. Porter, 181.

37. Michael Denning, *Mechanic Accents: Dime Novels and Working-Class Culture in America* (London: Verso 1987), 10.

38. Landrum, 6 (hereafter, this work is cited parenthetically in the text); Denning, 12.

39. Larry Landrum reports the impressive publication history of the Nick Carter series, such as the fact that, of the many writers producing these stories, Frederic Van Rensselaer Dey alone wrote 437 Carter novels (7).

40. Denning, 205.

41. Denning, 205.

42. Haut, 10.

43. Nolan, 26. Hereafter, this work is cited parenthetically in the text.

44. Raymond Chandler, "The Simple Art of Murder," rpt. in *Later Novels and Other Writings* (New York: Library of America, 1995), 992.

45. Cawelti, 176.

46. O'Brien, 53.

47. O'Brien, 42.

48. Quoted in O'Brien, 42.

49. Quoted in O'Brien, 116. O'Brien points out that the result of the committee was no "overt censorship" but that "local pressure"—presumably on newsstand owners—may have resulted in cover art becoming "steadily more restrained" after 1955 (45).

Chapter Two

1. William Graham Sumner, "The Forgotten Man (1883)" in *The Forgotten Man and Other Essays,* ed. Albert Galloway Keller (Freeport, New York: Books for Libraries Press, 1919, 1969), 491. Hereafter, this work is cited parenthetically in the text.

2. Franklin Delano Roosevelt, "The 'Forgotten Man' Radio Speech," in *The Roosevelt Reader: Selected Speeches, Messages, Press Conferences, and Letters of Franklin D. Roosevelt,* ed. Basil Rauch (New York: Rinehart, 1957), 66. Hereafter, this work is cited parenthetically in the text.

3. As one elderly man wrote in 1934, "Seemingly every body has been assisted but we the Forgotten Man"—using the term to refer not necessarily to the World War I veteran but to those who, like himself, "for 60 years or more have tried to carry the load without complaining, we have paid others['] pensions[,] we have educated and trained the youth, now as we are Old and down and out of no reason of our own, would it be asking to much of our Government and the young generation to do by us as we have tried our best to do by them even without complaint[?]" (quoted in *Down and Out in the Great Depression: Letters From the "Forgotten Man,"* ed. Robert McElvaine [Chapel Hill: University of North Carolina Press, 1983], 98). This configuration interestingly seems to borrow more from Sumner's original notion of the Forgotten Man than FDR's.

4. Robert S. McElvaine, *The Great Depression: America, 1929–1941* (New York: Times Books, 1984, 1993), 340. Hereafter, this work is cited parenthetically in the text.

5. Philip Abbott. 1998. "Who's Responsible?: The Thirties as a Contested Concept in American Political Thought." Paper presented at the Southwest Political Science Association, San Antonio, TX, March 1998: 2. Hereafter, this work is cited parenthetically in the text.

6. As McElvaine, Abbott, and other scholars, such as Warren Susman and David Kennedy, document, much anecdotal evidence—letters written to both Franklin and Eleanor Roosevelt, Studs Terkel's *Hard Times: An Oral History of the Great Depression* (New York: New Press, 1970, 1986), Mirra Kamarovosky's 1940 study, *The Unemployed Man and His Family: The Effect of Unemployment Upon the Status of the Man in Fifty-Nine Families* (New York: Dryden, 1940), and the accounts of Roosevelt Administration figures such as Harry Hopkins and Lorena Hickok—suggests feelings of impotence and a loss of authority on the part of men on relief.

7. Susan Faludi, *Stiffed: The Betrayal of the American Man* (New York: Perennial, 1999), 21.

8. James M. Cain's popular success is predominant here: Depression-era readers flocked to his novels, serialized in the hugely popular *Liberty* magazine; readers also consumed Chandler, Hammett, and other hardboiled purveyors in tough guy magazines such as *Black Mask* and *Dime Detective.*

9. An interesting parallel development exists within the proletariat literature of the day, which, instead of focusing on a masculinity defined through cooperative public service, reorients a masculinity through the rigor of one's struggle against the capitalist machine. Michael Gold coined the term "proletariat novel" in the 1920s, and the explicitly masculine cast he gave it mirrors that which we find in the hardboiled novel. As Paul Garon points out, "Michael Gold constructed the notion of proletarian literature as an almost completely masculine enterprise by drawing on standard rhetorical stereotypes wherein the bourgeoisie was associated with notions of femininity and decadence while the proletariat was linked to ideas of masculinity, strength, and purity" (Garon, "Radical Novel: 1900–1954," *Firsts* 4:3 [March 1994]: 24).

10. This binary has long-standing literary precedents. Consider, for example, the anxiety over female power in Bram Stoker's *Dracula* and other Gothic novels.

11. Walter Huff does work in a company, but, as we will see, he has merely been waiting for the opportunity to exit that system.

12. Kaja Silverman, *Male Subjectivity at the Margins* (New York: Routledge, 1992), 2. Hereafter, this work is cited parenthetically in the text.

13. In *Murder, My Sweet,* the film version of Chandler's *Farewell, My Lovely,* the potential love interest of Marlowe is transformed from an outsider to the stepdaughter of the femme fatale, thereby turning the triangle into a virtual recapitulation of the *Double Indemnity* family romance.

14. For instance, films noirs like *Lady from Shanghai* (1948), *Out of the Past* (1947), and *Scarlet Street* (1945).

15. James M. Cain, *Double Indemnity* (New York: Vintage, 1992), 32. Hereafter, this work is cited parenthetically in the text.

16. Frank Krutnik, *In a Lonely Street: Film Noir, Genre, Masculinity* (London: Routledge, 1991), 138. Hereafter, this work is cited parenthetically in the

text. Further, Krutnik argues that, in the film adaptation of *Double Indemnity,* Walter's "gamble is explicitly an attempt to impress Keyes with his potency. Keyes functions both as the one who must ultimately judge the transgression and as the one at whom the transgressive adventure is principally directed (Walter betraying his bonds of obligation to Keyes as 'father')" (142).

17. In Lacanian terms, we might consider what Walter "feels" (and what the investigatory Lola senses at the "back of" things) is the phallic signifier, the stain that, as Slavoj Žižek writes, "'denatures' [the picture], rendering all its constituents 'suspicious,' and thus opens up the abyss of the search for a meaning . . ." (91).

18. In this way, Walter and Phyllis are doubled. As Phyllis, to Walter's mind, threatens the codes of bourgeois business, the white-collar office, she also appears to threaten the family structure. William Luhr writes about the film version, "Phyllis . . . destroys the family unit at the most basic levels—the physical and the cultural"; she plots to murder the Nirdlingers one by one (succeeding twice) and, as Luhr adds, she "clearly destroys [the family's] cultural function as a unit of interpersonal cohesion, sexual containment and trust, and intergenerational support" (28). But what we need to consider here is whether it is Phyllis or Walter who is the true threat to the family. As discussed above, Walter recuses himself from the family romance that he has so actively entered.

19. Hélène Cixous and Catherine Clément, "The Untenable" in *In Dora's Case: Freud—Hysteria—Feminism,* eds. Charles Bernheimer and Claire Kahane (New York: Columbia University Press, 1995), 286.

20. Peter Brooks, *Body Work: Objects of Desire in Modern Narrative* (Cambridge: Harvard University Press, 1993), 244. Likewise, as Claire Kahane notes in her reading of Freud's Dora, "What Dora revealed was that sexual difference was a psychological problematic rather than a natural fact, that it existed within the individual psyche as well as between men and women in culture" ("Introduction: Part Two" in *In Dora's Case: Freud—Hysteria—Feminism,* eds. Charles Bernheimer and Claire Kahane [New York: Columbia University Press, 1995], 22).

21. As Freud offers in "General Remarks on Hysterical Attacks" (1909), "In a whole series of cases the hysterical neurosis is nothing but an excessive overaccentuation of the typical wave of repression through which the masculine type of sexuality is removed and the woman emerges" (124). See also Claire Kahane and Charles Bernheimer's *In Dora's Case.*

22. Elaine Showalter, "Hysteria, Feminism, and Gender," in *Hysteria Beyond Freud,* eds. Sander L. Gilman, Helen King, Roy Porter, G. S. Rousseau, and Elaine Showalter (Berkeley: University of California Press, 1993), 258. Showalter notes that the fact that we need to specify "*male* hysterics" demonstrates the extent to which, despite the number of male "cases," hysteria is still considered a female malady.

23. Paul Smith, "Action Movie Hysteria, or Eastwood Bound," *Differences* 1.3 (1989): 92.

24. Smith, 95.
25. One might consider the coincidence that so-called male hysteria was originally characterized by English doctors diagnosing men who had suffered traumas after railway accidents (Elaine Showalter, *Hystories: Hysterical Epidemics and Modern Media* [New York: Columbia University Press, 1997], 66–68). Huff's railway "accident" is of course staged, making him effectually engineering his own hysteria.
26. See David Madden, ed., *Tough Guy Writers of the Thirties* (Carbondale: Southern Illinois University Press, 1968); Joyce Carol Oates, "Man Under Sentence of Death: The Novels of James M. Cain," in *Tough Guy Writers of the Thirties,* ed. David Madden (Southern Illinois University Press: Carbondale, 1968), 110–128; Paul Skenazy, *James M. Cain* (New York: Continuum, 1989); Hilfer (1990); Marling (1995).
27. Mary Ann Doane, *Femmes Fatales: Feminism, Film Theory, Psychoanalysis* (New York: Routledge, 1991), 2. Hereafter, this work is cited parenthetically in the text.
28. I am referring here to an untheorized popular conception of the femme fatale, particularly in cinema and in the array of hardboiled texts that portray the femme fatale as "beautiful but deadly."
29. Phyllis's motivations and mental stability are normalized in the film version, her preformatted gothic aspects stripped away. Her motive becomes merely money, evacuating the uncanny element. See chapter five for further discussion.
30. Huff's job as an insurance salesman might seem to demonize him to Depression-era readers, but as passages like this one reveal, Walter is positioned as an insider exposing his industry's dark heart, and murdering an oil executive to boot. After all, in addition to the quickly made admission that he has indeed "gone nuts" working in his monotonous job, Huff is deconstructing a growth industry that thrives in a time of national depression on the miseries of its consumers. He strips it of any ad-man facade and exposes it as a coarse game of chance.
31. See D. A. Miller's seminal reading of hysteria in Wilkie Collins's *The Woman in White* for another model of male contamination by the female (*The Novel and the Police* [Berkeley: University of California Press, 1988]).
32. Walter explicitly likens Phyllis in this last scene to Coleridge's famous "Ancient Mariner" femme fatale.
33. Slavoj Žižek, *Looking Awry: An Introduction to Jacques Lacan through Popular Culture* (Cambridge: MIT Press, 1991).
34. Miller, 148.
35. Sigmund Freud, "The Uncanny" in *The Standard Edition of the Complete Psychological Works,* trans. James Strachey, vol. 17 (London: Hogarth Press, 1953), 240.
36. Jacques Lacan, "The Split Between the Eye and the Gaze," in *The Four Fundamental Concepts of Psycho-Analysis* (New York: W.W. Norton, 1981), 72–73.

37. Interestingly, the precise moment he notices this is the moment he first suspects she is out to grift, out to cheat the Company, twinning Company-related and sexual desires again.

38. The crutches are quite significant in terms of castration anxiety, a fact the film version makes clear in its credit sequence, wherein the shadowy figure of a man on crutches appears over the credits.

39. William Luhr, *Raymond Chandler and Film* (Tallahassee: Florida State University Press, 1991), 27. The film changes most character names: Walter Huff becomes Walter Neff, Nino Sachetti becomes Zachette (thereby losing the intriguing Sacco/Vanzetti connotation—a connotation Marling asserts is "compensatory retelling of their plight" [179–80]), and the Nirdlingers become the Dietrichsons.

40. In fact, Walter notes that Phyllis "seemed to have almost forgotten that there was a murder, and acted like the company was playing her some kind of dirty trick in not paying her right away" (81).

41. Michel Foucault, *The History of Sexuality, Volume I: An Introduction,* trans. Robert Hurley (New York: Vintage, 1990), 61–62.

42. Fred Pfeil, *White Guys: Studies in Postmodern Domination and Difference* (London: Verso, 1995), 110. Hereafter, this work is cited parenthetically in the text.

43. Pfeil importantly extends this point to the "male or male-identified reader as well," adding that "a large part of the pleasure of these texts must be the invitation they issue to dally with a violent yet carnivalesque world of dissolving distinctions and eroded authority that—though held at bay throughout . . . —need only in the last instance, at the climactic moment of resolutions, be firmly disavowed" (114).

44. Žižek, 60. Hereafter, this work is cited parenthetically in the text.

45. Raymond Chandler, *Farewell, My Lovely* (New York: Vintage, 1992), 34. Hereafter, this work is cited parenthetically in the text.

46. Fred Pfeil, in arguing for a latent homosexuality in Marlowe, notes the frequency of "times in Chandler's work the lethal yet seductive woman's tongue, in kissing or in speech, darts like a snake" (117).

47. Luhr, 116.

48. Luhr, 116–117.

49. There is analogy worth pursing here: Marlowe plies a black concierge with alcohol from the same bottle he later uses with Jessie Florian, yet his attitude toward the concierge is far more positive. There is no disgust, instead a vague admiration at the concierge's easily figuring out something Marlowe could not.

50. It seems no mistake that Marlowe's shadow in the novel—his client Moose Malloy—murders Florian. Malloy and Marlowe share desire for the same woman (Velma), share similar names, and cross paths over and over again. If we want to see Moose as, in some ways, a libidinal cathexis for Marlowe, then Moose's (accidental) murder of Florian seems a wish fulfillment.

51. Let us recall D. A. Miller's work on *The Woman in White.* Marlowe is, after all, incarcerated, forcibly held in an alcoholic/drug addict sanitarium soon after his encounter with Florian, suggesting he has indeed been "infected."

52. Raymond Chandler, *The Big Sleep* (New York: Vintage, 1992), 159. Hereafter, this work is cited parenthetically in the text.
53. Raymond Chandler, *The Long Goodbye* (New York: Vintage, 1992), 722. Hereafter, this work is cited parenthetically in the text.
54. Raymond Chandler, *The High Window,* rpt. in *Stories & Early Novels* (New York: Library of America, 1995), 1135. Hereafter, this work is cited parenthetically in the text.
55. Quoted in Jerry Speir, *Raymond Chandler* (New York: Frederick Unger, 1981), 1.
56. The exception being Fred Pfeil's comments, albeit brief ones, on Marlowe's unconscious episodes in *White Guys: Studies in Postmodern Domination and Difference* (1995).
57. Raymond Chandler, *The Little Sister,* rpt. in *Later Novels and Other Writings* (New York: Library of America, 1995), 328. Hereafter, this work is cited parenthetically in the text.
58. Raymond Chandler, *The Lady in the Lake* (New York: Vintage, 1992), 108. Hereafter, this work is cited parenthetically in the text.
59. Tania Modleski, *The Women Who Knew Too Much: Hitchcock and Feminist Film Theory* (New York: Methuen, 1988), 34.
60. Babener, 110.
61. Showalter (1997), 76.
62. We can see this connection, for instance, in Marlowe's characterizations of Velma in *Farewell, My Lovely.* At one point, he notes, "[Velma] hung up, leaving me with a curious feeling of having talked to somebody that didn't exist" (273). At the end, upon hearing of Velma's death, he reflects, "It was a cool day and very clear. You could see a long way—but not as far as Velma had gone" (292).

Chapter Three

1. James M. Cain, *Serenade,* rpt. in *The Five Great Novels of James M. Cain* (London: Picador, 1985), 191. Hereafter, this work is cited parenthetically in the text.
2. Miller, 148.
3. Note too Juana's conception of the power dynamics of heterosexual relationships: the male should "frighten" the woman, make her "heart beat fast"—female fear of masculine potency is the prelude to sexual consummation.
4. Quoted in Paul Skenazy, *James M. Cain* (New York: Continuum, 1989), 54–55. Hereafter, this work is cited parenthetically in the text.
5. This kind of unexamined slide can also be found in Joyce Carol Oates's piece on Cain. She writes of Cain's heroes: " . . . they are non-heroic heroes, animalistic or even mechanical in their responses *even (in the case of John Howard Sharp) masculine only by effort and luck,* and somehow losers in the economic struggle of America . . ." (114).

6. Sharp's claim that "That woman was in him" offers quite an echo of Karl Ul-richs's nineteenth-century formulation of the male homosexual as "a woman's soul trapped in a man's body" (see Miller, 154–55).

7. Of course one needs to be a bit dubious about Sharp's narratorial claim that it is only Hawes's musical talent that truly seduces him.

8. Oates, 115–116.

9. It is interesting to note that, in the 1956 Hollywood adaptation of *Serenade*, Cain's sexually tormented opera singer suffers no longer in the hands of for-mer lover and mentor Winston Hawes but in the slinky talons of Kendall Hale, as interpreted by Joan Fontaine.

10. Legman is a fascinating figure in post–World War II America. He published a two-volume psychoanalytic exploration of erotic and scatological humor. He was also editor of *Neurotica*, a Freudian quarterly. Other books include *The Horn Book: Studies in Erotic Folklore and Bibliography* and *Oralgenitalism*. Leg-man, according to his obituary in the *New York Times*, introduced origami to "the West" and also claimed to have "developed a vibrator in the late 1930's" and to have "coined the phrase 'Make love, not war' during a talk at the Uni-versity of Ohio in 1963" ("Gershon Legman, Anthologist of Erotic Humor, Is Dead at 81," *The New York Times*, March 14, 1999, Metro Section, 49).

11. Gershon Legman, *Love and Death: A Study in Censorship* (New York: Hacker, 1963), 24. Hereafter, this work is cited parenthetically in the text.

12. Diana Fuss, *Identification Papers* (New York: Routledge, 1995), 2.

13. Lana Turner starred as the adulterous Cora in the film version of Cain's *The Postman Always Rings Twice* (1946).

14. Quoted in Legman, 69; Chandler, "The Simple Art of Murder," 992.

15. Legman's claims do not entirely accord with the facts: for instance, Anne Riordan, the "Girl Friday" of *Farewell, My Lovely*, clearly fits none of these categories.

16. Quoted in Haut, 5.

17. Alan Nadel, *Containment Culture: American Narratives, Postmodernism, and the Atomic Age* (Durham: Duke University Press, 1995). Hereafter, this work is cited parenthetically in the text.

18. U.S. Congress. "Homosexuals in Government, 1950," *Congressional Record*, 96, part 4, 81st Cong., 2nd Session, March 29-April 24, 1950, 4527–4528. Hereafter, this work is cited parenthetically in the text.

19. One is reminded of Freud's slippage into French in "Fragment of a Case Study on Hysteria," as parsed memorably by Jane Gallop, among others, in *In Dora's Case*.

20. Quoted in J. K. Van Dover, "Introduction," in *The Critical Response to Ray-mond Chandler*, ed. Van Dover (Westport, CT: Greenwood Press, 1995), 9.

21. Quoted in *Selected Letters of Raymond Chandler*, ed. Frank MacShane (New York: Columbia University Press, 1981), 188.

22. Van Dover, 10.

23. Johanna M. Smith, "Raymond Chandler and the Business of Literature," rpt. in *The Critical Response to Raymond Chandler*, ed. J. K. Van Dover (Westport, CT: Greenwood Press, 1995), 184.

24. Quoted in MacShane, *Letters,* 229.
25. Smith, 184.
26. Smith, 184.
27. Quoted in MacShane, *Letters,* 203.
28. Michael Mason, "Deadlier Than the Male," *Times Literary Supplement,* September 17, 1976, 1147. Hereafter, this work is cited parenthetically in the text.
29. One might note the general sloppiness of Mason's article. For instance, he refers to Red Norgaard in *Farewell, My Lovely* as Red Olsen (1147).
30. An interesting side note is Mason's final claim that Robert Altman's revisionary adaptation of *The Long Goodbye* (which I will discuss at length in the epilogue) is a "brilliant film [that] was the first cinematic version of a Marlowe novel to discern the hero's sexual nature" (1147).
31. Peter Wolfe, *Something More Than Night: The Case of Raymond Chandler* (Bowling Green, OH: Popular, 1985), 51. Hereafter, this work is cited parenthetically in the text.
32. This power of the reading of Marlowe as repressed homosexual is such that nearly all critics dealing with Marlowe at length now feel they need to dismiss the reading. Witness Stephen Knight in his well-known work on Chandler in *Form and Ideology in Crime Fiction:* " . . . I feel to classify Marlowe—and so Chandler—as a latent homosexual is to give too definite, even too positive a description of the negative, self-defensive feelings the persona shows towards others. He fears interference with the exercise of his untrammelled freedom whether it comes from women, homosexuals, doctors or police" (158).
33. In his discussion of Howard Hawks's film version of *The Big Sleep,* Michael Walker analyzes the scene in which Marlowe seizes Geiger's lover Carol Lundgren in terms of its similarity to a pick-up ("Film Noir: Introduction," in *The Book of Film Noir,* ed. Ian Cameron [New York: Continuum, 1992], 198). Carol Lundgren is a pretty clear riff on Hammett's character of the "gunsel" Wilmer in *The Maltese Falcon.* Both Spade's interactions with Wilmer and Marlowe's with Carol smack of alarmingly hostile gay-bashing.
34. One might consider Eve Kosofsky Sedgwick's work on Victorian bachelor characters in this regard. In *Epistemology of the Closet* (Berkeley: University of California Press, 1990), she discusses William Thackeray's bachelor protagonists, for instance, as a response to "the strangulation of homosexual panic," characterizing the strategy as "a preference of atomized male individualism to the nuclear family (and a corresponding demonization of women, especially mothers); a garrulous and visible refusal of anything that could be interpreted as genital sexuality, toward objects male or female; a corresponding emphasis on the pleasures of other senses; and a well-defended social facility that freights with a good deal of magnetism its proneness to parody and to unpredictable sadism" (192).
35. Fred Pfeil offers a different take on much of the same aspects of Chandler, arguing, "It is not enough (though true enough, as far as it goes) to speak here of the latent and violently repressed homosexual desire charging [Chandler's] writing, or even more generally of its homosociality. Rather, the fear

that obsessively links women, blacks, overt homosexuals, and doctors within the same underworld through a complex chain of equivalences and affinities in Chandler's work must be understood as the flip side of a desire to yield to and to be penetrated by the infernally disordering dissolving force they serve and represent, to suffer and enjoy the violation of precisely that hard-shell masculinity which must be defended at all cost. Here I can only remind readers in passing of the number of times in Chandler's work the lethal yet seductive woman's tongue, in kissing or in speech, darts like a snake; of his deadly fear of doctors' injections, of the scarcely concealed sensual pleasure encoded in Chandler's descriptions of passing out" (117).

Chapter Four

1. Andrew Ross, *No Respect: Intellectuals and Popular Culture* (New York: Routledge, 1989), 65–101.
2. Jack Kerouac, "On the Road Again," *The New Yorker* (June 22 & 29, 1998): 56. Hereafter, this work is cited parenthetically in the text.
3. Richard Dyer, "White," *Screen* 29.4 (Autumn 1988): 46.
4. Sylvia Wynter, "Sambos and Minstrels," *Social Text* 1 (1979): 149–156.
5. See Toni Morrison, *Playing in the Dark: Whiteness and the Literary Imagination* (New York: Vintage, 1993); Robyn Wiegman, *American Anatomies: Theorizing Race and Gender* (Durham: Duke University Press, 1995); Harryette Mullen, "Optic White: Blackness and the Production of Whiteness," *diacritics* 24.2–3 (Summer-Fall 1994): 71–89; David Roediger, *The Wages of Whiteness: Race and the Making of the American Working Class* (London: Verso, 1991); and Eric Lott, *Love and Theft: Blackface Minstrelsy and the American Working Class* (New York: Oxford University Press, 1993) and "The Whiteness of Film Noir," in *Whiteness: A Critical Reader,* ed. Mike Hill (New York: New York University Press, 1997), 81–101.
6. George Lipsitz, *The Possessive Investment in Whiteness: How White People Profit from Identity Politics* (Philadelphia: Temple University Press, 1998), 1.
7. Dyer (1988), 45.
8. Frankie Y. Bailey, *Out of the Woodpile: Black Characters in Crime and Detective Fiction* (Westport, CT: Greenwood Pandarus, 1991), 49.
9. As an example of the governmentally sanctioned racial inequality in Los Angeles, consider how homeowners' associations sprang up in the 1920s to prevent blacks and other minorities from buying homes outside the ghettoes; so effective were these mobilizations that "95 per cent of the city's housing stock in the 1920s was effectively put off limits to Blacks and Asians" (Davis, 161). Mike Davis adds, "Until the U.S. Supreme Court finally ruled against restrictive covenants in 1948, white homeowner groups in Los Angeles had ample sanction in the law" (162), even finding help in the New Deal, whose Federal Housing Authority, as Davis points out, "not only sanctioned restrictions" but offered suggestions for how to include them in contracts (163).

10. Rodolfo Acuña, *Occupied America: The Chicano's Struggle Toward Liberation* (San Francisco: Canfield, 1972), 202. Hereafter, this work is cited parenthetically in the text. Carey McWilliams also discusses these comments, made by Captain Ed Durán Ayres, who prefaced his claims by citing Rudyard Kipling. In particular, McWilliams, the one-time chair of the Sleepy Lagoon Defense Committee, likens Ayres' comments to "another amateur anthropologist," Adolf Hitler. Ayres' comments, to his chagrin, were used by Radio Berlin, Radio Tokyo, and Radio Madrid to, according to McWilliams, "show that Americans actually shared the same doctrines as those advocated by Hitler" (*North from Mexico: The Spanish-Speaking People of the United States* [New York: Greenwood Press, 1990], 212).

11. Bethany Ogden, "Hard-Boiled Ideology," *Critical Quarterly* 34.1 (Spring 1992): 77.

12. Quoted in Davis, 116.

13. Roediger, 25. Hereafter, this work is cited parenthetically in the text.

14. Lipsitz, 5.

15. See letters, recollections, and analysis of letters written to FDR and New Deal administrators in Terkel (1970, 1986), McElvaine (1983;1993), Kennedy (1999), and discussion in chapter two. As an example, consider one such letter, written by a New York resident to President Roosevelt: "From what we see around here not much of the [relief] money goes to those who actually are patriotic and Americans and real good-living people. Most of it is *handed* out to European Wasps, Jews, and a certain class of Irish. Outside of these and the niggers, a real White-Man has very little chance for help" (McElvaine [1993], 199).

16. Warren I. Susman, "The Thirties," in *The Development of an American Culture,* eds. Stanley Cohen and Lorman Ratner (Englewood Cliffs, NJ: Prentice-Hall, 1970), 205.

17. James M. Cain, *The Postman Always Rings Twice* (New York: Vintage, 1992), 6. Hereafter, this work is cited parenthetically in the text.

18. Consider that Cain writes *Postman* in 1934, a time of extensive Mexican immigration. In 1920, the number of Californians either born in Mexico or having Mexican-born parents grew from 121,176 in 1920 to 368,013 in 1930 (Carey McWilliams, *Southern California County: An Island on the Land* [New York: Duell, Sloan & Pearce, 1946], 316). In the 1920s, these were predominantly migrant workers who returned to Mexico each winter, but during the Depression Mexican laborers began settling in Los Angeles. Tensions between white American workers and Mexican workers resulted in the County of Los Angeles "repatriating" thousands of Mexicans on relief (McWilliams, 316). As Rodolf Acuña observes, between 1931 and 1934, Los Angeles County repatriated 12,668 Chicanos (193). The motives were clear: as Acuña writes, "Many Anglo-Americans became concerned about the growing cost of welfare and unemployment and resented the 'brown men' in their midst who, after all, were not Anglo-Americans" (190). The "Mexican problem" continued to flare up, reaching a particularly brutal

peak, as noted earlier, in 1942 when the notorious Sleepy Lagoon case dominated headlines and in 1943 when the Zoot Suit riots occurred. Carey McWilliams, who was chair of the Sleepy Lagoon Defense Committee, offered a well-known recounting of both events (*Southern California County,* 318–321 and McWilliams, *North from Mexico,* 206–231). See also Acuña, 199–208.

19. William Marling notes, "'Nick the Greek' is a seme for blacks, for Mexicans, for Italians, for eastern Europeans, for all immigrants" (172).

20. This dynamic is similar to the one Toni Morrison locates in Hemingway's *To Have and Have Not.* When Marie asks Harry what it is like to have sex with a "nigger wench," Harry replies that it is "[l]ike nurse shark" (quoted in Morrison, *Playing in the Dark: Whiteness and the Literary Imagination* [New York: Vintage, 1993], 85). Morrison observes, "The kindness [Harry] has done Marie is palpable. His projection of black female sexuality has provided her with solace, for which she is properly grateful" (85).

21. We certainly see this anti-Mexican fear in Chandler, especially *The Little Sister* and *The Long Goodbye.*

22. The function of *language* in the construction of whiteness has been explored by David Roediger, who persuasively traces shifts in language used to describe work in nineteenth-century America. The shift, for instance, from "servant" to "worker" is shown to be emblematic of efforts on the part of the white working class to distance themselves from associations with slaves. Likewise, the term "freeman" emerges, with efforts made to "make the literal legal title of *freeman* absolutely congruent with *white* adult maleness" (58).

23. Wiegman, 9.

24. Richard Dyer, *White* (London: Routledge, 1997), 28. Hereafter, this work is cited parenthetically in the text.

25. Wynter, 150. Hereafter, this work is cited parenthetically in the text.

26. One is reminded of the repeated use of "the nigger" to describe the character, Wesley, in Hemingway's hardboiled novel, *To Have and Have Not.* Toni Morrison offers a compelling discussion of the narrative anxieties at work in the repeated use of the slur by both first-person and later omniscient third-person narrators. See *Playing in the Dark,* 70–76.

27. Mullen, 78–79.

28. Ross MacDonald has sweepingly referred to the hardboiled detective as the "classless, restless man of American Democracy" (quoted in Willett, 23).

29. Quoted in Bailey, 47. Hereafter, this work is cited parenthetically in the text.

30. Eric Lott reads the film version of *Farewell, My Lovely, Murder, My Sweet,* as "depict[ing] with varying degrees of self-consciousness a specifically racial deviance at the center of the domestic sphere" ([1997], 96). He notes particularly that the film "races" Moose as Mexican—and locates a "similarly ethnically resonant Velma Valento" ([1997], 96).

31. See Bailey (1991), Marling (1995), Peter J. Rabinowitz, "Chandler Comes to Harlem: Racial Politics in the Thrillers of Chester Himes," in *The Sleuth and the Scholar: Origins, Evolution, and Current Trends in Detective Fiction,*

eds. Barbara A. Rader and Howard G. Zettler (Westport, CT: Greenwood Press, 1988), 19–30.

32. Consider Marlowe's ruminations in *The Lady in the Lake* (1943) about a "nice girl" he knows who lives on a "nice street," shielded from the "Mexican and Negro slums stretched out on the dismal flats south of the old interurban tracks" (177).

33. As Robert Storey points out in his book *Pierrot: A Critical History of a Mask*, the Pierrot figure originates in seventeenth-century *commedia dell'arte*. A Pierrot was a fool in pantomimes with a floured face and white costume, the opposite of the black-masked harlequin (*Pierrot: A Critical History of a Mask*. Princeton: Princeton University Press, 1978, 19).

34. Dyer in fact references a still from *The Big Sleep* as an example: Lauren Bacall is dressed in dark clothing thus "heightening the whiteness of her face, wrist and hands," while Humphrey Bogart is "greyer overall" ([1997], 133–34).

35. Dyer defines three "senses of whiteness": whiteness as *hue* ("an observable distinction in the tints of the world"), as "a category *skin* color," and as *symbol* ([1997], 45).

36. The green sunglasses, referenced early in the scene by Marlowe, could be an early clue to the fact that the man in front of Marlowe is Lennox, as Lennox is characterized in large part by his love of the (green-colored) gimlet.

Chapter Five

1. *Raymond Chandler Speaking*, eds. Dorothy Gardiner and Katharine Sorley Walker (Berkeley: University of California Press, 1962, 1997), 221.

2. Foster Hirsch, *The Dark Side of the Screen: Film Noir* (San Diego: A. S. Barnes Co., 1981), 39. Hereafter, this work is cited parenthetically in the text.

3. In broad terms, the "woman's film," commonly featuring stars like Bette Davis and Joan Crawford, is a "term of convenience to describe a range of pictures commonly referred to as fallen-woman films, romantic dramas, Cinderella romances, and gold-digger or working-girl stories. . . . The conflicts of the pictures involve interpersonal relationships that present the heroine with dilemmas the resolutions of which usually entail loss" (Tino Balio, *Grand Design: Hollywood as a Modern Business Enterprise, 1930–1939*, History of the American Cinema series, vol. 5 [New York: Charles Scribner's Sons, 1993], 235).

4. Quoted in Karen Burroughs Hannsberry, *Femme Noir: Bad Girls of Film*. Jefferson, NC: McFarland & Co., 1998. Christine Gledhill writes that *The Postman Always Rings Twice*'s Cora is characteristic of noir's presentation of women as utterly changeable, characterologically unstable. Cora, for instance, "exhibits a remarkable series of unmotivated character switches and roles something as follows: 1) sex-bomb; 2) hardworking, ambitious woman; 3) loving playmate in an adulterous relationship; 4) fearful girl in need of

protection; 5) victim of male power; 6) hard, ruthless murderess; 7) mother-to-be; 8) sacrifice to law" ("*Klute* Part 1: A contemporary film noir and feminist criticism," in *Women in Film Noir,* ed. E. Ann Kaplan [London: British Film Institute, 1978], 18).

5. This pan shot up the body of a beautiful woman is heavily associated with (although far from limited to) noir. Frank Krutnik suggests that this prototypical pan is the means by which Hollywood films attempted to approximate the male narrators of the novels who describe the bodies of the femme fatale in violently erotic and objectifying terms. He writes, "the Hollywood film could not be explicit, but in the 1940s it did establish a codified means of instituting a similar kind of erotici[z]ed division—the equivalence of [the description of the female body] being the measured pan up the body of the woman, with the camera approximating the hero's look" (43).

6. The "angelically glowing woman" representation, according to Richard Dyer, "reached its apogee toward the end of the nineteenth century" during a "heightened perceived threat to the hegemony of whiteness"—specifically, the threats to British Imperialism, the rise of immigration, and the Southern ideal of womanhood, which was increasingly celebrated after the South's defeat in the Civil War (127).

7. Similarly, the class tensions of the novel are defused; the novel's Cora tries to claw her way out of her working-class roots while the film recasts the steely desires as generic, even crisp ambition: "I'm going to make something out of myself," Turner's Cora proclaims, shaking her head in jaunty emphasis.

8. Between 1930 and 1934, "compliance with the Code was a verbal agreement that, as producer Samuel Goldwyn might have said, wasn't worth the paper it was written on" (Doherty, 2). For an informative history, see Thomas Doherty's *Pre-Code Hollywood: Sex, Immorality and Insurrection in American Cinema, 1930–1934* (New York: Columbia University Press, 1999).

9. Quoted in Doherty, 353.

10. Quoted in Doherty, 362.

11. During the production of *Double Indemnity* in 1944, the Breen Office sent a letter to Paramount executives remonstrating the film for its supposedly sympathetic portrayal of Walter Neff and the film's "general low tone and sordid flavor [which] makes it, in our judgement, thoroughly unacceptable for screen presentation" (quoted in Richard Schickel, *Double Indemnity* [London: BFI Film Classics, 1992], 53. Hereafter, this work is cited parenthetically in the text.). In the end, however, the filmmakers only needed to make small changes, such as concealing details about the crime that could, the censors argued, encourage imitators. In his book on *Double Indemnity,* Richard Schickel argues that Billy Wilder and Raymond Chandler carefully managed the screenplay to avoid censorship problems, such as their choices of "adding the 'love story' between Neff and Keyes, [and] removing the psychopathic overtones from Phyllis's character" (56).

12. In particular, Richard Schickel attributes *Double Indemnity*'s production in 1944 after years of limbo to a "slight liberalization . . . of [the] interpretation of the Production Code by the Motion Picture Association's censors" (20).

13. Paul Schrader, "Notes on Film Noir," in *Film Noir Reader,* eds. Alain Silver and James Ursini (New York: Limelight Editions, 1996), 56. Hereafter, this work is cited parenthetically in the text.

14. Janey Place and Lowell Peterson, "Some Visual Motifs of Film Noir" in *Film Noir Reader,* eds. Alain Silver and James Ursini (New York: Limelight Editions, 1996), 65–68.

15. James Naremore, *More Than Night: Film Noir in Its Contexts* (Berkeley: University of California Press, 1998) and J. P. Telotte, *Voices in the Dark: The Narrative Patterns of Film Noir* (Urbana: University of Illinois Press, 1989), in addition to Alain Silver and Elizabeth Ward's exhaustive *Film Noir: An Encyclopedia of the American Style* (New York: Limelight Editions, 1996), offer useful discussions of the development of the term "film noir," including discussions of Nino Frank's coinage. Frank used the term in 1946 to compare particular American crime films to the novels published in France by Série Noire (which, not coincidentally, would later publish Chester Himes's detective novels). Raymond Borde and Étienne Chaumeton are crucial to the term's mass usage, publishing *Panorama du film noir américain* in 1955.

16. In fact, a lack of knowledge about source texts can often lead to embarrassing errors. Esteemed film writer Robin Wood mistakenly refers to the murderer in Chandler's *The Big Sleep* as Vivian Sternwood, played by Lauren Bacall in the film: "To have Bacall turn out to be the killer would certainly have gone against the whole spirit of the film . . ."(*Howard Hawks* [Garden City, N.J.: Doubleday, 1968], 170). Vivian Sternwood is neither the murderer in the book nor in the film.

17. Janey Place, "Women in Film Noir" in *Women in Film Noir,* ed. E. Ann Kaplan (London: British Film Institute, 1978), 45. Hereafter, this work is cited parenthetically in the text.

18. Richard Martin, *Mean Streets and Raging Bulls: The Legacy of Film Noir in Contemporary American Cinema* (Lanham, MD: Scarecrow Press, 1997), 14.

19. Quoted in Martin, 14.

20. Telotte, 93.

21. Telotte, 92–93.

22. This viewer alignment was made literal with Robert Montgomery's *Lady in the Lake,* which is famously shot with the camera (and therefore the viewer) as Marlowe.

23. We later learn Marlowe has been temporarily blinded when a gun is fired in front of his face.

24. Florian does regain the "step ahead" of Marlowe quickly. After he leaves, he sees her making a sudden, sober phone call that he cannot hear, and the viewer later learns that she has still more information then she reveals.

25. Elizabeth Cowie, "Film Noir and Women," in *Shades of Noir,* ed. Joan Copjec (New York: Verso, 1993), 135. Hereafter, this work is cited parenthetically in the text.

26. While one might see Chandler as a fitting choice to adapt fellow hardboiler Cain, their styles, as we have seen, are quite different. Chandler himself found Cain's work salacious and unpleasant, writing to a publisher, "Everything

[Cain] touches smells like a billygoat. He is every kind of writer I detest, a faux naif, a Proust in overalls, a dirty little boy with a piece of chalk and a board fence and nobody looking. Such people are the offal of literature, not because they write about dirty things, but because they do it in a dirty way. Nothing hard and clean and ventilated. A brothel with a smell of cheap scent in the front parlor and a bucket of slops at the back door. Do I, for God's sake, sound like that?" (*Letters*, 101).

27. Lola's hat-modeling recollection, too, comes from the book, but it appears the filmmakers favored its comparatively mild impact over the gruesome death mask scene.

28. As discussed in chapter two, Phyllis's grip is in part the grip of the Company. The role of the Company decreases greatly in the film as well. While Keyes rants and rails against the Company and particularly its ignorant president, Walter seems too uninterested and uninvolved in the Company to feel trapped by it.

29. Quoted in Ed Sikov, *On Sunset Boulevard: The Life and Times of Billy Wilder* (New York: Hyperion, 1998), 203. Hereafter, this work is cited parenthetically in the text.

30. Schickel, 62.

31. Naremore, 89. Hereafter, this work is cited parenthetically in the text.

32. Specifically, after *The Big Sleep* finished principal shooting, but before it was released, Bacall turned in what was considered a subpar performance in *Confidential Agent* (1945). Re-edits and re-shooting were then made on *The Big Sleep* to increase Bacall's presence in the film and to essentially make her "look good," as her best work tended to occur with Bogart.

33. Brian Gallagher, "Howard Hawks's *The Big Sleep*: A Paradigm for the Postwar American Family," reprinted in *The Critical Response to Raymond Chandler*, ed. J. K. Van Dover (Westport, CT: Greenwood Press, 1995), 152. Hereafter, this work is cited parenthetically in the text.

34. In the novel, Vivian's most recent husband is the missing Rusty Regan, whom we later learn has been killed by Vivian's sister, Carmen. In the film, Vivian has never been married to Regan, but to a man named Rutledge, whom she has divorced. The change makes Vivian's relative indifference about Regan's disappearance less morally problematic, while also making her more romantically available.

35. According to the brief documentary that accompanies the pre-release version, studio executives hated the veil.

36. David Thomson, *The Big Sleep* (London: BFI Classics, 1997), 208.

37. Michael Walker, "Film Noir: Introduction," in *The Book of Film Noir*, ed. Ian Cameron (New York: Continuum, 1992), 197.

38. In 1999, I presented a conference paper on gendered space and the private eye apartment, using Philip Marlowe's relationship with his domestic space as my primary example. In the paper, I discussed Marlowe's reliance on *domestic* activity (making coffee, most particularly) when he feels his home is being threatened. The traditionally feminine tasks serve ironically to restore

threatened masculine authority, reflecting just the kind of gender ambivalence that repeatedly characterizes domesticity in the hardboiled texts. During the question and answer session, a woman said, "Who best portrayed Marlowe on screen? Humphrey Bogart, right?" The suggestion seemed to be that an argument pursing a potential gender ambivalence in Marlowe falls apart in the face of Bogart's performance. As such, in a curious way, Bogart has trumped Chandler in terms of an accurate presentation of Marlowe.

39. Paul Jensen notes, "Although Bogart remains the definitive Forties toughguy, Dick Powell is really the more accurate Marlowe. A lot of Bogart's Marlowe is really Hammett's Sam Spade and most of it consists of the Bogart Mystique. . . . Powell came to the genre fresh, and could more easily adapt himself to the Marlowe persona—some would say because there was less to adapt" ("Raymond Chandler: The World You Live In," *Film Comment* 10.6 [November-December 1974]: 22).

40. Sylvia Harvey, "Woman's Place: The Absent Family of Film Noir," in *Women in Film Noir*, ed. E. Ann Kaplan (London: British Film Institute, 1978), 33. Hereafter, this work is cited parenthetically in the text.

41. Harvey does consider *Double Indemnity* in her article, but fails to correlate it to the source text.

42. In *Poodle Springs Story*, Chandler's unfinished Marlowe novel (later "finished" by Ross MacDonald), Chandler marries Marlowe off to *The Long Goodbye* love interest, wealthy Linda Loring. He wrote only a few chapters and then, according to biographer Frank MacShane, "beg[a]n to regret marrying Marlowe off" (*Life of Raymond Chandler*, 265).

43. *Raymond Chandler Speaking*, 249.

44. Rather inexplicably, the "e" is dropped off Anne's name in the film version. I will retain the "e" to refer to both the novel and film characters to avoid confusion.

45. Jonathan Buchsbaum, "Tame Wolves and Phoney Claims: Paranoia and Film Noir," in *The Book of Film Noir*, ed. Ian Cameron (New York: Continuum, 1992), 94.

46. James Maxfield, *The Fatal Woman: Sources of Male Anxiety in American Film Noir, 1941–1991* (Madison: Farleigh Dickinson University Press, 1996), 40. Hereafter, this work is cited parenthetically in the text.

47. Claire Johnston writes about this final scene, in which Keyes lights Walter's cigar for the first time: "The challenge to the patriarchal order eliminated and the internal contradictions of that order contained, a sublimated homosexuality between the men can now be signified. But there can be no more words—only The End" (*"Double Indemnity"* in *Women in Film Noir*, ed. E. Ann Kaplan [London: British Film Institute, 1978], 111).

48. Annette Kuhn, *"The Big Sleep:* A Disturbance in the Sphere of Sexuality," *Wide Angle* 4.3 (1982): 94. Hereafter, this work is cited parenthetically in the text.

49. Walker, 197.

50. Deborah Thomas, "How Hollywood Deals with the Deviant Male," in *The Book of Film Noir,* ed. Ian Cameron (New York: Continuum, 1992), 79. Frank Krutnik discusses filmic attempts to incorporate a traditional love story into hardboiled adaptations, noting "this grafting of the love story onto the 'hardboiled' detective story meant that the films had to confront what the written fiction could much more easily repress or elide: precisely the question of how heterosexuality could possibly be accommodated within the parameters of such an obsessively phallocentric fantasy, without causing it to collapse" (97).

51. When critics do refer (which is infrequently) to this tic it is usually ascribed to Bogart's persona in the large sense, rather than viewed in the context of the film. An exception is Brian Gallagher, who notes in passing that Marlowe's "most characteristic gesture throughout the film is his pulling at his earlobe and murmuring 'hmmm' when he learns something" (151).

52. Along with Marlowe and Carmen, we have Vivian rubbing her knee surreptitiously in Marlowe's office. Rejecting the lady-like concealment, Marlowe makes sure she knows she is hiding nothing: "Go ahead and scratch."

53. Haut, 99.

Chapter Six

1. Although published in the United States for the first time in 1966, *Run Man Run* was initially published in France in 1959 as *Dare-dare (Double-quick Time).*

2. Chester Himes, *Run Man Run* (New York: Carroll & Graf, 1995). Hereafter, this work is cited parenthetically in the text.

3. Dashiell Hammett's Sam Spade (*The Maltese Falcon*) is repeatedly described as resembling a "devil," though the comparison is playful.

4. The passage continues, "The thought came to him that white folks could believe anything, no matter how foolish or impossible, where a Negro was concerned" (7), echoing Himes's comments on French readers' delectation of negative portrayals of American life.

5. Interestingly, Himes suggested in a letter to Dell publishers that the apparently salacious cover art and text for the Dell paperback version of *Run Man Run* was "offensive" to his "black heroine Linda Lou," as it implied a more mutually desired sexual liaison between Linda and Walker. Himes insisted Linda Lou's sexual encounter with Matt Walker was inspired by her devotion for Jimmy, "whose life she hopes to save by sleeping with a white policeman" (quoted in Stephen F. Milliken, *Chester Himes: A Critical Appraisal* [Columbia: University of Missouri Press, 1976], 254. Hereafter, this work is cited parenthetically in the text.). The actual description of the affair is more equivocal, however: "Suddenly his hand closed over her breast. She shuddered spasmodically. His lips found hers in a hot blind kiss. She put her arms about him and pressed her breasts against his coat. She felt the room going away in a stifling flood of desire. . . . It was like taking candy from a baby, he thought" (143).

6. Interesting too is Stephen Milliken's suggestion that Himes "put a great deal of himself into Matt Walker," from the alcoholic blackouts to the scene where Walker slaps his mistress, which, Milliken argues, echoes Himes's description of slapping his girlfriend in his autobiography (255).

7. Work by Toni Morrison (1993) and Eric Lott (1993) also figures prominently in this area.

8. Wiegman, 14.

9. Chester Himes, *My Life of Absurdity: The Autobiography of Chester Himes Volume II* (Garden City, New York: Doubleday, 1976), 102, 105. Hereafter, this work is cited parenthetically in the text.

10. Chester Himes, *Conversations with Chester Himes,* eds. Michael Fabre and Robert E. Skinner (Jackson: University Press of Mississippi, 1995), 84, 108.

11. As an example of the kind of absurdist violence these texts offer, consider the headless motorcycle rider in *All Shot Up* (New York: Thunder's Mouth Press, 1996): "His head rolled halfway up the sheets of metal while his body kept astride the seat and his hands gripped the handlebars. A stream of blood spurted from his severed jugular, but his body completed the maneuver which his head had ordered and went past the truck as planned. The truck driver glanced from his window to watch the passing truck as he kept braking to a stop. But instead he saw a man without a head passing on a motorcycle with a sidecar and a stream of steaming red blood flowing back in the wind" (88–89).

12. The exception is the aforementioned *Run Man Run,* which does not feature Coffin Ed and Grave Digger.

13. As Himes would later write, his participation in the Série Noire was a risky move, as the "usual French intellectuals would resent a black American writing what they would call an Uncle Tom book that defied the tradition of Richard Wright and treated the American black as absurd instead of hurt. From their point of view the black American writer should always consider France as an escape no matter what actually happened to him in France" (158).

14. Most critics cite Rudolph Fisher's *The Conjure Man Dies* (1932) as the first black detective novel. For instance, John M. Reilly, in his 1976 article on Himes and the tough guy tradition, writes, " . . . before Himes only one black writer used black culture as a setting in a full-length published mystery novel. That was Rudolph Fisher whose novel *The Conjure Man Dies* appeared in 1932" (935). Reilly, however, considers Fisher's novel more of a "whodunit" than "tough guy fiction" (936). Stephen Soitos recently made the case for several works that predate Fisher, including Pauline Hopkins's *Hagar's Daughter* (1901–2) and J. E. Bruce's *Black Sleuth* (1907–9)—both serial novels (59).

15. Edward Margolies, *Native Sons: A Critical Study of Twentieth Century Black American Authors* (Philadelphia: J. B. Lipincott, 1968), 69. Hereafter, this work is cited parenthetically in the text.

16. Chester Himes, *The Real Cool Killers* (New York: Berkley Medallion, 1966), 28–29.

17. In a 1970 interview, John A. Williams asks Himes if he feels that the new rise of black detectives in books makes him feel "these people are sort of swiping your ideas" (*Conversations with Chester Himes*, 47). Himes responds, "No, no. It's a wonder to me why they haven't written about black detectives many years ago. . . . There's no reason why the black American, who is also an American, like all other Americans, and brought up in this sphere of violence which is the main sphere of American detective stories, there's no reason why he shouldn't write them. . . . They would not be imitating me because when I went into it, into the detective story field, I was just imitating all the other American detective story writers, other than the fact that I introduced various new angles which were my own. But on the whole, I mean the detective story originally in the plain narrative form—straightforward violence—is an American product. So I haven't created anything whatsoever; I just made the faces black, that's all" (*Conversations with Chester Himes*, 47–48).

18. George Kennan, "The Sources of Soviet Conduct," *Foreign Affairs* 25 (1947): 575.

19. Kennan, 575.

20. See Andrew Ross, *No Respect: Intellectuals and Popular Culture* (New York: Routledge, 1989) and Elaine Tyler May, *Homeward Bound: American Families in the Cold War Era* (New York: Basic Books/HarperCollins, 1988). Hereafter, these works are cited parenthetically in the text.

21. *Not June Cleaver: Women and Gender in Postwar America, 1945–1960*, ed. Joanne Meyerowitz (Philadelphia: Temple University Press, 1994) provides an important response to May's emphasis on bourgeois white women. In her introduction, Meyerowitz writes that May and other historians' "sustained focus on a white middle-class domestic ideal and on suburban middle-class housewives sometimes renders other ideals and other women invisible" (4).

22. The late fifties would produce a more culturally acceptable male retreat from the patriarch position in the bachelor figure, exemplified by *Playboy* magazine and by characters such as Dean Martin's Matt Helm, Ian Fleming's James Bond, and the swinger culture of the Rat Pack.

23. Mary Beth Haralovich, "Sit-coms and Suburbans," in *Private Screenings: Television and the Female Consumer*, eds. Lynn Spigel and Denise Mann (Minneapolis: University of Minnesota Press, 1992): 118.

24. Haralovich, 118. According to Dolores Hayden, late-1940s housing policies led to the exclusion of five groups from single-family housing: single white women, the white elderly working and lower class; minority men of all classes; minority women of all classes; and minority elderly (*Redesigning the American Dream: The Future of Housing, Work and Family Life* [New York: Norton, 1984]: 17–18).

25. Willfried Feuser, "Prophets of Violence: Chester Himes," *African Literature Today* 9 (1978): 60.

26. Quoted in Stephen F. Soitos, *The Blues Detective: A Study of African American Detective Fiction* (Amherst: University of Massachusetts Press, 1996), 156. Hereafter, this work is cited parenthetically in the text.

27. For example, as Roger Berger has shown, Walter Mosley rewrites the scene in his *Devil in a Blue Dress* (Berger, "The Black Dick: Race, Sexuality, and Discourse in the L.A. Novels of Walter Mosley," *African American Review* 31.2 [1997]: 281–294). Hereafter, this work is cited parenthetically in the text.

28. Chester Himes, *The Real Cool Killers* (New York: Berkley Medallion, 1966). Hereafter, this work is cited parenthetically in the text.

29. One significant example occurs in *Cotton Comes to Harlem* (New York: Vintage, 1988). Coffin Ed and Grave Digger are listening to jazz and the two discuss rather emotionally its effect on them (33–34). The exchange ends with Coffin Ed confiding, "Jazz talks too much to me." Grave Digger returns, "It ain't so much what it says. . . . It's what you can't do about it" (34).

30. Exceptions include *Cotton Comes to Harlem,* which offers a few scenes of the detectives' domestic lives, and *The Real Cool Killers* features Coffin Ed's daughter in the plot.

31. In an interview with Willi Hochkeppel, Himes talks about real life models for Coffin Ed and Grave Digger: " . . . the prototypes were a pair of black police lieutenants in Los Angeles. They were more or less the lords of the L.A. ghetto in the late 1930s, just before the war. They were the most brutal cops I ever heard of" (*Conversations, 27*).

32. Chester Himes, *For Love of Imabelle* (Chatham, NJ: Chatham, 1973), 116. Hereafter, this work is cited parenthetically in the text.

33. bell hooks, "Reconstructing Black Masculinity," *Black Looks: Race and Representation* (Boston: South End Press,1992), 89.

34. hooks, 98.

35. Himes is more closely affiliated, in this respect, with Mickey Spillane's gender representation, where detective Mike Hammer often ends up killing the purported femme fatale.

36. This tendency echoes white hardboiled novels wherein the detective seeks to avenge his partner's death by capturing the femme fatale. Sam Spade famously sends Brigid O'Shaugnessy to prison in *The Maltese Falcon,* though he does not physically abuse her nor does he express more than passing motivation to loyalty to the partner she killed.

37. In this way, Himes is far closer to Mickey Spillane's Mike Hammer novels, a product of the 1950s shift in hardboiled fiction away from dominating femme fatales in favor of according all power and agency to the male protagonist.

38. Accompanying this particular exposure pattern are incidents in which the unveiling of female genitalia is more disgusting than erotic. In *Blind Man with a Pistol,* two such incidents, both with random women, occur. A naked woman (who is actually named Poon) pushes the sheets of her bed away, "revealing her big hairy nest. Suddenly the room was flooded with the strong alkaloid scent of continuous sexual intercourse. Sergeant Ryan threw up his hands" (81). Later, Coffin Ed will punch his wife's cousin, knocking her on the floor, merely to stop her from screaming. When she falls, her "robe flew

open and her legs flew apart as though it were her natural reaction to getting punched. Grave Digger noticed that the pubic hair in the seam of her crotch was the color of old iron rust, ether from unrinsed soap or unwashed sweat" (149).

39. Perhaps a testament to the speed with which Himes produced these novels, *All Shot Up* features an almost identical comment about vixen Leila Baron: "All of her life she had played sex for kicks; now she was playing it for her life and it didn't work the same" (155).

40. Chester Himes, *Blind Man with a Pistol* (New York: Vintage Press, 1989), 29. Hereafter, this work is cited parenthetically in the text.

41. Himes writes in *The Quality of Hurt*, in the context of discussing his own parents' marriage (his mother was light-skinned and his father dark-skinned), that "light-complexioned house slaves" "considered themselves more beautiful, more intelligent, and of a higher class. This color class within the black race prevailed long after the slaves were freed, and there are still remnants of it left among black people. The 'light-bright-and-damn-near-white' blacks were offered the best jobs by whites; they maintained an exclusive social clique, their own manners and morals" (15–16).

42. Robert E. Skinner, *Two Guns from Harlem: The Detective Fiction of Chester Himes* (Bowling Green, OH: Bowling Green State University Popular Press, 1989), 22.

43. This is not to imply that gay characters are not exoticized in Chandler, Cain, or Hammett. Often, gay characters are "orientalized," for instance—as we see in the representation of Arthur Gwynn Geiger's home in *The Big Sleep*.

44. Ira Elliott, "Performance Art: Jake Barnes and 'Masculine' Signification in *The Sun Also Rises*," *American Literature* 67.1 (March 1995): 80. Hereafter, this work is cited parenthetically in the text.

45. Chester Himes, *The Heat's On* (New York: Vintage Press, 1988), 145.

46. Let us recall chapter two's discussion of male hysteria. As Elaine Showalter points out, "shell shock" as a disorder arose when English military doctor Charles S. Myers began noticing World War I soldiers with seeming hysterical symptoms: " . . . Myers did not want to describe British soldiers as hysterical, and so he suggested that the symptoms might be caused by the physical or chemical effects or proximity to the exploding shell," thus coining the disease free of hysteria's feminizing connotation (72–75). Showalter goes on to link shell shock with post-traumatic stress disorder and, controversially and rather sweepingly, with Gulf War Syndrome.

47. Once again, consider the stigma of "male hysteria" or men suffering from "shell shock." As psychoanalyst Lucien Israel says, the diagnosis of hysteria, and thereby presumably its symptoms, "became for a man . . . the real injury, a sign of weakness, a castration in a word. To say to a man, 'You are hysterical,' became under these conditions a way of saying to him, 'You are not a man'" (quoted in Showalter, 77).

48. Chester Himes, *The Crazy Kill* (Chatham, NJ: The Chatham Bookseller, 1973), 106. Hereafter, this work is cited parenthetically in the text.

49. Rabinowitz, 20. Hereafter, this work is cited parenthetically in the text.

50. Rabinowitz goes on to argue that not only did Himes make significant formal revisions to the genre but that those revisions were necessitated by his "political situation as a self-aware radical black writer" (191), and that those revisions reveal significant "contradictions between the Chandlerian thriller and American racial reality" (19).

51. Himes himself claimed at one point that he only added the characters of Coffin Ed and Grave Digger to his first novel because, forty pages in, his editor Marcel Duhamel reminded him that a roman policier needed to have police in it (*My Life of Absurdity,* 105).

52. John M. Reilly, "Chester Himes' Harlem Tough Guys," *Journal of Popular Culture* 9.4 (Spring 1976): 938. Hereafter, this work is cited parenthetically in the text.

53. One hears an echo in Raymond Chandler's comment that "[Marlowe] is a creature of fantasy. He is in a false position because I put him there. In real life a man of his type would no more be a private detective than he would be a university don. Your private detective in real life is usually either an ex-policeman with a lot of hard practical experience and the brains of a turtle or else a shabby little hack who runs around trying to find out where people have moved to" (*Raymond Chandler Speaking,* 232).

54. An interesting side note: in a 1992 interview with rapper/actor Ice-T, Ice-T discusses the flak he received from his fans for playing a cop in *New Jack City:* "Me playing that was sacrilegious in the ghetto. ' Why did you have to be a cop? You could have hated dope, well hate dope, but why do you got to give credit to the Man? Why couldn't you have just been a brother that went out there and handled it?' I had to tell them it wasn't my movie. I had to get in the movie, and this is the laws of Hollywood: the only way you can run around with a gun is to be a cop" (quoted in Ed Guerrero, *Framing Blackness: The African American Image in Film* [Philadelphia: Temple University Press, 1993], 235 fn. 39).

Epilogue

1. Portions of this chapter derive from my article "'Nothing You Can't Fix': Screening Marlowe Masculinity," which is scheduled to appear in the Winter 2002 issue of *Studies in the Novel.*

2. Fredric Jameson, "Postmodernism and Consumer Society" in *The Anti-Aesthetic,* ed. Hal Foster (Port Townsend, WA: Bay Press, 1983), 117. Hereafter, this work is cited parenthetically in the text.

3. Michael Eaton criticizes Jameson for his characterization of *Chinatown* as a "stylistic recuperation" of 1930s America, pointing out the various technical means by which Polanski avoided the look and style of film noir in favor of a more classic, "untricksy" look, not to mention its avoidance of a "retrospective soundtrack" (*Chinatown* [London: BFI Film Classics, 1997], 50, 51). Hereafter, this work is cited parenthetically in the text.

4. For instance, the adaptation of James Ellroy's novel *L.A. Confidential* was released to critical acclaim in 1998, but scarcely was the film referenced without mention of its similarity to (or even differences from) *Chinatown*. *Chinatown* has become the pivot to the past, to "original" noir or even the 1930s and 40s themselves. Indeed, when Fredric Jameson discusses the Art Deco–style credit titles of the neo-noir *Body Heat*, he suggests that they are designed to "trigger nostalgic reactions (first to *Chinatown*, no doubt, and then beyond it to some more historical referent)" ("Postmodernism and Consumer Society," 117).

5. See James Naremore (1998), John Cawelti, "*Chinatown* and Generic Transformation in Recent American Films," *Film Genre Reader II*, ed. Barry Keith Grant (Austin: University of Texas Press, 1995), 227–245, Paul Jensen (1974), Richard T. Jameson, "Son of Noir," *Film Comment* 10.6 (November-December 1974): 30–33.

6. Quoted in Jan Dawson, "Robert Altman Speaking," *Film Comment* (March-April 1974): 41

7. Jensen, 26.

8. Richard T. Jameson, 31.

9. Leigh Brackett, "From *The Big Sleep* to *The Long Goodbye* and More or Less How We Got There," *Take One* (January 23, 1974): 27. Hereafter, this work is cited parenthetically in the text.

10. Cawelti (1995), 238. Hereafter, this work is cited parenthetically in the text.

11. Michael Eaton points out that both Polanski and screenwriter Robert Towne "want to take credit for insisting that the detective's wound would not make a miraculous movie overnight recovery. Whoever had the idea, it was by displaying the various bandages which cover the proboscis, whilst—like displaced codpieces—continually drawing attention towards it, the consequences of an act of violence remain on parade" (45–46).

12. Anthony Easthope, *Literary Into Cultural Studies* (London: Routledge, 1991), 146.

13. Peter Biskind, *Easy Rider, Raging Bulls: How the Sex-Drugs-and-Rock 'n' Roll Generation Saved Hollywood* (New York: Touchstone Press, 1998), 268.

Bibliography

Primary Texts

Cain, James M. *Double Indemnity.* 1936. New York: Vintage, 1992.
———. *Mildred Pierce.* 1943. Rpt. in *The Five Great Novels of James M. Cain.* London: Picador Books, 1985.
———. *The Postman Always Rings Twice.* 1934. New York: Vintage, 1992.
———. *Serenade.* 1937. Rpt. in *The Five Great Novels of James M. Cain.* London: Picador Books, 1985.
Chandler, Raymond. *The Big Sleep.* 1939. New York: Vintage, 1992.
———. *Farewell, My Lovely.* 1940. New York: Vintage, 1992.
———. *The High Window.* 1942. Rpt. in *Stories & Early Novels.* New York: Library of America, 1995. 987–1177.
———. *The Lady in the Lake.* 1943. New York: Vintage, 1992.
———. *The Little Sister.* 1949. Rpt. in *Later Novels and Other Writings.* New York: Library of America, 1995. 201–416.
———. *The Long Goodbye.* 1953. New York: Vintage, 1992.
———. *Playback.* 1958. Rpt. in *Later Novels and Other Writings.* New York: Library of America, 1995. 737–871.
———. *Trouble Is My Business.* 1950. New York: Vintage, 1992.
Himes, Chester. *All Shot Up.* 1960. New York: Thunder's Mouth Press, 1996.
———. *The Big Gold Dream.* 1960. Chatham, NJ: Chatham, 1973.
———. *Blind Man with a Pistol.* 1969. New York: Vintage, 1989.
———. *Cotton Comes to Harlem.* 1965. New York: Vintage, 1988.
———. *The Crazy Kill.* 1959. Chatham, NJ: Chatham, 1973.
———. *For Love of Imabelle.* 1957. Chatham, NJ: Chatham, 1973.
———. *The Heat's On.* 1966. New York: Vintage, 1988.
———. *My Life of Absurdity: The Autobiography of Chester Himes Volume II.* Garden City, NY: Doubleday, 1976.
———. *The Quality of Hurt: The Autobiography of Chester Himes Volume I.* New York: Thunder's Mouth Press, 1971.
———. *The Real Cool Killers.* 1958/1959. New York: Berkley Medallion, 1966.
———. *Run Man Run.* 1959 (France). 1966. New York: Carroll & Graf, 1995.

Secondary Texts

Abbott, Philip. "Who's Responsible?: The Thirties as a Contested Concept in American Political Thought." Paper presented at the Southwest Political Science Association, San Antonio, TX, March 1998.

Acuña, Rodolfo. *Occupied America: The Chicano's Struggle Toward Liberation.* San Francisco: Canfield, 1972.

Babener, Liahna K. "Raymond Chandler's City of Lies." In *Los Angeles in Fiction: A Collection of Original Essays,* ed. David Fine, 109–131. Albuquerque: University of New Mexico Press, 1984.

Bailey, Frankie Y. *Out of the Woodpile: Black Characters in Crime and Detective Fiction.* Westport, CT: Greenwood Pandarus, 1991.

Balio, Tino. *Grand Design: Hollywood as a Modern Business Enterprise, 1930–1939.* History of the American Cinema series, gen. ed. Charles Harpole. Vol. 5. New York: Charles Scribner's Sons, 1993.

Baym, Nina. "Melodramas of Beset Manhood: How Theories of American Fiction Exclude Women Authors." *American Quarterly* 33.2 (Summer 1981): 123–139.

Beekman, E. M. "Raymond Chandler and an American Genre." *Massachusetts Review* 14 (1973): 149–173. Rpt. in *The Critical Response to Raymond Chandler,* ed. J. K. Van Dover, 89–99. Westport, CT: Greenwood Press, 1995.

Bellour, Raymond. "The Obvious and the Code." *Screen* 15.4 (Winter 1974–75): 7–17.

Berger, Roger A. "The Black Dick: Race, Sexuality, and Discourse in the L.A. Novels of Walter Mosley." *African American Review* 31.2 (1997): 281–294.

Bernheimer, Charles and Claire Kahane. *In Dora's Case: Freud—Hysteria—Feminism.* New York: Columbia University Press, 1995.

Berry, Jay R., Jr. "Chester Himes and the Hard-Boiled Tradition." *Armchair Detective* 15 (1982): 38–43.

Biskind, Peter. *Easy Rider, Raging Bulls: How the Sex-Drugs-and-Rock 'n' Roll Generation Saved Hollywood.* New York: Touchstone Press, 1998.

Bonitzer, Pascal. "Partial Vision: Film and the Labyrinth." *Cahiers du Cinema* 301 (June 1979): 35–41. Rpt. in *Wide Angle* 4.4 (1981): 56–63.

Borde, Raymond and Étienne Chaumeton. "The Sources of Film Noir." *Film Reader* 3 (February 1978): 58–66.

———. "Towards a Definition of Film Noir." In *Film Noir Reader,* eds. Alain Silver and James Ursini, 53–64. New York: Limelight Editions, 1996.

Brackett, Leigh. "From *The Big Sleep* to *The Long Goodbye* and More or Less How We Got There." *Take One* (January 23, 1974): 26–28.

Brooks, Peter. *Body Work: Objects of Desire in Modern Narrative.* Cambridge: Harvard University Press, 1993.

Buchsbaum, Jonathan. "Tame Wolves and Phoney Claims: Paranoia and Film Noir." In *The Book of Film Noir,* ed. Ian Cameron, 88–97. New York: Continuum, 1992.

Butler, Judith. *Gender Trouble: Feminism and the Subversion of Identity.* New York: Routledge, 1990.

————. *Bodies That Matter: On the Discursive Limits of "Sex."* New York: Routledge, 1993.

————. "Melancholy Gender/Refused Identification." In *Constructing Masculinity,* eds. Maurice Berger, Brian Wallis, Simon Watson, 21–36. New York: Routledge, 1995.

Cameron, Ian, ed. *The Book of Film Noir.* New York: Continuum, 1992.

Cawelti, John G. *Adventure, Mystery, and Romance.* Chicago: University of Chicago Press, 1976.

————. "*Chinatown* and Generic Transformation in Recent American Films." In *Film Genre Reader II,* ed. Barry Keith Grant, 227–245. Austin: University of Texas Press, 1995.

Chandler, Raymond. "Introduction to 'The Simple Art of Murder.'" Rpt. in *Later Novels and Other Writings,* 1016–1019. New York: Library of America, 1995.

————. "The Simple Art of Murder." 977–992. Rpt. in *Later Novels and Other Writings.* New York: Library of America, 1995.

Cixous, Hélène and Catherine Clément. "The Untenable." In *In Dora's Case: Freud—Hysteria—Feminism,* eds. Charles Bernheimer and Claire Kahane, 276–293. New York: Columbia University Press, 1995.

Cowie, Elizabeth. "Film Noir and Women." In *Shades of Noir,* ed. Joan Copjec, 121–166. New York: Verso, 1993.

Crooks, Robert. "From the Far Side of the Urban Frontier: The Detective Fiction of Chester Himes and Walter Mosley." In *Race-ing Representation: Voice, History and Sexuality,* eds. Kostas Myrsiades and Linda Myrsiades, 175–199. Lanham, MD: Rowan and Littlefield, 1998.

Damico, James. "Film Noir: A Modest Proposal." *Film Reader* 3 (February 1978): 48–57.

Davis, Mike. *City of Quartz: Excavating the Future in Los Angeles.* New York: Random House, 1992.

Dawson, Jan. "Robert Altman Speaking." *Film Comment* (March-April 1974): 41.

Denning, Michael. *Mechanic Accents: Dime Novels and Working-Class Culture in America.* London: Verso, 1987.

Diawara, Manthia. "Noir By Noirs: Toward a New Realism in Black Cinema." In *Shades of Noir,* ed. Joan Copjec, 261–278. London: Verso, 1993.

Doane, Mary Ann. *Femmes Fatales: Feminism, Film Theory, Psychoanalysis.* New York: Routledge, 1991.

Doherty, Thomas. *Pre-Code Hollywood: Sex, Immorality and Insurrection in American Cinema, 1930–1934.* New York: Columbia University Press, 1999.

Dove, George N. "The Complex Art of Raymond Chandler." *Armchair Detective* 8 (1974–75): 271–74. Rpt. in *The Critical Response to Raymond Chandler,* ed. J. K. Van Dover, 101–107. Westport, CT: Greenwood Press, 1995.

Durham, Philip. *The Boys in the Black Mask.* Los Angeles: UCLA Library, 1961.

————. *Down These Mean Streets a Man Must Go.* Chapel Hill: University of North Carolina Press, 1963.

Dyer, Richard. "White." *Screen* 29.4 (Autumn 1988): 44–64.

————. *White.* London: Routledge, 1997.

Easthope, Anthony. *Literary Into Cultural Studies.* London: Routledge, 1991.

Eaton, Michael. *Chinatown.* London: BFI Film Classics, 1997.

Fabre, Michael and Robert E. Skinner, eds. *Conversations with Chester Himes.* Jackson: University Press of Mississippi, 1995.

Faludi, Susan. *Stiffed: The Betrayal of the American Man.* New York: Perennial, 1999.

Farber, Stephen. "Violence and the Bitch Goddess." *Film Comment* 10.6 (Nov.-Dec. 1974): 8–11.

Feuser, Willfried. "Prophets of Violence: Chester Himes." *African Literature Today* 9 (1978): 58–76.

Fine, David. "Beginning in the Thirties: The Los Angeles Fiction of James M. Cain and Horace McCoy." In *Los Angeles in Fiction: A Collection of Original Essays,* ed. David Fine, 43–66. Albuquerque: University of New Mexico Press, 1984.

Flint, R. W. "A Cato of the Cruelties." *Partisan Review* 14 (1947): 328–30. Rpt. in *The Critical Response to Raymond Chandler,* ed. J. K. Van Dover, 39–41. Westport, CT: Greenwood Press, 1995.

Fontana, Ernest. "Chivalry and Modernity in Raymond Chandler's *The Big Sleep.*" *Western American Literature* 19.3 (1984): 179–86. Rpt. in *The Critical Response to Raymond Chandler,* ed. J. K. Van Dover, 159–65. Westport, CT: Greenwood Press, 1995.

Freud, Sigmund. *Beyond the Pleasure Principle.* Trans. James Strachey. New York: W. W. Norton, 1961.

———. *Dora: An Analysis of a Case of Hysteria.* New York: Collier, 1993.

———. *The Freud Reader.* Ed. Peter Gay. New York: W. W. Norton, 1989.

———. "The Uncanny." In *The Standard Edition of the Complete Psychological Works,* trans. James Strachey, vol. 17, 218–255. London: Hogarth Press, 1953.

Friedrich, Otto. *City of Nets: A Portrait of Hollywood in the 1940s.* New York: Harper & Row, 1986.

Fuss, Diana. *Identification Papers.* New York: Routledge, 1995.

Gaines, Jane. "White Privilege and Looking Relations—Race and Gender in Feminist Film Theory." *Screen* 29.4 (Autumn 1988): 12–27.

Gallagher, Brian. "Howard Hawks's *The Big Sleep:* A Paradigm for the Postwar American Family." *North Dakota Quarterly* 51.3 (1983): 78–91. Rpt. in *The Critical Response to Raymond Chandler,* ed. J. K. Van Dover, 145–57. Westport, CT: Greenwood Press, 1995.

Gardiner, Dorothy and Katharine Sorley Walker, eds. *Raymond Chandler Speaking.* Berkeley: University of California Press, 1962, 1997.

Garon, Paul. "Radical Novel: 1900–1954." *Firsts* 4:3 (March 1994).

Gledhill, Christine. "*Klute* Part 1: A Contemporary Film Noir and Feminist Criticism." In *Women in Film Noir,* ed. E. Ann Kaplan, 6–21. London: British Film Institute, 1978.

Gregory, Charles. "Knight Without Meaning?" *Sight and Sound* 42.3 (Summer 1973): 155–59.

Gross, Miriam, ed. *The World of Raymond Chandler.* New York: A & W Publishing, 1977.

Guerrero, Ed. *Framing Blackness: The African American Image in Film.* Philadelphia: Temple University Press, 1993.

Hannsberry, Karen Burroughs. *Femme Noir: Bad Girls of Film*. Jefferson, NC: Mc-Farland & Co., 1998.

Haralovich, Mary Beth. "Sit-coms and Suburbans." In *Private Screenings: Television and the Female Consumer*, eds. Lynn Spigel and Denise Mann, 111–141. Minneapolis: University of Minnesota Press, 1992.

Harvey, Sylvia. "Woman's Place: The Absent Family of Film Noir." In *Women in Film Noir*, ed. E. Ann Kaplan, 22–34. London: British Film Institute, 1978.

Haut, Woody. *Pulp Culture: Hardboiled Fiction and the Cold War*. London: Serpent's Tail, 1995.

Hayden, Dolores. *Redesigning the American Dream: The Future of Housing, Work and Family Life*. New York: Norton, 1984.

Hilfer, Tony. *The Crime Novel: A Deviant Genre*. Austin: University of Texas Press, 1990.

Hiney, Tom. *Raymond Chandler: A Biography*. New York: Atlantic Monthly Press, 1997.

Hirsch, Foster. *The Dark Side of the Screen: Film Noir*. San Diego: A. S. Barnes Co., 1981.

hooks, bell. "Reconstructing Black Masculinity." *Black Looks: Race and Representation*, 87–114. Boston: South End Press, 1992.

Jameson, Fredric. "On Raymond Chandler." *Southern Review* 6.3 (1970): 624–30. Rpt. in *The Critical Response to Raymond Chandler*, ed. J. K. Van Dover, 65–87. Westport, CT: Greenwood Press, 1995.

———. "Postmodernism and Consumer Society." In *The Anti-Aesthetic*, ed. Hal Foster, 11–125. Port Townsend, WA: Bay Press, 1983.

Jameson, Richard T. "Son of Noir." *Film Comment* 10.6 (Nov.-Dec. 1974): 30–33.

Jensen, Paul. "Raymond Chandler: The World You Live In." *Film Comment* 10.6 (Nov.-Dec. 1974): 18–26.

Johnston, Claire. *"Double Indemnity."* In *Women in Film Noir*, ed. E. Ann Kaplan, 100–111. London: British Film Institute, 1978.

Kahane, Claire. "Introduction: Part Two." In *In Dora's Case: Freud—Hysteria—Feminism*, eds. Charles Bernheimer and Claire Kahane, 19–32. New York: Columbia University Press, 1995.

Kamarovosky, Mirra. *The Unemployed Man and His Family: The Effect of Unemployment Upon the Status of the Man in Fifty-Nine Families*. New York: Dryden, 1940.

Kaplan, E. Ann, ed. *Women in Film Noir*. London: British Film Institute, 1978.

Kennan, George. Interview [online]. *CNN: Cold War*. CNN. Available from World Wide Web: ⟨http://cnn.com/SPECIALS/cold.war/episodes/01/interviews/kennan⟩.

———. "Sources of Soviet Conduct." *Foreign Affairs* 25 (1947): 566–82.

Kennedy, David M. *Freedom From Fear: The American People in Depression and War, 1929–1945*. New York: Oxford University Press, 1999.

Kennedy, Liam. "Black Noir: Race and Urban Space in Walter Mosley's Detective Fiction." In *Criminal Proceedings: The Contemporary American Crime Novel*, ed. Peter Messent, 42–61. London: Pluto Press, 1997.

Kerouac, Jack. "On the Road Again." *The New Yorker*. (June 22 & 29, 1998): 46–59.

Knight, Stephen. *Form and Ideology in Crime Fiction*. Bloomington: Indiana University Press, 1980.

Krutnik, Frank. *In a Lonely Street: Film Noir, Genre, Masculinity*. London: Routlege, 1991.

Kuhn, Annette. "*The Big Sleep:* A Disturbance in the Sphere of Sexuality." *Wide Angle* 4.3 (1982): 4–11.

Lacan, Jacques. "The Split Between the Eye and the Gaze." *The Four Fundamental Concepts of Psycho-Analysis,* 67–78. New York: W. W. Norton, 1981.

Landrum, Larry. *American Mystery and Detective Novels: A Reference Guide.* Westport, CT: Greenwood Press, 1999.

Lee, Robert A. "Making New: Styles of Innovation in the Contemporary Black Novel." In *Black Fiction: New Studies in the Afro-American Novel Since 1975,* ed. Lee, 222–50. New York: Barnes and Noble, 1980.

Legman, Gershon. *Love and Death: A Study in Censorship.* New York: Hacker, 1963.

Lid, R. W. "Philip Marlowe Speaking." *Kenyon Review* 31 (1977): 153–78. Rpt. in *The Critical Response to Raymond Chandler,* ed. J. K. Van Dover, 43–63. Westport, CT: Greenwood Press, 1995.

Lipsitz, George. *The Possessive Investment in Whiteness: How White People Profit from Identity Politics.* Philadelphia: Temple University Press, 1998.

Lott, Eric. *Love and Theft: Blackface Minstrelsy and the American Working Class.* New York: Oxford University Press, 1993.

———. "The Whiteness of Film Noir." In *Whiteness: A Critical Reader,* ed. Mike Hill, 81–101. New York: New York University Press, 1997.

Luhr, William. *Raymond Chandler and Film.* Tallahassee: Florida State University Press, 1991.

Lundquist, James. *Chester Himes.* New York: Frederick Ungar, 1976.

MacShane, Frank. *The Life of Raymond Chandler.* New York: Dutton, 1976.

———, ed. *Selected Letters of Raymond Chandler.* New York: Columbia University Press, 1981.

Madden, David. "James M. Cain: Twenty-Minute Egg of the Hard-Boiled School." *Journal of Popular Culture* 1 (1967): 178–92.

———, ed. *Tough Guy Writers of the Thirties.* Carbondale: Southern Illinois University Press, 1968.

———. *Cain's Craft.* Metuchen, NJ: Scarecrow Press, 1985.

Margolies, Edward. *Native Sons: A Critical Study of Twentieth Century Black American Authors,* 87–101. Philadelphia: J. B. Lipincott, 1968.

———and Michel Fabre. *The Several Lives of Chester Himes.* Jackson: University Press of Mississippi, 1997.

———. *Which Way Did He Go?: The Private Eye in Dashiell Hammett, Raymond Chandler, Chester Himes, and Ross MacDonald.* New York: Holmes and Meier, 1982.

Marling, William. *The American Roman Noir: Hammett, Cain, and Chandler.* Athens: University of Georgia Press, 1995.

Martin, Richard. *Mean Streets and Raging Bulls: The Legacy of Film Noir in Contemporary American Cinema.* Lanham, MD: Scarecrow Press, 1997.

Mason, Michael. "Deadlier Than the Male." *Times Literary Supplement,* September 17, 1976, 1147.

Maxfield, James. *The Fatal Woman: Sources of Male Anxiety in American Film Noir, 1941–1991.* Madison: Farleigh Dickinson University Press, 1996.

May, Elaine Tyler. *Homeward Bound: American Families in the Cold War Era*. New York: Basic Books/HarperCollins, 1988.

McElvaine, Robert S. *The Great Depression: America, 1929–1941*. New York: Times Books, 1984, 1993.

———, ed. *Down and Out in the Great Depression: Letters From the "Forgotten Man."* Chapel Hill: University of North Carolina Press, 1983.

McWilliams, Carey. *Southern California County: An Island on the Land*. New York: Duell, Sloan & Pearce, 1946.

———, *North from Mexico: The Spanish-Speaking People of the United States*. New Edition. Updated by Matt S. Meier. New York: Greenwood Press, 1949, 1990.

Meyerowitz, Joanne, ed. *Not June Cleaver: Women and Gender in Postwar America, 1945–1960*. Philadelphia: Temple University Press, 1994.

Miller, D. A. *The Novel and the Police*. Berkeley: University of California Press, 1988.

Milliken, Stephen F. *Chester Himes: A Critical Appraisal*. Columbia: University of Missouri Press, 1976.

Modleski, Tania. *The Women Who Knew Too Much: Hitchcock and Feminist Film Theory*, New York: Methuen, 1988.

Monaco, James. "Notes on *The Big Sleep:* Thirty Years After." *Sight and Sound* 44:1 (Winter 1974–75): 34–38.

Morrison, Toni. *Playing in the Dark: Whiteness and the Literary Imagination*. New York: Vintage, 1993.

Mullen, Harryette. "Optic White: Blackness and the Production of Whiteness." *diacritics* 24.2–3 (Summer-Fall 1994): 71–89.

Muller, Gilbert H. *Chester Himes*. Twayne United States Authors Series. Boston: Twayne, 1989.

Nadel, Alan. *Containment Culture: American Narratives, Postmodernism, and the Atomic Age*. Durham: Duke University Press, 1995.

Naremore, James. *More Than Night: Film Noir in Its Contexts*. Berkeley: University of California Press, 1998.

Nolan, William F. *The Black Mask Boys*. New York: Morrow, 1985.

Nyman, Jopi. *Men Alone: Masculinity, Individualism and Hard-Boiled Fiction*. Costerus New Series 111. Amsterdam: Rodopi, 1997.

Oates, Joyce Carol. "Man Under Sentence of Death: The Novels of James M. Cain." In *Tough Guy Writers of the Thirties*, ed. David Madden, 110–128. Southern Illinois University Press: Carbondale, 1968.

O'Brien, Geoffrey. *Hardboiled America: The Lurid Years of Paperbacks*. New York: Van Nostrand Reinhold, 1981.

Ogden, Bethany. "Hard-Boiled Ideology." *Critical Quarterly* 34.1 (Spring 1992): 71–87.

Omi, Michael and Howard Winant. *Racial Formation in the United States from the 1960s to the 1990s*. 2nd ed. New York: Routledge, 1994.

Pellegrini, Ann. *Performance Anxieties: Staging Psychoanalysis, Staging Race*. London: Routledge, 1997.

Pendo, Stephen. *Raymond Chandler On Screen: His Novels Into Film*. Metuchen, NJ: Scarecrow Press, 1976.

Pfeil, Fred. *White Guys: Studies in Postmodern Domination and Difference.* London: Verso, 1995.

Place, Janey. "Women in Film Noir." In *Women in Film Noir,* ed. E. Ann Kaplan, 35–54. London: British Film Institute, 1978.

———and Lowell Peterson. "Some Visual Motifs of Film Noir." In *Film Noir Reader,* eds. Alain Silver and James Ursini, 65–76. New York: Limelight Editions, 1996.

Porter, Dennis. *The Pursuit of Crime: Art and Ideology in Detective Fiction.* New Haven: Yale University Press, 1981.

Rabinowitz, Peter J. "Chandler Comes to Harlem: Racial Politics in the Thrillers of Chester Himes." In *The Sleuth and the Scholar: Origins, Evolution, and Current Trends in Detective Fiction,* eds. Barbara A. Rader and Howard G. Zettler, 19–30. Westport, CT: Greenwood, 1988.

———. "Rats Behind the Wainscoting: Politics, Convention, and Chandler's *The Big Sleep.*" *Texas Studies in Language and Literature* 22 (Summer 1980): 224–245. Rpt. in *The Critical Response to Raymond Chandler,* ed. J. K. Van Dover, 117–137. Westport, CT: Greenwood Press, 1995.

Reck, Thomas S. "Raymond Chandler's Los Angeles." *The Nation* (December 20, 1975): 661–63. Rpt. in *The Critical Response to Raymond Chandler,* ed. J. K. Van Dover, 109–115. Westport, CT: Greenwood Press, 1995.

Reilly, John M. "Chester Himes' Harlem Tough Guys." *Journal of Popular Culture* 9.4 (Spring 1976): 935–47.

Reinders, Robert C. "The New Deal: Relief, Recovery, and Reform." In *The Thirties: Politics and Culture in a Time of Broken Dreams,* eds. Heinz Ickstadt, Rob Kroes, and Brian Lee, 11–34. Amsterdam: Free University Press, 1987.

Roediger, David. *The Wages of Whiteness: Race and the Making of the American Working Class.* London: Verso, 1991.

———. *Towards the Abolition of Whiteness: Essays on Race, Politics, and Working Class History.* London: Verso, 1994.

Roosevelt, Franklin Delano. "The 'Forgotten Man' Radio Speech." In *The Roosevelt Reader: Selected Speeches, Messages, Press Conferences, and Letters of Franklin D. Roosevelt,* ed. Basil Rauch, 65–69. New York: Rinehart, 1957.

Ross, Andrew. *No Respect: Intellectuals and Popular Culture.* New York: Routledge, 1989.

Ruhm, Herbert. "Raymond Chandler: From Bloomsbury to the Jungle—and Beyond." In *Tough Guy Writers of the Thirties,* ed. David Madden, 171–185. Carbondale: Southern Illinois University Press, 1968.

Sandoe, James. *The Hard-Boiled Dick: A Personal Checklist.* Chicago: Lovell, 1952.

Schickel, Richard. *Double Indemnity.* London: BFI Film Classics, 1992.

Schrader, Paul. "Notes on Film Noir." In *Film Noir Reader,* eds. Alain Silver and James Ursini, 53–64. New York: Limelight Editions, 1996.

Scorsese, Martin and Michael Henry Wilson. *A Personal Journey with Martin Scorsese Through American Movies.* New York: Miramax Books, 1997.

Sedgwick, Eve Kosofsky. *Epistemology of the Closet.* Berkeley: University of California Press, 1990.

Showalter, Elaine. "Hysteria, Feminism, and Gender." In *Hysteria Beyond Freud,* eds. Sander L. Gilman, Helen King, Roy Porter, G. S. Rousseau, and Elaine Showalter, 286–344. Berkeley: University of California Press, 1993.

———. *Hystories: Hysterical Epidemics and Modern Media.* New York: Columbia University Press, 1997.

Sikov, Ed. *On Sunset Boulevard: The Life and Times of Billy Wilder.* New York: Hyperion, 1998.

Silver, Alain and James Ursini. *Film Noir Reader.* New York: Limelight Editions, 1996.

Silverman, Kaja. *Male Subjectivity at the Margins.* New York: Routledge, 1992.

Simpson, Hassell. "'So Long, Beautiful Hunk': Ambiguous Gender and Songs of Parting in Chandler's Fictions." *Journal of Popular Culture* 28.2 (Fall 1994): 37–48.

Skenazy, Paul. *James M. Cain.* New York: Continuum, 1989.

Skinner, Robert E. *Two Guns from Harlem: The Detective Fiction of Chester Himes.* Bowling Green, OH: Bowling Green State University Popular Press, 1989.

Sklar, Robert. *City Boys: Cagney, Bogart, Garfield.* Princeton, NJ: Princeton University Press, 1992.

Slotkin, Richard. "The Hard-Boiled Detective Story: From the Open Range to the Mean Streets." In *The Sleuth and the Scholar: Origins, Evolution, and Current Trends in Detective Fiction,* eds. Barbara A. Rader and Howard G. Zettler, 91–100. Westport, CT: Greenwood Press, 1988.

Smith, David. "The Public Eye of Raymond Chandler." *Journal of American Studies* 14 (1980): 423–441.

Smith, Johanna M. "Raymond Chandler and the Business of Literature." *Texas Studies in Language and Literature* 31 (1989): 592–610. Rpt. in *The Critical Response to Raymond Chandler,* ed. J. K. Van Dover, 183–201. Westport, CT: Greenwood Press, 1995.

Smith, Paul. "Action Movie Hysteria, or Eastwood Bound." *Differences* 1.3 (1989): 88–107.

Soitos, Stephen F. *The Blues Detective: A Study of African American Detective Fiction.* Amherst: University of Massachusetts Press, 1996.

Speir, Jerry. *Raymond Chandler.* New York: Frederick Unger, 1981.

State Department Information Program, *Proceedings of Permanent Subcommittee Investigation of the Senate Committee on Government Operations,* March 1953, 83–88.

Storey, Robert. *Pierrot: A Critical History of a Mask.* Princeton: Princeton University Press, 1978.

Sumner, William Graham. "The Forgotten Man (1883)." In *The Forgotten Man and Other Essays,* ed. Albert Galloway Keller, 465–495. Freeport, New York: Books for Libraries Press, 1919, 1969.

Susman, Warren I. "The Thirties." In *The Development of an American Culture,* eds. Stanley Cohen and Lorman Ratner, 204–205. Englewood Cliffs, NJ: Prentice-Hall, 1970.

———. *Culture as History: The Transformation of American Society in the Twentieth Century.* New York: Pantheon, 1973, 1984.

Telotte, J. P. *Voices in the Dark: The Narrative Patterns of Film Noir.* Urbana: University of Illinois Press, 1989.

Terkel, Studs. *Hard Times: An Oral History of the Great Depression.* New York: New Press, 1970, 1986.

Thomas, Deborah. "How Hollywood Deals with the Deviant Male." In *The Book of Film Noir,* ed. Ian Cameron, 59–70. New York: Continuum, 1992.

———. "Psychoanalysis and Film Noir." In *The Book of Film Noir,* ed. Ian Cameron, 71–87. New York: Continuum, 1992.

Thomson, David. *The Big Sleep.* London: BFI Classics, 1997.

Thorpe, Edward. *Chandlertown: The Los Angeles of Philip Marlowe.* London: Vermilion, 1983.

U.S. Congress. "Homosexuals in Government, 1950," *Congressional Record,* 96, part 4. 81st Cong., 2nd Session, March 29-April 24, 1950, 4527–4528.

Van Dover, J. K. Introduction. In *The Critical Response to Raymond Chandler,* ed. Van Dover, 1–17. Westport, CT: Greenwood Press, 1995.

Walker, Michael. "Film Noir: Introduction." In *The Book of Film Noir,* ed. Ian Cameron, 8–38. New York: Continuum, 1992.

Wiegman, Robyn. *American Anatomies: Theorizing Race and Gender.* Durham: Duke University Press, 1995.

Willett, Ralph. *Hard-Boiled Detective Fiction.* British Association for American Studies, *Pamphlets in American Studies 23.* Halifax, England: Ryburn Book Productions, 1992.

Wilson, Edmund. *Classics and Commercials: A Literary Chronicle of the Forties.* New York: Farrar, Straus, 1950.

Wolfe, Peter. *Something More Than Night: The Case of Raymond Chandler.* Bowling Green, OH: Popular, 1985.

Wood, Robin. *Howard Hawks.* Garden City, NJ: Doubleday, 1968.

Wynter, Sylvia. "Sambos and Minstrels." *Social Text* 1 (1979): 149–156.

Žižek, Slavoj. *Looking Awry: An Introduction to Jacques Lacan through Popular Culture.* Cambridge: MIT Press, 1991.

INDEX

Books are to be returned on or before
the last date below.

7 – DAY
LOAN